Praise for

any time, any place

Book Two in the Billionaire Builders Series

"Jennifer Probst is an absolute auto-buy author for me, and *Any Time, Any Place* is a prime example of why. Full of sensuality, humor, heart, and a deliciously sexy hero, *Any Time, Any Place* sucked me in from page one. Grab a copy—you won't be disappointed!"

—*New York Times* bestselling author Julie Kenner

"Probst creates a realistic, incredibly relatable couple whose mistakes might be anyone's, surrounding them with a stellar cast of characters, including a setup of the relationship that will likely feature in the sequel to this well-plotted, endearing story."

—*Publishers Weekly*

"The chemistry between the two of them is so palpable I could feel it in my soul."

—*Books and Boys Book Blog*, 5 stars

"I found the story to be an exciting *mixture* of ingredients resulting in a *cocktail* of tasty tidbits guaranteed to bring a smile to your face."

—*iScream Books*, 5 stars

"This new series, the Billionaire Builders series, is a new passion of mine. This woman knows how to write raw emotion, create amazing characters with deep connection, and get to the intense feelings of love, passion, and understanding of the delicate balance of trust. She writes in a manner that completely engrosses you in the story and leaves you breathless for more. I crave her stories because she understands so much about the human psyche and is able to put that into words like no other author. This story deals with deep emotion and pain, and yet she gives us a beautiful side of love, which comes from healing, trust, and fiery passion. If you love reading contemporary romance, and you have not experienced a Jennifer Probst book, you are seriously missing out. Do yourself a favor and grab a copy."

—*A Midlife Wife*

"*Any Time, Any Place* is a warm, sexy, gritty blockbuster of a book. Hear that sucking sound? That's *New York Times* bestseller Jennifer Probst pulling me into *Any Time, Any Place*, the second book in her Billionaire Builders series."

—*BookPage*

Praise for

everywhere
and every way

Book One in the Billionaire Builders Series

"Probst tugs at the heartstrings with feisty Morgan, strong and silent Caleb, and an array of appealing supporting characters. Readers will root for Caleb and Morgan's quest for happily ever after and will eagerly await the next in the series."

—*Publishers Weekly*

"Probst's fans will enjoy the unusual setup of her latest romance."

—*Kirkus Reviews*

"The passion just about sets the pages on fire."

—*RT Book Reviews*

"Ms. Probst, with her clever characters, fast-paced story, and humorous dialogue, made me a very happy camper. . . . The backstory of Caleb's family issues and [Morgan's] control issues added to the appeal of this sexy, sassy, and seductive read. The Billionaire Builders series is off to a good start."

—*Night Owl Reviews*, Top Pick

ALSO BY JENNIFER PROBST

The Billionaire Builders Series

Everywhere and Every Way

Any Time, Any Place

The Searching For Series

Searching for Someday

Searching for Perfect

"Searching for You" in *Baby, It's Cold Outside*

Searching for Beautiful

Searching for Always

Searching for Disaster

The Marriage to a Billionaire Series

The Marriage Bargain

The Marriage Trap

The Marriage Mistake

The Marriage Merger

all or nothing at all

JENNIFER PROBST

G

GALLERY BOOKS

New York   London   Toronto   Sydney   New Delhi

G

Gallery Books
An Imprint of Simon & Schuster, Inc.
1230 Avenue of the Americas
New York, NY 10020

First Gallery Books trade paperback edition July 2017

GALLERY BOOKS and colophon are registered trademarks of Simon & Schuster, Inc.

For information about special discounts for bulk purchases, please contact Simon & Schuster Special Sales at 1-866-506-1949 or business@simonandschuster.com.

The Simon & Schuster Speakers Bureau can bring authors to your live event. For more information or to book an event, contact the Simon & Schuster Speakers Bureau at 1-866-248-3049 or visit our website at www.simonspeakers.com.

Manufactured in the United States of America

10 9 8 7 6 5 4 3 2 1

Library of Congress Cataloging-in-Publication Data is available.

ISBN 978-1-5011-2429-7
ISBN 978-1-5011-2430-3 (ebook)

A man deserves a second chance, but keep an eye on him.

—John Wayne

One is not born, but rather becomes, a woman.

—Simone de Beauvoir

I love to see a young girl go out and grab the world by its lapels. Life's a bitch. You've got to go out and kick ass.

—Maya Angelou

———————

This book is dedicated to all the young women
in my family ready to take on the world.

My nieces: Taylor, Kaitlyn, Amanda, and Anna.

You are strong and beautiful, fearless
and magnificent. Never forget that, my dear ones.
I am proud of you. Now go kick some ass.

prologue

SEVEN YEARS AGO . . .

The darkness masked everything that was wrong and allowed her to bare not only her body but her very soul.

Her hands slid over sleek muscles and dampened skin. She arched under the heat of his mouth, at first demanding and rough, then gentling to an aching tenderness that broke her apart piece by piece. His name whispered from her lips in a prayer and a chant, wanting him, needing him . . .

"Tristan."

He parted her thighs and slid home. She cried out at the burning fullness crowding all the empty spaces inside until there was only him, his beloved face inches from hers, tight with tension and a raw possession that thrilled her.

"Give me everything."

She couldn't fight his words or his body. His hands gripped her hips. His amber eyes glinted with masculine demand as he pushed her higher, wringing agonizing pleasure with each step toward climax, and she gave up, gave in, and let him catch her as she shattered with release.

He followed her over, groaning her name, and she clung to him with a vulnerable need she tried desperately to hide in the light of day. He rolled to the side, and for a few precious moments, he held her. She breathed in the delicious scent of sweat, sex, and musk, cuddling into his powerful strength.

Tears stung her eyes. God, how she loved him. When he held her like this, the confusion and fear calmed, and she was able to reach an inner peace. But he was slipping further away with each passing day, and she didn't know how to stop the slide.

Maybe when he knew about the baby, things would change.

They'd get better. They'd make a commitment and move forward, and it would be like this all the time.

As if he caught her thought, he suddenly released her, turning away to sit up in the bed amid the tangled sheets.

The fragile hope was crushed like new spring grass under a booted heel.

"I have to tell you something, Syd."

She gathered her courage. "I have to tell you something, too," she said quietly.

He stood up. The moonlight trickled through the window and drenched him in a silvery glow. He pulled on his jeans with a quick precision that told her he wouldn't be staying the night. Again.

"I'm leaving."

Shock hit her like a sharp slap. She propped herself up on her elbow and stared. Panic stirred. "What are you talking about?"

He turned. His face looked like it was set in stone, as

if he hadn't been buried inside her a few minutes ago. "I'm done with this family. Done with this town. My asshole father just informed me he refuses to let me buy the real estate I wanted to flip. He wants me to be like Cal. To take his orders and build his cookie-cutter houses for the rest of my life. My own brother took his side, and we just had a blowout."

Heart beating wildly, she tried to find a solution. The family construction business, Pierce Brothers, was legendary in Harrington, but Christian Pierce ran his empire with a fierce hand and an even fiercer tongue. As the middle sibling, Tristan had been struggling to find his place for years and to show his father what he could bring to the company. "Your dad has a temper. If you keep showing him how you can help Pierce Brothers, I'm sure he'll come around."

He spit out a curse and shook his head. "Would you stop defending my father, Syd? He fucking hates me. God, I could take that if he respected me, but he thinks I'm a joke. Dalton is already leaving for California, my mother is dead, and I refuse to spend the rest of my life being a lackey. I'm going to New York City and doing real estate."

She winced, her heart twisting with pain. His mother, Diane, had been the heart of the family. The car crash that took her life a few months earlier ripped everyone apart, including Sydney. Diane had been like her own mother, and she was still reeling with grief. She struggled to put her thoughts into words. "Right now? Why don't you give it a little more time? Go over all your options. It's been hard for everyone."

"There are no other options here! Don't you understand nothing is ever going to change? I'm trapped. Trapped by my damn family and responsibilities and—" He broke off, shoving his fingers through his hair. "I can't wait any longer. I'm leaving this week."

Her breath backed up in her lungs. No. This was going all wrong. He couldn't just leave after the past few months together. Could he? Yes, he'd been in pain after losing his mother and constantly fighting with his two brothers. They all were struggling to put the pieces back together. But she'd thought he was leaning on her to help him through it. Not running away to some new place with new people.

Not running away from her.

He felt trapped. Is that the way he felt about her? When she'd turned nineteen, her dream had finally come true. After all these years, he'd finally *seen* her. Wanted her. Stopped looking at her as a child and saw her all grown up. They'd shared something extraordinary, but now he looked at her like she was holding him back, comparing her to his family.

"What about—what about me?" She hated the weak whine to her voice. Why couldn't she be strong and fierce? A woman confident in their relationship? She always reverted to that young girl who used to follow him around like a lost puppy, begging for attention. Shame filled her at the question, but she couldn't look away. She needed his answer.

"Come with me."

They were the words she craved to hear. She could accept them and run away like in her youthful fantasies. Leave her home and follow him to New York. They'd be together and be happy. Right?

The inner voice rose from her core and whispered in her ear.

What about the baby?

Trapped. His baby would make him feel like he was being strangled. Like she did. He'd never wanted her to go, or she wouldn't have had to ask. It was his guilt over leaving her behind. There was a shiny new life calling to him, and she wasn't a part of it. No, she was a part of his past, a part he wanted to forget. Their brief affair hadn't been as life changing for him. He didn't love her the way she so desperately needed him to.

Still, sheer stubbornness and habit kept her hoping.

"My grandmother is sick," she said. "She's been in and out of the hospital, and I need to take care of her."

"My father can help out. You can visit her. I'm sure she'd want you to go."

Once again, there was no passion or urgency in his voice. It was as if he was stating facts, giving rational reasons why she could join him. Her hands floated around to land on her flat tummy.

Trapped . . .

She'd go to New York and have his baby, and he'd be miserable. Or he'd decide to stay to be a father and be miserable. She'd be a mistake, along with his child. Could she live with that? She'd been one of those kids, with her junkie mother and a father who took off, leaving her in the care of her grandparents. Always feeling unwanted. Was this what she dreamed for her future?

Coldness lodged in her gut. No. She couldn't do that to any of them. Even if she had to lose the man she loved in the process.

"I don't want to go to New York, Tristan. This is my home.

I like my job at Pierce Brothers, and I can't leave my grand-mother. She took care of me my whole life, and I owe her. I want to enroll in business school and get my degree. I can't start all over in the city."

"Of course, you can! Don't you want more for yourself, Syd? More from your life?" Frustration clung to his aura. He clenched his fists and faced her down. "Is this it for you? Working for my father and settling in the same town you were born in? You can be anything in New York. I thought you weren't going to be that scared little girl anymore. Just take the chance, and let's do this. Let's leave together."

If he'd told her he loved her, she'd probably fly off the bed and follow him to Siberia. If he'd given her any indica-tion emotion ruled his speech, she'd tell him about the baby and take a leap of faith.

Instead, she looked deep into those gorgeous amber eyes and saw . . .

Nothing.

The numbness took over. She knew the pain would come much later. Right now, she needed to do this and set him free. He didn't love her the way she did him. There was something bigger out there for him. His dreams weren't about her. And damned if she'd spend the rest of her life trying to be someone who always doubted she was enough. Someone who trapped him into a life of what-ifs and regret.

"I can't leave, Tristan. I'm sorry. This is my home. I need to stay. And to be honest, I don't think you really want me to go."

He spun away from her. Anger beat from him in waves she could almost touch. "Are you kidding me? I ask you to go away with me, and you say you don't believe me? Are we playing these ridiculous games again, Sydney? 'Cause I'm tired. You can do anything you want, and nothing is keeping you here except yourself. But I'm not about to beg."

He grabbed his shirt, quickly dressed, and walked to the door. "Just remember you made your choice. I tried. I'm leaving on Friday, and I'm not looking back."

The door shut behind him.

She wrapped the sheets tight around her and bowed her head. Body shaking, she let the surge of pain and fear wash over her and wondered if she'd made the biggest mistake of her life.

chapter one

Sydney Greene-Seymour rushed into the office of Pierce Brothers Construction, frantically calculating how she'd make up the twenty minutes she'd lost in morning madness. Her daughter, Becca, had insisted on wearing her hair in a French braid, then raced back to her closet to change twice before school. If she acted like this at six years old, what would happen when she reached high school?

Sydney shuddered at the thought. Juggling her purse, laptop, and briefcase, she dug for the key. She was a bit of a control freak when it came to running the office where she'd worked since she was sixteen years old, and she liked to arrive before everyone else started. Order was the key to dealing with chaos. Her life had been such a series of sharp turns and fear-inducing hills, her soul was soothed in the one place she could not only control but thrive in.

Her job.

And finally, she was ready to take it to the next level.

The office was quiet, immediately calming her. She dropped her stuff on her desk, then headed to the kitchen in a hunt for sanity.

Or, at least, some clarity.

The kitchen was high-tech, from the stainless steel refrigerator to the cappuccino maker, soda machine, and various vending machines. With skilled motions, she quickly brewed the coffee, then grabbed her fave Muppets mug and filled it to the brim.

Trying not to gulp the wicked-hot liquid, she sipped and breathed, bringing her focus to the upcoming presentation. After years of running Pierce Brothers as executive assistant and general office guru, she was about to make the pitch of a lifetime. It was time to take the next step and prove her worth.

It was time to be promoted to CFO.

And they had no idea it was coming.

Nerves fluttered in her stomach, but she ignored them. She walked back into her office with her coffee, her Jimmy Choo high heels sinking into the plush carpet. She'd dressed to impress in her designer Donna Karan apple-green suit and even managed to pin up her crazed curls in a semblance of professionalism. Her black-framed glasses added a flair of style and seriousness. After grabbing her flash drive with her PowerPoint presentation loaded, she quickly set up the conference room with her handouts and laptop, then brought in a tray of pastries from Andrea's Bakery with a pitcher of water. Nothing wrong with a little bribing, especially when it involved sweets. She double-checked the room.

Perfect. She was ready. She picked up her mug for another sip. She'd calculated this quarter's profits and could clearly show the margin of growth once she brought in this new—

"Morning."

She jerked at the deep, cultured voice breaking into her

thoughts. Coffee splashed over the edge of her mug onto her jacket. Cursing, she swiveled her head, her gaze crashing into whiskey-colored eyes that were as familiar as her own beating heart. Familiar yet deadly, to both her past and her present. Why did he have to be the one who was here first? The man possessed an inner alarm clock that detested lateness.

She still hated the little leap of her heart when she was in his company, but it'd just become part of her routine. Kind of like eating and breathing.

Anyone else would've brought a smile and a bit of chatter. But Tristan Pierce didn't talk to her. Not really. Oh, he lectured and demanded and judged, but he refused to actually have a conversation with her. Not that she cared. It was better for both of them to keep their distance.

"You scared me," she accused. "Why don't you ever make any noise when you walk into a room?"

Those carved lips twitched with the need to smile. Unfortunately, her presence rarely allowed the man to connect with any of his softer emotions, so he kept his expression grim. They'd been dancing around each other for two years now, and still struggled with discomfort in each other's presence. Well, he experienced discomfort in the form of awkwardness.

She experienced discomfort in the form of sexual torture.

"I'll work on it." He gestured to the new brown stain on her clothes. "Need help?"

"I got it." Her body wept at the thought of him touching her, even for a moment. *Down, girl.* She grabbed a napkin, dipped it in water, and dabbed at her suit jacket.

"I didn't realize we were having a meeting today. I have some appointments."

"I rearranged your schedule. This is the only time that everyone was able to meet."

"Another board meeting?"

"Sort of."

He didn't ask any other questions. He rarely did.

She tried to ignore the waves of masculine energy that emanated from his figure. He'd always been the quiet one of his brothers, but he never needed words or noise to make his presence known. When he walked into a room, everyone noticed—men and women. He held a demeanor of competence and power in a whole different way from his brothers, Caleb and Dalton. As the middle child, he was a peacemaker and able to make decisions with a confident quickness most admired but never duplicated. His thoroughness was legendary. Tristan was able to see a problem from all angles and attack it with a single-minded intensity and level of control. He'd once brought that same talent to the bedroom, concentrating on wringing pleasure from her body with a thoroughness that ruined her for other lovers.

She studied him from under heavy-lidded eyes. His suits were legendary—custom made from the best fabrics and cut to emphasize his powerful, lean body. Today he wore a charcoal-gray suit, a snowy-white shirt, and a vivid purple tie. Engraved gold cuff links. His shoes were polished to a high sheen and made of soft leather. He always reminded her of one of those jungle cats who prowled with litheness, amber eyes lit with intention, taking their time before deciding what to do with prey. His analytical mind was as droolworthy as his body. Hard, supple muscles balanced with a beautiful grace most men could never pull off. His hair was thick, perfectly groomed, and a deep reddish brown. His face was an artistry of elegance, from the sharp blade of his nose to his square jaw, full lips, and high cheekbones. Lush lashes set off eyes that practically glowed, darkening to an intensity that made a woman's heart beat madly. He was beauty incarnate, a feast for the senses a woman could never bore of while spending the rest of eternity studying every angle and curve and drowning in his cognac gaze.

She'd once been that woman. Of course, that was centuries ago, before the ugliness between them sprouted from dark corners and swallowed them up whole.

Didn't matter. She only dealt with Tristan for work now, though the past two years had been more difficult, as she was forced to spend so much time in his presence. Those five years after he'd moved to New York and been away from Harrington were hard, but she'd finally grown up. Become a mother and made her own niche in life, rather than waiting for him to dictate her wants and needs.

If only she weren't still attracted to the man.

Already the room surged with the innate connection between them. Some things never disappeared. They'd always had chemistry. Now it was just a matter of accepting it as fact and ignoring it.

Most of the time she managed.

"Let me settle in. We'll start in fifteen?" he asked.

"Yes, that's fine."

She turned away, discarding the napkin, and he left. She practically sagged in relief. Having him too close threw her off, and this morning she needed to be a poised, cool, confident professional.

Twenty minutes later, the team was assembled around the conference table. She tried to keep a smug smile from her face as they immediately attacked the tray of pastries, arguing good-naturedly over who got what and who saw which first. She'd decided on a sneak attack for her presentation. She knew these men well, and taking them by surprise would lower their defenses and allow them to really listen to her presentation without preliminary assumptions. The biggest problem with working for Pierce Brothers for the past decade was also her greatest asset.

She was like family. Unfortunately, this meant being treated like a little sister, which was also frustrating. She needed to convince them she was the best person for the job of CFO based on her business history. Not because of familial relations.

"Who called this meeting?" Cal asked between bites of his favorite cinnamon bun. "It wasn't on my schedule originally." As the oldest brother of the crew, he was the most nononsense, with a simple, rugged manner. He wore his usual uniform of old, ripped jeans, a white T-shirt, and work boots. His face was as rough as his appearance, from his hooked nose to his bushy brows and gunmetal-gray eyes, but he was always protective and held the wisest counsel she knew. He'd led the company along with his brothers when it was almost lost due to his father's will, but now they stood together, bonded once again by affection.

"Not me." Dalton had his legs stretched out and propped up on the opposite-facing leather chair. She held back a sigh at the lack of professionalism. "I have no issues to discuss." As the youngest, he'd always been the wildest, and his woodworking talent was legendary. Stinging-blue eyes, long blond surfer-type hair, and an easy charm made women fall happily in line to warm his bed. Of course, now he was settled and in love with Raven. He'd grown and matured over the past year, and she had never seen him so happy.

They both looked at Tristan, who shrugged. Elegantly, of course. "I was told my calendar was rearranged just for this meeting."

The final member in the crew, not related by blood, was Brady. He lifted his hands in the air. "Nope. Have no idea what this is about." As the architect and a longtime family friend, he'd carved his own niche for himself in the company. With his dark Latin looks and commanding manner, he'd been essential to their success and easily held his own.

Time to gain control of this meeting and do what she came for.

"I did."

All gazes turned and focused on her. She gave them a cool smile and flipped on her laptop so the first slide of her PowerPoint presentation flashed on the screen. After quickly distributing the stack of handouts, she stood at the head of the conference table. Already she took in Tristan's fierce frown as he began flipping through the pages of her proposal.

"What's this about, Syd?" Cal asked, finishing up his pastry.

"As you know, I've been working at Pierce Brothers a long time. I started as file clerk, worked my way up to secretary, then executive assistant. I've been in charge of accounting, marketing, and managing the office staff."

Cal cocked his head. "You want a raise. You don't need to hold a meeting for this. You deserve a pay bump."

"I don't want just a raise, Cal. I want to be promoted to CFO of Pierce Brothers. I want to be part of the board of directors."

Dalton whistled. A grin curved his lips. "Man, this is gonna be good," he drawled, taking a bite of a simple jelly doughnut.

Brady sat back in his seat, a thoughtful look on his face. Cal nodded, urging her to go on. She refused to glance over at Tristan. She didn't need any negative energy affecting her presentation.

"I've been in charge of the accounts at Pierce Brothers for years, which goes beyond the standard accounts receivables and payables. Besides budgeting, I'm involved in negotiating with our local vendors for discounts and securing new jobs, and I have built solid relationships that keep productivity at increased levels. I've included a breakdown of the past quarter's profit margin." She brought up the graphs, which were also included in the work sheets. "As Pierce Brothers has evolved, the workload has doubled, and all of you are consistently in the field. I've been able to fill in the gap by being more involved in the design aspect. Three months ago, I secured a new contract with Grey's Custom Flooring with a significant discount to our clients. I was able to do this because of my relationship with Anthony Moretti. Building up my main base of contacts keeps Pierce Brothers viable and able to keep offering unique materials to our clients."

Cal tapped his pen against the desk. "I was impressed with Grey's. The quality is top-notch, and they've been easy to work with. You did a great job."

She gave a slight nod. "Thank you. I'd like to show you

how those savings affected our bottom line." She clicked steadily through the slides, breaking down each of her skills and leading up to the main event.

It was time to bring it home.

"I believe it's time to move forward. We're financially stable and ready to take on a bigger job with our redesigning and renovation projects." Tristan glanced up, frowning. This was the delicate part of negotiations. She was stepping directly into Tristan's territory, but it was time he realized what she could bring to the organization on her own. "I've been in talks with Adam Cushman. He's been very interested in securing some homes in the Harrington area and on the lookout for an opportunity. I believe he's finally found one."

"Cushman?" Tristan narrowed his gaze. "He's a big developer in New York City. I worked with him briefly. How is it you know him well enough to be involved in such a conversation without my knowledge?"

His voice was chilled, like one of those frosty mugs Raven used in her bar. Sydney fought a shiver, determined not to let him intimidate her. Not anymore. "If you remember, you were in a bidding war with him for the property on Allerton. He came into the office one day, but no one was here, so I took the meeting. You ended up winning the property, but he kept in contact with me regarding future opportunities in Harrington. We both hold a similar vision on developing more family-friendly homes with touches of unique design to court a solid middle-class income bracket."

"What properties is he interested in?" Tristan flicked out the demanding question with a touch of impatience.

She gave a tight smile. "It's there in the proposal you're

holding." She clicked to the next slide of her PowerPoint, sketching out a block of houses. "He'll be purchasing a total of eight houses on Bakery Street."

Dalton stared at the screen, shaking his head. "Bakery? Those houses are in bad shape. Most of the tenants abandoned them, and no one's been interested in renovation for an entire block."

"Exactly." She pushed the button for the next screen. "Adam has been able to purchase the entire lot and plans to renovate them all together, then flip them. This is the breakdown of approximate costs. We still need architectural proposals drawn up and design specifics discussed, but he's on board and wants Pierce Brothers to take the job."

Tristan studied the papers in front of him as if he were a lawyer about to take the bar exam. Brady scribbled notes in the margins, nodding. Dalton shot her a proud grin. It took everything she had not to smile back at his obvious admiration, but she kept her gaze focused on Cal.

"Ambitious," he said slowly. "And brilliant. How'd you sell him Pierce?"

"I want to use local suppliers for the entire project. I convinced Adam to go local instead of using the main manufacturing plants. We're concentrating on unique kitchen and bath features to appeal to middle income. Fenced-in yards, smaller-type decks, and appealing front porches for the lot."

"Have you confirmed all our local suppliers will be on board with this?" Tristan demanded. "Many of them refuse to work with the bigwigs. They prefer local developers. Not city slickers, as they term them."

"I've made initial contact and received definite interest.

I'd meet with them and get everything in writing before moving forward."

"Well done," Cal murmured, still tapping his pen. "This is a huge job, Sydney. Do you have specifics?"

She clicked to the next screen, which showed an organized calendar of tasks, assignments, and proposed time slots. "This is the working plan, but of course it will be tweaked as we discuss further."

"I would've appreciated a heads-up before this meeting," Tristan clipped out. "I have another project in the works, and this will take up my calendar for the next several months. Why didn't Adam reach out to me before this?"

She practically purred with satisfaction as she delivered the crushing words. "Because Adam wants me to lead this project. Not you."

The men stared at her in slightly shocked silence.

She smoothly continued her pitch. "Adam trusts me. He knows I'll retain his vision and be the main contact throughout the project. The only way he'll give Pierce Brothers the job is if I'm in charge. And the only way I'll agree to be in charge is if you promote me to CFO."

Sydney snapped the laptop closed. The screen went dark.

"I need something more. I deserve this opportunity. I know we'll need to hire another person to take over more office responsibilities, but I think Charlie may be interested. I know her primary love is doing renovation and rehab, but learning the business from the ground up intrigues her."

Brady nodded. Charlie had come to Pierce Brothers as an intern, then slowly made her way to becoming indispensable for her skill in pulling apart houses and putting them back together. She and Brady had experienced their own fireworks, beginning with intense dislike and moving to grudging respect and then something much more. Though they seemed like opposites, they fit together perfectly, and it was obvious how in love each was with the other.

"Charlie actually mentioned she'd like to take on more work," he said. "It's definitely a possibility."

"I have no problem hiring another person," Cal said. "Securing this project could be a big asset, especially for the future."

Dalton grabbed another jelly doughnut. "I think it's amazing, Syd. Great presentation."

"Thank you."

Suddenly burning amber eyes pierced into hers. Tristan's lips pressed together in a thin line of disapproval. "You giving us an ultimatum?"

She met his gaze head-on, refusing to flinch. Refusing to back down. "I'm giving you a proposal. A smart one. And I'll be waiting for your decision. Adam wants to move quickly on this, so I'd like to be able to get back to him."

"Fair enough." Cal rose to his feet. "Give us some time to discuss. We'll have an answer for you soon."

She smiled. "I appreciate it." Scooping up her laptop and empty coffee mug, she walked out of the conference room with her head held high.

She'd done it. Whatever happened next, she'd made her pitch and fought for what she deserved, for both her and Becca. After all these years in the background, she finally had her chance.

She intended to take it.

chapter two

Tristan stared at the stack of papers in front of him, neatly typed out, with impressive charts, graphs, and cost analyses. She'd handled herself like a true professional, reflecting a calm demeanor during his questions and delivering an adept presentation of exactly why she should be promoted to CFO.

Too bad she still pissed him off.

"Well, that was interesting," Dalton commented, finishing off his third jelly doughnut. "I had no idea Sydney wanted to move up. She always seemed pretty happy with her duties."

Cal leaned back in his chair. "I'm not surprised. Been waiting for this awhile now. Guess she was finally ready."

Tristan regarded his brother from across the table. "You knew about this deal she concocted with Cushman?" he asked. "A deal she deliberately worked on behind my back?"

One bushy brow shot up. "No, I didn't know about Cushman, but you gotta give her credit. We certainly weren't pursuing the opportunity. Because she put herself out there and followed through, we may gain a lucrative contract."

"I can't believe you knew she was going for a promotion

and you never told us," Tristan muttered. "You may be president, Cal, but we're all equal members at this table."

Cal cocked his head. "Damn, bro, why are you so pissed? I didn't know she wanted to be CFO, but I knew she's been working for this company for years, ran the office from the ground up, and is probably getting bored with her job. She's smart and ambitious. Why shouldn't she go for CFO?"

"She's definitely qualified," Brady offered. "To be honest, not one of us has ever competently pitched our projects in this manner. I think we'd be smart to vote her in."

"Agreed," Dalton said. "Cushman is just an extra benefit. Letting her lead on this job will allow her to spread her wings a bit. She's always been great with figures, but there's a creative vision she never gets to follow through on. This will do it."

Irritation spiked through Tristan. The worst part was he wasn't sure why. But Sydney had always irritated him, whether it had been as a young girl following him around with those sweet, longing glances or as a mouthy teen with a body that had filled out with luscious curves and tempted him at every turn.

It certainly didn't help how she'd only blossomed with age. She walked with the power of a woman who knew how to get what she wanted, perfectly demonstrated by today's meeting. Her strawberry-colored hair now hung halfway down her back, still curly and wild as ever, like silk trapped in fire. She liked to wear it up now, shoving those strands into a neat chignon. Her face had always been a bit too round, her mouth and eyes a bit too wide, and she'd always despised the scattering of freckles across her nose and dotted generously over her white skin. He hated those black-framed glasses that hid her jade-green eyes and gave him fantasies about sexy librarians. Her wardrobe drove him slightly mad, with her tight designer suits, short skirts, and sexy high heels. She'd never been petite or small boned—no, her body was all Eve, lush and ripe like the apple that tempted her. In New York, he'd had a hard time meeting a woman over a size 6. Their makeup was always flawless, they regularly attended blow-out salons to kill any curls, and they were all vegetarians who believed in saving the earth. They never looked at him with adoration and always paid their own check and would instruct the bartender exactly how to make their Skinnygirl martini.

No, much easier to concentrate on the way she treated him like a bug she'd rather squash or her refusal to talk to him during Sunday dinners at the mansion or the cool tone of her throaty voice when she answered his demands, like he was slightly brain damaged.

Much easier to remember the depth of her betrayal.

If he concentrated on that truth, it was easier to ignore the persistent electricity crackling between them and the low thrum of arousal beating through each cold, deliberate word spoken.

Just lingering stuff from the past, he told himself. They worked better together when they avoided each other and stayed in their private corners.

But now she was challenging the corner he'd put her in.

"Listen, I'm not saying Sydney's not competent at her job," he said steadily. "But she's never headed a project with flipped properties, renovation, and design. I've always been the one in charge, and I don't like that ultimatum she threw out at us. She has no right."

Dalton shrugged. "You would've done it," he pointed out. "It's good business. Offer something we want and present the hook to get it. Would've thought you'd admire her moves."

"It's different," he gritted out.

"How?" Cal asked.

He clenched his fists under the table. Frustration rippled through him. "She tricked us. Plus, if she fails, we lose Cushman for future projects and put ourselves in a serious financial hole. It's too risky."

"I don't think so," Cal said. "She'll have to be lead, but it's critical you work with her at every step. That will confirm our success."

He refused to acknowledge the slight trickle of panic threatening. "I'm too busy to babysit. I have my own shit going on."

"Like what?" Dalton asked. "You said in another week you'd be clear. Did you take something else on?"

He tamped down the urge to pound on his brother. "I was planning on investigating some houses outside of town." The vague explanation only made it more obvious he was full of crap. Dalton and Caleb shared a knowing look.

"Why are you so against this?" Cal demanded. "Don't you think she's earned CFO? Or is your problem personal?"

He jerked and smothered a curse word. His brothers knew they'd had a fling years ago, but he'd kept most of the details a secret. Being with Sydney had been almost taboo—she'd been a soft spot for his parents and had practically grown up in their household like a younger sister.

Of course, his brothers had been barely talking back then, anyway. When he took off to New York to carve out his own path, they lost all contact for five full years. It was only when Christian Pierce died that Tristan returned to Harrington to discover his father's will stated Pierce Brothers would be sold unless they all ran the company together for one full year.

The memory of that first year made Tristan shake his head. They'd barely been able to be civil to one another, let alone run a company. It was a hard year, full of painful fights and realizations that had changed them all. Finally, they'd healed the past, and he'd gotten his brothers back. There was still the occasional blowup or argument, but underneath was a respect and love that guided them through. Finally Pierce Brothers was a true family company again, and he'd decided to stay in Harrington.

Unfortunately, he hadn't been able to move forward with Sydney.

"Not personal," he shot back. "Just trying to present a full view of the obstacles. I know we all admire Sydney, but this is a big decision."

Cal's gunmetal eyes flickered as if he knew what the real problem was but wasn't going to force his brother to say it. "I say it's an easy decision to make," Cal said. "But we all have to be in agreement. Those in favor of offering Sydney the CFO position and taking on Cushman's project, say yes."

"Yes," Brady said.

"Hell yes," Dalton called out.

"It's a yes for me, too," Cal said.

Tristan remained silent. Everyone turned to look at him. A strange stirring in the pit of his stomach warned him that if he agreed, things were going to change. He wouldn't be able to constantly avoid her. He'd be in her presence, day after day, working closely with her.

But even he couldn't deny her the promotion she deserved, no matter his doubts. No matter how much he didn't like it.

"Agreed."

"Good. I'll bring her in." Cal headed out the door and returned with Sydney. Tristan had to give her credit. Even at the moment of truth, she gave off the confident vibe of a woman deserving of success. When had that happened? When had she changed from the insecure, tentative young girl who looked to him for all the answers?

"It's official. Welcome to the board, Sydney. Congratulations."

Her joyous smile poked at Tristan's heart, but he kept it firmly barricaded. Cal gave her a warm hug, Dalton picked her up for a quick spin in his arms, and Brady squeezed her shoulder.

Tristan remained seated, somehow frozen in place.

"Why don't you talk to Tristan about your next step with Cushman?" Cal suggested. "I know we have to move fast, so I'll leave you both to work out those details."

"Of course."

Everyone else filed out, shutting the door behind them. Silence descended. Tristan watched her smooth down her skirt, grab some papers, and gracefully sit in the leather chair.

He forced himself to speak. "Congratulations."

She nodded. Tilted her head. And met his gaze with full force. "You didn't want to vote for me, did you?"

He tried to keep his expression neutral. No need for her to see any type of weakness at this point. Not when they were about to spend too many hours together on a regular basis. "No," he admitted.

Her banked anger shot out at him in sparks. "Don't like sharing the spotlight?" she challenged. "Or does my being boss bother you?"

His jaw clenched. "My ego has nothing to do with my reservations."

"Then why?" she demanded. "Haven't I proved myself at this point? Or will I never be good enough for you?"

He refused to squirm in his chair. The familiar scent of orange blossoms drifted in the air and teased his nostrils. The smooth expanse of her bare legs in those ridiculous heels bothered the hell out of him. Why couldn't she wear pants? Why did she consistently emanate sensuality with every breath? He tried to snap back his focus. "It's not that you don't deserve the promotion. You've never taken on such an ambitious project, and you forced us to make a decision based on how bad we want Cushman to sign. That isn't fair."

"Bullshit," she bit out. "I forced you to make a decision you would've dragged on for way too long. And I'll relish showing you how well I can run this project on my own. I'm not about to fail, Tristan. I worked too hard to get here, and one day I'll get the satisfaction of hearing you say you were wrong. Wrong about me and my ability to handle anything you throw at me."

His dick stirred in his pants at the raw hunger carving out the lines of her face, the sizzling heat in her eyes. The same hunger and heat she used to express when looking at him, begging him with her body and voice and eyes to take her, fuck her, claim her.

The space between them shrank, filling the air with a crackling, sexual tension that exploded in the room and tried to drag him under. He sucked in a breath, got himself under control, and swore he'd do whatever he needed to keep his distance. No way was he going back down that path. He'd once begged her to choose him, and she'd turned away.

He'd never beg again.

"I'd advise us to stick to future business," he said coldly. "We'll need to set up a conference call with Cushman and get Brady working on specific plans. I hope you'll be able to work late and on weekends. This will take up all of your spare time."

Her voice went back to its rigid distance, as if she was barely able to tolerate his company. "I'll handle it."

"Good. Let's start with the first house."

For the next hour, Tristan concentrated on the task at hand, putting his body on lockdown. Work was primary. The goal was the only thing that mattered, not this strange relationship that imprisoned his body and stirred his mind.

But the past still drifted between them, curling and wispy like smoke that eventually disappears into nothing.

"Tristan! Wait for me!"

Impatience snapped at him, but he stopped running and turned. Her chubby legs pumped with effort, but the determination on her face confirmed she would have followed even if he hadn't stopped. Sydney never took no for an answer, even if it meant ruining his game.

"Why don't you find Dalton?" he hissed, trying to keep his voice low. Playing zombie tag required a delicate balance of

swiftness, savvy, and sheer luck. The acres of woods around his house were perfect but also known to hide a good sneak attack. With her wild red hair, clumsy motions, and high voice, she'd get him caught in no time.

"I want to stay with you," she said stubbornly. She reached him, her breath coming out in ragged pants.

"Fine, but you gotta keep up."

"I will. I saw Carl over by the shed."

"Good. Let's head this way." He took off with her at his heels but made himself go a tad slower. Why did he always have to look out for her? Having two brothers was already a pain in the butt, and now he got stuck with a girl. Mom always warned him to be nice, and he liked Syd, but she was always trailing him, asking him to play and stuff. He was fifteen—practically a grown-up—yet she kept trying to join in, whether it was to play video games or baseball or to watch movies. "Keep your ears out for any sounds."

"I will."

They walked through the brush in silence, listening to the chatter of birds, the snap of branches, and the wind in the trees. The rich scents of earth and rotting leaves rose to his nostrils. Voices echoed, but they were to the left, so they must be heading in a good direction.

"I saw a zombie movie once," she said. "It was really gross. They wanted to eat brains."

"Your grandmother let you watch it?" he asked.

"No, I snuck out of my bed at night and watched it. I'm more grown up than you think."

He snorted. As if. "You're only eleven. Still in elementary school."

"So? Diane says I'm mature for my age."

"Mom's just trying to make you feel better. Besides, wouldn't you rather be playing with dolls and princesses and stuff?"

She wrinkled her nose and shot him a disgusted look. "Ugh, I hate that stuff. I'd rather hang with you. Your dad said he's going to bring me to the job site so I can see how the houses are built. I'm going to work for him one day and run the whole company."

"Why? Don't you want to get out of here when you get older? Go somewhere cool?"

She shrugged and picked at a hangnail. Her sneakers dragged through the leaves. "No. I like it here. And I'm gonna like working for your dad."

Annoyance flooded him. He was trapped with nowhere to go. If it were up to him, he'd travel and do something great. Something just for him. He was sick of always taking his father's orders and being ignored. His father only listened to Cal and never him. Dalton was always with Mom. Tristan had no one, but he didn't care. Sydney had the freedom he always wanted, but she just wanted to stay in stupid Harrington. "Well, I'm going off to college soon." If he could get far enough away, maybe things could change. But already his father was warning him he'd need to go local so he could continue working for Pierce Brothers.

"But you'll come back, right?" Her green eyes held a worried glint and something else, something deeper that made his stomach tighten in a weird way. Like he was important.

"Maybe."

She opened her mouth to say something, but voices broke through the woods, and he shushed her. Looking around wildly, *he dragged her over to a massive oak tree with thick, gnarled branches.*

"They're coming," he whispered. "We gotta climb this tree." Her eyes widened. He shinnied up the trunk and got to the first branch. "Come on, hurry before they spot you."

"I can't get up there!"

The voices got louder.

He muttered a curse word that made him feel manly and glared. She was going to get him caught. "Yes, you can. Try."

She scrunched up her face and tried to crawl up the fat trunk, but her arms and legs weren't long enough to get a decent grip. "Tristan, help me!"

He groaned, leaning down to offer his hand. She grabbed on, and he yanked her up to the first branch, her legs scraping against the rough bark, drawing blood.

"I hear them! Over here!" Carl's voice was full of triumph. Feet pounded in the brush.

"Damn, Syd, they heard you!"

Her lower lip trembled. "Sorry."

Annoyance warred with sympathy. "Is your leg okay?"

She looked so miserable. "Yeah."

Guilt struck. "Just forget it. You stay here, and I'll jump off and head toward the creek."

Sheer stubbornness flickered over her face. She shook her head so her red curls slapped her ruddy cheeks. "No. I can help you. Run."

"What are you—"

With a wild whoop, she jumped down from the tree branch and started waving her hands in the air. "You can't catch me, you can't catch me!"

"There she is—get her!"

With one last glance, Sydney took off in the opposite direction, leading the boys away. Tristan quickly leapt down, taking off to safety. He heard victory yells as they caught her, and she turned into a zombie, but he already knew she'd never lead them back to him. She liked to make him happy, which made him feel bad when he was mean to her.

Oh well. At least he'd win the game.

He pushed the thought of Sydney from his mind and concentrated on winning.

chapter three

"Mama, it's almost my birthday! Can we get an ice-cream cake?"

Sydney laughed, grabbing her daughter and pulling her onto her lap. "Of course. You know that's my favorite. What do you want to do, sweetheart? Have you decided?"

Her daughter tilted her face and scrunched up her nose. "Can we go to Chuck E. Cheese?"

Sydney couldn't help wincing. It may be a kid's paradise, but it was a mother's nightmare. The loud, flashing games, overexcited children hunting for prize tickets and winning only enough for a spider ring, and a large mouse character that danced in a purple sweater. She always left with a headache.

Maybe she could sneak in a flask and fill it with wine.

"Sure. Just get me a list, and we'll send out some invitations."

"Okay. And I want to see Uncle Cal and Morgan and Dalton and Tristan and Uncle Brady. Can they come to my party? 'Cause they're my family."

Her chest tightened, but she managed a breath. The guilt was manageable this time. Practice did make perfect. "Yes, honey. But we'll have a cake for you at Uncle Cal's house, and Morgan said she's making your favorite dish."

"Spaghetti and meatballs?"

"Yep." She savored her daughter's soft body sprawled over her lap and the scent of her coconut shampoo. Her pink T-shirt boasted her favorite Disney princess: Ariel, because she had the same color hair. Her jeans had pink sparkles and matched the glittery nail polish on her fingers and toes. Already Becca was moving away from her cuddling, demanding more alone time and independence to read, draw, or play on her Kindle. How had so much time flashed by without Sydney realizing it? She used to laugh at mothers warning her to enjoy the toddler years, when she'd just prayed to be out of diapers and formula and sleepless nights. Now her daughter was reading on her own and had a group of friends she insisted on seeing at regular revolving playdates. She was going to be a powerhouse one day, but until she grew into that power, Sydney tried to keep her daughter's temper, and independence, in check. "I can't believe you're going to be seven," she murmured, stroking her daughter's hair.

"Was Matilda in the movie seven?" Becca asked. "'Cause I want to be like her."

"I think so. Wait a minute—you want to have terrible parents who lock you up, are mean to you, and don't let you go to school?"

Her daughter giggled. "No, but she gets to watch TV all the time. I'd like that part."

"Brat." Another giggle. Becca was always trying to finagle more television time. "For now, I need to get started on dinner. Sorry I've been working late this week. This new job will be a bit challenging, so I'll need you to help out more and understand I won't be home as much. Just for a while."

"That's okay, Mommy. I'm happy you got a premition."

"Promotion."

"Yeah, that. But don't forget about my ballet recital."

"I'd never forget your recital. Are you nervous?"

"A little."

"We'll get there early so I can be in the front row, okay?"

Her daughter's smile was Sydney's heaven and earth, making her heart explode with a fierce emotion that still humbled her. The moment Becca had pushed her way into the world, wailing in fury, Sydney had tumbled into a love that knew no bounds.

The voice she'd shoved deep inside, trapped in a locked box of her own making, slithered up to whisper.

She doesn't just belong to you . . .

Dear God, it was getting worse. Every day since the Pierce brothers had come home, she'd struggled. Her peaceful, ordered existence was shredded. Now she was haunted every day. Every night. Haunted by the truth she'd sworn to hide when Becca was born.

Her thoughts broke off as her daughter shot out of her lap, snuggling complete. "I'm hungry, Mama. Can I go play?"

"Yes, I'll call you when dinner's ready." She watched her daughter bound up the stairs, and with a sigh, she headed to the kitchen. Her home was small but perfect for the two of them, a yellow-shingled bi-level on a dead end. With a fenced-in yard, she had no worries about traffic, and she felt safe and secure, tucked away from the world. She'd decorated the house with all the girly stuff she loved—from throw pillows in bright teal to cozy afghans and fuzzy rugs supersoft under bare feet. She liked her work ruthlessly organized and her house casually messy. A good thing, because Becca was a whirlwind of activity, and Sydney was constantly remind-ing her to pick up her toys so she didn't trip on Barbie dolls, DVDs, and books.

Sydney opened the refrigerator, removing the thawed tilapia and slipping into mechanical mode. She still told Becca it was special chicken, since Becca gave her a hard time about eating fish. Dumping the fish into a pan, she doctored it with citrus, dill, and basil, olive oil, fresh gar-lic, and Himalayan salt. She scrubbed the potatoes and slid them in the oven, then grabbed a bag of frozen peas to steam—her child's only accommodation with green vegeta-bles. She pulled a bottle of Chardonnay from the refrigerator and poured herself half a glass, sighing with pleasure at the first cold, fruity sip.

As she moved around the kitchen in a dance she could complete with her eyes closed, she mentally ticked down the list of items to finish before the weekend. Time was a chal-lenge, but Charlie was a quick learner and taking on more re-sponsibility in the office. Sydney and Tristan were visiting the site tomorrow, and she'd need to meet Adam in the city soon for final contracts. She relished being more hands-on with the renovation and creative process, but she'd stepped right into Tristan's territory, and he wasn't letting her forget it.

He was always . . . around. Questioning every move. Lift-ing that arched brow in silent regard, forcing her to doubt her initial instincts. Trying to check up on her like she was a child and hadn't been working for the company since she was sixteen. He drove her mad, and eventually something was going to break. It was more than his judging stares and intense amber eyes. No, he seemed to be analyzing where she fit, as if trying to figure her out on a deeper level.

And that scared the hell out of her.

She set the timer and sipped her wine. God, she missed Diane. Whenever there was a problem, Sydney could sit in her cozy kitchen, talk, and be fed warm, filling food that always made her feel better. Grief struck like a stinging slap. Her grandparents had raised her with love and care, but Diane had been the mother figure she'd been missing. Growing up in the Pierce household gave her a sense of belonging, and working for the company only cemented her place. Funny, she'd always known exactly what she wanted to do with her life. She'd had no dreams of going away to college or leaving Harrington.

It had been Tristan who wanted to leave.

She stared out the window into the early-evening darkness. She'd spent her entire youth trying to force him to see her—really see her—and he'd spent most of his youth treating her like an annoying younger sister. What was it about him that had called to her from the very first day they met? Dalton was closer in age, but it was always Tristan who fascinated her. His quiet personality hid a fierceness of heart and loyalty she craved. No matter how mad his brothers made him, he was the peacemaker. As chaos reigned around him, he was the calm in a storm that soothed, offering a protection she'd always dreamed about. She'd tumbled into love with him at only eight years old, and he'd been haunting her ever since. How hard she had tried to hide her feelings, especially from Diane, not wanting to cause disapproval or concern with either of Tristan's parents, since they were so close.

But Diane knew. Had probably always sensed her desperate longing for a man who was destined to hurt her . . .

She sat at the counter, trying to nibble on the warm chocolate chip cookie fresh from the oven. But her stomach tumbled in that sick kind of way, so she settled on sipping iced tea from the yellow sunflower cup.

"You look pretty today," Diane said with a smile. Her dark, reddish hair was pinned up, and she looked comfortable in jeans and a loose T-shirt. She smelled of sugar, chocolate, and home. "Going somewhere special?"

Sydney tried for a casual tone. "Maybe. It's Friday night, so some of my friends want to go out."

"Ah, I forgot. You're growing up so fast. Any cute boys you have your eye on?"

A blush rose to her cheeks. She shifted on the stool. "Um . . . no, well, maybe. There's a boy in my science class. He's smart and helps me with lab work sometimes. He may be at the movies tonight."

"That's my girl, going for the brains."

"Is that what you did?" Sydney teased, trying another bite of the cookie.

Diane laughed, eyes sparkling. "Eventually. But first I started off with the bad boys. They were more fun for my wild soul." She winked, and Sydney laughed with her.

The bang of the door echoed through the room. She stiffened, trying to breathe normally. Her heart pounded in a wild rhythm. Her inner voice hissed a reminder: Don't look eager. Be cool.

Tristan was home.

"*Mom!*"

Diane shook her head and sighed. "In the kitchen, where I always am."

He came into the kitchen. Sydney's breath caught, and her belly did a slow tumble. His jeans were snug, emphasizing the muscled length of his thighs, and his black T-shirt stretched across his chest, showing off corded biceps and toasty-golden skin. His hair reminded her of hazelnut, a mix of brown with a hint of red, and always fell in perfect, thick waves over his brow. He smelled of pine, fall leaves, and s'mores. But that was probably just her imagination, because those were some of her favorite things in the whole world.

Sydney tried to act casual yet sophisticated as she waited for him to greet her. She propped up an elbow to tilt her head to the side, making sure her hair fell over her cheek in neat curls. God knows she'd spent hours this morning with the curling iron making sure it didn't frizz. She'd also been careful with her makeup. Pink lips, blush, mascara, and a touch of liner made her look older. The short denim skirt showed off her bare legs, and her trendy black top was cut to emphasize the swell of her breasts. Even her girlfriends had said how good she looked today. Maybe this time he'd notice?

"Mom, can you make dinner early tonight?"

She kept her position, but he still hadn't acknowledged her. She forced herself to speak. "Hi, Tris." Was her tone cool and casual enough? She crossed her legs deliberately so her skirt rode up an inch higher. "How are you?"

"Oh, hey, Syd. Mom? Can you?"

Diane kissed his cheek, which he allowed because he'd

learned the alternative was a big bear hug that went on for too many seconds. "Sure. How was school this week?"

"Astronomy test. Science sucks."

She raised a brow at his language but let it slide. "Maybe Dalton can help you. He's starting to know more than me ever since he got that telescope." She slid the cookies from the tray onto a large plate and set it in the middle of the marble table.

"Nah, I'll manage. Are those chocolate chip?" He snatched a few from the plate and leaned over to eat. Sydney studied him from under lashes that still seemed sticky from too much mascara. Had he even looked at her yet?

She cleared her throat. "Hey, Tristan, a few of us are going to the movies tonight. Wanna come?"

He swiveled his gaze around. Piercing amber eyes glinted with amusement and . . . tolerance. "Huh? No, thanks, I have a date tonight. Going to a concert. But you have fun."

His indulgent smile flattened her hopes like a deflated float. "Oh, sure. A date, huh? Sounds nice."

"Hopefully she's not."

Diane hit him in the arm, and he laughed, face filled with a mischief Sydney didn't understand, but she forced herself to laugh with him like she got the joke. She'd seen some of the girls he dated before. They always had shiny straight hair and lithe, athletic bodies. They talked about things like art history and finding artistic expression without societal constrictions and paraded in and out of the house on a regular basis. But none of them stayed more than a week or two, and then Tristan would show up with a new girl.

Sydney hated every single one of them.

Suddenly she felt stupid with her too-short skirt and

mascaraed lashes and lame invitation. Tristan was in college. He dated older girls who knew how to talk and dress and flirt. They probably kissed him in the front seat of the car and made out. Maybe even got to second base. She was nothing to him but a family friend who hung around his house too much. Jealousy mixed with misery for a depressing cocktail that slumped her shoulders.

Her self-flagellation was interrupted by a booming voice that made Tristan stiffen as if preparing himself for something unpleasant. "Cookies! Why am I always the last to know around here?" Christian Pierce strode in, his usual gruff face softening into a relaxed grin when he caught sight of her. "Hey, sweetheart." He gave a whistle as he took in her outfit. "You look gorgeous! Whose heart you gonna break tonight?"

She couldn't help smiling back, a bit of her confidence lifted. Tristan's father treated her like she was his daughter. He was sometimes rough with his boys, but to her he remained sweet, making her feel special. "Hopefully no one's."

"Well, if anyone tries to break yours, I'll make him regret it." He patted her cheek fondly, then grabbed a cookie from the plate. "I invited your grandparents to dinner tomorrow. Can you join us?"

"Of course."

"Good. I'm looking for some redemption from our last poker game. I still think he cheats."

He glanced over at Tristan, and his easy smile disappeared, replaced by a hard expression. "Glad you're back this weekend. Have a big job coming up, so you need to work tomorrow."

"I can give you a few hours, but I need to leave by three."

Christian practically spit with disgust. "Boy, you'll work till *the job's done. I'm allowing you to run off to your fancy college, but your future is right here. Houses don't get built by themselves. Have your fun on someone else's time—not mine."*

Tristan threw his head back in challenge. Rebellion shone from his eyes. *"I'm taking seventeen credits this semester, and I work my ass off. I come back each weekend to help out. Why is it never enough for you?"*

Dread trickled through her veins. Tristan and his dad were constantly fighting, and it seemed to be getting worse. Diane tried to run interference, but Christian usually ended up yelling at her, too, and then Sydney felt bad for everyone. What was happening to the family she loved?

His father seemed so cold as he stared back. *"'Cause it's not good enough. Lately, boy, nothing you do ever is."*

Raw pain flickered in Tristan's amber eyes. She ached to get up and go to him, but he'd only shake her off. Diane put a hand on her son's arm. *"That's enough,"* she told Christian, her voice edged with warning. *"He just got home. His studies come first. If we need to hire someone else, we will."*

The tension between them practically vibrated in the air, nothing resembling the easy camaraderie a husband and wife should exhibit. *"If our sons did their jobs properly, we wouldn't need outsiders. Babying them does no good for any of us."*

"Leave Mom out of this," Tristan clipped out.

"Fine. I'll have your brothers take up the slack while you go enjoy yourself. I'm going back to work."

Christian walked out. Silence fell over the kitchen.

Tristan cursed under his breath. *"I'm going up to my room."*

Diane took a step forward. *"Honey, wait—"*

But he shot off, disappearing up the stairs.

Sydney couldn't stand it. Seeing him in pain was too much. "I'll check on him," she said, sliding off the stool.

But Diane caught her hand, shaking her head. "No. Sit back down, Syd. I want to talk to you about something."

Heart pounding, she sat. Diane took the stool next to her. She seemed to be mulling over her words carefully. "Am I in trouble?" Sydney asked.

Diane squeezed her hand, smiling. "Of course not. You, my sweet girl, are a light around here. You help balance all this male energy in the house. I think I would've gone a bit crazy if I wasn't able to talk about makeup or clothes or Matthew Mc-Conaughey."

Sydney relaxed, soaking in the warmth that emanated from Diane's figure. This kitchen was her safe haven. She couldn't imagine not having the Pierce family in her life forever. "I feel the same way about you. Actually, all of you. I never lacked for siblings because of the boys."

"Even Tristan?"

Sydney sucked in a breath. Had she betrayed herself? The knowing look on Diane's face panicked her. "Wh-wh-what do you mean?"

Diane reached out and stroked her curls. The tender gesture allowed Sydney to lean into the embrace. "Oh, honey, I know how you feel about Tristan. I knew it from day one. There was always a connection between you two."

Her face flamed. As embarrassing as Diane's words were, a flood of relief poured through her. It had been a secret for so long she craved to talk to someone she trusted. Even if it was Tristan's mom. "Is it that obvious?" she asked miserably.

"Only to me. No one else suspects." She gave a long sigh.

Her eyes filled with concern and an understanding that made Sydney feel like Diane really got it. "It's hard right now. The age difference between you makes things difficult. And Tristan is going through a stage right now—figuring out who he is and what he wants in this life."

"Is that why he's always with a different girl?"

"Yes. That's what boys do. They date to figure out who they are and what they're really looking for."

"He doesn't even notice me. He never did."

Diane nodded. "I know. He's not ready yet, sweetheart. He needs to grow up a bit, and so do you."

"I just have all these feelings," she whispered. "I think about him all the time. And I want him to be happy. I think I'd do anything to make him happy. Is that messed up?"

Diane reached out and hugged her tight. "No, that's what happens when you love someone. And you have all these hormones pumping through, making you even more confused. Tristan cares about you, sweetheart, more than I think he knows. But you need to be patient. If it's meant to be, it will happen at the right time. But don't lose yourself in trying to make him happy. You need to find yourself, too, and that takes time."

She heard the words, but her heart didn't care. Sydney only knew if she could get Tristan to be interested, she'd do anything necessary to keep him. Diane pulled away. Sydney spotted a sheen of tears in her eyes, but his mom just laughed and shook her head. "My son is a kindhearted, strong man who I love more than my life. But I also know there's something within him I can't reach. I've never been able to." Frustration tinged her voice. "He keeps himself distant. Protected. He feels responsible in ways I can't explain and is harder on himself than anyone else could be. And one day, he's going to need to break that barrier open to have a full life. That's the day I hope you're right there to help him, my sweet girl."

Sydney sat with her in the kitchen for a long time. They talked and ate chocolate chip cookies, and she dreamed about the future.

One day, Tristan would fall in love with her.

And then everything would be perfect.

The memory floated away, jarring her back to the present.

She finished her wine and shook her head to clear her thoughts. She'd just have to live with her lingering feelings and bury the attraction. Stick to business. Be polite but distant. Eventually she'd find a nice man to date and fall in love and leave Tristan Pierce and all her memories behind for good.

Because he could never know.

chapter four

Sydney looked at the long trail of abandoned houses lining Bakery Street and wondered if she'd been an idiot to take on such a project.

It was bad. Real bad.

"What do you think?"

She practically felt the challenge tingeing his tone, as if he was looking forward to her freak-out. Yes, it was a massive undertaking, but she was of the mantra "Go big or go home."

She was going big—with or without his support.

"I think we'll have our difficulties but will deliver. Why? What do you think?"

His gorgeous lip curled up. "I think we're fucked."

She shoved down her irritation and spun on her heel, stabbing her pen into the air. "Listen, I don't need your negative energy on my project. If you don't think you can get it done, I'll be happy to grab Dalton or Cal."

"They can't handle a flip like this. Dalton will get obsessed with creating the perfect cabinet, and Cal will just want to rebuild everything. You're stuck with me."

His smug attitude only pissed her off further. She refused

to deal with his snarky comments and his ridiculous polished appearance. She'd donned ripped, old jeans and a purple flannel shirt. At least her sneakers were pink with a small wedge heel for some type of femininity. Her hair was pulled back in a ponytail. He'd shown up sporting a designer suit in crisp navy with a pink tie. What man had the guts to wear pink, especially to a job site? He should look metrosexual. Instead, he looked sexy and a touch bored, as if he'd just grabbed the first thing in his closet and thrown it on without care. She wished briefly for her own power suit and heels for some type of armor. She felt like a sixteen-year-old in her outfit, but she bucked up and refused to back down.

"Fine. Then I'd suggest an attitude adjustment. Let's start with number thirty-two. I want to do a complete walk-through and tweak some of my designs."

"It's your party."

She gnashed her teeth and stalked toward the first house. Her folder bulged with notes, Brady's plans, and various sketches. She strode over remnants of trash and weeds in the front lawn, avoided the broken second step, and unlocked the front door. The rusty squeak scraped at her nerve endings.

"Ever see that horror movie with the guy who lives in a run-down house on an empty block and snatches women to keep in his basement?" he asked casually.

"No."

"That's good. 'Cause you would be freaked out right now."

She shot him a warning glance and climbed the set of stairs leading to the first level. The raised ranch needed the most work out of all of them. With old shag carpeting, gold fixtures, and cheap countertops, the place screamed *help me*. They walked down the hallway. Each room seemed squeezed into its own private space, giving off the vibe of claustrophobia. The kitchen was a cube with white-finish appliances, peeling paint, and a vinyl floor.

"We need to open this wall," she murmured, tapping the main one blocking up the view to the kitchen. "Brady said it's not load bearing, so it's a possibility."

Tristan regarded the setup, tapping his index finger against his bottom lip. "Yes, but if you remove this wall, the moment you climb the stairs you're staring into the kitchen. Sure, it gives you open concept, but it's not aesthetically pleasing, and that's the first moment you get to impress a visitor."

She cocked her head, considering. He'd always been brilliant in his vision for what worked well in a house. He respected each one for its individuality and never tried to force a concept for either ease or stubbornness.

It was so much easier to fight an attraction when the man didn't have a brain.

She never got tired of learning about the give-and-take of redesigning a home. It was endlessly challenging and creative, with no black-and-white answers. It was strictly a personal preference, yet when flipping, the design needed to appeal to the general consumer. In this case, she needed to have Adam's goal in mind, yet keep to cost while offering Realtors something unique to sell.

"What would you suggest, then?"

He crossed his arms, leaned against the same wall they discussed, and cocked his head. "What do you think?"

She clenched her fists under her clipboard. It was obvious

he didn't think she could handle this job and was testing her. He wanted to play games? Fine. Maybe it was time to show him what she'd learned while he was away all those years.

Sydney spoke in cold, clipped tones. "I'd suggest removing not only this wall here but this one separating out the living room. We'd do a built-in wall cabinet here so they don't lose organization space." Her pink Skechers made no noise as she walked farther into the kitchen. "We keep the appliances on the right wall, upgraded to stainless steel, but on the far wall, we add a small back deck with glass sliding doors. The view is gorgeous with all the trees in the background. Then when you climb the stairs, your first impression is of the deck."

He kept his face expressionless, but the gleam of interest in his amber eyes gave him away. He followed her in and peeked out the small window hiding the glory of the backyard, now shrouded in overgrowth. "A deck and glass doors is another expense for Adam. It may be well over budget."

"Not if we keep it average size with basic materials. We keep the luxury items to the finishes in the kitchen and bath. Dalton can build the deck and cabinetry quickly enough, with an incremental increase. It'll be worth it."

"Are you going to be the one to tell Dalton he needs to build an *average* deck and cabinet without getting creative?"

It was hard keeping the small smile from her lips. Dalton was known as the Wood Whisperer, and his projects compared to works of fine art. He had a bit of an artistic temperament and despised cookie-cutter projects that didn't add to the visual appeal of a home.

"With a plate of brownies, I convinced Brady to deliver plans in twenty-four hours."

Amusement laced his words. "Brady was always an easy target. Dalton is more temperamental."

"Not if I deliver the five-layer chocolate cake," she said with a sigh.

His brow shot up. They both knew about Dalton's obsession with Hershey's Kisses and any type of baked goods. "The one with the shavings and cherries in the middle?"

"That's the one."

"Damn, you are serious. Will you have time?"

"If I want the damn deck done, I'll find the time."

Their gazes met, and they shared a smile. For one second, pure understanding passed between them, bringing her back to the days when they'd meshed perfectly—both in and out of bed. She'd always appreciated his subtle sense of humor. He was more laid-back and reserved than his brothers. Too often it translated to him not being noticed amid his noisy, loud family. How many times had she gazed at him while he stood on the sidelines, wishing he realized how truly special he was?

Her smile faded, and she shoved away the memories. They no longer had a place here, and she needed to stick to work. "I have to do a quick check in the attic. Need to see whether it's viable space that can be renovated or just enough for storage."

"I'll go with you."

His phone rang. Glancing at the screen, he waved his hand in the air. "Give me a minute. I need to take this."

He drifted away, talking to a client, and Sydney dropped her purse on the floor. Silly to wait for him when it would only take a minute. She headed down the hall, grabbing the step stool Brady had placed during his last visit, and climbed up. It took her a while to work the rusty lock the past family had installed, which made her wonder what they'd kept up here. A shiver worked down her spine. Creepy stuff.

The door was barely functional, so that would need replacement ASAP. Definitely a safety hazard.

With a quick jump, she managed to wiggle up the last foot, barely making it thanks to her lack of height, and got in. Grabbing a large stick nearby, she propped open the hatch. Damn, she'd forgotten a flashlight. She'd tell Tristan to bring up his cell phone when he was done.

She walked the attic with slow, careful steps, noting the rotted wood, low beams hanging with cobwebs, and the one dirty window. Hmm, definitely not worth restoring for an extra room. They'd need to replace the door and lock, clean it up, and call it a day.

What was that on the window?

She squinted, moving closer, then stopped. Her mouth fell open.

Bars.

Holy hell. Maybe someone had been locked up here!

Not usually spooked, she felt goose bumps pepper her arms. Nope, she was outta here. Enough recon done for now.

She turned, but a low scratching suddenly rose in the air.

What was that?

"Tristan?" she squeaked. His voice rumbled from outside. No, still on the phone. "Hello?"

Another movement. Was that red cloth thing moving? Frozen to the floor, she watched in horror as the bulge shook, and another scratch echoed.

Oh, my God.

She had just managed to unstick one of her feet to run for her life when the red cloth jumped. With a high-pitched squeak, a furry body shot out across the attic, heading right for her.

"Agh! Help!"

The scream exploded from her lips. She jumped up and down, still screaming, as the creature passed her and frantically scuttled around, bumping against the walls in a desperate attempt at escape.

Mouse.

"Sydney!" Her name split the air, and suddenly Tristan was diving upward through the space. "What's wrong? Are you hurt?"

"Mouse! Mouse!" A whimper broke through her lips. "Get it!"

"You gave me a heart attack for a mouse? Woman, I thought you were in real trouble!"

She hissed through gritted teeth, "I am! Get the damn mouse or I'm going to lose it."

Muttering under his breath, he turned toward the frantic creature and grabbed a wooden stick. "Come on, buddy, out this way."

"You're not going to kill it?"

"Do you want me to hurt an innocent creature of God?"

She shot him a withering look. "Fine, just get it. I have to get out of here!"

He took the stick, urging the mouse toward the open hole of the exit, and she watched in horror as the creature dove out of the attic, falling through the empty space, and disappeared.

She jumped up and down, rubbing her hands over her arms to rid herself of the chills. "Oh, my God, that was so gross. Now he's in the house!"

Tristan shook his head. "I cannot believe you're afraid of a mouse. I swear, Syd, don't do that to me again." He walked over to the attic door and turned, and the stick knocked out the flimsy support, swinging the hatch closed.

The loud crash made her jump, and she glared at him. "Nice work," she gibed. "This place is creepy. I want out of here now."

He glared with pure disgust. "Fine. I told you to wait for me in the first place, but no, not you. Miss Independent has to climb into the attic all by herself and disturb the poor mouse."

Irritated and still jumpy, she pushed him aside and leaned over to pull open the door. "I'll be sure not to call you if I ever need saving," she shot out, yanking at the flimsy handle.

The door didn't budge.

"It's stuck."

"I'll get it." He pulled. Nothing. Frowning, he knelt down and jerked the handle hard.

The metal ripped off the rotted wood.

Blinking in confusion, he stared at the handle in his hands. Then down at the door. "It broke."

"Yeah, so just bust through it or something."

He gave her a withering look. "I can't just bust through it like in the movies. The damn handle came off. That's how we get out."

She stared at him, her heart beginning to pound. "What do you mean? Just get us out!"

"Give me a minute, okay?" He took his time trying to

jiggle the door open, then examined the handle. When there seemed to be no movement, he took the stick and began crashing it against the wood.

The door held tight.

He rose to his knees. "I think we're locked in."

"No. We can't be locked in here. It's impossible."

"Well, since the door isn't opening and we're stuck in the attic, I guess it is possible."

She took the stick and began smashing it against the door, like a crazed person on a mission to break open a birthday piñata. "Whoa—slow down, slugger," he said, grabbing her arms. Out of breath, she glared at him, then the door. "Are you afraid of small spaces or something? You never had those fears before."

"No, but I think something bad happened in this attic. There are bars on the window. And that lock on the outside is just plain weird. What if there are ghosts in here?"

His lips twitched. "I don't believe in ghosts. Just relax. We'll call someone. Where's your cell?"

"In my purse."

"Where's your purse?"

She glowered. "Downstairs."

"Fuck." The amusement faded to frustration. "Why would you leave your purse downstairs? You take it everywhere."

She blew out a breath. "Not in an attic! Let's just use your cell to call someone. Have them come spring us."

A strange expression flickered over his face. "I can't."

"Why not?"

"Because I dropped my cell phone in a race to save your life when you started screaming."

It took a few moments to realize they were trapped together in a haunted attic with no idea who would eventually come looking for them—or when.

Then she really did want to scream.

Tristan had an urge to pull her against his chest, wrap his arms tight, and whisper in her ear that everything would be okay. She infused a raw need in him to either fuck her senseless or shower her with tenderness. It was like a pendulum— he never knew which need would hit him first, but it always came with a degree of intensity that surprised him.

Like it did right now.

Instead, he kept his hands firmly tucked away from temptation and spoke with authority. "I mentioned our trip to Cal, so I'm sure he'll know where to look when we don't answer our cell phones. Is your daughter okay?"

"Yes. Thank God, she's with the sitter."

"Good. So, all we have to do is sit tight and wait for someone to get us."

"Great. Unless the demon ghost kills us first," she muttered. She began pacing. The wood under her feet creaked dangerously.

"Let's not test the floor foundation, too," he said. Dragging over a dusty trunk, he swiped the surface halfway clean. "Sit."

Blowing out a breath, she plunked herself down on the trunk and stretched her pink-clad feet out in front of her. Her ponytail had flopped to the side of her head, and fiery curls had sprung loose. Her purple flannel shirt was wrinkled and missing a bottom button. Her jeans had a hole in the knee.

His dick shot to life, and he smothered a groan. Great. She rocked the sexy librarian role in the office, and the girl-next-door look was even more appealing. His fingers itched to grab that ponytail, drag her toward him, and feast on those luscious, sulky lips. Unbutton that farmer-type shirt, yank her jeans down, and figure out the quickest way to stroke her to orgasm. It had never taken him long before. In fact, he'd just kiss her, and she'd be dripping wet, ready for his fingers to slide into her tight heat until she begged for more.

But that was then, and this was now.

He turned his back on her and pretended to check out the window so she wouldn't spot his current condition.

"Hey, can you break the window and call for help?"

"Hard to shatter glass between steel bars. And since the block is deserted, yelling won't help."

"At least I'm trying to come up with ideas," she shot back. "Why'd you have to go waving that stick around like a messed-up Jedi? If you hadn't hit the door, we wouldn't be in this mess and stuck with each other."

He turned back around. Guess being locked in a room with him wasn't her favorite thing. Her desperation to get away from him would've been funny if it didn't bring a touch of annoyance. "Are you kidding me? First you didn't listen to me when I told you to wait. Then you lost it over a silly mouse. This whole thing is your fault."

Her chin rose a few notches. Emerald fire shot out at him. "You've been testing me from the moment we got here. I think you want me to fail so you can go back to your brothers and tell them 'I told you so.' You voted against me for CFO!"

The jab hit home. Guilt sprung up. "I don't want you to

fail," he retorted. "And I just wasn't sure if you were ready, that's all. I had no idea you wanted more."

"Why would you? You don't know who I am anymore. You haven't even talked to me since you got back home two years ago!"

He jerked back. She slapped a hand over her mouth, eyes wide with shock. Obviously she hadn't planned to let out such a truth. They'd become masters at the art of non-conversation, avoidance, and the occasional snipe. When he'd been forced to return to Harrington for his father's will and found himself back working for the company, he'd intended to keep the tension between them to a minimum. In the beginning, her betrayal had still bothered him. He was reminded of that scene each time he looked at her or her daughter.

But she wasn't the same person who'd sent him away. Nor was he the same person who'd left. And maybe this distance was tearing apart pieces of them in a long, torturous process. Maybe it was time to try to move forward instead of living in the past.

"I didn't know it bothered you," he said quietly. She tore her gaze away. He waited for a few moments in silence, gathering his thoughts. "Syd?"

"It didn't. Not at first. But I'm getting tired of the boxing match." He lifted a brow in question. "A jab here. Uppercut there. I keep waiting for the knockout punch, but then we may not be able to work together. And we need to find a way to do that, Tristan."

He let out a breath, then slowly nodded. She was right. He'd been so focused on fighting their physical attraction he'd forgotten his ruthless ability to close himself off. It was easier to treat her with a cold distance to keep her locked safely in the box of his past. He hadn't allowed himself to really get to know the woman she'd become while he was away those five years.

"You're right." She looked at him with surprise. "I don't think either of us were able to deal with each other at first. Then it became habit to avoid you or keep communication limited."

"I want to be able to work together again." A tentative smile touched her lips. "Or at least, I want us to try. I need you on my team for this project to succeed. I'm not pretending I can do this all alone, but I want a chance to prove myself and show what I can do for Pierce Brothers."

His gut clenched. He might still have doubts, but he admired her tenacity and determination. She'd changed from the shy, uncertain girl who'd once looked to him to make all her decisions. This company meant something important to her. And God knows, she'd grown up in his household—more of a family member than a casual friend. She deserved his respect, and it was time he stopped questioning her abilities.

"I can give you that," he said. "I want us to be able to work together. Move forward. I can try if you will."

"I can try." Her husky voice scraped across his nerve endings. The tentative smile grew bigger, until those lush lips were stretched into a joyous grin that did strange things to his insides. She'd always been an emotional giver—never afraid to soothe, nurture, touch. She cried big, laughed loud, and refused to shy away from silliness. It had been a long time since he'd been on the receiving end of one of her true smiles, and he remembered how special it felt, as if he were the only man in the world to make her happy.

He smiled back.

The connection always humming in the background exploded full force, filling the musty attic with an electric sexual surge that practically charged the air. Suddenly lust hit him, sending him to his knees with the urge to close the distance between them and kiss her, strip her, claim her. Because she'd always been his.

He stumbled back a step. The raw, primitive thoughts tangled with his arousal and put him into a brief panic. No, dammit. He'd just agreed to a truce, and he wasn't going to get sidelined again by a connection fueled by the past.

"Can I ask you something?"

He shuddered and prayed she wouldn't. What if she felt the same energy pulsing between them? What if she asked him questions he couldn't answer—questions that haunted him in the night when his defenses were gone? His voice came out rusty. "What?"

Her beautiful face tilted up toward him. Her lips parted. Her eyes flickered with longing.

"You don't happen to have a granola bar in your pocket, do you?"

He blinked. "Huh?"

"I'm so damn hungry."

Her meaning cut through his clogged thoughts.

And then he laughed. She joined in, and for a little while, everything was good.

"What time is it?"

He shifted his weight. "About five minutes after the last time you asked me."

She groaned. "It smells in here. I'm still hungry. And bored. What time is it?"

He glanced at the watch on his right wrist. "Five twenty-five. Six minutes after the last time you asked me."

"Why do you wear expensive suits and jewelry to a job site?"

He frowned. "I don't wear jewelry. You must have confused me with Dalton."

"That silver watch has some bling," she pointed out. "And your matching cuff links can be spotted a mile away."

Irritation trickled through him. "This is man stuff, not jewelry. Dalton wore an earring and a man bun. Go give him a hard time."

"I don't like it when you look better than me," she grumbled.

"Why don't women understand how hot they are in a natural state? Sure, I love the suits and heels and red lips, but this is real. I'll take this outfit on you any time." Her mouth fell open, and he quickly backtracked, realizing he'd given too much away. "I mean, on all women," he said.

"Right. Well, right now I have a headache, and I'd give my left arm for a bottle of water." She reached up, ripping out her hair tie, and those fiery red strands broke free in abandoned glory. His gut clenched with the need to reach out and touch her hair. It had been so long. He'd always been obsessed with her curls and the way they wrapped tight around his fingers and hung on.

His mouth dried up. "Yeah, wish I had water, too," he muttered. "We should be rescued soon. I heard my cell phone ringing down there steadily."

She massaged her temples and stretched. "Distract me."

Unfortunately, he could think of many pleasurable ways to distract her. Most of them involved his mouth, hands, and tongue. He bit back a groan and tried to focus. "Wanna tell scary stories?"

She shuddered and wrapped her arms around her bent knees. "Hell no. Are you happy about Morgan and Cal getting married?"

He relaxed. This subject he could handle. "Definitely. It's going to get lonely rattling around in the mansion alone. Dalton just moved in with Raven, and Cal will be closing on the new house. Lots of changes lately."

"Is Cal taking the dogs?"

He nodded. "They belong to Cal, though we all love those goofballs." Cal had rescued two mastiff puppies found chained to a tree and taken them in as his own. Now those puppies towered as big and tall as Tristan. They'd flunked out of obedience school twice and failed at listening to any commands, but they were full of love and affection, making everyone around them smile.

"Maybe you can get a dog, too."

"Maybe. I'm more worried about what I'm going to do about dinner. Morgan spoiled all of us."

"You didn't cook when you were in the city?"

"Most of the time I was too busy. There were a ton of restaurants that delivered, and I ate out a lot with clients."

"Your mom would be ashamed."

He smiled, even though his heart felt a pang. His mom had been the only soft spot in his life, always there to support, comfort, or listen. Many times he wished for just one more day with her so he'd be able to apologize for ever taking her for granted. "She would've just told me to get married so my wife would cook."

Sydney rolled her eyes. "That comment alone would've gotten you smacked. Your mom didn't raise you to be like Brady."

"True. Though, Brady has certainly changed since meeting Charlie." He'd never seen his architect so smitten with a woman. Usually he was the one who was walking away if she didn't follow the rules of what he believed was the perfect mate for him. "I wish Mom could've met Morgan, Raven, and Charlie. I think she would've liked them."

"Me too." A short silence descended. "I miss her so much. I miss sitting in her kitchen and watching her cook while she talked about you guys."

His breath caught at the surge of warmth flowing between them. How many times had he entered his house to find Sydney in the kitchen laughing with his mom? She'd been the one to hold and comfort him when they found out about Diane's death. She was the only one to truly understand what a hole his mother had left in all of their lives. His throat tightened with emotion. "I miss her, too," he said softly. "You were like the daughter she never had. She used to warn me all the time about you."

"Me? What could she have possibly warned you about?"

The words burst free, refusing to be caged. "She told me not to break your heart."

Sydney sucked in her breath. Shock kept him still. His confession had come from deep within, but he wasn't ready to accept or examine the memory. It was too raw, too fresh, and too terrifying.

He opened his mouth to change the subject or to make a lame joke—anything to change the emotional charge sizzling between them.

A loud creaking noise rose in the air, as if a rocking chair had begun to move or a footstep had struck a loose floorboard. An icy draft whooshed through, carrying a deep chill that prickled his skin with goose bumps.

WTF?

Sydney froze, eyes wide with fear. "Tristan?" she whispered, lips trembling. "Wh-wh-what was that?"

"Nothing. Just the attic settling. It's an old house."

A loud bang exploded in the room.

Suddenly Sydney screamed and hurtled through the air, right into his arms.

He staggered back a step, her legs and arms wrapped around him, clinging to him while she buried her face into the crook of his neck. He found his balance, hitched her higher, and settled his hands on her ass to keep her close.

"We're going to die," she moaned, her thighs clenching around his hips.

In that moment, Tristan realized he might.

Five foot five inches of pure woman surrounded him. The scent of orange blossoms filled his nostrils, and her wild curls caressed his mouth and cheeks. The imprint of her full lips burned into the skin of his neck, her breath hot and ragged. Her ripe breasts pressed against his chest, the flannel a flimsy barrier to mask the hard tips of her nipples. His hands sank into the glorious full curves of her ass, and his dick notched in the perfect opening of her thighs.

His head exploded with sensual stimuli. He battled

through the muck, desperately seeking focus. "Not gonna die," he managed to mutter. "Just the wind."

"That's no wind or house settling. It's a ghost, and he's pissed at us for encroaching on his territory." Her arms entwined around his shoulders, ripping a tortured groan from his lips.

"Sweetheart, you're not going to die. I got you. See, the noise stopped already."

Slowly she lifted her head.

Their gazes crashed together.

He watched her pupils dilate as fear turned to arousal. Her lips parted, and she arched into him. Her nails dug into his shoulders, the simmering heat cranked up to a scorching fire, and in moments he was rock hard and crazed for more. The past merged with the present until nothing mattered but tasting her honeyed sweetness just once. Just once . . .

"Tristan?"

It was a question. It was a demand. It was surrender.

He ducked his head and covered her lips with his.

Home.

The word repeated in his mind like a mantra as he plunged his tongue between her lips and rediscovered her. She was hot and wet, tasting like spun sugar, and he explored her mouth, licking and sucking in a mad quest to devour her whole. This was no polite introduction or tentative curiosity. This was no-holds-barred hunger, dragging him down into a dark abyss where pleasure demanded and ruled.

She welcomed every stroke of his tongue and gave it all back, moaning wildly against him, clutching at his shoulders and squeezing her thighs tight in her own feminine demand.

Man to woman, mate to mate, the primitive carnality of the kiss shook him to the core, ripping away his illusions of his previous lovers and leaving him aching for her and only her—the woman who'd broken his heart years ago. The woman who he'd never truly been able to forget.

He bit her lower lip, captured her sexy little moan, and slid his tongue back in, plundering the depths of her mouth in a possessive, explosive kiss that went on and on and—

"Sydney! Tris! You up there?"

The voices penetrated the sexual fog like the clean slice of a knife. He ripped his mouth from hers, breathing hard, and stared down at her. Shock filled her dazed emerald eyes. Her lips were swollen and moist, and her breath came in tiny pants. As if in a dream, he slowly let her slide down his length until her feet hit the ground.

Oh, fuck.

What had they done?

She backed away like he was the ghost who'd terrified her and quickly turned from him.

He cleared his throat. "Here!" he managed to call out. "We're up here in the attic!"

The clatter of the ladder and a curse drifted upward. After a few hard bangs, the door crashed open. Footsteps clattered on the steps.

His brother's head poked in. "What the hell happened?" Cal demanded. "Everyone's been worried sick, trying to track you down."

"We got stuck," he said.

Cal glanced back and forth between them, a frown creasing his brow. "You gotta be kidding me. Where're your cell phones?"

"We left them downstairs," Sydney said. Her voice was back to regular pitch, solid and coolly calm. Not breathy, with that sexy little hitch she gave when he kissed her. "The door handle broke off. Thank God you figured out where we were."

Cal shook his head. "Took us a while to realize you were both MIA. This is one for the record books. Wait till Dalton finds out."

Tristan groaned at his brother's poorly hidden glee. "Yeah, and you can't wait to tell him, like a little tattletale. Now move. We want to get the hell out of here."

Cal disappeared. Tristan looked at Sydney. Her face told him everything he needed to know.

The kiss had never happened.

Slowly he acknowledged the hit, refusing to analyze the strange curl of pain in his gut. She met his gaze with a calm detachment that pissed him off. Like she'd never jumped into his arms, kissed him back, and practically begged for more.

He followed her down the stairs and told himself it was better this way. But on the car ride home, the memories leaked through, reminding him of how things had started . . .

"Where's the Ackerson contract?" Tristan called out. His fingers flipped through the cabinet with pure impatience. "It's missing. Is anyone listening to me?"

"I am." The throaty voice came from behind his left shoulder. The scent of orange blossoms and musk drifted in the air. It took him a moment to realize it was her. When had she stopped smelling like baby powder? And her high-pitched voice had somehow deepened, reminding him of smoke and sex. "Here it is. Cal had it to finalize some of the building permits."

He spun around and found her way too close. Practically bumping into the cabinet, he took the file and tried to ignore the naked interest in her green eyes as she looked at him. That had changed, too. From a girlish adoration to a young woman's eagerness to experiment. His pants tightened, and he barely held back an embarrassed flush. Holy shit, when had he started thinking of Sydney Greene as a woman? She was a baby, right? Well, not that eighteen was a baby any longer, but this shift of dynamics was starting to throw him.

She was off-limits, and he'd better get his shit together.

"Thanks. Sorry, I'm in a hurry."

"You always are." Her smile was less look at me *and more* I'm in charge. *Even her wardrobe had changed. She'd taken to wearing business suits, with short skirts, white button-down blouses, and proper jackets. The combination had a strange effect of making him want to discover what lay beneath. Her bare legs and heels were now a tease. "Hey, I need to go over some things with you. Have time to share a sandwich with me?"*

Uneasiness slithered down his spine. Of course, it was stupid. He usually shared lunch with Sydney when they needed to work. It was no big deal. "Sure. Order me a—"

"Chicken with roasted peppers. Got it."

She tilted her head, and those curls slid over her cheek. He used to pull on them when he teased her. Lately he'd held back, because he wanted to linger and see if they felt as silky as they looked. "Yeah. Thanks."

She retreated, her ass swinging, and he smothered a groan. If his brothers had a clue about the way his thoughts were rearing, they'd beat the crap out of him. His father, too. Sydney was like his daughter, and he treated her like a pampered princess.

And his mother? Well, his mother already seemed to suspect his sudden interest. The last time Syd had come to dinner, Diane spent most of the night staring at both of them with a thoughtful expression on her face.

Maybe he just needed to get laid. It had been a while.

He pushed away his confusing thoughts and worked for the next hour, trying to set up a proposal to get his father to finally allow him to flip a property and see how they could make money. It was getting old the way Christian only listened to Cal. Dalton was happy enough working on the wood aspects, but Tristan was left cleaning up all the leftover details, from paperwork and accounting to dealing with suppliers. He wanted to get dirty and renovate houses, implementing some new designs.

The door opened, and Sydney came in. As usual, she'd laid out the sandwiches on plates and plopped an iced tea on the blotter. She slid gracefully into the leather chair opposite his desk and glanced at her planner. He tried not to focus on the couple of inches of bare thigh exposed by her crossed legs.

"Your dad wants you to take a meeting tomorrow at three p.m. with the new granite place," she said, pursing her red lips. *When had she switched from bubblegum gloss?* He shifted in his chair and grabbed his sandwich.

"Not doing it. I have a meeting to see if I can secure some property."

A tiny frown creased her brow. "He's gonna be mad."

"I don't give a shit. I'm getting tired of not having my voice heard around here. I'm not a lackey to take his meetings."

Pure empathy radiated from her jade-green eyes. He relaxed an inch. Sydney always understood and backed him at every turn. Even now he could tell her brain was clicking to try to find *a way to help him.* "Do you want me to take the meeting? I can take notes, and if there's a problem, I can text or call you."

He could go toe-to-toe with his father again or allow her to do it. This time it'd be easier to keep the peace until he knew he could purchase the property. "Thanks, Syd. That would be great."

"Welcome." *She smiled, and their gazes met, and his heart suddenly started beating way too fast.* "I need to get out of here on time tonight, though."

"Sure. Going out with your friends?"

"Nope. Got a date."

He stilled. "Didn't know you were dating someone," *he said casually.* "What's the matter? Hiding him from us for some reason?"

His teasing seemed to fall flat, but she just shrugged, shifting a little so her skirt slid higher. He couldn't keep his gaze from flicking down for one brief moment. Her golden skin looked smooth and soft, and those wicked heels seemed too mature for her to wear. What was going on with her lately?

What the hell was going on with him? Sydney was . . . family. An annoying little sister but someone he loved. Lately she made him uncomfortable, and he didn't know how to handle it.

"Christian wouldn't approve," *she flung out.* "He's a bit of a bad boy. Rides a bike."

A low growl rose from his chest. "Syd, that's not a good idea. Where the hell did you meet him?"

"That bar down on South."

His ears rang. His blood pressure cranked up a notch. "You're not legal drinking age! Are you fucking kidding me?"

She rolled her eyes. "Tris, you and your brothers have been *drinking at that bar since you were seventeen. I'm careful. I always go with a group of girlfriends."*

"Are they going on your date with you tonight?" A touch of bitterness leaked into his voice.

"No. But I can take care of myself."

"No, you can't, dammit. Cancel."

Suddenly she leaned forward. Her proper white blouse gaped open, giving him a glimpse of her lacy white bra cupping full breasts. Dear God, when had she filled out? "If you want me to cancel, Tris, you need to give me a good reason."

Shock hit him. The woman across the desk was barely recognizable, from her flirty eyes to her pouty mouth and crackling sensuality. For a while, he couldn't move. He just stared into her heated green eyes and fought a surging arousal that was strangling him, pulling him down into a seething pit of pure temptation. He imagined himself walking around his desk, pulling her to her feet, and taking her mouth in a punishing kiss.

He also knew she wouldn't fight him. Oh, no, she'd open her mouth under his and take his tongue deep and arch into him, her hot little body for the taking.

Because she was meant for him.

The shock morphed into panic. His sandwich dropped from his hands, and he rolled his chair back, desperately needing more distance. "Umm, how about we talk about this later? Listen, I'm sorry, I forgot I have to make an important call on this deal."

Disappointment flashed in her eyes. "Sure. No problem." She grabbed her stuff and stood up. "Let me know if you need anything."

Her words dripped with meaning. His dick pulsed, making him feel like a damn teen boy. "Yep. Thanks," he choked out.

When she shut the door behind her, he was able to breathe, but he knew in that moment everything had changed.

Sydney had grown up, and he'd finally noticed. The real problem would be keeping the necessary distance between them until the urge faded. Besides being part of his family, she worked at Pierce Brothers. Getting involved with her would be an epic disaster, and he had enough to deal with lately with his father and brothers. They were fighting all the time, having different views of how the company should go. The closeness among them had vanished. Even his mother was having trouble getting them to communicate or even to spend a meal together any longer. Something was going to break, and soon.

He needed to make sure he stayed away from Sydney.

chapter five

On Friday morning, Sydney waited outside her house, trying to ignore the sickening twirls in her belly. She felt like she'd just gone on the teacup ride and was ready to hurl. Embarrassed at her childish reaction, she kept reminding herself this was a business trip. Adam Cushman wanted a face-to-face in Manhattan to go over some important details and to begin moving forward. Since the attic incident, she and Tristan had spent the last few days working separately or in the office surrounded by people. The tension between them had turned from cool distance to shattering awareness.

Today would be the first time they'd be alone since the kiss. She chided herself mentally for her worry. They'd chat politely in the car, listen to some music, have their client lunch, and go home. There was no reason to feel as if she was going to be held hostage and tortured. She'd set the tone, he'd follow her lead, and they'd get this thing done. Nothing to worry about. It was just a kiss.

The kiss. Oh, God, the kiss.

She burned just from the memory of that hot, soul-stirring, wicked kiss. He'd tasted like musk and sin. Smelled like the ocean and sun-warmed sand. Her fingers gripped rock-hard muscles trapped under soft, elegant fabric. He kissed her with the same raw passion and dominant control that always made her panties wet. It was everything she'd remembered but more. So much more.

Damn that stupid ghost.

He pulled up to her door in his silver Lincoln Crossover— both practical and elegant. Just like him, her mind reminded her. Whether he was closing a deal or stripping off his clothes, he'd always held an innate animal grace that buckled her knees.

Don't think about it.

He strode around the car toward her dressed in a black pin-striped suit and red tie. Timber-colored hair swept back from his face, showing off his broad forehead, arched brows, and gleaming whiskey eyes. He opened the car door for her. She swallowed. Maybe he'd forget that moment of weakness and intimacy. They'd just managed a truce to promote their business relationship. Neither of them was prepared for more. "Morning," she offered.

"Morning. I brought you coffee and a fruit cup."

"Thank you."

"You ready for this?"

She turned and found him standing close. His hand propped the door open, and a tiny smirk rested on his full lips. His jaw was clean shaven, and the delicious ocean scent of his cologne drifted from his skin. Her fingers itched to trace the faint scar that ran down his right cheek—evidence of a rock fight with his brothers that hadn't gone well. A reluctant smile got past her. Did his question hold a hidden meaning, or was she being paranoid? She fought the blush and ducked her head anyway. "Ready."

She got in the car, and he came back around, pulling out. The smell of leather and his cologne wrapped around her. Jazz music played softly from the speakers, soothing her ears. "You can put on the seat warmers if you'd like. It's a bit chilly this morning."

"March is temperamental."

"Yes, it is."

Silence descended. Sydney tried not to wring her fingers and stared out the window. One hour and twenty-eight minutes left to their destination. Could she pretend to doze? There should be plenty of room in such a spacious car, but it felt as if his powerful thigh was just inches from hers. Why had she worn a skirt? Her legs were practically naked and vulnerable to his gaze. He kept his attention on the road, sipping his coffee, not seeming to care that the tension between them was knotted so tight, she might choke. The chunky silver watch emphasized the sinewy muscle of his wrist and his long tapered fingers. She'd always believed he could be a concert pianist. Lord knows he'd played her body like a maestro. With his lips, too.

Don't think about it.

"Do you know what the goal is for this meeting?" he asked.

She clung to the subject like a jumper to a parachute. "Contracts are finalized on three houses, but he's holding out on the others. I think he's giving me pushback for price. My margin is limited in order for this to be worthwhile for our local suppliers, so I'll need to be ready for negotiations."

"Smart. I've met him a few times when I worked in the city. He has an excellent reputation but is well-known to be ruthless. Most good businessmen are."

"Are you?"

"A good businessman?"

"No, ruthless." Sydney wished she could take the words back. They'd just popped out. The boy she'd loved was no longer here, but the man he'd become still intrigued her. For years, he'd been held under his father's rule, until his ambition turned into a ruthless need to escape everything he'd once loved. Including her.

"When I need to be."

She believed him. "Did New York teach you that?"

His grip tightened on the wheel. They were in new territory. Since his return they hadn't discussed his time in the city or anything that could lead them back to their past relationship. But now, with their working truce, she admitted to being a bit curious about those five years when he'd grown into his own man.

His answer reflected no hidden tension. "Yes. I needed to go to New York and find out who I was without my family. Dad would never have allowed me to explore real estate. It was difficult at first, but I hooked up with a decent firm and began learning. In my spare time, I took some extra home-design courses and built my skills. After two years, I was ready to step out on my own. I recruited a small clientele and kept growing."

"Did you enjoy living in the city?"

She didn't ask the question she really wanted to know:

Did he regret coming home to stay?

"The city is a beast. It's big and powerful and tries to devour you whole. But if you work hard, take your punches, and fight back, the rewards make it worth it. I found my niche. Sometimes it was brutal, because this business is cutthroat and you have to be able to make some hard decisions. There are people who get right in your face and say you'll fail. You have to get past the negative junk." His voice held a bit of self-mockery. "Dear old Dad helped me with that."

She smiled. Christian had been hard on him, but like with everything else, Tristan was able to take the bad and change it into a life lesson. "He did have a way with words," she said drily.

He smiled back. The bitterness and hatred toward his father had softened over the two years since his death. In a way, Sydney wondered if Tristan was able to see him more as a man than as a father. Diane had eventually left Christian for another lover, only to die in that fateful car crash. The events had trapped Christian in such bitterness, he alienated his family one by one. It was as if he ended up only punishing himself, and Tristan had finally moved past it.

"I loved the cultural benefits in New York. Great restaurants. Theater. Opera. Museums. Endless opportunities to meet interesting people and have unique experiences."

A pang hit her. She'd never traveled. Sure, she'd been to the city for a few events. She'd visited Boston, and Philly, and even taken a short ski trip to Vermont. But that was as far as she'd gone. She'd never longed to see beyond the borders of Harrington and used to look at it as a lack within herself. Especially compared with Tristan's burning need to see the world and flee his home. After birthing Becca, she'd learned more about herself and refused to apologize any longer for her own dreams. She'd been lucky to be raised by grandparents who loved her, but knowing her parents never cared about her broke something deep inside. She'd always felt . . . needy. Needy for love and security. For comfort. For assurances that everything would work out.

When she was pregnant with Becca, Sydney had needed to provide a home and security for her daughter. She'd known Jason for years, as he worked construction for a competitor, but when he seriously began pursuing her after Tristan left, he seemed like the answer to everything. He was kind, happily settled in town, and wanted a wife and family. When he learned of her pregnancy, he didn't run but offered a future they both seemed to want. It was a whirlwind courtship so they could be married quickly. Unfortunately, it didn't take long to discover that friendship and good intentions did not make a marriage. How badly she'd wanted to lay a strong foundation of home for herself and Becca. They'd tried so hard to make it work, but when Becca turned six months old, Jason was offered a unique opportunity to move overseas to do underwater construction, and everything fell apart.

Besides refusing to move her daughter to a new country, they realized there was too much missing in their marriage to endure a long-distance relationship. Their decision to part was painful, but there'd been no resentment. Just a sadness they weren't meant to be together. Becca still retained her exhusband's name, but Jason was no longer a part of their lives. Becca was truly, solely hers. One day, she intended to explain to her daughter the details of her past, but Becca was still too young to understand. One day, questions would be raised and answers demanded.

After all, the truth was clearly revealed on the birth certificate.

But not now. Not with Tristan refusing to even interact
with her daughter and not with the distance between them.

Her brief marriage taught her so much. Sydney had spent
her entire life consistently looking to others, usually men, to
fill the empty, aching void inside.

Now she knew only one person could fill it.

Herself.

She refocused on the conversation. "I guess you miss
New York." Her voice sounded calm and analytical, with a
touch of interest.

"Not anymore." She glanced at him, startled to find his
gaze swiveled to meet hers. "I know I belong here. With my
brothers. Running Pierce Brothers." His amber eyes flared
with intensity. "I'm finally home."

The tension knotted a few notches tighter. She fought
the urge to roll down her window for air. Instead, she reached
for her coffee with trembling hands. Okay, no more questions. She didn't like playing with matches that could cause a
bad fire. She still carried the scars from the last one.

"What about you? Do you regret never leaving Harrington?"

The past rose up like a tsunami, but she fought the waves
and held on. "No. I never needed to leave to find myself."

"Plus you had Becca."

She froze. Her daughter's name on his lips caused a deep
shudder to wrack her body. She cleared her throat. "Yes. I had
Becca to think of."

"Do you ever see *him*?"

Her voice broke. "No."

The pause between them was rife with memory. "He never comes back to see her?"

Her head spun in sudden sickness. She put her coffee down and concentrated on breathing. She needed to pull it together. "He lives overseas now and isn't part of our lives. Becca's mine and no one else's. And I'd rather not discuss my ex-husband."

He drove in silence. This was the reason she couldn't be alone with him. The questions were too dangerous—the mess of the past better left untouched. The soothing jazz coming from the stereo mocked the seething tension between them. "Syd?"

"Yeah?"

"Have you thought about that kiss?"

Sydney sucked in her breath. Instantly, the chemistry flickered, caught, and burned hot. All of her senses were trained on him, his body heat practically pulling her in. Her nostrils flared at his scent, and her body surged to life, still conditioned to her first love, her first lover, her first heartbreak.

Yes. She wanted to scream, fight, surrender, beg. Instead, she locked her muscles and fought with everything she had left.

"No."

"You're lying."

"It doesn't matter."

"It does to me."

A cry caught in her throat. She would not do this with him. She made sure to inflect her voice with her only defense: coldness. "Then I'd suggest you get over it. Because nothing is going to happen between us again. We agreed to a working truce and no more."

"Fine."

She kept her gaze averted for the rest of the ride, counting down the miles and praying she hadn't made a huge mistake.

He shouldn't have mentioned the kiss.

Tristan drove and tried to ignore the screaming silence between them. He'd sworn to push the encounter out of his mind, chalking it up to impulse, fear, and curiosity about the past. But he'd never expected such an intense reaction, from either of them. It was as if the kiss was bigger than them, swallowing good intentions and reminding him of all the wonderful things Sydney had brought to his life. Besides the most powerful physical chemistry he'd ever experienced with a woman, there was an emotional connection bridged from their shared memories. They knew each other. Had experienced great love and great pain. She was the only one who'd stripped down all of his layers and truly seen the man he was.

And she'd loved him anyway.

Though, she ended up betraying him.

Once she'd turned nineteen, he began to lose the battle not to touch her. They worked together for almost a year while he fought his body with a crazed intention. But eventually, it was too much for either of them. She used every opportunity to get close and tortured him with sweeping generalizations about her *dates* with other men, hinting at physical intimacy. Her eyes told him she wanted him if only he had the balls to ask. To seduce. To take.

The lines had blurred, until he walked around with a constant erection and woke from lustful dreams of her naked in his bed. He was slowly being driven insane, until that one late night in the office pushed them both over the edge.

"I hate this software system," he grumbled, banging on the keyboard as columns of numbers flashed in front of him. "It sucks. Why did we have to upgrade?"

"Because it's better, and once we're trained, it'll be worth it."

Her calm dismissal of his grumpiness only irritated him further. Her outfit was driving him nuts. Weren't redheads supposed to stay away from pink? Well, she'd broken that damn rule. The hot-pink little suit barely covered her curves, and the conservative white blouse only emphasized the illegal length of her skirt. Her hair was loose today, and extra wild, as if teasing him to try to tame the strands.

To try to tame her.

He told himself to focus, but he was really directing the order at his dick.

"It's not calculating the supply orders properly. I don't have time for this, Syd."

"Here, let me show you." Her scent whispered behind him, tantalizing. She leaned over behind his chair, her breath rushing against his ear, the full curve of her breast pressing into his shoulder. "You need to hit the equal button and make sure you highlight this column. Then drag it over. See?"

Her scarlet-tipped nails clicked deftly over the keys. His muscles tensed as her hair brushed his cheek. Both her arms stretched forward, caging in his body.

He bit back a tortured groan. Slowly she withdrew and placed her soft hands on his biceps. Then squeezed.

He stilled. Dragged in a breath. And waited for her to move away.

She didn't.

"Tristan?"

His name on her lips was a question that burned with need. Smothering a vicious curse, head pounding with desire, he swiveled his chair around to look at her. His dick strained against his pants at the naked want gleaming in her green eyes.

"Be sure you know what you're doing, Syd." His body craved to pull her into his arms and show her every pleasure a man could bring. "I don't fool around with little girls."

She surprised him with her boldness. Though her hands shook, she slid onto his lap, looping her arms around his neck. Her touch burned through his shirt. He could practically smell her arousal, her nipples straining against her blouse, begging for his mouth. "I'm not a little girl anymore, Tristan." Her voice was full of smoke and sex, leaving innocence behind. "I know things you don't think I do."

The rage that shook through him at the idea of her being with some clumsy boy egged him on. He growled and twisted his fingers in her hair, tugging back her head. Her pupils dilated with arousal, no fear reflected on her face. "I don't like a tease, either." He gave in to the need to taste her, bending to swipe his tongue down the exposed curve of her neck. She shuddered. "Are you a virgin?"

Color flooded her cheeks. He was ready to stop right then and there, but she arched toward him, gaze fastened on his. "Yes. I've been waiting for you."

He closed his eyes, fighting for control. His ego screamed with satisfaction that he'd be her first, that he'd be carved in her memory for the rest of her life, that he could make it so good for her, she'd never forget him. "Be sure," he said again. "Your virginity is a gift, Syd. I don't intend to screw with it."

"I know exactly what I want, Tristan Pierce." She looked him straight in the eye with resolve and a raw ache that ripped at his heart. "I want you."

He didn't need any more convincing. Keeping her head still, he took her lips with his and drowned in pure sweetness and exotic spice. He devoured her with a hunger he'd never experienced before. She burned up in his arms, her skin blistering hot, her mouth and tongue and lips giving back to him with both inexperience and eagerness. The kiss became an explosion of hidden wants he never even knew he had, and Tristan feasted on her body without regret or apology.

His fingers dove under her tight little skirt, brushing against the lace of her panties, savoring the sopping wetness he found there. She jerked in his arms, eyes wide open in pure surprise. "You like that?" he murmured, moving his thumb to rub softly against her clit. She writhed in questing need, grinding her sweet pussy against his thumb, trying to get there. He refused to take her virginity tonight. Sydney didn't deserve a quickie on the office chair, but God, his entire body pulsed with a raw ache that desperately needed fulfillment. "Answer me, baby."

Her face turned red, but she gave him what he needed. "Yes. Oh, I need—more—"

"I know. Let me play a bit. Show you how good I can make you feel." His index finger slipped under the elastic at the same time that he opened the top buttons on her shirt to reveal her breasts. Clad in delicate white lace, she was a vision in front of him, and he wondered if he was going to come in his pants like a kid. He closed his mouth around one stiff nipple and sucked her through the lace while his finger traced the swollen folds of her sex, ramping up her need. She writhed in his lap, dragging her thigh against his erection, caught in the pleasure only he could give her. Mesmerized by each expression flickering over her face, he pushed his finger inside her tight channel, groaning at the way she tightened around him.

"You're so damn beautiful," he growled, his teeth scraping against her hard nipple. "Give me more. Don't hold back."

"Tristan, oh, God, it feels so good."

He pulled down her bra and sucked on her nipple, adding another finger inside of her. With controlled motions, he played her, bringing her slowly to the edge and keeping her there, until her clit throbbed with need and her teeth sank into her lower lip, her head thrashing back and forth as she reached desperately for climax.

His blood roared in his veins, and he knew he couldn't take another moment. "Let go, baby. Come for me."

He rubbed her clit and bit down on her nipple at the same time.

She screamed, jerking in his arms as the release washed over her. He cursed and studied her face, drinking in the shocked satisfaction, reveling in her response to his touch. He kissed her again, murmuring softly against her lips, taking her down with care.

She collapsed on his lap, still holding him. Tristan wrapped his arms around her and held her just as tight, not wanting her to regret a single act they'd done together. She'd surprised him

*with her erotic surrender mixed with the pure honesty she al-
ways reflected. It was a heady combination.*

*"Are you okay?" he asked, pressing a kiss to the top of her
head.*

"Mmm," she murmured against his chest.

*"I don't know if this is a good idea." He stroked her, and she
purred like a cat, and all he could think about was how fast he
could make her come again. "We work together. My brothers
would freak. My father would kill me. Baby, I don't know where
this can go between us, and I don't want to hurt you. I'd rather
die than hurt you."*

*"I know. But I can handle it, Tristan. Why can't we take it
slow and see what happens? We don't have to tell anyone. It can
be our secret."*

"Is that what you want?"

*He held his breath. His head warned him if he took this road
with her, everything could change. But something in his gut
drove him forward: a need to dive deep and discover everything
this woman had to give. He waited for her answer, swearing that
if there was even a glint of wariness, he would let her go.*

*Slowly she raised her head and treated him to a sexy, sleepy
smile. "What I want is for you to do that again."*

So he did.

"The parking garage is that way. We can walk to Carmine's,"
she said, interrupting his thoughts.

He got himself together. This was about business. Not
stolen kisses in attics or hot memories of bringing her to
climax as she sat sprawled on his lap. He needed to bring
his A game to Cushman, and he didn't intend to let his little
head dictate the next couple of hours.

"Got it." He parked. She climbed out of the car, hitching her purse over her shoulder and smoothing down her black skirt. They walked the few blocks to the popular Italian place, known for good Chianti, generous family-size portions of food, and solid service. He tried not to notice the way her skirt hugged her lush ass or the stretch of those muscled legs, flexing due to her high strappy heels. She'd put her hair up in a bun today, reminding him of a sexy librarian he ached to mess up.

He was sure she wouldn't appreciate his thoughts.

They walked inside, where Adam was already seated. The dining room was richly decorated, from the glittering chandelier to the numerous portraits of celebrities and the sprawling wooden bar that took up half of the front room. Adam stood up to greet them. The man was a dynamo when it came to real estate, preferring to sweep up good property and trust builders and design teams to increase the value. "Adam, good to see you again," Tristan said. They shook hands with mutual respect. "I'm so glad we're able to work this deal together."

"Me too. Sydney, you look wonderful as always." He pressed a kiss to both of her cheeks in the European manner. With his neatly trimmed goatee, dark hair, and muscled body, he was known to turn a woman's head, then keep her attention with his intelligent conversation. He'd already ordered a bottle of wine. "I started off with a red but can easily order a bottle of white if you prefer."

Sydney smiled. "Red is perfect, thank you."

They exchanged polite chitchat, then Adam swung the conversation to business. "I love that I finally got an investment property in Harrington. Lots of activity going on, especially after the Rosenthals moved there. You're close to New York, near a marina, and have a pick of artsy stores. Plus there's money. Everything I want to invest in."

The Rosenthals were a celebrity couple who'd filmed a movie in Harrington and hired Morgan to build them a custom dream house. She'd done the job side by side with Cal and become an even bigger name in home design. Now Harrington seemed to be the new buzz city for the up-and-coming.

Tristan hated thinking about his small town getting overrun, but he also understood that if he helped with the design and locations, at least he had input. Sydney smoothly cut in. "It's a great place to live," she said. "Problem is good land is getting scarce, especially around the harbor. Buying up the Bakery block to renovate a string of custom houses that look upscale is a brilliant idea. Tristan and I already solidified the plans for the first three houses, and we're ready to move forward. Were you able to go over the cost estimates we sent?"

Adam nodded. "Yes. I love the designs and being able to work with local suppliers. But I'm not sure if that's going to work out. I'm thinking of going with the Builders Loft warehouse out in Jersey. They were able to offer a very competitive proposal."

Tristan's radar began to ping. He knew Cushman always threw a curveball, and this one was a biggie. He'd given them the sample, hooked them like a fish, then reeled Pierce Brothers in. Sydney wouldn't have been prepared for such a strategy. New York had taught him about the ruthlessness and touch of greed within the property development segment.

The waiter dropped off platters of stuffed artichokes, cala-mari with marinara sauce, and salad, then smoothly retreated.

He decided to wait it out, hoping Syd would have time to wrap her mind around Adam's challenge. Tristan hoped he wouldn't have to dive in to save her, and be forced to engage in the main contest that all males knew best:

Who had the biggest dick.

Sydney filled her plate, nodding thoughtfully. "I under-stand why you'd be concerned, Adam. Working with an es-tablished warehouse definitely drives down costs, but then we're missing out on the big picture and the true goal of this project. Hiring local brings in a unique perspective, product control, quality, and the loyalty of the town. Depending on one warehouse to complete all eight houses is risky."

Hmm. Nice volley. He decided to play backup until she needed him to jump in and take the reins. "She's right. You've already expressed reservations about the cookie-cutter products available. Our suppliers will give you houses with a custom feel, and that sells properties fast."

Adam glanced back and forth, considering. He broke off a piece of bread, buttered it, and took a bite. Sydney took his lead and began to eat, not pressing him for a quick response. Damn, when had she learned the fine art of patience when negotiating? Many grown men weren't able to stop talking to save a deal for their lives.

"Local suppliers are sometimes difficult to work with," Adam finally commented. "I'm unsure if it will be worth it. How about this? I'll give you the first three houses. The rest I'll move to the warehouse and tweak the plans accordingly. It's a win-win."

Tristan admired his savvy, but he knew compromising on a half deal wasn't the way to go. Splitting the jobs would bring chaos and resentment from the locals. It was a breeding ground for disaster. Pierce might need to walk away from the entire deal. He'd learned that not compromising sometimes led to better profits that he could make up in the future. Pierce wasn't desperate. And beginning this relationship with Adam on an unbalanced foundation was unacceptable.

A flash of regret settled over him. He'd still try to save the deal, but he hoped Sydney wouldn't be too disappointed.

Platters of chicken parmigiana and spaghetti were placed on the table. Water and wine were topped off. Sydney filled her plate, rotating her fork with deft expertise, seeming to relish the meal with no nerves. She dabbed at her lips with her white napkin.

"Sorry, Adam. Pierce won't be able to compromise on that issue. I'm afraid this is an all-or-nothing deal."

The businessman blinked, suddenly looking curious. "You'd give up three solid houses just for the other five? It doesn't make good business sense. You'll still be ahead with profit margins, and if this works out, I'll consider a future deal."

"This is the deal we need to close," she said firmly. "I'm not screwing my suppliers, who already agreed to take a discount in order to meet your needs on this project. And please don't forget the zoning in Harrington is extremely strict. Problematic, actually. Fortunately, Pierce Brothers is well-known and can smooth over a lot of bumps."

Tristan tried not to gape like an idiot. Why didn't she seem off balance? She'd threatened Cushman. Oh, it was subtle, but the consequences were clearly stated beneath the fluff. He was used to her glancing at him for support and following his lead. When he used to occasionally force her to meet clients, she'd duck her head, a lovely blush staining her cheeks. He'd nod in encouragement and help her through the discussion, then sit back and revel in her wide-open admiration of his skill.

Now he'd been neatly pushed to the sidelines.

She simply didn't need him like that anymore.

Adam considered her words, swirling the wine around in his glass. "Interesting. I hadn't expected any . . . problems in that area."

She kept her smile flawless, as if she had no idea what he meant. Tristan bit back a chuckle. "Oh, you wouldn't have any of those problems with Pierce. What did you think of the actual design plans for the remaining homes?"

"I like them," he said almost grudgingly. "I like a lot you've done, and that's why I want to work with you." Respect edged his gaze. "So, I'll give you my final proposition. I want an additional five percent cut if we use all your suppliers. Get me that, and I'll sign the rest of the contracts. Then we're in business."

She shook her head. "They've already taken a substantial cut."

"An additional five percent for this job is what I'm asking. Let's get it done."

She took her time. Forked up more pasta. Tristan waited for her to check in with him, even via a veiled glance, but she seemed to be running this whole deal on her own. He kept quiet, not wanting to ruin her mojo at the moment.

"I'll discuss it with them. Give me three days."

"You have two. I need to get moving on this." His shark smile was hidden under buckets of charm. "You understand how much I want you to take this deal, don't you?"

This time, she glanced over. He jumped right in.

"We do, too, Adam, but you're still looking for a lot. We'll get back to you in two days, but then I want copies of the contract expressed to us in a twenty-four-hour time frame. We need to know about your commitment, too."

"Agreed." Adam grinned. "Let's have a toast." They raised their glasses. "To a fruitful prospective partnership."

Crystal clinked. They spent the rest of lunch going over details, and Tristan and Adam shared stories of their time in Manhattan when they had tried to take the real estate world by storm. But the whole time he was aware of the woman sitting beside him. She'd come into her full power.

It was sexy as hell.

And he didn't know what he wanted to do about it anymore.

chapter six

Maybe she'd made a mistake.

Sydney tried not to chew her lower lip and lengthened her stride to keep up with Tristan. After lunch, he'd been eerily quiet. His stare had shredded her neat barriers, and then he'd turned on his polished heel and begun walking, forcing her to follow. The swish of his pressed pants and the tap of his shoes on pavement rose to her ears. She concentrated on the hypnotic pace and keeping up.

Swish, swish, swish.

Tap, tap, tap.

The March wind tugged at her neat bun, but she was already overheated from the wine and the stress of what she'd done. He was probably pissed. She'd basically risked the entire deal on a game of chicken, and now she had to convince those suppliers to take an additional 5 percent discount. She hadn't once asked Tristan for permission to push Cushman. Tristan was a control freak when it came to running a deal, whether or not he'd agreed to let her take the lead.

But she had to go with her gut and do it on her own.

Adam wouldn't have respected her if she'd looked to

Tristan. She had to set the rules up front and make sure he knew she wouldn't deal with his bullshit.

They passed the parking garage and headed toward Bryant Park. The familiar sounds of the city wrapped around them, softening the silence between them. With its raw power, naked ugliness, and glorious elegance, New York was home to the very best. From Adam's stories, which she'd greedily gobbled up, Tristan had been quite the star in the real estate market, building an important list of contacts and securing a stellar reputation.

Not that she was surprised. Looking back, she was ashamed of her need for him to fill all her empty spaces. God knows she wanted to teach Becca to be her own self before belonging to another. The thought of her daughter tightened her stomach, so she quickened her pace and concentrated on walking.

Pedestrians crowded the sidewalks, pressing into an impatient mass as they waited for the walk lights. Many ignored the flashing warnings, jumping into the street to beat a rushing cab, turning up a middle finger at the beeping and loud insults from the cabbie. Vendors took up street corners selling knockoff designer bags, pashmina scarves, and sunglasses. Artists sketched and ticket scalpers shouted amid homeless people with handmade signs begging for money. The smells of exhaust, hot dogs, and grease filled the air. She jumped over a steaming metal grate to avoid getting her heel caught, then turned right where the park opened up like a cool drink of water in the desert.

Up the stairs past 'Wichcraft, the famous sandwich shop by *Top Chef* judge Tom Colicchio. More vendor booths spilled out and lined the grassy center, boasting painted iPhone covers, custom jewelry, and pretty hair bands with bright ribbons and crystals. Hot soup was ladled into paper cups, served alongside churros, chili, chicken kebabs, and anything else a New Yorker could possibly crave. The ice rink would soon turn to green grass and become host to concerts and other events. Tristan stopped, lowering himself onto a bench. Still not speaking, she sat next to him.

His shoulder pressed against hers. Even in the March chill, the burn of his body heat tempted her to move closer. The delicious scent of salty ocean and warm sand filled her nostrils. Where had he discovered that cologne? She cursed the designer for creating it and driving her mad with lust. She'd never realized the beach could smell so damn good.

Slowly her body began to relax as he remained silent. They'd shared many wonderful things together she still missed. Passionate nights, engaging conversation, and raunchy humor. But what she grieved over the most were the gorgeous silences between them, filled with endless possibilities, deep understanding, and the fragility of the passing moment.

The sun skipped through the half-bare trees, and occasional chirps blasted from unseen perches from the birds returning from migration. Branches rustled, and a fat gray squirrel shot out from the brush to cross the pathway. A couple linked arm in arm strolled by, heads bent together, whispering with an intimacy that bespoke bliss. Two men in red plaid hats and heavy winter coats sat at a metal table, involved in a game of chess. She breathed in a lungful of air, feeling it penetrate all the closed parts of her body, then slowly released it. She remembered how they used to sit by the marina at the hidden spot they'd claimed. Hands clasped together, they'd sit in utter quiet while they studied the bright moon and listened to the gentle slurps of water sloshing against the boats.

God, how she'd missed him.

"You surprised me."

His voice was full of all the things that seduced her. Gravel lined with silk. Smoke edged with flame. Grace entwined with raw power. A shudder wracked her body, but she fought through it. "Why? Because I actually handled him without asking for permission?" she said with a touch of defensiveness. She waited for his temper, ready to fight back. This was her deal, and he needed to accept it.

"No. Because you were magnificent."

Her mouth fell open. "Huh?"

"I was wrong. You can handle this deal. You did everything I would have. You challenged him, held your ground, and gave where you could. You are ready for CFO. I just didn't see it."

The words settled into her soul and spread warmth through her body. Gaining Tristan's respect was priceless. He was a tough taskmaster and held everyone to the highest standard, including himself. She knew how much it had taken for him to admit he'd been wrong.

She also realized the past two years of avoiding him was also her fault. Yes, she had a big secret to protect, but she'd never allowed him to see how much more she was capable of. How much she could handle.

How much she wanted.

"That's because I never told you what I could do," she admitted. "I kept it from everyone, then got frustrated when no one would give me a chance to prove myself. Thank you for backing me up today. It meant a lot."

"You're welcome."

His arm pressed against her thigh, the tips of his fingers resting lightly against her bare calf. She shivered. His brows snapped in a frown. "You're cold. I'm sorry, I didn't think. You aren't wearing a coat."

"No, I'm fine, I don't need—"

He ignored her, stripping off his suit jacket and placing it around her shoulders. The snowy-white shirt molded to his broad chest, emphasizing the lean cut of his hips and the hardness of his stomach. The line of his bright red tie was like a matador's cape luring over a bull. Oh, how she wished she could rip open those buttons with her teeth and strip off that damn tie. Oh, the things they could do with it . . .

"You okay?"

Did she have a moony look on her face? Ugh. Knowing it was a battle she'd lose due to his innate chivalry, she huddled into the jacket, savoring the deliciousness of his lingering body warmth and scent. "Fine. Thank you."

"Think we can convince our suppliers to cut another five percent off the top?" he asked.

She winced. "Not going to be easy. I'll meet with Anthony Moretti. He's the main leader, though he denies it. If he agrees, he'll convince the others to work with us."

"Good plan."

They sat together on the bench, enjoying each other's presence. Her eyes burned with emotion, but she chalked it up to fierce satisfaction at having this man finally see her for the woman she'd become. On his level.

"I know you don't want to talk about this now. I know we're in the midst of a big project. I know we just started a tentative truce. But there's still something between us, Syd. And I'm telling you right now, I'm not sure what I'm going to do about it."

His stark words fell between them in a challenge. He'd always been brutally honest. He went after what he wanted, or who, when he was truly ready. He'd fought their chemistry for over a year before he'd finally succumbed to the intense attraction. But when he broke, he'd bound her to him for life.

She refused to look at him. Her insides shivered with dread. With anticipation. With want.

But there was no way to follow that path without telling him he was Becca's father. And she didn't know if either of them was ready to handle such a truth.

How she had loved this man with every part of her being. She shook with the need to make contact but knew the rules must be set to chart the course. Temptation didn't matter. If they gave in to their physical cravings to stroll down memory lane, it could destroy them both.

She reached deep for strength and followed the conversation through. "You need to know nothing has changed, Tristan. This is business. I'm not interested in dredging up the past or scratching any itches."

"Neither am I. I'm talking about something more. Something brand-new." His eyes glittered with shards of gold. "I've been thinking about that damn kiss, and I know you have, too."

Her breath came out in uneven bursts. The memory of those carved lips over hers was stamped in her brain. The rush of his warm breath, the thrust of his hot tongue claiming her as his, the glorious strength of his arms holding her tight as he devoured her on his own terms. Damn him. He couldn't rip away her life twice. Once was enough, and playing this dangerous game threatened to steal her very sanity.

She avoided the question and concentrated on her frustrated fury. "We both have an opportunity to work on something important, and I refuse to let a fit of lust ruin my chance. I have a daughter to think of, and a life I built on my own. So, no, Tristan, I have no desire to revisit the past or move forward with you. There's too much at stake for me to blow it up for a quick roll in the hay."

"It would never be quick. And I'd never let it affect the work."

The confident, masculine response weakened her knees. He'd always been a controlled, demanding lover who liked to be in charge—and didn't believe in the quickie. She was so glad she was sitting. "I need you to back off and respect my wishes. I can't—I can't do this with you again." She lifted her chin and met his stare head-on. "Ever."

The flash of regret was gone so quickly she'd probably imagined it. He nodded quickly, then stood. "We'd better head back."

They walked back to the car in the same silence they'd begun with.

Because of rush hour, construction, and an accident that blocked up a lane on 287, they reached Harrington hours past their ETA. Most of the drive had been spent discussing the project and making a preliminary list of things to accomplish. After their walk back from the park, Tristan had steered the conversation toward business to keep the peace. He'd forgotten how nice it was to talk shop with a woman. Sydney had always been sharp, but watching her take charge and exhibit ambition simply turned him on.

He kept wondering what she'd be like once he dragged her back into bed.

Dangerous thoughts, especially since she had made her intentions well-known. At least her intentions not to sleep with him.

"We're so late," she said. Her foot shook nervously over her crossed leg. "What time is it?"

"Almost eight. Got big plans for the evening?"

"Yep. I have to pick up my dress from the cleaner's and head back to the city for the Met Gala. Then I made a cocktail date afterward on top of the Marriott Marquis."

"I sense sarcasm."

She rolled her eyes. "You sense right. Such is the plight of the single mom. I have to get up early tomorrow and get my oil changed in the car, grocery shop, pick up extra tights at Target, do laundry, and get to a dance recital at night."

"For Becca?"

"No, it's my debut at the Paramount Theater."

"I sense much anger within you."

A strangled laugh escaped her lips. "Sorry, I'm stressed. I get bitchy sometimes."

"Wow, and I thought I was busy. Now I feel like a slug. I can't even seem to get to my workout with Raven's trainer without bitching, and I only have to take care of myself."

"And you said yes?" she practically screeched. "Xavier is legendary. What if you damage yourself?"

Disgust laced his voice. "Dalton manages. I think I'm just as equipped."

"Dalton's younger."

"You're right. You are bitchy when you're stressed."

He enjoyed the sound of her laugh, open and infectious. She didn't laugh as much around him anymore. She was too buttoned up and afraid to show any emotion.

"Dalton's never babysat this long for Becca before."

"I'm sure they're both fine. There's never been a female Dalton couldn't handle."

He pulled into the winding pathway of the Pierce family mansion and cut the engine. The glow of headlights flashed on the two giant figures perched in perfect stillness, flanking the massive door.

Sydney sucked in a breath. "Oh, no, what should we do?"

He considered the problem, but even now, he watched their twin bodies shake with suppressed emotion. They rose to full height, which was intimidating as hell, since they reached all the way to his shoulders. Their muscles were brutal and built to withstand any type of attack.

"We have no choice. I'll get out first. Stay here till I signal it's safe."

"Will you be okay?"

"I got this."

He turned off the lights and opened the car door quietly. With deliberate, slow movements meant not to threaten, he climbed out and put his hands in the suddenly charged air. "Hey, guys. It's me. No need to freak out, now. Right?"

They quivered. A low wail broke from their lips, like that of a coyote suddenly faced with a juicy steak.

"I mean it, no more of this behavior. I've had enough. Now I'm going to walk toward you, and you are going to stay—stay—STAY—ah, hell!"

They leapt through the air like Santa's flying reindeer and hit him full force, sending him staggering backward. As he flailed his hands in total indignity, they whipped him with a tongue bath, shoving their warm bodies against him with abandon in affection and canine joy.

Sydney's laugh echoed through the air, but most of the dogs' insane energy had lost its sharp edge. They only bumped into her with gentle affection, offering a few licks. "Are they ever going to outgrow this behavior?" she asked.

He lifted hands coated with saliva and looked down at his once-perfect pants, now covered in dog hair. "Ugh. Cal sent them to a third obedience school, but they were dismissed early for a refund."

"They never trample Becca, though," she commented.

"They must sense she's like a tiny mouse they want to protect rather than eat." They headed to the door, and the dogs accompanied them in, jumping in happiness to get more company. The sound of Dalton's voice drifted in the air, followed by a giggle.

They rounded the corner, and Becca let out a squeal, running into her mother's arms. "Mama! Uncle Dalton and I had so much fun, I had chicken for dinner with the potato fries I like, and we made friendship bracelets, and I made you one!"

"You did? Let me see. Oh, I love it."

He watched Sydney examine the bright pink-and-yellow-braided fabric, face alight with genuine pleasure. Watching their heads bent together, arms entwined, faces close, he felt a pain rip at his gut and a yearning that knocked him off his ass.

It was like seeing Sydney young again. He studied her daughter, with her bright red hair now contained in a pony-tail. Already the curly strands broke free in rebellion and fell across her cheeks and nape. Fair skin with a generous smat-tering of freckles. Bright green eyes swirled with gold, full of curiosity and a zest for life that humbled him. She was all long, lanky legs like a young colt out of the gate. Her favorite color seemed to be pink, from her leggings, sneakers, and long-sleeved T-shirt with a cat in a tiara.

"Say hi," Sydney prodded.

"Oh, sorry, hi, Tristan!"

"Hi, Becca." She called his brothers Uncle. Not him. For some reason, she only used his first name. Not that he was great with kids. They puzzled him, and he'd always preferred the company of adults and cocktails to children's games and juice boxes.

Becca made him . . . uncomfortable. He never knew what to say to her or how to act. He tried to avoid her. Looking at her face hurt. She was a reminder of Sydney moving on and marrying another man, but he never wanted his raw emotions to leak out in the way he treated her daughter.

He looked over at Dalton, who sported a bright blue braided bracelet. It went perfectly with his man bun. "Nice look, dude."

His brother rolled his eyes. "I'm secure in my manhood."

"Uncle Dalton says real men wear jewelry," Becca recited with wide eyes.

"You're right," he said seriously. "I remember the day Uncle Dalton got his ear pierced and screamed like the Cowardly Lion. A scary sight."

"Mama said I did good when they pierced my ears, but I don't really remember. Where's your earring?" she asked Dalton.

His brother shot him a look. "Took it out. I'm into friendship bracelets now."

Becca giggled.

"Thanks for watching her, Dalton. Sorry we were so late."

His brother stood up from the stool and stretched. "No problem. I had a blast. How did your meeting go?"

"Good. Sydney killed it," Tristan offered.

Pride flashed in Dalton's blue eyes. "Not surprised, Ms. CFO."

"Thanks. Your brother wasn't too bad himself. But I'd better get the princess home. We have a big day tomorrow."

"Are you coming to my ballet recital?" Becca asked Dalton.

"I'm sorry, sweetheart, I have to work with Raven tomorrow at the restaurant."

"Oh." Disappointment reflected in Becca's eyes. "Morgan can't go, either." Suddenly that green-gold gaze swiveled to snare Tristan in its grip. A shiver raced down his spine at the contact. "Are you coming, Tristan?"

He hadn't been invited. Not that it mattered. Sure, Dalton and Cal and even Brady liked to attend her recitals and plays and stuff. But he'd set himself up as a more distant figure, too busy with work and other things to take the time out for such activities. And of course, Sydney never wanted him there. Not when they'd barely cobbled together a conversation since he'd returned to Harrington.

He shifted his feet, suddenly uncomfortable. "Umm, sorry, Becca, I can't. I'm busy."

An awkward silence descended. Dalton shot him a withering look, but he didn't know what they wanted from him. He wasn't about to go to a ballet for Sydney's daughter. He had no clue how to relate, and it was better he kept his distance.

"Oh. Okay." Her soft words carried a touch of hurt.

Sydney gave her daughter a hug and a blinding smile. "I'll be there in the front row, and you'll be with all your friends. Maybe we can all go out for ice cream together afterward?"

Becca's face brightened. "Cool."

He pushed away the guilt. How did he get to be the bad guy in this? The idea of being trapped in a car with both of them for the ride home touched off a flicker of panic. Becca was known for her chatter, and he wasn't good at conversation with kids. "Hey, Dalton, can you drive them home for me? I have to make a few calls. For business."

"Sure. Come on, ladies. My chariot awaits."

"Bye, Tristan," Becca called out, linking her hand with Syd's as she headed toward the door.

"See you later."

He noticed Sydney didn't look back or offer a good-bye.

chapter seven

Sydney? I need you down here now to talk about this deal.
I won't be available tomorrow or Monday, so if we're going
to discuss, we need to do it now."

She looked down at her out-of-date Valentine's Day Lu-
LaRoe leggings, faded oversize T-shirt, and furry boots. She'd
squeezed in the oil change this morning, bought the tights,
and picked up some groceries, and she didn't have much time
left before Becca needed to get ready for the recital. Especially
since scoring a front seat meant getting there an hour early.

Swallowing past the panic, she kept her voice calm. Anthony Moretti was known for his quality tile, workmanship,
and theatrics. She'd been able to reach out to him briefly
about the deal, but he liked face-to-face encounters. Her
plan to approach him on Monday obviously wasn't going to
work, since he refused to wait. "No problem. Can you give
me half an hour?"

"See you then."

She clicked off her cell phone and dragged in a breath.
Okay, she could do this. Her brain madly rushed through the
options as she crammed her hair into a halfhearted bun and

hunted for her files. "Becca!" she yelled. "Honey, I need you down here now!"

"What?"

"I have to drop you off at My Place for a little bit while I run out." She frantically pushed away catalogs, school bulletins, and Becca's artwork and found her work folder. Thank God. "We have to go now!"

Her daughter came down with her Nintendo DS and a big frown. "But we have to get ready for my recital!"

"We'll have time. I promise it'll be fine. I'll swing by and pick you up in an hour."

Becca gave a grumble but began tugging on her pink boots. "Okay. Can I get sweet potato fries? And play darts?"

"Yes, anything you want." She grabbed Becca's jacket and her own, then hurried into the car. She dialed Raven's number on her Bluetooth, praying it wouldn't be a problem. Raven adored Becca, as did the restaurant staff, and was always happy to babysit when Sydney was in trouble. Raven's voice came over the line. "Raven? It's Sydney. Can I drop Becca off for a little while? A work thing came up."

"Sure, I'll get a platter of the fries she loves ready. Can't wait."

"Thank you. See you in five."

She hurried to My Place, dropped her daughter off, and drove like a bat out of hell to the granite place. Slipping into work mode, she allowed herself a few seconds of quiet meditation, then walked inside.

In her hot-pink heart leggings.

Anthony greeted her with warmth, shooting her a puzzled look at her wardrobe, but at least he kept quiet. The older man had a clean-shaven head, ruddy cheeks, and a nice belly that screamed of his love for pasta and beer. His networking ability was legendary in Harrington. Thank goodness he displayed pure loyalty to Pierce Brothers.

His only problem was working with "city slickers" who were going to beat him, rob him, and leave him in the gutter to die.

"I can't go another five percent, Syd," he said with a worried expression. "It's not worth it."

She'd prepped for this battle and was ready. "Anthony, I fought him on this, but it's the only way to compete with the warehouse. You have to look at the bigger picture for Harrington. For the first time, we'll be showcasing local suppliers for the bigger jobs. We nail this, and you can pick and choose from projects you've never been able to bid on before."

She knew Anthony was a bit of an egotist when it came to his work. Another reason he loved Pierce—they weren't the type of builders who threw up cheap houses for cost. "I don't know."

"Then let me convince you."

She spent the next half hour going over design plans, costs, and benefits. Slowly he began nodding his head, beginning to grasp the bigger vision she'd been desperate to communicate.

Then she went for her close.

"Let me be honest. Adam is going to begin building in Harrington whether we want him to or not. He'd rather bring in crappy chain distributors and put up cookie-cutter houses that will eventually insult both of our businesses. This is a way to stop him without a feud. On our terms. You have the ability to make something spectacular happen. But I'm afraid if you don't bend on this final condition, we'll not only be cut out but cut up."

Anthony tapped his finger against the papers, then slurped his coffee. "Bastards," he grumbled.

"I know. So let's do this our way."

A reluctant smile curved his lips. "Ah, hell, why not?"

"Do you think you can get Brenda and Sam on board?" The other two granite, textile, and wood suppliers usually followed Anthony's lead on projects.

"Yeah, I'll call them today. But you'll have to pay them a visit."

"I will. Monday. I promise."

"Good."

She managed to peek at her watch. She was running a bit late, but nothing some deft driving and organization couldn't handle. Saying her good-byes to Anthony, she headed to her car. She wished My Place weren't on the edge of Harrington. Easing on the accelerator, she whizzed out of town, until a loud *pop* exploded in the air.

"What the hell?" Her car pulled to the left, and she angled into the spin. Thank God the road was basically clear, since she spun once, then landed on the side of the road. With shaking hands, she climbed out of the car and walked to the back.

Flat tire.

Completely. There was no saving this one. She must've run over something, maybe a busted glass bottle. Good thing she knew how to change a tire, thanks to Christian, who had always wanted her prepared to be safe on the road.

She opened the trunk, pulled off the cover, and stared into the empty space.

No spare.

Holy shit.

With horror, she remembered she'd taken the spare in to get it patched, but she'd never picked it up and put it back in the car. Which meant she was officially stranded on the side of the road with no spare and her daughter's recital in an hour.

Okay, don't freak. She had Triple A. She'd call them, and they'd give her a tow, or fix it, and get her home. Not in time for the recital, but maybe Brady or Charlie could take Becca and she'd meet them there. Morgan and Cal were gone for the weekend, so they couldn't help. Raven always had a fully packed restaurant on a Saturday night, and Dalton wasn't available. She began dialing numbers and kept getting voice mail.

When she finally reached Brady and Charlie, she discovered they were at a family dinner and over an hour away. Her regular sitter was off for the night. There was no one left to call.

Groaning, she frantically searched for anyone else in her contacts list who'd be able to get Becca to that recital. She'd been practicing so hard, and it would devastate her to miss it. She didn't have Becca's friends in her cell phone, or she'd be able to hunt down another mom who'd sympathize with her predicament. Maybe—

Tristan.

She squeezed her eyes shut. She couldn't. It was a terrible idea. It could lead to disaster.

God, she'd hated the distant way he'd treated Becca last

night. His bumbling excuse of being busy during her recital was a total lie—his left brow always quirked upward—and Becca had sensed his untruth. Not that Sydney wanted them to be buddies, but hurting her daughter's feelings stirred up her protective instincts. His asking Dalton to drive them home was a secondary punch. It was obvious he wanted nothing more to do with either of them last night, and the rejection stung.

More than she anticipated.

Fine with her. She should feel relief she'd shut down his advances in the park. Sticking them together could be a monumental mistake.

But her daughter's face haunted her.

She had to ask. She had to try. Then at least she could tell Becca she'd exhausted all possibilities.

With shaking fingers and a pounding heart, she made the call.

A fucking ballet recital.

Tristan didn't experience fear very often, but right now, his heart was slamming against his chest. He was going to be trapped with Becca, and he had no idea how to behave. When Sydney called him, he'd been ready to say no immediately but then stopped at the hint of desperation in her voice. His entire family was busy. It seemed this recital was a big thing to her daughter, and there was no way she'd be able to get home in time. If he drove across town to get her, then went back to pick up Becca, she'd end up missing the recital. He'd already been close to My Place and had no big plans tonight he'd have to break. His lie from last night mocked him. But how could he say no?

His fingers gripped the steering wheel. Thank goodness Raven always kept an extra booster seat at the restaurant. Becca sat in the booster seat in the back, obviously upset her mother was going to be late. He cleared his throat. What could he say?

"Umm, don't worry. Your mom will get there in time."

"Do you know what to do?"

No. "Yes, no problem. I've handled recitals before." He waited for the lie to strike him dead, but nothing happened. "Piece of cake."

"You have kids?" she asked in amazement.

He coughed. "No. I mean, I've gone to recitals when I used to live in New York." He decided not to tell her those were at Lincoln Center with professional ballerinas in *The Nutcracker*.

"Oh. But you said you were too busy to come."

He'd go to confession later. Right now, he needed to save face. "My appointment got canceled."

"My hair has to be in a tight bun. My teacher said it's important to look the part because then you feel the character and can tap into your ability to dance the character."

Huh. She was smart. Big words. Still, his palms sweated at the idea of doing her hair. He'd never get through this. "I'm good at hair. No problem."

"Did you ever take ballet when you were little?" she asked. "Mama said boys and girls can do anything. Boys dance ballet, and girls build houses."

"Yep, they do, but I was never a good dancer. I was better at basketball."

He pulled up to Sydney's house. He'd gotten the code to the alarm, so he quickly escorted Becca in, punched in the correct numbers, and shut the door behind him. Okay, he'd just need to focus. He was sure she already knew what to do.

He turned around, and she stood in front of him, staring.

He stared back. "Umm, so I guess you should get dressed."

She nodded like she understood. "I have my leotard and my tights upstairs."

He almost sank to his knees in gratitude. This whole thing would be easy. He knew mothers complained all the time about taking care of kids, but honestly? They only needed structure and discipline. Raising kids wasn't brain surgery. Tristan began to relax. "Great. You get dressed, I'll do your hair, and then we'll drive to the recital. Sound good?"

"Yes!" She bounded upstairs, and he let out a breath. Flexed his fingers. He grabbed his cell and quickly texted Sydney that everything was okay, adding a smiley face. No need for her to worry. He had it under control.

"Tristan!"

He jumped. "Yeah?"

Her voice seemed tearful. "I got a run in my tights! I need help!"

"Oh, okay. Coming," he called out. He eyed the staircase with pure trepidation but decided he had no choice. When he hit the top of the stairs, she showed him a small hole in her upper thigh. He frowned. "Won't the lacy thing cover it?"

She shook her head. "No, the hole will end up running, and I'll be onstage and look awful."

"Do you have an extra pair?"

"Mama bought pink, but it's way too much pink, and I just can't wear it. I'll look ridiculous!"

"Uh, okay. Maybe we can Krazy Glue it?"

"Mama said nail polish does it. She keeps her polish in the bathroom, under the sink in a big brown basket."

"Got it." He headed toward the bathroom and stopped short. *Whoa.* It was damn scary in there. Endless jars in various shapes cluttered the long counter, and the claw-footed tub held an array of body lotions and bath soaps, emitting a fragrance that was too familiar. Orange blossoms. He'd always wondered how she managed to cloak herself in the fragrance. Loose clothing was hung over the shower rod, and he immediately spotted a black lace thong that froze his brain for several precious seconds. *Focus,* he reminded himself. *Nail polish.*

He rummaged under the sink and yanked out a big basket, and a ton of other stuff tumbled out with it. Smothering a groan, he began stuffing junk back in, until his hand closed around a large object that had a familiar shape, encased in a plastic bag. He stared at it for a few moments before his brain slammed into high gear.

A vibrator.

His mouth hung open. The contraption featured several interesting buttons and was an impressive size. He had a searing image of Sydney soaking in the tub, thighs spread, head thrown back, vibrator humming as she stroked herself to climax. Heat exploded through him, and he clenched his fingers around the object. So, she kept it in the bathroom instead of the bedroom drawer. Interesting choice. He thought of all the fun ways they could engage in all sorts of fun play together and put this piece to good use.

"Tristan! Did you find it?"

He shoved the bag to the back of the cabinet and grabbed a bottle of red polish. "Got it." He walked out and began twisting open the bottle.

"No!" He stopped, staring at her in confusion, and she began giggling. "You can't use red nail polish. It needs to be clear, or I'll have a red spot on my tights."

"Right. Sorry." He went back in, found the bottle of clear, and painted around the hole. One crisis down. "Surgery complete. Do you have your shoes?"

"Downstairs. Can you do my hair now? And spray it with the pink glitter? Mama said I could for the recital."

"Yep. Can't dance onstage without glitter." She followed him into the bathroom, and he gazed at the riotous curls framing her face. Hmm. "Umm, does Mom use a special hair tie or something?"

"You can use these." She gave him a bunch of silky pink ribbons and a contraption outfitted with fake diamonds and a bunch of claw teeth that snapped open. He wished he'd paid more attention to how a woman fixed her hair. He was only familiar with bobby pins and scrunchies.

But he'd handle it. It was just hair. He gathered all the loose strands into a fist, and twisted the bundle twice to keep it together. Then, using his other hand, he opened the claw thing and slid it on in the center of her head. He wrapped the pink ribbon twice around the bump and tied it with a bow. A grin split his lips. "Done. Want me to spray you now?"

Her green eyes—which looked much more like gold, and a lot like his—widened in horror. "It's crooked. And there's a big bump. It needs to be smooth. And if I do my pirouette, it won't hold." She demonstrated, bouncing once in the air, and he watched an array of curls merrily escape the knot and spring back around her face.

"I'll try again. Don't worry, we'll get it."

He tried again. And again. On the fifth attempt, they were both hopped up on nerves and beginning to panic. "Use the curling iron!" she suggested. "Mama says sometimes the strands need to be straightened to get it in a tight bun."

His throat dried up, but he nodded. "Sure. Curling iron. Where is it?"

Becca pulled the weapon out of the closet. "Here, I'm not allowed to plug stuff in."

He set it up, refusing to be intimidated by a tool that was hot pink. He was a builder, for God's sake. He used power tools on a regular basis. He could handle a curling iron.

But hair was very different than houses. The silky, springy curls bounced away when he tried to grasp them between the two segments, and they slid off on a merry chase. He burned his finger twice, and his stomach was in knots about possibly burning Becca. Precious minutes ticked by.

"The pink ribbons don't work. Does your mom have rubber bands anywhere?"

"All the hair stuff is here." She pulled open the top middle drawer, and numerous items sprung forth. Hair bands, headbands, clips, barrettes, ribbons, and even a damn scrunchie. He grabbed a simple rubber band in pink and prayed hard he could do this. Finally he managed to get the strands in a tighter type of bun with the band, then he added the clip thing. The pink ribbons were casualties.

Becca announced it was acceptable.

His shoulders sagged in relief.

"Now the sparkle," she instructed.

He grabbed the can, shook it madly, and began spraying. A cloud of sparkles burst from the hose and exploded around them, drenching them in shimmery pink crystals. Becca's mouth fell open. "You weren't supposed to shake it," she whispered.

Tristan looked in the mirror. It was as if he'd been dipped in a vault of sparkles. They shone from his hair, reflected off his suit, and clung to his face. He looked like a deranged princess.

Their gazes met in the mirror with horror.

Then they both laughed.

Tristan had never laughed so hard in his life. The ridiculousness of the entire situation struck him full force, and Becca clung to him, bent over, as tears rolled down her face. A sense of pure joy filled him at her reaction and the open way she was able to view the situation.

Just like Sydney.

When they calmed down, he hurried her into the car, and he followed his GPS to the dance hall. Already the parking lot was a madhouse, with little girls in tutus gripping their mothers' hands, carrying bags and large bouquets of flowers.

"Were we supposed to bring anything?" he asked. "Flowers or something?"

"No. Daddies bring flowers for their girls sometimes after they dance," she said matter-of-factly. "Sometimes Mama picks me up sunflowers. I like them. They're happy."

A pang hit deep. "I like sunflowers, too. Okay, let's do this."

They walked into the hall, where chaos reigned, girls chattered madly, and moms filled the empty spaces in tight clusters. "Do you know where to go?" he asked. "Do you need me to check in with your teacher?"

Becca raised her hand and waved to a little girl across the room. "No, I'm okay. My friend Lyndsey is over there—her mom will help me. You need to get a seat—Mama says it gets crazy in there, and she likes to be in the front row."

"Got it. Okay, break a leg."

Her eyes widened. "What?"

"Never mind. Good luck. You'll be great, and your mom will be here soon."

"Thanks, Tristan!"

She skipped over to her friend. Ignoring the pointed looks he got owing to his sparkle incident, he headed down the aisle and grabbed the last two seats on the end. Lowering himself into one of them, he shrugged off his jacket and laid it on the other. Relief coursed through him. He'd done it. They'd had some hiccups, but Becca was dressed and here on time, and he had seats in the front row.

"Excuse me? You can't save that seat."

He looked up. A woman with dark blond hair, heavily lined eyes, and bright red lipstick stood over him. She was dressed in an expensive cream sweater set, with oatmeal pants, and had a ton of sparkly gold jewelry dripping from every bare inch of skin. Her perfume was expensive and too obvious.

He was used to dealing with all types of personalities in his business, so he shot her a charming smile. "Oh, I'm saving it for one of the girls' mothers. She had a flat tire, so she wasn't able to get here in time."

She gave him a tight smile. "It's still against the rules. No saving seats for anyone in the family. It's not fair. I'll need to sit there."

He made sure he kept the smile on his face. "I understand the rules, but this is a unique circumstance. I'm sure the teacher will agree this time it would be okay to hold one seat."

"Not in the front row," she retorted. "You can save her a seat in the back. You only get the front if you're here in person."

His gaze narrowed. So did hers.

"Sydney Greene-Seymour had an emergency. Do you know her? And her daughter, Becca? I'm sure Sydney will be appreciative of your flexibility—it really is an emergency."

Uh-oh. He'd figured name-dropping would help, but her face got all scrunched up, and a venomous glee glinted from her eyes. "I see. Are you a *friend* of Sydney's?" she practically sneered.

"Yes."

"Well, *friends* can't save seats, either. My daughter Lucy is the lead, and I plan to sit in this seat." With a sharklike smile, she reached out to move his jacket.

His hand shot out to keep it there. "Sorry. This seat is saved."

She gasped. "I tried being polite. Now I'm getting Ms. Benneton. Stay here." She jabbed a sharp bloodred fingernail in his direction and stalked away.

Was he in trouble? His stress level shot up. This was supposed to be a supportive, creative community, yet he felt like he'd gotten dropped into the Hunger Games arena. Then again, he'd seen clips of the movie *Bad Moms*. He figured it was fiction, but maybe it was reality? PTA moms going psycho and blackmailing others not in the clique? He fought a shudder. Still, no one was getting Sydney's seat without a fight. He'd managed to battle Realtors, developers, and clients that would scare Satan himself. No local ballet mother was getting the best of him.

A few minutes later, a tall woman with dark hair twisted into a bun and kind features appeared before him. She looked a bit stressed, so he pegged her as the head teacher. "Here! See, he's saving a seat for Sydney, and he's just the boyfriend."

"Friend," he corrected patiently. He gave Ms. Benneton his best smile and oozed extra charm into his voice. "Forgive me for causing any trouble. Sydney had a flat tire, and she'll be here soon. She asked if I could take Becca to her recital and save a seat. I'm sure you understand."

"There are no exceptions to the rule," *Bad Moms* Lady snapped out. "One exception leads to another, and then it is unfair to us all. I insist you give up this seat so I can watch my daughter dance the lead."

Ms. Benneton looked like she'd rather get a root canal than be next to Bad Mom, but she managed to pat her arm and keep her patient expression. "We do have that rule for a good reason, but this is a special circumstance that has never occurred before. Cynthia, how about we set up one extra folding chair in the front row, and allow—"

"Tristan," he cut in smoothly.

"Tristan to save Sydney a seat. Will that satisfy everyone?"

"Yes."

"No."

They glared at each other. Ms. Benneton glanced back and he saw a crowd was gathering over the debacle. Shit. He didn't want the bad moms to target Sydney, but he wasn't giving up this damn chair.

"I demand you move," Bad Mom aka Cynthia hissed.

"I'm sure the other chair will be perfectly fine, and you'll be able to see your daughter," he said reasonably.

She leaned in. Ruthlessness gleamed from her eyes. "Then you take the other chair. I'm taking this one."

She grabbed his jacket and tossed it to the side. Then started to sit.

He immediately threw his leg up and over to take up the empty seat.

She yelped in outrage.

"I don't have time for this right now," Ms. Benneton practically wailed. "Cynthia, I need you to be reasonable. Help me. I have girls who need help with their costumes, and hair ties have broken, and I am begging you to be the voice of reason and the leader you always are. Please."

Wow. She was good.

Tristan caught the look the teacher tossed him, and he realized the reverse psychology was actually working. Bad Mom Cynthia seemed to calm, composing her features in a mask of reason and hiding the crazy. Giving him one last murderous glance, she nodded and straightened her sweater set. "You're right. This isn't worth it when there's so much to be done. If you keep that extra seat open for me on the aisle, I'll help you and then sneak back quietly to my special seat."

His lips twitched. Ah, now it was a special seat, huh? Ms. Benneton nodded and escorted her away, leaving Tristan alone with his leg hiked up on the metal folding chair and a throbbing headache.

Son of a bitch. This was more stressful than real estate.

When the lights went out, he realized he should be videotaping the show, so he took out his iPhone and began recording. About ten minutes into the performance, Becca still hadn't danced, and he was falling asleep. All the little girls looked similar, and it was no *Swan Lake*. At times, it was almost painful.

A warm body slid beside him. Her breath whispered in his ear. "Thank you so much for helping me out. Any problems?"

He studied her in the flickering shadows. The fall of her fiery hair, the soft dew of her white skin, the smattering of freckles bridging her nose. She was wearing an interesting outfit of tight, bright leggings, furry boots, and an oversize shirt. She was sexy and adorable, and in that moment, he had so much respect for her for raising a daughter on her own and doing a slam-dunk job of it.

'Cause after only a few hours, he was ready to raise the white flag.

Slowly he smiled and reached out to squeeze her hand.

"Everything was perfect."

She relaxed and let him hold her hand for a little while longer.

And he remembered.

"My mother is dead."

He uttered the words with a numbness that caused a flash of guilt. He should be more upset. It had been two weeks of non-stop chaos, grief, and anger, and then nothing. He hadn't cried at his own mother's funeral. Cal had. So had Dalton. Not him. He'd just stood there on the muddy ground, staring at the casket while the priest muttered words that meant nothing. Her death should have brought him closer to his brothers and healed the growing rift between them.

Instead, the rift had only widened, until they could barely stand being in the same room with one another. They fought and blamed, and their father was in the background, muttering about their beloved mother's betrayal.

She'd left them all. Left her family. Left him.

For some strange man he didn't even know. She was going to run away with him with two tickets to Paris found in the wreckage.

One-way. She wasn't planning on coming back.

His entire life swiveled on its axis and shattered into fragments. He didn't know what was real any longer or what to believe in. He had no one to talk to. He had nowhere to go with this burning emptiness that slowly ate at his gut and devoured his soul.

He'd come to Sydney because she was the only one who'd loved his mother with a depth that shadowed his own. His secret affair with Syd had started off as a sexy, intense interlude that lasted through the summer months, but when fall returned and it still raged on, his brothers had discovered the secret. After an explosive fight during which he'd punched Dalton in the nose and Cal had given him a black eye, they'd reached an understanding. They stayed out of his business and backed him up by not telling his father. He'd convinced them he and Syd were friends, respected and cared about each other, but it wouldn't be a long-lasting relationship. Sydney had confirmed it. With a blush on her cheeks, she told his brothers to mind their own damn business.

Eventually they stopped giving him a hard time. The months drifted into almost a year, and he and Syd were still going strong. Tristan didn't like to think about it or classify what they had. Yes, she was young. Yes, sometimes they fell into ridiculous arguments because she was jealous of every other woman he talked to. Yes, she was insecure, and sometimes clung a bit too hard despite her guise of not caring.

But then his mom had died, and everything had changed. He was floating out there in space with no anchor to Earth, and for the first time, he was scared of who he was becoming.

There'd always been a coldness deep within him, an ability to shut himself off from the world to avoid messy emotions. But lately he'd been living in that place. His mother had always been able to pull him out.

So had Sydney.

As he stared down into her face, she did the only thing he needed in that moment.

She said no words of inane comfort. She reached up, gathered him in her arms, and held him. He leaned his cheek against the top of her head, breathing in the scent of orange blossoms while he soaked up the warmth of her body heat. Her fingers stroked the nape of his neck, and she whispered low murmurings of nonsense into his ear.

The block of ice trembled, and chips began to fall away.

"Why? Why did she betray us all, Syd?"

"I don't know. All I know is she's been unhappy with your

dad for a long time. But I swear to you on everything I know and believe, Tristan, she was coming back to you."

"She never said anything to you? Not a word about this guy she was seeing on the side?"

"No, nothing. I knew she was going to an art class she loved, but that's all. I didn't know about the teacher."

"She said nothing to us about this man. She had no return ticket. She was going to lose herself in Paris and forget her sons."

She yanked her head back from his chest, stood on tiptoe, and met his gaze with a fierceness that took his breath away. "She was coming back," Sydney repeated. "I know Diane, and you were everything to her. If you believe only one thing, you must believe me."

He stared at her for a long time and found only a knowledge and resolve that eased some of the tightness in his gut. The words spilled from him in all their raw, awful, naked truth. "I'm so lost, Syd. I don't what to do anymore."

Her eyes shone with tears. "You're going to believe what I tell you, Tristan. She was coming back."

Every time she repeated the phrase, he seemed to believe it more. His head spun, and his heart ached, and with a low groan, he dipped his head, desperate to feel alive again.

She welcomed his tongue, clung to his shoulders, and kissed him back full force. Slowly the kiss grew to something bigger, until they were ripping away clothes, falling on each other with a vicious hunger they needed to sate. Her hands burned on his skin as she fisted his throbbing length, lowered her head, and took him deep in her mouth. He threw his head back in surrender, loving the scrape of her teeth, the wet cave of her mouth sucking him tight, the slow lick of her tongue.

He reached down in a frenzy, picking her up and laying her out on the bed. Parting her thighs, he donned a condom and slid deep within her hot, swollen folds, burying himself balls-deep, taking her completely.

She cried out. Biting down on her lip, she seemed to try to fight him off, but he plundered her lips, sinking his tongue as deep as his cock, chaining her to the bed, chaining her to him.

"No, tonight I need all of you, baby. Give me all of you," he grated against her mouth.

His words caused her to tremble wildly, but then her muscles relaxed, and her hips arched for more. With a low growl of satisfaction, he pulled out in one slow slide, then pounded back into her with a ruthless desperation he couldn't control.

She matched him thrust for thrust, not only giving him everything she had but demanding everything from him. He fucked her and made love to her in a way he never had before, opening himself up to every delicious sensation wrecking his body and mind, until she screamed her release, shuddering underneath him, and he allowed himself to let go.

His orgasm burst through him. Her name ripped from his lips in a curse and a prayer. His body shook helplessly in the grip of the most intense pleasure of his life, going on and on, until he was emptied completely.

He didn't remember how long it took him to pull out and roll to the side. A strange ache filled him up, traveling through his body like wildfire, and he gripped her arms, gazing into her beautiful face, which was filled with so much love he was instantly humbled.

"I love you, Tristan Pierce," she whispered, stroking his cheek. "And I will always be here for you when you need me."

There was nothing in her voice but calm certainty and the need to give him everything he needed, with no thought as to what he was able to give back.

The block trembled and broke apart inside his chest.

He lowered his forehead to hers, and tears began slipping from his eyes as he finally cried for the first time since he'd heard the first love of his life had left him forever.

She stroked his hair and kissed his cheeks and held him through his tears. And he knew then that Sydney was part of his soul and had changed him forever.

chapter eight

*T**hey were holding hands.*

Sydney tried not to focus on the connection that hummed between them and felt completely right.

The early-spring recital revolved around a fairy tale, so each of the girls wore a colored tutu, taking her turn for a brief solo across the stage. When Becca came out in shimmery pink—her favorite color of all—her face radiant under the beaming lights, Sydney's insides shifted and an overwhelming flow of love and pride held her in its grip.

It was always like this when she gazed at her daughter, but watching her grow and change in front of her was awe-inspiring. Her throat tightened and she grinned madly as Becca spun and floated to the music without error. Those were five of the happiest minutes in Sydney's life.

Then it was over, and the other groups of dancers took their turns. When the lights came up, chaos erupted and she and Tristan quickly dropped hands. She tried to control the heat rising to her cheeks and blamed it on the stuffiness in the recital hall rather than the hand-holding.

She turned, ready to dive into organized-mom mode. "I

have to go backstage and pick her up. I can't thank you enough for— Why are you covered in pink sparkles?"

With the lights now shining full force, she took in his ruined suit and the hazelnut strands of hair highlighted in pink.

His lower lip twitched. "Just a little incident with the aerosol can."

She narrowed her gaze suspiciously. "Anything else happen?"

His left brow rose in his trademark giveaway of a bald-faced lie. "Nope."

Oh, she so didn't believe him. She hoped it wasn't a disaster that couldn't be fixed. Sticking him with the ballet recital was intense. Not many regular parents managed well, let alone someone who wasn't often around children. "Okay. Shall I meet you out front?"

He nodded, then paused. "She was good."

His voice sounded a tad wobbly. An odd expression flickered across his face, like he wasn't used to communicating his feelings. Her heart pounded so hard she swore he glanced at her chest. "Thanks. She likes to dance."

"I was bored the first half, though."

A laugh escaped at his obvious truth. "Most parents are," she confided. "We only want to see our own children perform, but we pretend we're all about the group."

"Moms are kind of hard-core, aren't they?"

"You have no idea."

"Now I think I do."

She frowned at the strange words, but then she was getting pushed by the crowd and had to go with the flow. "I'll meet you out front," she said again. Scrambling past chairs and proud, bragging moms, she dove into the madness and finally reached her daughter in the back room, standing with her friends, talking excitedly.

"Mama! I didn't stumble, not once!"

Sydney held her tight but was forced to let go way too quickly. She'd been given new rules about showing too much motherly affection in front of Becca's friends. "I'm so proud of you girls!" She gave each of them a quick hug. "You worked so hard, and it really showed."

"Thanks, Ms. Seymour," they all chanted in unison. Becca's three best friends had grown up with her from preschool into elementary school and were very close. Their mothers were responsible and down-to-earth, but she didn't get to attend many mommy dates due to her work schedule.

"Mr. and Mrs. Ellison are taking everyone out for ice cream. Can I go? Please?"

She hesitated, more for her than for Becca. She'd been looking forward to having some time alone to go over the recital. Maybe make some popcorn and rent a movie. She'd even originally planned on inviting all the girls out so she could soak up her daughter's excitement. But Becca's face was all puppy-dog eager, matched by the trio surrounding her, so Sydney gave in.

"Sure. Lyndsey, is your mom outside, so I can talk to her?"

"Yes."

"Okay, grab your bags, and let's head out. Becca, don't forget to thank Tristan for taking you."

"I won't."

They pushed their way out the front door, and she gulped in the crisp air washing over her heated skin. The girls huddled together in excitement, and she said a few quick words to Lyndsey's parents, who looked happy enough to escort four girls into their maroon minivan.

Becca ran back and stopped in front of Tristan. He sank to his knees so he was on her level. His smile flashed a set of straight white teeth. He had the grace of old-school Cary Grant and the handsome charm of Leonardo DiCaprio rolled into one. Sydney's heart hitched when her daughter practically beamed in front of him. "Thank you for taking me, Tristan."

"You're welcome. You were magnificent."

Her cheeks pinkened. "You didn't think it was too boring?"

"Absolutely not. What was that twirly move where you lifted your right leg?"

"A pirouette!" she said proudly.

"Yes. I have no idea how you didn't fall over."

"They teach you about using a focal point, but my teacher said you need to let go of your mind and trust your body."

"Excellent advice."

They stared at each other, smiling. "Well, I have to go with my friends now. We're getting ice cream."

"Sounds fun. Do you have your ID handy?"

Her daughter's silly giggle floated in the air. "You don't need ID for ice cream! Just stuff for when you become an adult and can get away with tons of things and don't have anyone telling you no."

He sighed with fake suffering. "You're forgetting about all the boring stuff they make you do when you're old. Like paying bills and going to work and being responsible. Trust me, it's no fun."

Becca snorted. "Tragic."

He laughed, a big, booming sound Sydney rarely heard

from him. She fought her shock. Tristan rarely spoke to her daughter, let alone laughed with so much emotion. Even his awkwardness seemed to have disappeared. What had happened between them tonight?

"I gotta go! Bye, Tristan, bye, Mama!"

She blew kisses, gave her mom one last hug, and raced off to the minivan, where the doors slid slowly shut. Sydney turned to face him, intent on getting more answers to her questions about what they had spoken about tonight, when Cynthia suddenly appeared by her side, obviously fuming, dressed in her perfect clothes, with her perfect makeup. Sydney winced but was determined to be nice to her. Cynthia was a control-freak mom, always causing trouble and wanting to be in charge of decisions in ballet school and on the PTA. Sydney found it much easier to stay out of her line of attention, rather than fighting over silly things she had little time or patience for. She forced a smile.

"Hi, Cynthia. Lucy did wonderful. Did you enjoy the show?"

The woman shot Tristan a look of loathing, then pressed her lips together tightly. "I must say, Sydney, I'm disappointed in your lack of respect for the rules here," she said snottily. "Saving seats is not allowed, but having your *friend* here accost me in front of children is shocking."

"I did not accost you," Tristan replied. "I just refused to let you take her seat."

Sydney gasped, glancing back and forth between them. He'd had a fight with Cynthia? Oh, this was bad. So bad. And why did Cynthia sneer when she uttered the word *friend*? "There must have been a misunderstanding. My car had a flat, so Tristan was doing me a favor. There was no deliberate intention to break the rules here."

"Yet you did. We lecture our children on the perils of bullying, yet your *friend* here humiliated me and used intimidation to scare me. It's unacceptable."

"I did not bully you!"

Trying to get a grip on the down-the-rabbit-hole conversation, she shook her head and spoke calmly. "Tristan doesn't bully people. Let's let this go and chalk it up to an unfortunate miscommunication. I'm truly sorry you felt you were being bullied."

Tristan glared but remained silent. She'd never seen him so aggravated. It must've been an epic encounter.

Cynthia regarded them both with her nose in the air. She was so cliché it was almost ridiculous. She had too much money, too much time, and too much ego. "Fine. We'll put this incident behind us. Perhaps you should leave your intimate *friends* at home from now on. It reflects poorly on you and Becca. We wouldn't want rumors to begin circulating at the school, now, would we?"

Oh, she did not just say that. Everyone knew Cynthia's husband was having an affair with his accountant. And she had the nerve to judge who Sydney brought to Becca's recital? Anger punched through her, and she took a few steps forward and got in the woman's face. She practically snarled the words against Cynthia's red, Botoxed lips.

"Listen up, chickie. You keep out of my and Becca's business. And if I ever hear a word about me, or Tristan, or Becca from your mouth, I promise you, I will kick your ass so hard, I will make Christian Grey look like an amateur. Got it?"

Cynthia gasped and stumbled back. "You're crazy," she whispered. "Both of you."

Tristan grinned. "Nice to meet you."

The woman turned on her smart nude-colored heel and took off, grabbing her daughter's arm and pulling her away, ignoring her loud protests.

They watched her leave, the final headlights pulling out of the exit. Then they stood alone in the empty parking lot.

"Christian Grey, huh?" he asked. "That was good."

She sighed. "It was kind of lame, but I was too mad to be clever."

"No, I liked it."

"I'm sorry I put you in that position. I didn't know you got in a fight with her over saving a seat."

He gave an elegant half shrug. "It was fun. Sharpened my warrior skills. Had no idea moms had to be this tough. Or so good with hair."

Her lips twitched, and her muscles relaxed. "It stayed up during her pirouette, so you did great."

Did he puff out in pride or was she imagining things? "Thanks."

This whole conversation was getting too weird. And way too intimate. She needed to put back the distance between them. "Well, thanks again for helping me out. My car is okay, so I'd better head home. We need to meet with the rest of the suppliers to get them to sign contracts. I got Anthony Moretti on board."

He lifted an eyebrow. "You're kidding? That fast?"

"Yes. That's where I was coming from when my tire blew. Can we meet at the site to hammer out some details this week?"

"That works."

"Great. Well, have a good night."

His arm shot out. Strong fingers wrapped around her upper arm, encasing her in a firm grip. "Have coffee with me."

His touch jolted her like a hit from Iron Man. She tried to mask her reaction by looking at the ground. "I don't drink coffee this late at night. It keeps me up."

"Wine?"

"My Place is too far a drive. I need to be back for Becca."

"We can go down by the marina. Just one cocktail and then home. You can take your own car."

She casually stepped back, breaking his hold. Her skin burned. "Umm, I'm sure you have better things to do on a Saturday night after a rocking ballet," she joked. "People to call. Lively places to go. Hot girls to hang with."

"Actually, I don't." There was a seriousness that clung to his manner, to his words. Those beautiful golden eyes seemed haunted as he stared at her. Why, oh why, had they declared a tentative truce? It was much harder to be nice to him than snippy. Being nice opened up all sorts of nasty things inside of her. Weepy things. Needy things.

Girly things.

He continued, each word chipping away at another piece of her finely built armor. "I don't feel like going home to an empty house."

Direct hit. More of her barriers shook, but she crossed her arms in front of her chest and regarded him suspiciously. "Why are you trying to make me feel guilty? You used to tell me your greatest moments were spent alone."

He winced. "That's when we were young and my brothers

drove me insane. Now I like some company while I drink my wine. Come on. Just one drink."

This man rarely asked. He demanded, cajoled, and sneered his orders. But the genuine need in his voice threw her off balance. "Fine. One drink. A quick one."

Straight white teeth flashed in the shadows. Those braces had done him wonders. "Thanks. I'll follow you to the marina."

The whole time Sydney drove she cursed herself for being a half-wit. This was not a good idea. Oh, sure, she'd get to steep herself in the glory of his cologne and feast her eyes on his beautiful face and enjoy his sharp dialogue, but the barrier was wavering, and she needed to keep him firmly on the other side.

The marina was busy with its usual weekend crowd. The harbor was the main highlight, with boats bobbing gently in the waves, the pier and lampposts strung with tiny white lights to give off a festive air. Restaurants and shops surrounded the water, and the outdoor bars were lively with music and groups relaxing on the decks.

They parked in the lot and walked over to Andy's Tiki Bar. Since spring still hadn't fully bloomed, a plastic covering blocked the wind from the water, and heat lamps were set out so people could enjoy the outside space. She found an empty cocktail table off to the side, away from the main action, and saved it for them as he got their drinks.

He strolled through the crowd with two wineglasses, cutting a path just by his presence. He'd always radiated power, even when he was young. It was an innate confidence in who he was and his abilities that made him so damn sexy.

Plus his delectable body. The man had an ass that should be worshipped.

"Now that's a thought I need to know. You've got quite an intense expression on your face."

His teasing words caused a flush to rise to her cheeks. Thank goodness it was dark so he couldn't see it. She took her glass of Cabernet Sauvignon and busied herself with taking a few sips. The rich flavors of earth and blackberry and heavy tannins coated her tongue. So good. He knew how to pick the best reds; he shipped his favorite vintages direct from France.

"Just thinking about how bad I want to dance." The horrified expression on his face made her laugh out loud. "Are you telling me you didn't bring back some wicked moves from the city you want to show me?"

He sipped his wine and shuddered. "Dancing is the most unnatural thing for a man to do. Flailing around like an idiot to impress a girl." His gaze crashed with hers. "There are better ways."

Her belly dropped to her toes, but she ignored it. "It's a sign of being willing to compromise," she pointed out. "We already know the majority of men are uncomfortable on the dance floor. But the ones willing to look like an idiot to impress a girl may stick around longer than one night."

"Ouch. Are you mad because I never danced with you?"

She sighed. Memories stirred. "I never asked. We were still sneaking around a lot."

"Cal and Dalton eventually knew. I think Mom did, too, but she never challenged me on it. I felt like I was living out the theme of don't ask, don't tell." He traced the rim of his glass with the tip of his index finger. "It wasn't fair to you. Hiding our relationship for so long. Meeting after hours and at the marina and in the woods. I'm sorry, Syd. I hope I never treated you like you didn't matter. Because you did."

Her throat closed up. The music pounded in the background, and a rowdy group of men at the bar were calling out for shots. But right here, right now, it was as if they were completely alone, caught up in a protected bubble. This was the first time he'd ever brought up their relationship. The end had been so spectacularly bad, she'd figured they'd never be able to discuss the in-between.

"I don't think it would've worked as long if we weren't keeping it a secret," she said honestly. "Between work and your family and the age difference, we were able to protect what we had from the outside world. I don't blame you for that, Tristan. I never did."

His other hand slid across the table. His fingers brushed hers, then withdrew an inch. The space between them seemed endless. The space between them seemed nonexistent.

"It all blew up on us, didn't it?" he asked softly. "After Mom died, my family splintered. I felt as if there was no real foundation anymore, and getting out of Harrington meant everything." He shook his head, trapped in the past. "I was so mad you wouldn't just come with me. It was easy for me to think like that, you know. I was caught up in my own shit, and when you said no, something broke."

The cold lump in her stomach tightened. They'd gone straight from idyllic affair to fighting nonstop. The slide down had been just as spectacular as the slide into intimacy—all consuming, overwhelming, and scary as hell. "My grand-mother just got back from the hospital, remember? I didn't want to leave her alone."

"I remember."

"But that was an excuse, too. I was afraid to leave Har-rington, Tristan. I didn't have your crazy desire to see the world or make my own way somewhere else. I always knew this was my home, and I stopped apologizing for not wanting to leave it."

He flinched, his face tight from her confession. How long had she held in her feelings, never having the opportunity to really talk to the man she once loved so wholeheartedly? Yes, it was dangerous, but long past due. Seeing him really listen to her and understand eased some of the rawness she'd kept hidden inside.

The words trembled on her lips, refusing to be held back any longer. "There was something else that kept me from going with you," she whispered.

He leaned forward, studying her face with intensity. "Tell me."

"You never said it."

He frowned. "Said what?"

"Said you loved me. I told you, but you never repeated the words back. How was I supposed to take such a leap with you when you gave me nothing?"

He jerked. Wine splashed over the rim of his glass. She watched as pure grief carved out the lines of his face. He didn't speak for a long time, seemingly caught up in the pain of the past. "No, I didn't. I felt it. But after Mom died, I be-came almost like a ghost. You were the only thing that made me feel again, and as much as I needed you, I was scared shitless. I wasn't ready to admit such things when my life was falling apart. It was easier to blame you, or fight with you, rather than love you." Regret flickered in his golden eyes. "It was easier to leave."

Her heart cracked open and bled clean. It was the answer she'd always needed to hear when she lay in bed, going over and over that night he'd walked away and everything had ended. "Yes. It was easier for both of us, I guess."

The sounds of the music pounded around them. People laughed. Glasses clinked. Couples danced.

"But I came back."

She dropped her gaze, terrified to let him see her face. "It was too late," she managed to say.

"Three months. Only three months until I realized I wasn't whole without you. I came back to ask you one more time to come with me, and you were getting married. You'd already moved on."

Oh, God, she couldn't do this. Not now. She thought it would help, but the past swallowed her whole, and she fought madly to free herself from the strings of her greatest omission. "I don't want to talk about it. I think we've had enough of going down memory lane, don't you?"

"I have one more question. Something that's been bothering me for a very long time."

Fear cut through her. No. No, no, no. "I think it's time we go. I should get home." Breaking eye contact, she finished her wine and swiveled around in her chair, ready to flee.

"You were divorced after a year and a half. Why, Syd?"

She froze. The question hung in the air, ripe with

meaning and hidden inflections. Oh, God, she couldn't do this now. Her shaking hands clutched her purse. Some of the past should never be dredged up again. There were too many secrets threatening to rip everyone apart like the *Walking Dead* zombies.

"I have to go," she said again.

"I need to know. Please."

She stood up. Took a few steps. Stopped. Then made herself look at him.

"Because I could never love him the way I loved you."

He opened his mouth, but she didn't wait around to hear his response.

She fled.

As she drove home, she allowed the tears to burn her eyes. And she allowed the memory to take hold for just a little while . . .

The blinding-white dress hurt her vision, so she averted her gaze in the mirror. It was perfect, of course. Everything was. The wedding might be small, but it would be tasteful, with just the right touches she'd always imagined. She wore her grandmother's veil and splurged on designer shoes with more bling than even Cinderella could stand. The dress fell perfectly away from her hips, hiding the tiny bulge she was still able to conceal. The venue was her favorite restaurant in Harrington. They'd recite their vows overlooking the marina, then settle into a happy, cozy life.

Her stomach lurched. She refused to think it was anything but a case of bridal nerves.

A discreet knock at the door to the changing suite interrupted her thoughts. The sales associate peeked in. "Sorry, Sydney, but the groom is out here to see you. I told him you wouldn't allow him to see your dress. Shall I tell him to wait outside?"

She forced a smile. She didn't believe in any superstitions. This marriage was based on friendship, respect, and a common goal. "It's okay, you can send him in."

The sales associate looked a bit disapproving, but she nodded. Sydney reached down to move her pile of clothes to the side and heard the door open and shut. "You just couldn't wait, could you?" she teased. "I hope this won't bring us years of bad luck."

"I think we've already had our share, don't you?"

She froze. Heart hammering, head spinning, she slowly raised her gaze to meet his.

Tristan stood before her. Dressed in a sleek charcoal suit, snowy-white shirt, and red tie, he cut an intimidating, sexy figure. The scent of the ocean filled the dressing room, driving the breath from her lungs. Timber hair fell back from his forehead in perfect waves, the red highlights visible in the bright light. Whiskey-colored eyes filled with a swirl of rage, and something more, something that beat down his usual distant control and whipped at her in waves of male power. A muscle in his jaw ticked. His hands clasped into tight fists.

He was overwhelmingly pure, primitive male, and her body immediately flared to life, weeping to move closer and take him into her arms as she'd done so many times before.

Instead, she locked down those messy emotions and forced herself to stand her ground. It was crucial to get him to understand it was over. She had too much to protect.

"What are you doing here, Tristan?" she asked quietly.

His gaze snapped over her, taking in the wedding dress and veil. "I don't believe this," he ground out. "You're getting married?"

"Yes."

"The hell you are! First you tell me you can't join me in New York, and then you go and marry someone else? Are you fucking kidding me?"

Her palms were drenched in sweat. She swayed on her heels but managed to fight for control. *"You left me,"* she reminded him with a touch of bitterness. *"I haven't heard from you in three months."*

"I thought we needed a cooling-off period," he muttered.

She gave a humorless laugh. *"Oh, is that your line? No call or text or even an email? No Facebook post? Nothing for three months. Did you really think I was back here waiting for you to one day realize what you threw away? Sorry. I've moved on. I'm happy, and I'm getting married this Saturday."*

He tunneled his fingers through his hair, cursing viciously. *"I came back for you. I realized what we had was too good to throw away, and I wanted to try again. I want you to move to New York with me, Sydney. We'll be together. We can make this work."*

Her whole being cracked and bled. A throbbing loss flowed through her, and Sydney ached to drop to her knees and weep, rage, grieve. How badly had she wanted to hear those words months ago? But even now, in his outrage and sudden return to bring her back with him, she didn't believe him. If he'd truly loved her, it wouldn't have taken three months for him to contact her. He was still stuck on her living his life, miles away, on his terms. It was the usual routine—she bent to Tristan's will because she would do anything to make him happy.

But now there was someone else to take care of. Someone more important than either of them.

It was her baby growing in her belly that gave her the strength to look him in the eye and finish it.

"This is over, Tristan. My God, am I supposed to sink to my knees and be grateful that you missed me after three months? It was over when you stormed out after making love to me and never returned. Do you know how long I waited for you to contact me that week? I waited for you to come back so we could talk or at least say a real good-bye. I thought I was owed that after the time we spent together. But you didn't. And I never heard from you, so I moved on."

"I needed you!" he said furiously. "I asked you to go and you weren't there for me!"

"I have always been there for you," she gritted out. "Always. But you left me, and I'll never forgive you for that. I'm happy now. I'm starting a brand-new life, in Harrington, and I'm going to have everything I want. So, I'm asking you to leave. Leave me alone, and go back to New York."

His shocked expression made her want to wail in pain, but she bit it back, tilted her chin, and faced him down in her white dress. Slowly his eyes drained of emotion. His voice was flat when he finally spoke.

"You're right. I made a mistake. It won't happen again."

For the second time, Tristan left her. But this time, there were no more tears left to cry. This time, she had something bigger to protect, and she intended to give her all to this marriage to make it work.

For everyone's sake.

chapter nine

Tristan sat out on the porch. Balin and Gandalf flanked him with a serious demeanor, as if knowing he needed the support. Even when a suspicious rustle in the woods pricked their ears, they never budged. Just kept tight on their vigil.

He sipped his second glass of wine and pondered Sydney's words. She had no idea, but with her confession, she'd changed all the rules of the game.

Now there were no rules.

It was time to see what they could have moving forward and leave the past firmly behind. For the five years he was away from her, he'd been twisted inside at the thought of her making a life with someone else. Having his baby. Being happy in Harrington when once she'd belonged solely to him.

Her refusal to go with him to New York had helped cleanse the pain. He reminded himself that Sydney never could have loved him if she was getting married so quickly after their breakup.

But she'd finally told him a different truth. She'd tried to make a life with her husband but hadn't loved him the same way. She'd never truly been able to move on from what they'd had. Neither had he. None of the women he'd dated over the years held his attention long. His affairs held a shallowness he despised as he surged forward, constantly looking for depth and purpose in his relationships.

All roads seemed to lead back to Sydney. It may not have been their time before, but they'd grown up, and it was time to face the reality.

They still cared about each other.

He closed his eyes and wished his brothers were here. They balanced him, able to use snarky humor and a deep love to take him away from the clouds of the memories. But now, in the dark, alone, the past came back for him.

He remembered the first few months in New York City away from her. He'd landed a decent apartment and begun working with an up-and-coming real estate agency that had been impressed with his background and credentials. For the first time, he was truly on his own. He'd fallen in love with the raw glory of Manhattan and left his father's tight rule behind to build his own future.

But Sydney wasn't with him.

A gaping hole in his gut haunted him. He rarely slept, thinking over and over of their terrible fight and how he'd left. The poisonous words launched at each other like darts. The wounds still bled, and he realized he wasn't whole without her. He needed to go back and make things right. He needed to find a way to see if their relationship could move forward, because he'd made a huge mistake leaving her behind. Yes, she was young. But sometimes fate wasn't neat and tidy. He was beginning to realize certain things didn't look good on paper but felt perfect within the heart.

So he decided to go back to Harrington to see if she'd come to New York with him. When he couldn't find her in the office, the assistant had told him she was getting married. That she was at that very moment at her bridal fitting.

Not believing it, Tristan headed to the bridal shop and discovered her in the dress. But she wasn't the same Sydney. This new Sydney was cold, and distant. There was no warmth or welcome in her eyes. No love.

No forgiveness.

When he left, he swore he'd never think of her again. It was time to start his new life. It was easier to focus on her betrayal.

Tristan finished his wine and stood. But so much had changed. Time softened the past and made him realize how many mistakes they'd both made. Maybe it was time to create a new path for them and forgive. They'd both been young and temperamental. The world was cruel to people in love. The years had ripened them and allowed enough time for them to heal. Tristan knew he'd regret not trying to see if there was a way to write a brand-new story.

With a brand-new ending.

The next morning, Sydney opened her door to a man holding a bunch of sunflowers. Puzzled, she tipped him, carried them inside, and read the card.

Dear Becca,

    You danced beautifully. Congratulations.

        Love, Tristan

Sydney stared at the flowers. Read the card again.

The trembling started deep inside her body and spread everywhere, until her fingers were shaking as she gripped the note.

He'd sent her daughter flowers. How many times had she ached when Becca stared at the fathers gifting their little girls bouquets of roses on recital night? She'd sworn it didn't matter because she was able to give Becca so much more than flowers. She was able to give her a beautiful life with stability and love and comfort.

But right now, her axis shifted, and she realized everything had suddenly changed.

She just didn't know what to do about it yet.

Dragging in a breath, she called out to her daughter. As Becca raced down the stairs, she caught sight of the sunflowers, and her eyes widened. "Mama, did you buy me flowers?" she asked with delight.

Her throat closed up with emotion. "No, honey, someone else did. Here's your card."

Becca read the note and gave a whoop, grabbing the bouquet and sticking her nose deep into the flowers. "I love them! Can I call Tristan to tell him I got them?"

Sydney nodded, handing her the phone. "The number's right here. Just click on this and see if he answers."

As Becca bounced around the room with her blooms, Sydney heard her begin to chatter with excitement. Finally the phone was thrust into her hands. "Tristan wants to talk to you!"

She put the phone to her ear. Thank goodness he couldn't hear the wild thrum of her heart. "Hello?"

"She seemed to like them."

His voice was smooth and poured over her like hot fudge and creamy caramel. Her thighs squeezed together. "She loved them. Thank you. How did you know her favorite flower?"

"She told me. We shared a moment over the explosion of pink sparkles."

A chuckle escaped her lips. "What I would've given to see that."

"I discovered a few other surprises. But I'll tell you about them another time."

"That sounds ominous." His wicked laugh tickled low in her belly and brought a rush of heat. Oh, he was dangerous. She had to get off the phone. She tried to stick to business. "I intend to get the suppliers to sign off tomorrow and scheduled a Friday trip into the city."

"Works for me." He paused. "What are you doing today?"

The low rumble over the phone screamed of intimacy. Her nipples tightened. Damn him. "Exciting stuff," she drawled. "More laundry, cleaning toilets, and prepping meals for the week."

"I can take you both out to lunch."

The casual offer was dangerous. It seethed with possibility and a male curiosity that hadn't been there before. He'd invited her daughter. He wanted to share a meal with them. They'd barely been on speaking terms a week ago, and now a connection had formed.

"Thanks for the invite, but I can't. Too much going on. I'll see you tomorrow?"

"Sure."

"Bye."

She clicked off the phone and practically threw it across the table.

She would not get moon-eyed again over Tristan Pierce.

Not with this much to lose.

chapter ten

They walked out of the supplier's office with a signed contract.

One more to go.

Pride burned deep. It had taken many hours, but she'd gotten the majority to agree to a further 5 percent reduction. With Anthony Moretti on board, it was much easier to convince them to agree as a group and make this the first large-scale experiment working with a big property developer.

Tristan had been brilliant.

He let her lead, but his support was crucial. When the suppliers came back with complaints, he pondered their comments with a thoughtfulness that caused them to feel respected. She always admired his patience. It was a completely underrated virtue, but Tristan never made final decisions without carefully weighing all the options. That hard-won patience made him a brilliant businessman.

And in the bedroom, it made him a devastating lover.

They walked down Main Street. The lunch crowd was out, grabbing caffé mochas and paninis as they strolled the quaint sidewalks. Shop doors were flung open, even with the brisk air, and boats cut smoothly through the calm waters to head out to bigger horizons.

"Need to take a break?"

She hadn't slept enough, had grabbed only a protein bar and apple for breakfast, and was still jumpy in his presence. But damned if she'd allow him to see weakness. "No. I'm good. Let's go."

They hit the last supplier, made their presentation, and closed the deal. In the hours they were gone, she fielded desperate calls from Charlie, who was just learning the office routine, and Dalton, who thought he'd already invoiced the order for teakwood but never received it. She managed to text her sitter to make sure Sydney got off the bus okay and chat with her daughter regarding getting her homework done earlier rather than later.

She rubbed her forehead, trying to ward off the faint headache threatening. She'd have to find a decent way to deal with the higher stress load. Maybe she should take up working out with Xavier with Raven. Maybe punching the crap out of a bag would make her feel like a limp biscuit and she wouldn't care if she dropped one of the balls she constantly juggled in the air.

"You okay?"

His gentle concern bothered her. "Fine. I can handle this."

"Never said you couldn't. I just know you do that when you're getting a headache. Follow me."

He turned into the Millennium Café and ordered her a cappuccino with skim, an almond biscotti, and a bottle of water. After leading her over to a small bistro table, he sat down across from her and snapped open his leather briefcase.

"I should have insisted we stop for lunch." He reached in and pulled out a bottle of Advil. Shaking out two tablets, he held out his palm. "Here. Take these."

Frustration nipped. How did he still know her so well? She had low blood sugar, and a skipped meal could occasionally affect her with a brutal headache. When they had been dating, she'd loved the way he fussed over her and made sure she'd had regular meals. Now it only made her feel silly, like she didn't know how to take care of her own self.

He raised an eyebrow as if he knew her stubborn thoughts, then motioned toward the pills. Like a good girl, she took the tablets with a sip of water and began nibbling at the cookie.

"I hate when you act superior," she grumbled. "I can handle a simple headache, Tristan. I'm not going to fall apart or wither onto the ground."

He studied her with a sharp, assessing gaze, those gorgeous golden eyes roving over her features, then dropping to take in the snug fit of her polished black suit. Immediately her nipples tightened into hard points, and she squeezed her thighs together in punishment. He'd always had a way of looking at her as if he owned her. As if he knew he could casually slip his hand under her skirt, in a public place, and she wouldn't be able to tell him no.

She'd never been able to tell him no.

"I'm sorry." Her eyes widened in shock. Had he just apologized? "I keep forgetting you don't need me to tell you things any longer. Not when to eat or how to close a deal, or what to say to a difficult customer. I just don't like to see you in pain if I can help it, Sydney. That's all this is about."

His tenderness ripped away her strong protective walls, leaving her flapping back and forth in a restless wind. The fight left her body. This was the Tristan who'd stolen her heart. The one who deeply cared about the people around him and would do anything to keep them from harm. He was a caretaker, a peacemaker, and a man who loved to give. That was the man staring back at her right now, and there was no way she could turn from him.

"Then I'll just say thank you."

His full lips curved in a warm smile. She smiled back, cupping her mug between her hands, enjoying the sweet, hot brew. Silence settled around them like a comfy blanket. He checked his phone, his fingers flying over the screen in a flurry of texts. She took advantage of his distraction to study him with leisurely pleasure while she sipped her coffee.

"Now that we have everyone on board, are we ready to meet Adam on Friday?"

"Yes. Becca is sleeping over at her friend's house after school, so I'm covered. Bring on the traffic."

He grinned. "Slumber party, huh? Figured that wouldn't start until her early teens."

"There're only two people I'd trust to allow her to sleep over, besides Morgan. I know the parents well, and they're like family."

"I wasn't judging," he said quietly. "I had no idea how hard it was until I got a taste Saturday night." His face held a touch of apology. "I have a new level of respect for you being a single mom. She's a great kid, and you're amazing with her."

Intensity lit the air between them. Warmth flowed through her. "Thanks." She tried to lighten the mood. "Sometimes it's hard to remember there's no rule book for this. And the mom culture can be a bit judgy. Add that to the usual maternal guilt, and I'm a real bundle of fun."

"Actually, you are. Watching you go apeshit on Bad Mom was hearty entertainment."

She dropped her head into her open palm. "That wasn't me at my best. I'm usually so much more restrained."

"I always enjoyed when you lost your temper. Remember how pissed you were when I came to help when you had the flu last year?"

She groaned at the memory. "I wanted to kill you. You didn't even call me! Just showed up looking like you were going to some fancy party, with a container of soup in your hand. Meanwhile, I was in three-day-old pj's, sported crazy hair, and hadn't brushed my teeth."

"You were scary, but it wasn't your appearance. When I tried to get in, you practically handicapped me with the door, and that was you in weak form."

Humiliation burned. She'd barely been able to function, and he'd looked like Daniel Craig playing James Bond, all unruffled and sexy, unbuttoning his shirt sleeves like he was about to get dirty. "Never surprise a woman when she's sick and ugly."

"You've never been ugly a day in your life." His soft words brought a flush of pleasure and a touch of sudden shyness. They hadn't said nice things to each other in a long time. "And it just showed me how strong you really are. I ran over there because I figured you wouldn't be able to take care of Becca. But I was wrong. You had it handled."

"Then why did you stay?"

He'd spent the night on the lumpy couch. He'd done her laundry and left it all neatly folded in the basket. Becca slept nonstop, so he'd kept watch so Sydney could also get some sleep. The kind gesture only angered her further. She hadn't wanted him to be involved in any part of their lives, and by busting in to help, he'd tipped the scales. It was a dangerous game she hadn't wanted to play, so her fear came out as anger. When she'd woken up, she'd immediately thrown him out.

"Because you needed a break. I was figuring out you really could do it all. I just didn't want you to be forced to."

She swallowed past the lump in her throat. He gazed at her with sudden warmth and openness, and her heart squeezed. What was happening? His words broke her apart and put her back together. Isn't that what every woman wanted a man to recognize? Some shift had occurred since her confession Saturday night—a deeper understanding and connection—and she didn't know how to handle it.

Her voice emerged like she was talking through sticky peanut butter. "We'd better go."

He waited a bit, assessing her reaction, then nodded. She smothered her sigh of relief. "Sure. Let's head back to the office to do an assessment, then call it a day."

She followed him out, trying to ignore the faint clang of warning in her brain telling her she hadn't escaped the danger.

She'd just delayed it.

On Friday, they strode out of the Cushman Real Estate offices with a signed contract for Pierce Brothers.

It had been a hell of a week, but they'd done it. Tristan

noticed she looked a bit shell-shocked, but she'd hidden it deftly the entire meeting. When they exited the conference room and made their way down in the elevator, they hadn't talked. Walking out of the twenty-story building back into the March wind, they still didn't say a word. And when they stopped in front of the hot dog vendor at the Avenue of the Americas, they finally turned to each other and slowly grinned.

"We did it."

"Hell yes, we did it," he said. "Congratulations. You've just closed your first huge business deal, Ms. CFO."

The new Sydney he was finally getting to know was more controlled and didn't exhibit impulsive behavior. As much as he sometimes mourned the raw passion and enthusiasm of the past, his respect and fascination for the grown woman overpowered his memories. But when she let out a rip-roaring yell of victory and jumped into his arms, he tumbled hard for the entire package.

He was still crazy about this woman.

He caught her as she flew through the air and spun her around in the midst of the jaded city crowd. Eyes glowing with delight, she hugged him in triumph, the barrier between them ripped down in the joy of the moment. Tristan closed his eyes and savored the feel of her soft curves cradled against him, the smell of orange blossoms from her skin, the silky caress of her hair against his cheek. When he finally set her down, he already grieved the loss.

"I want two hot dogs!" she announced. "With toppings. And a Coke!"

"Now you're scaring me," he teased, quickly putting in his order with the vendor, who already looked impatient at their exchange. Every other woman he knew would have insisted on an expensive lunch with crystal and champagne to celebrate such a deal. But Syd liked the simple things as much as the fancy stuff. In her view, it was all magnificent because she had an uncanny ability to enjoy her life in the moment, no matter what it brought.

They sat on a bench and ate their dogs, slurping soda from the can and discussing the highlights of the meeting. It was the type of work Tristan had always craved. A perfect combination of real estate and design. The knowledge that Sydney would be involved in each step made the journey even more satisfying. Wasn't that what he had always wanted in life? A woman to be by his side every step of the way? A woman who could match him, challenge him, and accept him for all the good and bad and in-between? Wasn't that what every man dreamed of somewhere deep inside, during the night, where no one could judge the empty ache that seemed impossible to fill with short affairs and satisfying work?

It was time to show her how serious he was about moving their relationship forward. It was time to roll the dice and make his play. Tonight.

"Tristan?"

He turned toward her, shaken from his thoughts. "Yeah?"

"Not tonight, Rambo."

He jerked, spilling his soda over his fingers. Shock held him immobile. "What did you just say?"

She tossed him a teasing smile. "You've got that really intense look you get when you're planning a big coup. Your eyes squint up and you press your lips together, and you look kind of mad."

That was his sexy face? Ugh. He needed to work on a better seduction technique. Still, at least she hadn't guessed the real reason for his focus. "Never realized you knew my habits so well."

She shrugged. "We've known each other a long time. I also know when you lie."

Now, that was a terrifying thought. He gave a fierce frown. "Do not."

Was that a giggle that escaped or just his imagination? "Your left eyebrow hikes up."

Holy shit. Was she right? No one had ever told him before. Was that how his mother had always known when he skipped school, hit his brothers, or snuck in after curfew? "That's ridiculous. You're bluffing."

She shrugged, but her face danced with delight. "Think whatever you want. I'm just playing fair and warning you. Anyway, back to your intense face. Take the night off before you try to get off on another project."

This time he choked on his own spit, causing him to fall into a coughing fit. Crap, he had to get out of here. He was beginning to spiral down. "Good idea. How about we head to My Place to celebrate? My brothers will be there."

She stood up, discarding her trash and brushing off the crumbs from her red power suit. "Thanks for the offer, but I'm going to head home. I need to catch up on some serious sleep. It's been a long week."

He wanted to try to change her mind to extend his time with her, but she was right. She needed a night to relax on her own, especially since Becca was over at a friend's house.

But that wouldn't change his plans for later.

They drove home, but this time their trip was filled with chatter and discussion instead of charged silence. He turned into her driveway, noting her porch light flickering on and off.

"Thanks for driving. I'll touch base with you and— What are you doing?"

He'd already climbed out of the car. "Walking you to the door. It's dark, and your light is out."

She slammed the car door and walked over to him. Her lips twitched in a smile. "I know how to change a lightbulb."

"So do I. Becca's not home, and I'll feel better knowing you're safe inside. You should get a dog."

She sighed but let him accompany her. "I have an alarm, and don't you dare mention your thoughts to Becca. She's been torturing me. Who knew you were such an old-fashioned guy? You wouldn't even let me pay for the hot dogs."

"That was on the company account."

She laughed and opened the door before quickly tapping out the code to her alarm. He looked around the rooms, enjoying the simple comfort and warmth the feminine decor gave a visitor. His space was kept ruthlessly neat and organized, but he liked the joyous clutter of Sydney's home. These were rooms well lived in, played in, laughed in. Every object was used and held some sort of statement, from the Disney snow globes to the colorful vases filled with cheerful daisies and the explosion of vibrant throw pillows. A painting of a rowboat washed ashore on the beach hung slightly askew. The kitchen table held piles of books and crayon kits, a red Nintendo DS, glittery nail polish bottles, and three stuffed animals in shocking pink.

"Sorry, it's always a bit of a mess." She rummaged around in the closet and removed a bulb. "See, I got it covered."

"I'll change it for you."

"You don't have— Okay." She broke off when he plucked the bulb from her hand and went outside. It took him only a few minutes to change it out, and he was surprised at the satisfaction from such a simple task. Underneath his civilization lurked a caveman, content to take care of his woman. He returned with the empty package and stuffed it in the recyclables.

"Thank you. I appreciate it," she said.

"Where's my meat?"

His sense of humor was sometimes odd. Like his brothers, Sydney had always gotten it, and she laughed right away, catching the reference. Why did it make him so happy to know there was still a connection between them? Why did occupying the same space as her make him feel so damn complete?

"Would you settle for a drumstick as payment?" she teased.

"How about a different type of payment?"

She stilled. The relaxed air between them dissipated, but he didn't care. He had one intention tonight, and that was to make her uncomfortable. In a good way. In a sexual way.

"You're getting that intense look again," she practically whispered.

"I'm not thinking about work."

She took a step backward. Raised her chin. Rallied. "I'm not doing this with you," she stated. "We had our shot, and it became a disaster."

He took a step forward. "We were young and foolish. Now we're different."

"We're involved in an important project. I refuse to screw up this opportunity."

"We're adults. We've worked together before. I swear I'd never let personal interfere with business."

Her thighs hit the back of the sofa. She stood her ground, refusing to back off, and the way she fought only made his dick harder as his blood thickened in the heat of the chase. He practically shook to touch her, his mind wrecked from being in her presence all day, smelling her sweetness, the pull of her body heat driving him mad.

Her voice rumbled in a catlike growl that made him want to howl with lust. "I'm not your plaything any longer, Tristan Pierce. You don't snap your fingers, and I don't come running. Your best bet is to turn around and walk back out that door, and we'll forget this slipup ever happened."

He paused, letting his gaze linger, touching each part of her body as if he were using his fingers. The pulse in her neck beat rapidly, and her breath was erupting into ragged pants. A slight trembling shook her. But it was her eyes that confirmed his truth. Pupils dilated, the emerald green drowned to black, filled with emotion.

Anger. Frustration. Wariness.

Lust.

He would have left her alone if he'd only spotted the first three. But there was no way he'd walk out now when he guaranteed she wanted him as badly as he wanted her.

"Don't want to walk out," he drawled. "Want to kiss you instead."

Her eyes widened. A gasp erupted from her plump lips. "Don't you dare! I'm not playing games, you big jerk. You can't get what you want all the time just because you've got a sudden urge to walk down memory lane. Get out."

"Have no interest in living in the past. I'm more interested in the present. The woman you are and have become. The woman who is making me lose sleep every night. Wanna know what I see in my dreams?"

"No."

"I'll tell you anyway. I dream you walk into my room and slide into my bed. Of course, you're naked, 'cause it's my dream, and all that bare, silky skin slides over mine and drives me insane. Your hair spills into my fingers, and when I kiss you, you make this delicious whimper that makes me want to give you every pleasure imaginable."

"I've heard enough. You need to—"

"I kiss you deep and hard, making sure you know how much I want you. Your mouth is so wet and hot, just like I know your pussy will be. I can't wait any longer, so I trail my fingers between your thighs, and when I brush your swollen clit, I know how bad you need me to take away the ache."

He stopped a few inches away. Transfixed, her breath coming in choppy gasps, fists clenched, she seemed to struggle for sanity, but his words had already cast their spell. She'd always been turned on by his verbal foreplay, and a fierce flow of satisfaction rushed through him, knowing his voice could still drive her to the limit.

"But I don't. I let you wait. The tips of your breasts are tight and achy, so I bend my head and take them into my mouth and suck hard. At the same time, my finger plays in your sweetness, sliding inside your drenched, tight heat, feeling you clench around my finger and pull me back in. Your body goes wild for me, until I pin you to the mattress to keep you still, wrench your legs apart, and slide inside in one quick thrust."

She stayed perfectly still, caught up in the fantasy he wove around them. Lips parted, eyes glassy, she swayed slightly on her feet. He reached out slowly and tangled his fingers within her fiery curls, pulling her head back. Her neck arched in a perfect, vulnerable column. He lowered his head and breathed her in, drunk on the scent of musk and citrus. He pressed her slightly back so she was bent over the back of the couch. Her nipples stabbed through the silk of her blouse.

"Then I fuck you, Sydney. I bury my aching dick inside of you, thrusting like a wild man, needing to soak up and feast on every inch of your sweet body. Your pussy squeezes me, and you scream my name, and I feel you come all over me. I feel the sting of your nails digging into my shoulders and the way you shake underneath me, and I know the only thing I want in this world is to be able to do it again and again and again."

His lips halted an inch from hers. His fists clenched in her hair. Still, he waited, needing her to be a full partner, needing her to be as crazed as he for one tiny taste, needing her to say it.

She shuddered. Licked her lips. And whispered, "Do it."

His mouth crashed over hers.

Her lips opened under his, and their tongues tangled together while he drank her honeyed nectar with a hungry impatience as if making up for the time apart. Kissing her again was a primitive, animalistic leap into the unknown with no markers set up on the path. It was darkness and light, past and present, vicious hunger and aching tenderness. He couldn't get enough.

Her hands were all over him, ripping his suit jacket off his shoulders and sliding her palms up his back, dragging him closer. The bite of her nails urged him on as he removed his fingers from her hair and dragged her skirt up to her hips, sliding back down to cup her full ass and lift her hard up against his chest.

A moan spilled from her lips. He swallowed it, nipping at the swollen flesh. She nipped back and reached for his tie, yanking him down closer, her thighs wrapped around his hips, the scent of her feminine arousal drifting to his nostrils.

She engulfed him whole with her scorching heat and raw need, until he was desperate to bury himself between her thighs and mark her forever. He slid his hand up the back of her knee, squeezing gently, then bumped against the barrier that was her panties.

"Oh, God, you're soaked. I'm going to die." He bit between her shoulder and neck, and she convulsed, arching into his hand. He licked her hard nipple through her blouse, then tugged with his teeth.

"Not until you touch me." His tie was loosened, and she was struggling with the buttons on his shirt. He shifted her higher on top of the edge of the couch, and suddenly she yanked hard, popping the buttons off. They flew in every direction and skittered across the floor.

"Good girl."

He kissed her hard, ravaging her tender mouth as he hooked a finger under the elastic of her panties and slipped inside. Her wet, swollen folds gripped him and held tight. He added another digit and teased her, his thumb brushing her bud in light butterfly strokes.

She bit his lip in punishment while her hands explored his chest, tugging on the whorls of hair, flicking his nipples, dragging her nails downward toward his belt buckle. All the while, her body shook as if caught in a fever, reaching toward climax, but he kept her on edge, refusing to let her fall over too soon.

In retaliation, her hands gripped his erection through his pants and squeezed. He jumped in her grip, cursing as she traced his length, her thumb pressing against the straining fabric.

"That's it, you little witch. I'm done."

Her dazed eyes didn't register his next move. Pulling his fingers out of her dripping entrance, he lifted her high in the air and dumped her over the edge of the couch.

Her frustrated wail barely reached his ears before he followed her over. In seconds, he'd opened up her blouse and ripped down her panties so she was splayed before him in all her glory. Mad with lust, he gazed down at her. Skirt hiked up high around her hips, her pink flesh swollen and wet, heavy breasts straining against the white lace of her bra, hair tumbled around her shocked face. He savored every inch of her like a warrior claiming his spoils.

And she liked it. She had a hidden exhibitionist streak behind her sometimes-shy exterior, and it turned him on. He used to take her while he was still fully clothed, getting into the fantasy, but tonight he could only focus on burying himself deep inside her until he could rid himself of the brutal, throbbing ache of emptiness.

With slow, deliberate motions, he removed his belt. Unzipped his pants. Grabbed her fingers and placed them over his straining erection. Then pinned her with his gaze.

"You're the only woman that can wreck me, Syd. I need you tonight. Don't make me stop."

He waited for the hesitation and swore he'd back off if she changed her mind. He needed her to want him just as badly, so badly she didn't care about logic or the past or anything but how they craved each other until nothing else mattered.

She sat halfway up, her face inches from his. Gaze narrowed. Skin flushed, damp with perspiration, choppy breath rushing over his lips. His heart stopped, afraid she would send him away.

"Fuck me, Tristan."

She ripped down his underwear and covered his mouth with hers.

Tristan pressed her deep into the cushions. With their mouths fused, he jerked against her soft, hot hands as she tortured him, his skin stretched so tight it skated the fine line between pain and pleasure. Drunk on her taste, he kissed her with a brutal force, unable to get enough, and finally ripped his mouth away from hers to drop down the length of her body.

"No," she gasped, trying to wiggle away from his grip and force him against her.

"Yes."

"But I want—oh, God!"

Her slick flesh was heaven under his tongue. Growling deep in his throat with pleasure, he licked and sucked her, nibbling on her swollen clit, bringing her to the hard edge, then backing off. She begged and pleaded, twisted underneath him for more, for less, caught up in the brewing storm neither of them was going to escape.

Finally he rose up between her legs and fit himself with a condom. Grasping her knees, he pressed inch by inch inside her, needing to do this slow so he'd never forget a second. Her tight flesh squeezed him mercilessly, fighting his entrance, but he wouldn't be denied. When he was seated deep inside, he cupped her cheeks.

"Look at me."

The slight flare of panic in her green eyes faded under the sting of physical need, a gaping hole that demanded to be filled. She arched up, bringing him deeper, and clutched his shoulders. "I'm scared."

His heart shredded at her broken honesty. He kissed her slow and long, until her muscles relaxed and she melted against him, then rested his forehead against hers. "I am, too."

Understanding passed between them.

He moved.

The ride was a contradiction of their foreplay; a slower slide toward each edge, his gaze locked on hers, not allowing her to hide from any of it. The lust changed to something else, something deeper, and he let himself go and followed the path, until the tension tightened to a fine line, and they gripped each other in a frenzy, needing the release. His hips thrust faster, forcing her to the limit as he pinned her tight against the cushions, his fingers gripping her legs, hitching her higher, going deeper, until—

She broke open and screamed his name. With a rush of heady satisfaction, he watched her face shatter with her release, never slowing his pace, then let himself follow.

Brutal waves of pleasure seized his body, flooding his veins with a rush of sensation so intense he lost all control. He let it overtake him and hung on, eyes squeezed shut as he finally collapsed. He rolled to the side to keep from crushing her, his palm on her stomach, his head next to hers. Legs still entwined, they caught their breath, letting the air dry the sweat from their skin.

Silence settled. He stroked her gently, letting her gather her thoughts. He'd always known what she was thinking before. She'd been transparent to him, an open, beautiful book only he was allowed to read. Now life had done its job, and she was hidden in shadows.

Still, he understood. He'd need to earn his way back. Showing her how good they were in bed had only been the first step. The more time he spent with her, the more it proved what he already suspected.

They still belonged to each other.

"Are you going to freak out?"

She groaned, shutting her eyes and shaking her head back and forth. He enjoyed the view of her ripe breasts swaying with her movements, strawberry nipples ripe for a taste. "Yes. What have we done?"

"We had great sex. I don't regret it."

"I'm still in shock. We just kissed, and now we're naked on my couch like a pair of crazed, hormonal teens."

"Awesome, isn't it?" He kissed the line of her jaw, smoothing back her tangled hair. "You're so damn beautiful."

She opened her eyes and turned toward him. "Stop. This is bad. You need to go home. I need to think."

"That's exactly what you don't need." He stood up and discarded the condom. Then he lifted her from the couch, carrying her into the bedroom. Like the other rooms, it held purple and silver pillows. The furniture was creamy white, and the walls were a dark plum, offset by silvery accents. Pretty and feminine, yet comfortable. He pulled back the quilt and settled her in.

"What are you doing?" she asked, watching him with an adorable type of suspicion.

He shucked off his pants and climbed in beside her. "Making sure you don't kick me out before I'm done with you."

He watched her shudder in reaction to his words. Delighted by her response, he traced a finger down her arm and watched goose bumps pop up. Oh, yeah. She was still into him big-time. "We're done. There's no more. You have to go."

He laughed, trailing his fingers over to stroke her breasts, watching her pretty nipples pinch. "I will. In the morning. We'll talk about whatever you want then. You can analyze this, and yell at me, and deny this whole thing tomorrow. But I'm asking for tonight. I still ache for you, Syd."

Her lips trembled. A sheen of tears misted her eyes, and her voice was fierce with anger. "Damn you. You've ruined everything."

She reached for him, and he kissed her, swallowing the last of her denials, knowing he only had a few more hours to prove she was meant to be his.

chapter eleven

What had they done?

The room was quiet and shrouded in darkness. She sat on the edge of the bed, watching his muscular chest rise and fall with each breath he took. Even in sleep, his hair was perfectly mussed, combed by her fingers, the thick waves falling over his high forehead. His full lips were slightly parted.

His beautiful face reminded her of an angel at rest. His body reminded her of a sinful, delicious banquet she wanted to feast on.

The purple sheets had fallen to his waist. Her gaze took in each defined pec, his toasty-golden skin sprinkled with dark hair, leading down his flat, hard abs and disappearing from her sight. But she already knew what lay beneath the sheets. She'd touched him. Tasted him. Bitten him. Licked him. Rediscovered every glorious inch with a greed that still surprised her.

Dear God, what had they done?

She stumbled toward the window. Nerves shredded, on the verge of a panic attack, she tugged at the sash until it opened up halfway with a pop. She leaned over and sucked in a great lungful of cool air, pressing her palms flat to the glass pane.

The terrible truth twisted and writhed inside the darkest of places inside, wailing to finally escape.

Becca.

She moaned, and the memories attacked her like vicious ghosts in a haunted house.

She'd been able to deal with all the challenges of being a single mother because she was the one responsible for Becca's happiness, and that was her only goal in life.

But now everything had changed.

Because Tristan was in her bed, and in her life.

And the truth was finally going to come out.

She dropped her face into her hands. Maybe she could push him away. Pretend it was only about sex. Maybe it wasn't too late to backtrack and try to get back to the way things had been between them.

Because if she couldn't, she was going to have to tell him the truth.

It had been easier when he kept her at a distance. When he refused to talk to Becca. When he was the same cold man who'd made love to her and left without a glance back. Those reasons drove her forward, reassuring her she had made the best decision for all of them.

But now he was talking about second chances. Sending her daughter flowers. Trying to embrace the woman she'd become, not the young girl she'd been.

Sydney prayed for strength to weather what was ahead for all of them.

Tristan woke up to the scent of eggs and bacon.

He rolled over, confirming her empty space in the bed. He

mourned the chance to have woken her up properly this morning, but breakfast came in a close second. If his plans held, he'd have plenty of opportunities to seduce Sydney and watch her gorgeous face in the sunlight as he brought her to climax.

Groaning, he headed to the bathroom with his morning wood and took a quick cold shower. He wrapped a towel around his hips, wondering how he was going to handle going home in a shirt with no buttons. Talk about the walk of shame. Or as his brothers would term it, the walk of fame.

"Morning."

She whipped around. Damn, she was hot. Dressed in a faded gray Adam Levine T-shirt and tight Lycra bike shorts that cupped her glorious ass, she sported bare feet and wild, unbrushed hair. Oversize black-framed glasses perched on her nose, giving her the slightly sexy nerd look men found so intriguing.

He waited for her reaction, not knowing if he'd get shyness, distance, or panic. When she smiled at him slow and sweet, his knees almost buckled.

Oh, yeah. She still held witchlike power over him.

"Morning. Becca should be home in an hour. I made bacon omelets and wheat toast." She filled a mug with steaming brew and handed him his coffee. "I'm sorry about the shirt. I found some safety pins. Maybe if you button your jacket, it won't be so noticeable."

He slid onto a stool, still clad in only a towel, and stared at the perfect plate she put in front of him. "I'm not sorry at all. But I'll take the apology if I get a breakfast like this. I think I died and reached heaven."

She grinned. "You don't ask for much in the afterlife."

"Maybe just you naked, and then I'm good."

She sipped her coffee, regarding him above the rim of her mug. "Figured you would have had your fill last night. I think we slept a whole hour."

"One hour too much." He forked up a bite and moaned in happiness. "So good. Okay, I'm ready. Let's do this."

"Don't you want to finish your breakfast before a morning quickie?"

"Was talking about the morning-after discussion. I'm sure you have plenty of questions and would like an in-depth analysis of what is going to happen between us now that we've had carnal relations."

"Fancy words for a fancy guy."

"I try."

"Thanks anyway, but I'm good."

His fork clattered to the plate. "Huh?"

She shrugged and sipped more coffee. "I'm good. No need to freak out over a night of great sex. I say we acknowledge it and move on."

He gazed at her with suspicion. He should've known she'd throw him off. Sydney never did what was expected, and the moment he caught up, she was already ahead with a new curveball. "You're accepting that we're getting involved in a relationship?"

She blinked. "Of course we have a relationship. We work together, and I've known you for years. But last night was about sex. Now that we've satisfied ourselves we can move forward and concentrate on work. Not all that sexual tension. Don't you agree?"

"Hell no!" He stood up and glowered. No way was she going to use last night as a check mark on her list of things accomplished. He knew it was more than just scratching an itch, and he knew she knew that, too. Was she trying to protect herself by pretending it wasn't a big deal? "Last night blew my mind. I don't intend to walk away from you and not do it again. And I'm not just talking about sex. I'm talking about the connection between us. I'm talking about the whole package. Get it?"

Panic flared in her bright green eyes. Ah, there it was. That made more sense than the casual speech she'd thrown at him. She could handle thinking of him as a one-night stand, but anything more pushed her buttons.

Well, tough luck. He was going full throttle here and she'd just have to learn to deal with it.

He slid out of the chair and stalked toward her. The towel dropped to the floor. Her gaze slid down his body, noting his heavy erection, and she tried to hide the raw lust on her face.

Too late.

She was just as crazed for him as he was for her.

"I thought men liked simple," she shot at him, holding her hands in front of her to ward him off. "Why complicate things? I like my life the way it is, and I don't intend to blow things up. I'm sure you can appreciate that. Plus, I have a daughter to think of, and she comes first. You should love this new setup."

"I hate it."

"But why?" Frustration nipped at her tone. "Isn't this what you always wanted? Low maintenance and no strings? You can have it all this way!"

He grabbed her hands and pulled her in. She stumbled off balance and fell against his chest. He took the opportunity to hold her tight, his hand gripping the back of her head so she was forced to look up at him. "I don't want it all," he growled against her lips. "I just want you. I want a second chance at your heart. I know you're scared shitless because of what happened in the past, but we've both changed and grown, and I refuse to blow this because it's easier to pretend it's all about sex."

"But—"

He slammed his mouth over hers, kissing her with a fierce desperation he didn't want to hide any longer. He kissed her until she was bent over, her fingers in his hair, her lips soft and yielding, her body pressed against him, already begging for more.

Finally he broke away. "Do you want me?" he demanded.

She shuddered. "Yes."

He smiled and slid her hand down to his pulsing erection. "Good. But the only way you're going to get more of this is by agreeing to one thing." He whispered the words against her swollen lips. "You're gonna have to take me to dinner."

She blinked. "What?"

"You heard me. I refuse to be used and abused without getting fed properly and treated like more than a body. I'm a person." He grabbed his shirt, which she'd draped on a hanger, and put it on. Retrieved his pants, buckled his belt, and stepped into his shoes. "Oh, and I want Becca to join us, too. She's part of you, and it's a package deal. It's time we date, sweetheart. I won't take no for an answer." He shrugged into his jacket, tucked his tie in his pocket, and grinned. "Thanks for breakfast. I'll call you later."

She was still staring at him in shock when he shut the door behind him.

He headed to his car, determined to show her it was possible to have a second chance. He'd finally changed the rules of the game so they could both win. But he needed to talk it over with someone he trusted so he didn't make any mistakes in pursuing Syd.

There were two people he trusted more than anybody else.

His brothers.

When he arrived home, they were drinking their coffee on the porch. He grinned and walked up the stairs. "Oh, good. I wanted to talk to you both."

They took one look at him and shared a meaningful glance at the large safety pin hanging from the center of his shirt where the jacket gaped open.

"Walk of fame, bro," Dalton said. "Damn, your buttons got ripped off? That's one serious night. Probably not a lot of talking going on, then, huh?"

Tristan shook his head and grabbed his brother's coffee. At least he also took it black. "Real clever. Hey, I thought you were both heading to the new house today. Is it almost ready?"

Cal nodded. "We're closing in a few days. It's official. Dalton finished up the table last night, so we're indulging in a lazy morning. Raven and Morgan are in the kitchen, but I wouldn't go in there, 'cause they're talking about the wedding. Who're you banging?"

He shifted his feet. Great. He wanted to talk seriously, and they wanted the sex details. "Dating," he corrected. "Not banging."

"Sure. Did she pull those buttons off with her teeth? I always wondered if that could actually be done," Dalton said.

"It can," Cal offered.

Tristan held back a groan. Sometimes they were so damn juvenile. But this was bigger than the usual sibling banter, and he needed his brothers to help him navigate brand-new territory. For so long, he'd been alone, not trusting either of his brothers. Now he had his family back, and he wasn't ashamed to ask for help. "I need some advice," he said quietly.

Immediately their faces grew serious. Cal nodded. "We're listening."

"It's Sydney. I'm dating Sydney."

Cal choked on his coffee. Dalton just whistled.

"Whoa. Been waiting for that announcement, but I gotta say, I wasn't prepared. You two have been ignoring each other for so long, I got used to it," Dalton said.

"You're banging Sydney!" Cal shouted.

"Dating, asshole, not banging!"

"Same thing! Are you ready for this? She is not someone you just pick up and leave on a whim. She's got a kid. Do you really know what you're getting into?"

He fumed. As the oldest, Cal always liked to boss them around, and age hadn't softened his ways. "Yes. Not that it's your business. I just wanted you both to know I'm trying to pursue this on an honorable level."

Dalton spurted out a laugh. "Umm, I have a feeling last

night had nothing to do with honor. Your shirt looks like you were on a strip-club stage."

Tristan glowered. "Forget it. I'm done. I'll figure it out myself. I don't need your approval, I just figured you should know." He turned to stomp off, but Cal called out his name, forcing him to stop.

His brother blew out a breath. "All right, calm down. You just caught me by surprise. I know the two of you share a history. Sit down for a minute."

Tristan regarded them both, then plunked himself on the wicker chair. "Anything is better than dealing with wedding talk," he muttered. Dalton snatched his coffee back. "This is a fucking big deal to me, too, you know. I don't need any more crap from you boneheads."

Dalton patted him on the back. "You are real touchy, bro. We're here for you. Just tell us the whole story. We all knew you were sleeping together, but when Mom died, things got a bit out of control."

Tristan stretched his feet out, remembering that vulnerable time when they all scrambled to piece their lives back together. "It was tough," he admitted. He'd kept the secret from his brothers so long, his voice came out a bit rusty. "I was so pissed at both of you, I never shared what was really going on between me and Syd. Telling you we were having an affair was bad enough."

"Yeah, we all lost our way back then. But now is a good time to tell us everything," Cal said. He motioned over to Dalton, who grumbled but gave up his coffee mug for the greater good of gossip. Tristan nodded his thanks and took a sip.

"We began sleeping together and kept it quiet over the summer. You two were away most of the time, so it was easier. But then we were still together, so we figured you'd find out eventually. Sydney insisted we tell you together."

Dalton snorted. "I remember that scene. I gave you a black eye."

"That was me," Cal said. "Tris gave you a broken nose."

Dalton glared. "Did not."

"Can we get back to the subject?" Tris interrupted. "You agreed not to tell Dad, and that was my main concern. I knew he'd use it as some sick leverage against me, or completely lose his shit."

"Smart," Cal commented. "Did Mom know?"

Tristan's face softened. "I think so. She loved Syd like a daughter, but she never confronted me about our relationship. Once, when we were in the kitchen, she told me not to break Sydney's heart. That's all she said—just dropped that bomb on me and walked away. I think she figured we'd work it out on our own, and then she was gone, and things blew up."

They all pondered that dark time in quiet. Tristan was still grateful their relationship had healed and they were now a real family. He had no idea how truly lonely he'd been in New York until he came back to Harrington and claimed his place again.

"I fell apart. I couldn't deal with my feelings for Sydney because I was so enraged at Dad, and all I wanted to do was get out of Harrington. I began pulling away from her, and we ended up fighting a lot. All I could think about was getting out on my own to see what I could accomplish."

Dalton nodded. "That's how I felt when I fled to California. I needed that break."

"Sydney didn't want to go. I asked her, but her grandmother was in the hospital, and she wanted to stay. The thing is, I realized besides the constant fighting and age difference, she was happy in Harrington. She liked her job and her life. I was the one who craved a new start. Eventually things got so crappy, I left without her."

"Makes sense," Cal said. "I wonder if that's why she got married so fast after you two broke up."

The scar still throbbed, but Tristan understood so much more now. "I actually came back to town right before her wedding," he admitted. "I tried to stop her. Asked her to come to New York with me again."

"What happened?" Dalton asked.

"She said no. Said I'd never told her I loved her or offered her anything to fight for. She was right, even though I didn't want to believe that for a long time. We both screwed up, but I want a second chance. We've changed. Looking back, I doubt it would've worked between us during that time. She's still the woman I want, and I'm tired of fighting it. I just have to convince her to trust me and take the leap."

Dalton grinned and motioned to his ripped shirt. "Seems like you got a great head start."

"Coming from the man whore of the century," Tristan said, rolling his eyes.

"Hey, not anymore. Raven has made me a changed man, but it was a long road. I had to learn to forgive both of us for the past, and sometimes that screws you up. But I always felt like you and Sydney belonged to each other."

Cal nodded. "Agreed. You both going to be able to work together so closely while building a personal relationship? Want me or Dalton or Morgan to step in and help?"

"No, I think it will be a good thing for us. Force her to deal with me on a daily basis without running."

"You really are serious about her," Cal said thoughtfully. "Just a few weeks ago, you were against promoting her to CFO. Now you want to embark on a relationship. What happened to make you change?"

Tristan tried to express his emotions without getting too touchy-feely and embarrassing all of them. "I kept her at a distance because I was afraid. She made me feel things I wasn't comfortable with. I hated thinking about how things ended with us, but in the past weeks, I've felt different when I'm around her. It's hard to explain. When I watched her negotiate with Cushman, and the way she'd been handling her CFO position, I respected the hell out of her. And seeing her take care of Becca reminds me so much of Mom. She's grown into herself, and I fall deeper every day. It's almost as if all roads in my life were leading to her." He buried his face in his coffee, ready for them to tear him apart for his poetry.

Instead, they both shared a sigh. "Yep, you got it bad," Dalton declared. "Raven drove me to highs and lows I'd never experienced. But I can't imagine a day without her. She makes me whole."

"Morgan was such a pain in the ass," Cal said fondly. "She wrecked me. But it was fucking awesome, and I never want to be my old self again."

Tristan swallowed a lump of emotion, then cleared his throat. "Thanks, guys. I needed to hear that."

"We'll back you up, bro," Dalton said. "Just don't get impatient. Sometimes women need lots of time to settle things in their minds before their hearts catch up."

Tristan stared at his brother. He'd always been the closet poet in the group. "That was really sweet."

"Thanks. Now give me my fucking coffee. I have to get a refill now, and I'll be forced to answer some wedding questions that scare the hell out of me."

Tristan and Cal laughed as Dalton snatched his mug back and the door clattered behind him.

His brothers were right. He'd court her slow and steady, in the old-fashioned way. But he wasn't backing off with the sex. It was the best way to remind her they were meant to be together, so he'd grab every opportunity to bond her to him, until she stopped being spooked and realized the same truth he did.

They were meant to have a second chance.

chapter twelve

Sydney picked her way across the job site, her work boots crunching over wood fragments, twisted metal, and various items of junk. Sawdust flew madly in the air, and the sound of power saws, drills, and hammers rose to her ears.

"Syd! I need to know if we're keeping this wall or if you changed the plans?"

"Hey, there's a back order on those tiles for the kitchen—did you talk to Tony?"

"Got another dumpster coming in—this all has to be moved."

"Sydney, we found some mold problems in the basement—you need to come take a look."

Holy shit. She was never going to be able to pull this off.

It was total chaos. She'd been at job sites before but never with eight houses and never being the main lead. Swallowing back pure panic, she schooled her features into a confident expression, gripped her clipboard like a lifeline, and tried to figure out who to answer first.

Tristan was deep in a conversation regarding a plumbing

problem with the bathroom renovation, so she gave him a short nod of acknowledgment and headed to the basement to tackle the mold. The next few hours flew by in a mad rush as three houses were prepped and pulled apart and various crises were put to rest.

Temporarily.

The majority of workers finally trudged off-site in clumps, and she headed to the back bedroom to grab a moment of quiet.

What if she couldn't do this?

What if she failed?

She'd always been a perfectionist, and running the office was her safe haven. She was the queen and always felt completely in control. This project was hitting all her buttons, and the voices slithered in her head, questioning whether she had the talent to deliver Adam all these houses, completely renovated, on time and on budget.

Heart racing, palms sweating, she felt the clipboard slide from her hands, and she bent over to suck in a deep breath. Just one minute to freak out and she'd pull herself together. No one would see.

A strong, warm hand pressed into her lower back. "Breathe," he commanded in a silky, sexy masculine voice that caused goose bumps to break out over her skin.

"I'm fine, I just—"

"Don't talk. Just breathe."

His hand stroked her back firmly, soothing her as much as his confident tone that promised her everything would work out. She gulped in another breath, and slowly her muscles began to loosen again. Her lungs refilled in grateful bursts.

Finally she straightened up, avoiding his gaze. Ugh. He was probably kicking himself for letting her lead this project. Tristan never lost his calm. Why did she have to be so weak?

"Stop it, now." His voice flicked like a whiplash. Startled, she swung her gaze to his, swallowed whole by the stinging cognac of his eyes, burning with heat. "Don't ever psych yourself out again. Yes, it's a lot of work. Yes, it's going to be bad. Yes, we'll get it done. Together."

And just like that, Sydney ached to topple him to the ground, crawl over that gorgeous, muscled body, and do bad, bad things to him.

"Sorry," she muttered. "I freaked for a moment. I'm good."

His features softened. "The first time I got a house to flip, I couldn't eat for two days straight. I was sick to my stomach."

She smiled. Lord, he was kind. It was even more devastating under his cool, professional surface because it was safely tucked away where most couldn't see. But he'd always showered her with care, even in his frustrating, commanding manner. "Thanks." She retrieved her clipboard, already feeling more in control.

"Good. It wasn't bad for the first day. How serious is the mold problem? We going to need a French drainage system?"

"No, it wasn't as bad as we expected. No regular leaks, so it looks like an isolated incident. We'll begin the cleanup and install the new floor."

"Good. Plumbing is solid, too. We can begin moving forward on the kitchen by end of week unless we uncover more issues."

She wrinkled her nose. "Oh, please tell me there won't be any issues."

He laughed, playfully tugging at her curls. He hadn't touched her like that in years, and she tried desperately to ward off the sweetness of the memory. "Sweetheart, there are always issues. Remember the Reidy house? The electrical ended up being shit, and I ended up over budget."

She shuddered at the thought. "That's right. You had a bit of a tantrum that week."

He glowered. "I don't have tantrums," he corrected. "Toddlers have tantrums. Men blow off steam."

"Well, you rivaled Thomas the Tank Engine then," she teased, trying to keep a straight face. "Throwing files around, bitching at Cal for not hiring the right electrician. Bitching at Dalton for breathing."

"This business isn't for the weak." He cocked his head, frowning. "Did I bitch at you for something?"

"Yeah, I paid the bill for the electrician too fast. You wanted to negotiate for a discount."

"That's right. Why didn't you wait?"

She crossed her arms in front of her chest and frowned. "Because you never asked me."

He tried not to wince. "Oh, yeah. I don't think we were communicating well at that time."

"You think? If I didn't read your mind and stay out of your way, you behaved badly."

"I was working out some issues."

She was tempted to gloss over his answer, but a few days ago he'd been buried deep inside of her, wresting raw pleasure from her body. They both deserved more honesty from each other. She couldn't ever go back to the cold distance between them, even if they stopped at just one night of perfect sex. "Why now, Tristan?" she asked softly. "We barely spoke for two years when you got home. Now suddenly you're focused on trying to forge a relationship again. It's confusing. And it—"

"What?" He stepped closer and laid his hand on her cheek. The tender gesture tore down her barriers.

"It scares me."

He let out a ragged breath and nodded. "I know. Me too. I needed that time to sort through my feelings about what had happened between us. I think we needed that time. I'm sorry I treated you like shit, Syd. I really am. I was confused about still wanting you and didn't know what to do with those feelings."

Her breath caught at his honesty. This was what she'd missed. The Tristan who told her the truth and never flinched. She couldn't keep blaming him for the past. The only thing she could do was move forward and see if they had a shot at something beautiful, something they'd just missed so many years ago.

As long as she told him the truth.

She didn't think she had a choice any longer.

"I accept your apology." A smile touched her lips. "I never could stay mad at you for long."

"True, but you always did make me pay first."

Her brow lifted. "I made sure the punishment fit the crime."

"Sure you don't want me on my knees?"

The sexual tide surged and caught fire. Suddenly her body softened, ripening for his touch. The image of him on his knees before her, pulling down her jeans, giving her pleasure, made her sway slightly. His eyes darkened. "Ah, I see you do like that idea," he murmured. "I'll have to remedy my apology."

Pink flushed her cheeks. "Stop."

"You won't say that to me later."

He'd always been extremely sexual, and she'd always responded with ease. It was no different years later. The only thing that stopped her from stepping into his embrace and calling him on his dare was the presence of the trucks parked outside and the workers still tromping through the site. His gaze promised their discussion wasn't over.

She was looking forward to continuing it.

"Tris! Syd! Where are you guys?"

They headed toward the familiar voice and greeted Brady and Charlie. Sydney noticed they were holding hands. The pairing had astonished her at first. Brady was ten years older, with a defined view of how women acted in a romantic relationship. His Latino heritage and his strict father had limited his acceptance of a woman daring to challenge him, teaching him to prefer demure, submissive, and conservative females to pursue romantically.

Charlie was the complete opposite.

At twenty-five, she was addicted to her job and looked barely legal. With generous curves, a teen-type wardrobe, and long, straight honey-blond hair, she'd driven Brady nuts her first six months at the company. They'd fought consistently, challenging each other on various projects, while everyone stepped back and watched the fireworks.

Guess the real problem was they were crazy about each other. Once they stopped fighting their feelings, a true love had blossomed between them. Sydney had never seen the architect so happy with a woman she would've sworn was his opposite. It was another lesson learned.

Sometimes love was just meant to be.

"Is everything okay at the office?" she asked.

Charlie gave her a thumbs-up. "Yes. I have a bunch of contracts and invoices for you to look at. I put them in chronological order on your desk."

Brady grinned. "She was dying to get out here and get dirty," he explained. "The idea of so many houses being renovated without her made her a bit itchy."

Charlie nodded. "Guilty as charged. Could you use the extra help?"

The woman loved rehabbing houses like some women loved diamonds. She also had a gift for knowing which features could be saved in a house and which needed to go. In under a year, she'd gone from intern to full-time, and Pierce Brothers was lucky to have her.

"Are you kidding? All hands on deck. Would love you to take a look at house number seven and give me some feedback on design."

Her hazel eyes filled with zeal. "I'm on it."

"I'm sorry I had to contain you in the office, Charlie. I can always look to hire someone else part-time."

Charlie waved a hand in the air. "I don't mind at all. I think it'll be a great way to learn more about the business. My uncle used to say work the paperwork from the bottom up to learn what you need before going out in the field. But at least I'll get my hands on one of these babies on weekends."

Brady shook his head. "Why do I have a feeling I'll have to turn into a crappy house to get some attention from you now?"

Charlie laughed. "Babe, you're the one I'm coming home to. Think of all the aggression I'll get rid of destroying the walls and ripping out cabinets."

Brady grunted. "Maybe I can be convinced."

Tristan groaned. "I'm getting a cavity right now. Time to turn in your man card."

Brady gave him the finger.

Tristan laughed. "Fine. While you're here, let's go over the tweaked plans for the fireplace and the outside wall in this one. Follow me."

They spent the next hour gathering feedback on some outstanding issues. Sydney was excited about Charlie's vision for number seven, which included a bolder design aesthetic paired with brand-new dark wood floors. They didn't want a row of houses that looked too alike, or it would lower the price. No one wanted to feel like they were living in the same house as their neighbors. Charlie had a brilliant outlook on how to tweak a budget. She was one of the most budget-conscious women Sydney had ever met.

Charlie just laughed and called herself cheap.

When Brady and Charlie finally left, the other workers had gone, leaving the abandoned block in a quiet that hummed with exhausted energy. Sydney gave out a sigh. Her whole body hurt, and there were weeks of the same ambitious schedule unfolding ahead. Still, satisfaction flowed in the way hard work cleansed the soul. She headed toward the kitchen to grab her clipboard. Tristan followed. "I may have to rely on pizza delivery to get through this project. Thank God for chicken fingers and pasta to round things out."

"I think you owe me that dinner tonight."

She glanced over. He was studying her intently, as if he'd easily peeled off the surface and dove deep into her soul. A shudder wracked her. She couldn't keep the truth from him for much longer—not after their night together. She just needed to figure out the best way to present it and decide if her daughter should know first.

Time. She needed some extra time and distance to figure things out.

"Tonight's not good," she said lightly. "I think I should spend some quality time with Becca. Plus we have her birthday celebration this weekend."

"I remember. At our house, right?"

"Yes, I tried to convince her to have it at home but she loves the mansion. Morgan's going to help me come up with a special theme, but it's just family and three of her girlfriends. Trying to keep it simple."

"She turns eight?"

She stiffened. Her voice cracked. "Seven."

"Oops, sorry. Forgot."

His words held nuances of the past. Of pain and regret and words that could never be unsaid. She clutched her clipboard and turned away. "It's fine. We need to go."

"Not yet. Not when you throw up your shield and refuse to let me in. If we're going to move forward, we need to be open to each other, even when it hurts."

Temper came and she gratefully tugged it around her like a familiar blanket. "You've gotten quite demanding about how you see this so-called relationship," she snapped. "We slept together. Once. It doesn't give you the sudden right to define what we are to each other or tell me what I need to do."

"Better. I like you angry rather than cowering like a scared dog."

She pivoted on her heel and got in his face. "You're so arrogant. Just because you decide you want something doesn't mean it's going to happily fall in your lap. I'm not something you can handle or control."

"Never wanted to. The moment you began depending on me to make your decisions, things fell apart."

Her breath caught with rage. Oh, was that his party line for the reasons they'd broken up? It was time to settle some hard truths. "Nice and easy to reframe the past, isn't it? The bottom line is you started acting like I was a chain holding you down. Oh, you gave me some good orgasms, but you kept your heart locked up and uninvolved. Do you know how that made me feel? Like some stupid, foolish girl you used for physical release and then bitched about later. Do you know what it's like to want someone that badly, yet have them betray you?"

"Yes." He grabbed her upper arms and dragged her toward him. "I fucked up. You did, too. I don't care about then. I care about now. And the woman you are right now, right here, is the one I'm falling for all over again." He gave a bitter laugh. "You think I'm arrogant and controlling? That's because I'm terrified you're going to refuse to see me and declare this whole thing over. I know your body is the way to keep your heart in the game, and I'm playing for huge stakes, Syd. I'm playing for you."

Their gazes locked. Her heart stopped, and all the smart comebacks and good intentions to buy space evaporated and drifted into the cosmos.

This time she pulled him to her, desperate for his mouth and lips and tongue. He didn't make her wait, lifting her up to crush her to him, a low groan rumbling from his chest. He kissed her with full purpose and laser-like intention, his tongue thrusting through the seam of her lips and diving in, sweeping around in a hungry hunt for everything she had.

Desperate for more, she wrapped her arms around his shoulders and kissed him back, arching into his erection without apology, wanting it all. He turned and set her on the cheap countertop so he could step between her legs. Thighs splayed open, she grew wet in an instant, and the crazed need for him took over, pushing away any logical thoughts except to be close.

His teeth bit into her lower lip. She gasped, and he swallowed the sound, his tongue licking away the hurt. "Tristan, what's happening? We can't do this. Not here."

"Yes, we can." He unsnapped her jeans and pulled them down her legs, his hand sliding up her thigh and hitting the edge of her cotton panties, already damp. "No one's coming in."

She twisted for more even as she struggled for sanity. He played his fingers over her swollen flesh like a conductor. "It's not professional. We're on work premises."

"It's officially after hours. God, you're so wet. I need this. Need to show you how good we are together. I can't stop thinking about you."

Her fingernails bit into his shoulders as he traced an erotic pattern over her panties. "Oh, this is bad. This isn't healthy. This isn't— What are you doing?" She blinked through a haze as he slowly knelt before her. He was so tall, his head was directly facing her sweet spot at the perfect level. His eyes burned amber flame.

"I'm on my knees, and I'm gonna show you how good it is when I beg for forgiveness."

She cried out his name, tugging hard at his hair as he leaned in, his warm breath rushing over her sensitive tissues. With adept grace, he tugged her panties down her legs until they dangled from her ankle. He licked his lips.

"Oh, Tristan, you shouldn't—"

"Yes, I should."

His open mouth hit her sensitive clit, and she was gone.

Nothing mattered but the mastery of his swirling tongue, the pressure of his lips, the gentle scrape of his teeth. He pleasured her without apology, licking her essence until she was a wild thing, writhing to get closer, pushed toward climax and held ruthlessly at the edge by his skill.

"You taste so damn sweet," he growled, using his thumbs to open her wider. "Give in. Just let me take you where you want to go."

And she did. He gave her no choice as he sucked her clit and worshipped her dripping core, and then the convulsions seized her, wracking her body as if a storm tossed her from the waves to shore. She rode it out, his dirty, adoring words taking her to the limit, and then she sagged boneless in his arms.

He nuzzled her inner thighs, kissing her, then slowly pulled her panties back on. He fastened her jeans over her trembling thighs and slowly stood.

She blinked, dazed, still holding on to him with a desperate grip. "I'm not going anywhere, Syd," he said in his dark, deep voice. "You can push me away, but I'll push back. Now, I'm asking to take you and your daughter to dinner tonight. Will you go with me?"

It took her a while to answer. Words were something she still couldn't seem to form. "That was a dirty play."

He smiled wickedly, his fingers straightening her hair. "I like to play dirty. Think you can handle it?"

His remark held a deeper meaning. He was asking if she was willing to try to meet him on these new terms. He was giving her the choice of running scared or meeting him with her head held high, able to hold her own ground. It was a heady feeling, because it showed a respect for the woman she'd become. He'd use her body to win, but it was still up to her. Yes, he'd play dirty, but he also told her she could match him.

And she could.

A thrill shot through her. "No fancy steakhouses. Becca still likes mac and cheese or chicken fingers."

"Done."

"Seven p.m."

"Thank you."

She pressed her forehead to his. "Thank you. For, well, everything."

He laughed and lifted her from the counter. Licked his lips and winked.

"My pleasure."

They left the house holding hands.

chapter thirteen

Tristan smiled at the two females seated across from him and felt a sense of satisfaction. He'd decided to go to Raven's restaurant, My Place, where the chicken fingers were the best in town and the atmosphere was fun and comfortable. The sweet potato fries weren't bad, either. He'd begun to have a bit of a craving for them on a regular basis.

"Mama, when do you think I can come play poker with you?" Becca asked, busily attacking her coloring book with a handful of bright crayons.

Sydney met his amused look. "When you're twenty-one," she said.

"The same age I need to be to drink wine?"

Tristan laughed out loud at her cheeky question. He was more comfortable talking with her now after the recital.

"Correct," Sydney said.

He reached for a chip and swiped it in salsa. "I'm grown up, and even I don't want to play poker with your mom."

Her brow furrowed. "Why?"

"'Cause she cheats."

Her giggles charmed him. "She cheats at Monopoly

Junior, too. She always seems to have more money than me. I think she takes it when I'm not looking."

Sydney sniffed. "I invest my money properly so I get more in rent. I certainly do not cheat."

"And you always get mad if I land on Boardwalk and don't buy it."

"Because that's the best property!"

"It's too expensive."

"Bet you would buy it with my money," Sydney muttered, grabbing a chip.

"Your money is different."

Tristan clamped back a smile. The two of them could do stand-up comedy. "Are you looking forward to your birthday, Becca?"

Her eyes sparkled. "Yes, I can't wait. It's going to be a princess party, so we get to dress up in gowns and shoes and crowns! The cake will have pink frosting, too."

"I don't have to wear a costume, do I?" he asked with mock nervousness.

"No, that would be weird. Just the girls dress up." She studied him intently. "You may be bored."

"Will there be Cheez Doodles?"

She gasped. "Yes! Those are my favorite, but I like the crunchy, not the puffed, and Mama said I could have as much as I want 'cause it's a special occasion."

"As long as you share some, I won't be bored, and I like the crunchy, too."

Raven came over with their plates. "Personal delivery," she sang, setting down everyone's dinner. "Al said he gave you a few extra because you're his favorite customer, Becca. He also gave you two new dipping sauces to try out."

The chef was culinary-school trained and had become a close friend of the family's after Raven began dating Tristan's brother. Al had taken a shine to Becca and liked to send her special treats.

"Thank you!"

"Welcome."

"Is Al coming to my party, too?" Becca asked, her face solemn.

Raven sighed. "Honey, I'm so sorry, I know he'd love to, but he has to work and I can't close. But I'll be there. I'm dressing up in the coolest costume ever, but it's a secret. You won't know till I show up."

Becca clapped with delight. "I can't wait."

"Me either." Raven smiled at them. "Need anything else, guys?"

"No, we're good, thanks," Sydney said.

"Enjoy!"

She strode off on long legs clad in her usual denim, her wild black hair tied up on top of her head. Tristan had fallen hard for both of his future sisters-in-law. It wasn't official with Raven yet, but Dalton was already researching rings and brainstorming the best place to ask her. His brothers had done well finding the right women to fit them.

He looked at Sydney diving into her burger without a trace of ladylike restraint and felt that odd tugging in his gut. As if his instincts were trying to remind him not to use his head too much but listen to his heart. He might be a bit rusty from lack of practice, but he was determined to try. If he played this one safe, he'd end up regretting it.

They ate amid light chatter and humor. He watched Becca double-dip her chicken like a master, finally noticing the hand she favored. "Hey, you're a lefty, too." He wiggled his hand in the air. "Welcome to the exclusive club for geniuses."

Becca lit up. "Cool! I don't know many lefties. Mom's jealous. She said it proves I'll be a true creative."

He glanced at Sydney, expecting to see her grin, but she suddenly looked as if she'd spotted a ghost. Face pale, she gripped the fork midair, as if stuck in a strange place she couldn't break free from.

"Syd? You okay?"

She blinked. Then all traces of her freak-out seemed to disappear, so maybe he'd imagined it. "Fine. Sorry, was thinking about work."

He relaxed. "Plenty of time for that after dinner," he teased.

"Mama, can I go see Al in the kitchen? I want to tell him I loved my chicken fingers."

"Sure, honey. He'd like that."

"Can I play the jukebox, too?"

Tristan fished out a few quarters and handed them to her. "Play something good. I like Britney Spears."

Another giggle. It was easy to feel like a superhero to a young girl. Silly humor was easy to do. "Thanks, Tristan."

She scrambled out of the booth and left them alone.

Sydney reached for her pink cocktail, and he leaned over the table, dropping his voice.

"I still have your taste on my lips."

She choked on her first sip, quickly putting her glass back down. Color rushed to her face, emphasizing the cute freckles splattered over her nose and cheeks. "Don't say things like that!"

Amusement laced his tone. "Why? We're alone."

"Because it disturbs me."

He dropped one lid in a naughty wink. "That's why I do it. Getting you all hot and bothered is a highlight of mine."

She shook her head, letting out a frustrated sigh. "You're impossible." They stared at each other for a while, letting the heat build between them. "Can I ask you something?"

"You can ask me anything."

"Do you—do you enjoy being around Becca?" Her fingers twisted around her glass in a rare display of nervousness. "Or are you just trying to get along with her because of me?"

Instead of jumping to defend himself, he took the time to pull apart her words. "That's an excellent question. At first, I avoided both of you because things were complicated. I may even have been resentful of Becca."

She stiffened, but he forged on, owing her the complete truth.

"But not anymore. Now I find myself wanting to know more about her. She's a great kid—warm, funny, smart. She respects you, and it's obvious she loves her life. So, my answer is I do enjoy being with her. And you. This is still new to me, though, so I may do some stumbling, but I'm not trying to be nice to Becca to get to you."

She nodded, her shoulders relaxing. "I needed to hear that," she admitted. "It wouldn't be fair to either of us if you were pretending."

"I can't pretend," he said simply. "I never could."

Her lips parted. He reached out to snag her hand across the table, desperately craving contact. Her graceful fingers slid through his, her sleek, colorful nails giving him just a hint of a bite.

"I don't want to be that guy who tries to force my company

on your child to score points. She needs to get to know me just as much, so she doesn't feel overwhelmed. She's been more comfortable with Cal and Dalton, since I've never really taken the time to get to know her. I'm willing to take my time now, Syd. In fact, it's important to me."

He enjoyed the light in her beautiful eyes; the firm grip of her hand in his. The moment was to be savored: the loud music and laughter in the background, the smell of bacon and beer, the simple pleasure of sharing a meal with a woman who meant something. His life had been a roller coaster. It was nice to once again realize the simple pleasures were everything.

He only wanted more.

But certain questions still burned in his mind. With her hand tucked in his, he skirted around the issue that had bothered him for the past two years, trying to find an inroad. "I know you don't like talking about your previous marriage," he said calmly. "But I wanted to ask you why he doesn't want anything to do with Becca. Why won't he be at her birthday party?"

Her mouth opened, then shut. She seemed to be gathering her strength to answer, but her voice was firm when she finally spoke. "Jason lives overseas now and remarried. We decided it would be best for him not to confuse Becca, so he stays out of both our lives." A fierce light glimmered in her green eyes. "Becca belongs to me."

"But he's her father! Does he even call? Check on her? Ask for pictures?"

She yanked her hand back as if she'd been burned. "No. Please let it go for now. This is not the time to talk about it."

A curse blistered from his lips. He stared at her, knowing there was more to the story. But this wasn't the place—not with Becca here and no time to really delve into the past. He'd let her keep her secrets, but to move forward, they needed to trust each other again. Honesty was key.

"Fine. I'll let it go. For now."

She let out a breath. "Thank you."

He nodded and deliberately took her hand back in his. Her gaze was pure stubbornness, as if she was deciding whether or not to allow him to keep touching her, but then her muscles relaxed and a hint of a smile curved her lips.

Good. It was time she learned he wasn't going anywhere.

Becca ran back to the table, jumping up and down as the first stanza of Britney's classic schoolgirl hit blasted from the speakers. He pretended to know the lyrics, singing off-key and butchering the song so badly she broke into hysterics.

Maybe it was better this way. They were forging a new future, and that would take trust. Her marriage was in the past, and dredging up old memories sometimes wasn't the best way to create something brand-new.

He pushed aside the niggling worry in his gut and concentrated on enjoying his time with both of them.

"That was fun."

Sydney turned to her daughter, who'd paused on her way to her room. She'd shrugged off her pink cardigan, kicked off her sneakers, and now regarded Sydney with a curiosity that had never been in evidence before.

Sydney tried to act casual. "You've always liked Tristan, right, honey?"

Her daughter nodded, her red curls flopping with the

normal enthusiasm of youth. "Sure. He never talked to me as much as Uncle Cal and Uncle Dalton, though."

Nerves ripped through her. Sydney leaned against the counter, wondering how deep this conversation would go. Wondering if this was the time to have a talk. "True. Did that bother you?"

Becca shrugged. "No, I just didn't know he was so funny and nice." She tilted her head, as if coming to a decision. "I think I'm going to call him Uncle Tristan now. He took me to the recital and gave me flowers."

She chose her words carefully. "I think if you feel comfortable, that's a good idea."

"I saw you holding hands. Are you dating?"

Sydney's legs crumpled under her. She had to fight her way back to a standing position, leaning more heavily against the counter. "What? Where did you hear that? How do you know about dating?"

Her daughter gave a long, exaggerated sigh. "Mama, I'm not a baby. My friend Tracey's mom dates 'cause her dad left, just like mine. It's not a big deal. I just want to know."

The past surged up and threatened to drown her. She fought for a lungful of air. *Cool. She needed to play this smart, yet cool.* The ridiculous song from *West Side Story* rumbled through her thoughts, distracting her. Now was not the time to channel Broadway. She was definitely freaking.

But looking into her daughter's clear green eyes, Sydney realized she deserved honesty. She'd hidden the past to protect her daughter from hurt, but now that Tristan was not only back in their lives but becoming a part of them, she couldn't hide any longer. She simply didn't have the right.

Eventually she'd need to tell Becca the truth. For now, telling her Tristan would be in their lives was important.

She ignored her heart slamming crazily within her chest and spoke.

"Dating is something a man and woman do to get to know each other. By spending time, they both get to see how they feel, and if they want to see more or less of the other person. So, yes, at this point, I'd say Tristan and I are starting to date. How do you feel about that?"

Becca scrunched up her nose in deep thought. Then shrugged. "It's fine. Tracey says sometimes she doesn't like her mom going out with so many different boys. Will you do that?"

The overwhelming, tangled mess of the past was tricky to sort out, especially to a seven-year-old. She knelt down so she could look straight into her daughter's eyes.

"No. I'm not going to do anything that makes you uncomfortable. Tristan and I used to be good friends, so we're taking it slow. But he'll be around more. He'd like to take both of us out. Is that okay?"

Becca nodded. "Yes."

Her throat tightened. She took her daughter in her embrace, surrounded in comfort and love. The scent of coconut drifted from her bright curly hair, and her slender shoulders pressed against Sydney. Her daughter hugged back tightly. "Can I go play my DS for a little bit before bed now?"

Sydney laughed, letting her arms fall to her sides. "Of course. Brush your teeth. I'll be up in a bit."

Her daughter ran up the stairs, conversation already forgotten.

But Sydney thought about it all night, tossing and turning,

kept from sleep by the knowledge that all roads had led back to Tristan. Fate had stepped in and forced her hand. She'd made the only decision possible seven years ago, but would Tristan see it that way? Would his anger overshadow the fragile foundation they'd begun to build together?

Nausea turned in her belly. For two years, he'd ignored both of them. His innate coldness had confirmed over and over she'd made the right choice. But now he grew closer to them each day. How could she possibly have a second shot at happiness with him if she didn't tell him Becca was his?

Dear God, it was time.

She had to tell him the truth.

Fear gripped her like a vise, strangling her breath. How would he react? Would he hate her? Blame her? If she realized her child had been kept from her, she'd lose her mind. She needed to be prepared for an emotional fallout but be able to keep her calm and stay centered. She had to convince him she'd done the best thing for both him and her daughter. Eventually he'd see her intentions had been true. She'd never wanted to hurt him. She only wanted to give Becca the home and stability she herself had never had, and a father who resented them both would've destroyed them. She'd always planned to tell him the truth one day. It was just coming earlier than she'd expected.

After the party.

She'd talk to Tristan after the party. She'd tell him everything, and they'd talk and come up with a game plan for the future. In time, he'd have to realize she had done the only thing possible. Becca had to come first. Always.

Sydney didn't sleep for the rest of the night.

chapter fourteen

The mansion looked like it had puked up the color pink.

Tristan placed the platter of chips on the table, snatching a crunchy Cheez Doodle, and tried not to be intimidated. The estrogen pumping through the air was enough to keep him in check. Between the elaborate Happy Birthday signs and the pink glitter, streamers, and gaily wrapped favors, he didn't know where to look. Little girls in elaborate gowns and high-heeled "glass" slippers seemed to be everywhere. They carried purses and wands and all wore tiaras.

So did the grown women.

He figured he'd keep to the background, but Syd and Morgan kept him busy hustling food, fixing broken costume jewelry clasps, and refilling the bright pink punch bowl. Fake gems cluttered every table surface, and they'd already had a scavenger hunt for some type of magic mirror. Poisoned red apples bobbed in a jewel-encrusted bucket. The strains of "Bibbidi-Bobbidi-Boo" exploded from the speakers.

He was kind of in Disney hell.

"I'm scared."

Tristan turned toward Dalton. "Be cool," he said. "Stick to the walls, where they won't notice you."

His brother gave a shudder. "I tried, but they found me and made me be the prince. Raven tried to make me wear tights, but I told her no way. She's still a little pissed."

Tristan laughed. "Where is Raven anyway?"

"She wanted to finish up at My Place before picking up her costume. She still won't tell me what she's going to be, but . . ."

"What?" Dalton was looking at the front door, suddenly mute. Tristan glanced over to see what he was missing and stopped cold.

Oh, yeah. This party was getting outrageous, and there wasn't even any alcohol.

Raven was dressed up as Maleficent. Clad in a long black gown, with an elaborate headpiece that gave her black horns, she held a scepter and surveyed the crowd like she'd flown in on her wings and decided to crash a princess party. Her dark hair was pulled back tight from her face, emphasizing scarlet lips, pale skin, and heavily accented eyes that burned like dark coals.

He wouldn't have recognized her if it hadn't been for her wicked wink as four girls gasped and stared at her in pure wonder.

Her throaty voice hit the room with command. "Whose birthday is it today?"

Becca moved forward. Her turquoise gown swished around her ankles, and her hair glittered in the light, due to some heavy-handed sparkles. Tristan bet they'd never wash out. His suit had been unsalvageable from the pink sparkle incident, and it had been one of his favorites. "It's mine," Becca squeaked.

Staying in character, Raven lifted the scepter, her face carved in the arrogant lines of a true queen. "I've come to bestow a special gift on the princess. Please kneel."

Mouth open, Becca knelt on the floor and bowed her head. The audience tittered and giggled in excitement. Sydney was grinning and videotaping the whole thing.

Raven lowered her scepter and touched the top of Becca's head lightly. "I offer you the gift of wisdom, to decipher between good and evil. I also offer the power of bravery, to face the darkness and rise above, to be the guiding light to others and yourself. Do you accept these gifts, princess?"

"Damn, she's good," Cal whispered.

Dalton looked dazed, as if he'd been hit over the head with a blunt object. Tristan pressed his lips together to keep from laughing.

"I accept them," Becca said reverently.

Raven urged her to rise and kissed both of her cheeks. "Happy birthday, Rebecca Seymour."

The girl's smile was pure sunshine. Tristan's heart did a weird little flip-flop. "Thank you, Raven—er, Maleficent!"

The girls flocked around, touching her gown, chattering nonstop, while his brothers took in the scene. Cal cleared his throat. "I don't know about you, but I had no idea grown women who dress up as princesses were hot as hell."

Dalton shook his head as if trying to clear it. "My woman is a complete sexpot," he declared. "And if we disappear later, don't look for us. If you do, I'll beat your asses."

"Same here," Cal shot back. Morgan was dressed in a blinding-white dress, supposedly someone from the movie *Frozen*. With her blond hair, pink lips, and a silver tiara, she looked like some type of icy queen. "Do you know how bad I want to get her dirty?"

Tristan groaned. "We're at a kid's birthday party, dudes. Get your minds out of the damn gutter."

"Sorry," Cal said. "Course I saw the way you looked at Sydney. Seems like you want to be her beast, man. Bad."

"You're sick."

Cal and Dalton hooted with laughter. Tristan shook his head but had to take the jabs. Because they were right.

He sucked at his princess knowledge; all he knew was her gorgeous yellow dress was cut low in the front, nipped in at the waist, and spilled to the ground in satin glory. The thin material hugged and emphasized every curve. Her gorgeous hair seemed lit with flame, and she'd put some gold sparkles over her skin, which made him desperate to find every single one.

With his tongue.

God, she turned him on. And since their talk last night, his arousal was mixed with a craving to go deeper, exploring every facet of her that had been hidden these past years. It was sex and need and hunger and tenderness all rolled into one. It was glorious and sucky and scary as hell.

But he was gonna own his shit this time around.

This time, he wasn't going anywhere.

Sydney drifted over, turning off the videotape. "And that is why I still have a girl crush on Raven," she said with a grin. "I could never pull that off. She's such a badass."

"You're not supposed to. That's what cool aunts are for." He ran a finger down her soft cheek, catching a few sparkles with his thumb. "You're the one who pulled this entire party together. The one in the background who makes sure your daughter gets everything she needs without any thank-yous. You, Sydney Greene-Seymour, have a whole lot of badass in you."

She blinked, obviously startled. Cal and Dalton tittered like teenagers, clearly enjoying the show, but Tristan didn't care. He was making a big move, and being subtle wasn't the way to do it. He intended to claim her on all levels, and it began with his own family. No more hiding or sneaking around. He wanted their relationship in the full light of day.

"Thank you." He ached to kiss the blush from her face. "That was one of the nicest things anyone ever said to me."

Their gazes locked. Her jade eyes filled with emotion, but something dark still flickered there, as if an innate fear that hadn't been spoken was still lodged between them. He figured that with patience he'd be able to get her to trust him again.

Morgan joined Cal, slipping her arms around his waist and leaning in. "Tristan, I just swooned. That was so . . . romantic."

Cal scowled, possessively curling his arm around her waist. "He's just trying to get her into bed."

Morgan gasped. "Cal! There are children here!"

Dalton burst out laughing. "This is awesome. Usually I'm the one getting the crap."

Cal growled. "They're all huddled around the witch and can't hear me. I give you romance." He paused. "Right?"

She softened, reaching up to push back his mussed hair. "Every day," she said.

The caveman seemed satisfied and shot Tristan a look as if saying *beat that*. His brother was certifiably nuts about his fiancée. If it weren't so damn cute, Tristan would torture him endlessly.

The bell interrupted them, announcing the arrival of pizza. The next hours passed in a blur of princess games, endless eating, and a dance party that rivaled nothing he'd ever seen.

Though watching Sydney shimmy and shake to the beat of "Let It Go" was pretty hot.

When the three-tiered pink-frosted cake came out, and they all sang "Happy Birthday," he had to admit he got a little emotional. He had no idea why, unless it was the joy on Becca's face, and the way she looked at her mother, surrounded by friends and family.

It was probably all the estrogen in the room beginning to affect him.

Becca opened her presents the way she seemed to attack life: no-holds-barred. Pieces of wrapping paper scattered the floor as each new prize was revealed, and she gushed over each one, making each giver feel special. When she came to his, he shifted in his seat, wondering if he should take a break to get some air.

"This one's from Tristan," Becca read from the envelope. She looked up and smiled, and he sat back down, deciding to wait it out. It wasn't big or gaily wrapped, just a simple card with a pink bow stuck on it. She probably wouldn't even like it, but he knew she'd be polite anyway. He should've stuck with a doll or stuffed animal. Those always went over big with kids.

She pulled out the card and studied it. Slowly her expression changed from confusion to amazement to delight. With a whoop, she jumped up, waving her hands in the air like she'd won the lottery.

"It's horseback-riding lessons!" she screamed. "I'm going to ride a real horse!"

Her friends shared respectful glances, and he puffed up a bit. Guess he'd scored after all.

"Thank you, Tristan!" She flew across the room and jumped into his arms for a big hug. He caught her just in time, hugging back, the scent of coconut drifting from her glittery hair. A surge of fierce protectiveness took him in its grip. He didn't know where it came from or what it meant.

When she bounced back to her friends, his gaze met and held Sydney's. He hoped it was okay with her, since he hadn't vetted the present. Uh-oh, maybe he'd screwed up. Maybe riding a horse at her age was a bad idea?

"Excuse me," Sydney whispered, getting to her feet and leaving the room. Tristan quickly followed her out to the front porch.

She gripped the handrails, staring out at the woods. He moved up behind her and rested his hands gently on her shoulders.

"Are you okay, sweetheart? It's not like I got her an actual horse."

His halfhearted attempt to make her laugh failed. Frowning, he noticed her whole body trembled, so he pulled her back and wrapped his arms around her for warmth.

"Can you talk to me?" She stiffened. "Are you over-whelmed? Scared about us? Worried about Becca?"

"There's something we need to talk about, Tristan," she said. Her voice came out as if dipped in ice. "It's important."

His heartbeat sped up. He tried desperately to sound confident, but his only thought was she was going to say it couldn't work between them. "I didn't know I had to ask per-mission before getting a big gift. Wanna yell at me now?"

"After the party. Okay? I brought Becca's pajamas so we could stay tonight."

"Okay." Unease pitched his belly, but he swore no matter what excuses she came up with, he'd make her see the truth. They were meant to be together. He'd fight dirty and push hard if he had to, but nothing she had to say would stop him from convincing her he wasn't going anywhere. "Syd?"

"Yeah?"

He pressed a kiss to the top of her head. "You're not going to be able to scare me away," he murmured. "Tell me what-ever you need, and we'll work on it together."

She didn't respond. But she let him hold her for a bit lon-ger before stepping out of his embrace and making her way back inside.

He noticed she didn't meet his gaze.

Tristan pushed away the worry and tried to concentrate on the rest of the party. The second round of desserts came out, including pink cake pops and princess cookies. The girls dove in, and he managed to snatch one for himself without his brothers seeing. He had a weakness for sugar cookies, pink or not.

"Okay, girls, how about some actual fruit?" Morgan asked

with a smile. She passed around a tray of strawberries, and Sydney's friends scooped a few up like they were candy.

Becca raised her hands in the air. "Not me," she said.

"Not me," he said at the same exact time.

They shared a glance. "Jinx!" she yelled out.

"Darn, you were too fast for me." He grinned at her. "Don't like them?"

She shook her head. "No, I'm allergic."

"Me too. I blow up like a balloon."

"Me too! I look like the clown fish from *Finding Nemo!*" Her face was delighted, as if sharing a terrible allergy bonded them. He remembered being rushed to the hospital with his mom freaking out the first time he'd gotten a hold of a strawberry.

"Do you have an EpiPen?" he asked, finishing his sugar cookie.

"Yep, do you?"

"Nah, when I got bigger, I just knew how to avoid them. Want some coffee? You're seven now."

"I'm still too young!" Her friends burst into silly laughter with her. He'd had no idea how easy it was to get on with a young girl. Maybe he wasn't as terrible with children as he thought.

With a wink, he headed for the coffeepot. He'd been less exhausted after a twelve-hour workday than this kids' party. How did Sydney manage?

When the first of the parents began picking up the girls, he breathed a sigh of relief. Becca's friends left, and the grown-ups all began to clean up while she kept up a stream of nonstop chatter, showing them all of her gifts and twirling in her bright blue gown. They were halfway through the dishes when he noticed the quiet. He looked around, trying to find out why the talking had stopped.

And found Becca sprawled out on the living room couch, asleep.

Sydney smiled at her daughter, tucking a knitted afghan over her gown and slipping off her plastic high-heeled princess shoes. She tiptoed out, and they stepped back into the kitchen.

"She plays hard and sleeps harder," Sydney said with a laugh. "It'll be impossible to wake her up."

"You were smart to stay here tonight," Morgan said. "You'll have the place to yourselves. Cal and I are sleeping at the new house tonight."

"You close Tuesday, right?" Tristan asked.

"Yep, it's finally official. We should get back soon, though. We left the dynamic goofball duo there alone. It'll take them a while to get used to the new place, and I'm afraid they've been left alone too long."

"Should've brought them over," Tristan said with a laugh.

Morgan shook her head. "One of Becca's friends is afraid of dogs, and I didn't want her first introduction to be with Cujos, even though they're the sweetest dogs alive."

"Dalton and I are heading back, too," Raven said, wiping her hands on a dish towel. She'd ditched the horns and the headdress but still wore those wicked black boots. "Sydney, I'm madly in love with your daughter. Thank you for letting me be a part of this."

Sydney hugged her hard, and Morgan stepped into the circle until it was like three powerful princess/witches who were about to rule the world. He cut a glance over to his brothers, registering the tenderness on their faces while they looked upon the women they loved. For so many years, after their mother died, there was an emptiness and pain that filled up all the empty spaces. They'd lost one another for a long time. Somehow, beginning when Morgan came into their life, there was joy again in this house, and among them. He'd not only rediscovered his brothers but a whole new life of possibilities.

Finally they all left and Tristan shut the door behind them, then turned to Sydney. "How about I carry her up for you? Get her settled and then we can have that talk?"

Her skin turned vampire pale. "Thanks."

He lifted Becca into his arms. Her warm body cuddled automatically against him, and she mumbled in her sleep, frowning fiercely. He climbed the spiral staircase to the first room on the right—decorated in feminine lemon yellow with a floral bedspread. He smiled when she muttered and smooshed her face into the pillow, just like her mother did. He walked back downstairs, poured them both a glass of wine, and went into the living room.

Sydney came down ten minutes later and took the glass he offered with trembling fingers.

"Not gonna lie here," he finally said in the stretching silence. "I'm trying not to freak out, but when a woman says we need to talk, there's usually some type of trouble besides my gift. Is it us?"

She flinched. Then nodded. "Yes."

He let out a breath. "I know you're scared. I know we share a controversial past. But, Syd, I think you'll regret it if we don't try. We have something special here. A connection.

It gets stronger all the time, and I'll be damned if I'm going to let what happened between us when we were young and made mistakes affect us now. We're two different people. Do you really want to throw this away?"

She lifted her gaze. Raw emotion shimmered in her emerald eyes, along with a fear that made dread trickle down his spine. "I want you, Tristan. I thought I could control my feelings and keep you in a safe place. I even decided I'd use you for sex, to wring you out of my system. But you've always been more, and I can't lie to myself anymore. I'm tired of the lies. I'm falling in love with you all over again."

He put down the glass and reached out to her, but she stiffened, shaking her head and moving away. She set her own glass down, curling into herself for protection. The obvious distress cracked his heart. "What is it, baby?" he asked softly. "Just tell me. We can work through anything. I'm not running away anymore, no matter what's scaring you right now."

"I have to tell you something important. All I can do is hope you understand why and give me a chance to explain."

The dread grew to a roaring river when he looked into her face. Suddenly he knew. And in a matter of seconds, everything broke and splintered apart between them. The words dropped from her lips like bursts of gunfire, piercing tender flesh and drawing blood.

"It's about Becca."

A roaring began in his ears, but it was dull, so he shook his head to try to focus. His legs loosened, unable to hold his weight. "What about Becca?"

"You're her father, Tristan. Becca is yours."

The nausea in his gut burned like an ulcer, and his vision dimmed. Slowly he fell to the couch, blinking away the haze, his mind grasping at the only piece of knowledge that meant anything. That meant everything.

Becca was his daughter.

She watched the man she loved sit back in shock, his face ravaged by pain, and fought back the choked sob in her throat. No, she had to be strong. She had to try to make him understand.

"My daughter," he whispered. "Becca is my daughter."

"Yes."

"When? When did you find out you were pregnant? When did you know she was mine and not your husband's?"

She set her shoulders, determined to tell him everything. "The day you left me to go to New York."

He let out an animallike cry and rose to his feet, pacing madly in front of her. Waves of fury and confusion whipped from his figure. Fear knotted her belly, but she kept her breathing even, knowing this was going to be the hardest thing she'd ever done, getting him to understand. "You said nothing," he gritted out. "Never mentioned anything about a pregnancy."

"I was going to tell you that night, but then you said you were leaving, and I knew, Tristan, I just knew if I told you about the baby, you'd feel trapped. You didn't want to stay with me."

"I asked you to go to New York with me!" he shouted. "Is that the lie you've been telling yourself for seven fucking years? You never gave me a chance!"

"Lower your voice," she hissed. Fear choked her at the idea of Becca coming into this confrontation. She wrapped her shaking hands tight around her body. Somehow, she had to make him see what she had that night. "I saw your face. You were like an animal stuck in a cage, and I was your jailer. You would've hated me for trapping you into a life you resented. You would've hated both of us, and I swear to God, I was not going to do that to my child. My parents didn't want me, and I had to live with that. I refused to give Becca a life of regrets!"

"And what about the second time?" he practically spit out. "When I came to the dressing room and you were in your wedding dress? I asked you again to come with me! What are your excuses for not telling me you were pregnant and marrying some other guy to hide the truth?"

"He was ready to be a father to Becca. He wanted to marry me and build a life in Harrington. He gave me everything I thought I wanted, the type of security I dreamed about for our baby! He wanted what you didn't!"

"Then why did he leave?"

"Because I couldn't love him the way he deserved," she choked out. "He knew it, and so did I. We tried, but we realized after Becca was born, he could never take the place of you."

He whirled around, muttering a string of foul language that zinged her ears. "She doesn't know anything, does she?" he asked. "About me?"

Sydney prayed for calm to get through this. Already her idea of making him understand why she'd made such a decision burned in a cloud of smoke. Right now, he was wild, in pain, and ready to attack. She needed to keep her control so they didn't begin screaming at each other, dragging them back into their past. "No. Jason got a job in Australia when she was six months old. We talked about trying to make it work long-distance, but we both knew the marriage was over. We decided it would be best if he stayed out of her life so she didn't get confused. He's remarried now with a child of his own. When Becca was old enough to ask questions, I explained her father lived far away for his job and couldn't come home. I explained he may not be a part of her life, but she was celebrated the day she was born and she was a precious gift."

"And she just accepted your weak explanation? Never asked why? Never demanded to see him or talk to him?"

She dragged in a breath. "No. But I'm preparing for when she begins asking more questions and know I'll have to face a discussion when she gets old enough to truly understand."

"What did you plan on telling her? More lies? Were you gonna pretend I never existed?"

She held her ground. "No. I knew one day the truth needed to come out, for everyone. I just wasn't ready to face it all back then, and Becca was too young to understand. I thought you'd left for good, Tristan. When you came back because of your father's will, you were so cold to me. To Becca. You ignored me and acted like you wanted nothing to do with either of us. I couldn't take it. It was only recently when you began to mend our relationship that I knew the truth had to be told."

He gave a bitter laugh, staring at her with disdain and resentment. "Must be nice to control it all, huh? You got to decide everything. I don't think I believe you were going to tell me about Becca. If I hadn't pushed this relationship forward, you would've kept the truth from me forever. Dear God, I've been back for two years! I sat next to Becca, talked to her, took her to that damn recital, and all the time she was mine. The only reason you finally decided this was a good idea is because we ended up in bed with each other."

She winced but held firm. "I always intended to tell you eventually."

"I don't believe you. Do you know how much time I've lost? Time I can't get back. Do you know what that feels like, Sydney?"

Eyes glittering with fury, he stepped toward her, his muscled body tight with drawn tension. "How would you feel if you found out you had a daughter and missed the first seven years of her life? Missed her first step, first word, first smile? And you had no choice, because the person you once trusted decided to keep her from you?"

Tears stung her eyes. "I would be heartbroken," she whispered. "Angry. Full of pain. But I'm asking you to think back to that time, Tristan. I was so young, and scared, and our relationship had blown up after your mother's death. I didn't know what to do! The idea of you being trapped in Harrington, with me and a baby . . . That wasn't your future. I knew it, and you knew it. You can tell yourself whatever excuses you need and blame me, but I made the best decision I could. I needed to make sure this baby felt loved and not like an accident. Becca will always be my first priority."

He let out an agonized roar, and the tears flowed faster. God, she'd done this to him.

"You never gave me a chance. Even when I came back, and you had opportunities to tell me, you continued to lie." He backed away again, his face haunted. "Even in bed, with me buried inside of you, thinking we had this connection nothing could break, you lied."

A sob choked her. "I knew after that night together we had another chance. A chance to be a family. I wanted to tell you both the truth so we can move forward. Together."

In that moment, it was as if all the emotion drained out of him, leaving him lifeless. It was more terrifying than the rage. He stared at the wall, his voice completely dead. "You took her away from me. You allowed me to treat her like a stranger, when she's my flesh and blood—part of the Pierce dynasty—and I swear to God, I'll never forgive you for that. Never."

"Tristan."

"No, you're going to listen to me now. Because from now on, we're done playing things your way. We're done with you manipulating both of us. I'm going out for a while to wrap my head around this."

"I understand. We can talk more later."

"I can't stand looking at you right now," he said. The chill in his voice sliced her open and left her bleeding. "I need to get out of here before I do something I'll regret."

He never looked back. Just shut the door behind him.

Sydney slid down the wall and sank to the floor. Somehow, she had to stay strong. Convince him she'd made the best decisions for both of them at the time. Show him they could heal together and be a family.

Lowering her head on her bent knees, she prayed their second chance wasn't gone forever.

chapter fifteen

He drove.

With no idea of his destination, he turned onto dark roads that seemed vaguely familiar and chased sanity. Like shadows, his thoughts leapt out of his grasp, leading him further into madness.

He was a father.

Her words spun in his brain, causing more havoc. That little girl belonged to him, and he'd been kept from her. He didn't care about Sydney's tangled rationalizations or excuses. He deserved a chance to be a father and hadn't been given one. But underneath all the messy emotions lay the cord of rationale that would guide him through the chaos. He needed to rip away the pain, grief, and anger. He needed to make a decision on what to do next and where the future for all of them lay.

Her betrayal ate at his gut. God, how he'd trusted her. Believed in her. Believed in them as a couple. How stupid to think they could topple the past and build a future when it was all based on deceit. All this time he'd been patient, tearing down each one of her walls, pleasuring her body, and through every kiss, she'd known and deliberately held the most precious thing of all from him.

Family.

With shaking hands, he followed the twisting hill to the top and cut the engine. The spill of house and land soothed his ravaged soul, and he stumbled from the car, needing someone to talk to, someone who would keep him from drowning. The dogs barked crazily when he rang the doorbell, and when his brother flung open the door, they jumped on him in merry greeting.

"Down, Balin, down, Gandalf. Where's Raven when you need her?" Cal muttered, tucking them back in the house. Dressed in briefs and an old T-shirt, he blinked sleepily, pushing his fingers through his hair. "What's up, man? It'd better be important. That party was worse than my crew celebrating after a job and—" He broke off. Reached out and grabbed Tristan's arm. "What happened?"

Tristan shook his head. Once he would've handled this alone. He would sit by himself, think about all the options, quietly drink his wine, and make a decision. He was good at stamping down the tide of emotions that wrecked rational thinking. But tonight he realized he had his brothers back, and they might be the only things that could help him.

"I'm Becca's father." The words were choked out. He held on to Cal, feeling the ground tilt underneath him. "I'm Becca's father, and I don't know what to do."

The shock on Cal's face confirmed no one had known. They'd all been living alongside Becca with no clue she belonged to them. His brother gripped him like he did when he was drunk, holding him upright and guiding him through the door. "Okay, it's going to be okay, Tris. I swear it. I got you."

For some reason, he clung to his brother's words and allowed himself to be led inside.

It only took half an hour for Dalton to get there. They set him up in the man cave—a special room Cal had insisted the house include for entertaining male guests. Morgan had pointed out he only saw his brothers and Brady, but he hadn't cared. Decorated in rich wood and earth colors and packed with television screens, surround-sound speakers, elaborately carved game tables, and a fully stocked bar with leather stools, it was indulgent yet masculine.

Dalton sat beside him on the leather couch while Cal paced. They'd given Tristan a snifter full of Cal's expensive whiskey and insisted he drink it. He tried, but even though he technically knew it should be heating his throat and stomach with a burning sting, he felt nothing.

Maybe he'd never feel anything again.

Maybe that would be a good thing.

"You both never considered the idea she could be mine?" he asked for the third time, staring into his glass. Sydney used to tell him Cal's whiskey reminded her of his eyes. He'd pretend to be embarrassed, but her compliment pleased him. That had been a lifetime ago.

"Never," Cal bit out. "We weren't on speaking terms when you left, and she got married so quickly. I figured you guys had just moved on. Yeah, she got pregnant fast, but I never questioned it."

"I was in California at that point," Dalton said. "By the time I got back, I knew the story everyone did. It hadn't worked out with her husband, she had the baby, and he took a job overseas. She never said a bad word about him."

"I was so stupid," Tristan muttered. He drained his glass, and Cal quickly gave him another. "I asked her to come to New York with me and she said no. Said she wanted to stay in Harrington. We had a big fight and I left. But I came back three months later, because I realized I couldn't live without her."

Cal frowned. "I didn't know you came back," he said. "What happened?"

He lifted his head and gazed at his brothers. His heart felt like a barren wasteland where nothing would ever grow again. "She was having a wedding dress fitting and I asked her again to come with me. She told me she was getting married and had built her own life. And she never told me about her pregnancy."

Dalton shook his head. "I can't believe this. It just doesn't sound like something Sydney would do. Why? What was going on with you two?"

The past surged up with all the memories. The times he'd pushed her away. The statements he'd made to her about feeling trapped in Harrington. The subtle way he'd insulted the life she said she wanted, hoping to push her to want more, be more, go explore the world. His refusal to say he loved her. "We had different views of our lives back then," he said shortly. No way was he going to feel guilty or excuse her lies.

"I can never forgive her." He stated the words with certainty.

"But I have to make a decision about Becca. How we move forward. I want to be with my daughter. I deserve the time to make up for what I lost."

"You can share custody," Dalton suggested. "Work out a schedule."

"So I can grab small chunks of time like a part-time father?" he said bitterly. "No. I want more than that."

"When are you going to tell her?" Cal asked.

"I don't know. I left to get my head on straight. She doesn't deserve me flipping out when I need to be the role model. I don't know how she's going to react."

Cal stopped pacing and gave him a hard look. "She's going to wonder how she got so lucky."

"Maybe not. We were never as close as you guys were," he pointed out. "It's just recently I began to get to know her. She may not really like me. May not want me as her father."

"Shut the hell up," Dalton practically shouted. "Dude, you're going to be the best father. Look at who we lived with our whole lives. If it wasn't for Mom, we'd all be walking disasters. Becca has both you and Sydney, and she's going to recognize how lucky she is the moment you tell her."

His raw nerves were soothed a bit. Cal and Dalton were brutal with their honesty. If they believed he'd be a good father, he might actually be. The idea of Becca looking at him with disappointment haunted him. He pushed the image out of his mind and tried to concentrate on the bigger plan.

"Either way, you're going to have to eventually make peace with Sydney," Cal said. "I'm afraid when I tell Morgan, she'll lose it. She's very protective of you, and keeping such a secret is going to hit her hard."

Dalton nodded. "Same thing with Raven. Our women are quite like mama bears when it comes to us."

"I know." The memory of sinking to his knees to pleasure the woman he was falling for again shook him to the core. Damn her. "She's Becca's mother, and no matter how I feel about her now, I need to give her respect. Becca will be confused enough without me trying to blame her mother."

"You need some time to work through this," Cal said quietly. "You can't expect to know everything in a few hours."

His brother might be right, but Tristan already knew he wanted something bigger than stolen hours or weekends. He wanted to offer Becca a real family—one she deserved. And there was only one way to get there, whether he liked the scenario or not.

If he went through with the plan slowly blossoming in his mind, there would be consequences. His life would never be the same, but then again, the truth had ripped away any foundation he'd ever had. He had to begin thinking like a father and do the best he could for Becca.

Sydney wouldn't see it his way.

She'd fight him. She'd refuse. She'd threaten. She'd rant and rave and cry and push back.

But she was going to lose, because Tristan decided there was no other way, and nothing would keep him away from his daughter again.

Nothing and no one.

"You have a funny look on your face," Dalton said. "What do you want to do?"

"I need to close my eyes and rest a bit," he managed. He laid his pounding head against the leather cushions. "I think I've decided what I'm going to do."

His brothers didn't push him any further. Just shared a glance, then nodded. "Do you need to be alone or can we hang out with you?" Cal asked.

He clung to the sliver of peace that wriggled free and lit the way. His brothers had his back. Always.

The word barely escaped his throat, but it was a request from the heart.

"Stay."

They didn't ask again. Flanking him on the couch, they sat and waited together for dawn.

chapter sixteen

Sydney heard the door slam and sat up. Eyes gritty from lack of sleep, her jeans and sweatshirt wrinkled and creased, she pushed away her knotted tangle of hair and held her breath.

She'd eventually fallen asleep on the couch waiting for him to return. Tears long dried up, her heart bruised and aching, she prayed there was some way to reach him and make him understand. She'd carried the guilt every single day, many times sick about her decision to keep Becca a secret. But she'd done the best she could, her only focus giving her daughter a stable, happy life.

When he didn't come find her, she made her way into the kitchen and found him making coffee. Swallowing hard, she took a seat on a stool and waited for him to speak. Or yell. Or do something. Anything.

"I've made a decision."

He flung the words at her like they were chips of ice, and she knew there would be no understanding or compromise. This was the Tristan from the past—ruthless in business, distant in relationships, analyzing each situation to further himself on the path of success to achieve what he wanted. She was now the enemy and would be treated as such.

Dread coiled in her gut. "Becca's still sleeping," she said evenly. "I'd like us to be able to be on the same page before she gets up. I don't want her affected the morning after her birthday." She tried to sound calm, but her nerve endings were raw. Her question came out in a ragged whisper. "Are you okay? I was—worried."

He didn't even glance back. Just continued making coffee. "No, but I will be. I've thought about our options here, and there's only one way to give Becca what she needs and allow me to be the father I want to be."

"I understand. I have no problem sharing custody, Tristan. I want her to be a part of your life moving forward and would never fight you on this. We just need to take some time to figure things out."

The coffeepot began to brew merrily. He took a mug from the cabinet and lined it up neatly on the granite countertop. "Partial custody won't be enough. Not to make up for the last seven years. I'll have to be involved in her day-to-day schedule for us to get to know each other the way we both need."

She blinked, tamping down the rising panic threatening to choke her. "Becca needs me. There's no way you're going to take her away from me."

"I don't intend to as long as you agree to the plan."

Her mouth trembled, but she made herself speak. "What plan?"

He turned. Even mussed and wrinkled and dead tired, he retained an aura of competence and sexuality that reached across the room and grabbed her. Their connection had never been the problem between them. Unfortunately, now it made everything so much harder. His face was calmly set, with an implacable determination in his amber eyes that froze her in sheer fear.

"We're going to get married."

It took a few moments for his announcement to register. She figured she'd just heard wrong. "We're going to what?"

"Get married. It's the only way to ensure Becca gets the family and support she needs. It's cruel to rip either one of us away at this point. This way it's a win-win for her."

The kitchen spun, and she grabbed on to the edge of the counter. "Tristan, you must be joking. Or drunk. Or delusional. You're not thinking clearly about what you just proposed."

"Oh, but I am." He crossed his arms in front of his chest, cocked his hip, and stared at her. The heat and tenderness were gone. In their place were an icy resolution and faint distaste for his proposal. "We're going to face Becca and give her the happy news. I'll let you tell her how and why any way you wish, as long as the bottom line is we'll be getting married and completing our family."

Anger snapped up from her core, and she lowered her voice to a furious whisper. "We are not about to tell my daughter anything today. This is a delicate situation, and she needs to be thought of first. We need to plan when and how we'll tell her, and I'm open to feedback. But nothing will be happening right now. Things are too raw. We're not ready, and neither is she."

"Oh, I'm ready." She flinched at the cutting edge of his voice. "I don't intend to wait another year to be with my daughter. And we will get married, Syd. That's the only solution to this."

"You're not thinking clearly! It'll never work. She'll know we're miserable and unhappy and lying about our relationship. Kids can sense that. She'll only be more confused!"

"Not if we commit to giving her what she deserves. A real marriage. We both focus on creating a stable, happy home life. We're not strangers. It's worth the sacrifice for Becca."

She wondered if she'd just dropped into an alternate universe where arranged marriages were the norm. The idea of living with this man on a daily basis was impossible. Sleeping with him. Eating breakfast. Wearing old pajamas while she watched television. Those were the types of activities you did with a man you trusted and loved. There was no way they could pretend on such a scale. She'd go mental. She'd become . . . broken.

"It won't work," she repeated again. "We can't live together, Tristan. That type of give-and-take in a marriage, raising a child, isn't something you can just fake."

"I don't intend anything to be fake." He narrowed his gaze. "We'll mean every word of those vows we share. I intend to be faithful, show you respect, protect you and Becca, and provide a secure, nurturing environment. And you will do the same."

She had a crazy urge to laugh at the ridiculousness, but knowing he was dead serious stole away all humor. Oh, God, she couldn't do this. He stated his intentions like a Boy Scout or military person serving his country. Not like a husband, or a man who wanted to spend his life with a woman he loved.

Because he didn't love her.

Not anymore.

Maybe not ever. He'd never been able to say the words, no matter how intimate their time was together.

"You can't just bully me into a marriage. Listen, we don't need to rush into anything. We'll talk and decide the right time to tell Becca. Couples deal with two-parent households all the time, and Becca will understand. You can have plenty of time with her—pick her up from school, take her for sleepovers, a weekend getaway. Anything you need."

"What I need is to be with her every single day." The implacable determination carved out in his features told her he wouldn't change his mind. "I need to make up for what was taken away from me. And you will marry me, Sydney. One way or another."

"You have no right," she breathed in horror.

"Oh, but I do. You lost all your rights the moment you played God and kept me from making my own choice." A flick of temper leaked through the armor, but it was quickly brought under control. "You don't get to say no to this."

"And if I do?"

He poured his cup of coffee, lifted it to his lips, and took a lingering sip. "I take Becca from you. I hire the best legal team imaginable and make your life a living hell. I let the court decide who'll be the better parent. How does that sound?"

Her teeth rattled together like a poor imitation of a skeleton. If she hadn't been sitting, she would've sunk to the floor, boneless with fear. He wasn't making idle threats. Tristan never did. No, he was ruthless when he came to a decision, whether it be leaving for New York, walking away from a deal, or doling out punishment to those who wronged him. This was a man who trusted with his whole soul, but once betrayed, he locked the door and threw away the key.

She'd lost him forever.

The pain of such a loss was still secondary to the idea Becca could be dragged through a custody suit. Nothing was worth that.

Not even living in a sham of a marriage with a man she still loved.

"You would do that?" she asked quietly. "Even if it would tear Becca apart?"

His jaw clenched. His eyes were flat and devoid of all emotion.

"Yes."

She shuddered, wrapping her arms tight around her body. He'd do it. He wouldn't want to hurt Becca, but he was desperate. Betrayed. Savage. The worst was the empty vastness between them, reminding her the man she'd fallen for was no longer here. The one who'd taken his place was ruthless. "Don't do this to us," she whispered. "You'll destroy everything."

"You already did." He set his coffee down. "I want to hear you say the words. Say you agree."

"If you do this, you'll be giving up the opportunity to marry for love. Do you really want to wake up one day and feel trapped by your decision? Feel as if you missed out on an unknown future because of responsibility? You don't need to do this. We can work it out some other way if you give it a chance."

Her final plea lay between them. A part deep inside of

her fantasized he'd admit he did love her. If he gave her the tiniest indication there was a real chance for them, she'd marry him without question. But to be trapped with someone who'd never love you back? It would be the worst nightmare imaginable.

His gaze flicked over her with dismissive ease. "Love is overrated. I think a marriage based on shared commitment to the greater good is what this world is lacking. There will be no regrets on my part."

"And me? You're blackmailing me as punishment. How can our relationship stand a chance with such a start? Don't you want more for us?"

His words were as robotic as his tone. "No. This is all we have left."

Her heart fragmented into tiny pieces. She rocked back and forth, searching for any loophole or offer she could beg him to accept. And came back to the same shattering conclusion.

She was going to have to marry him and forfeit her very soul.

"Say you agree," he said again.

No. She wouldn't do it. Wouldn't hold both of them and Becca hostage in a marriage that could never be real, at least on his end. She grabbed on to her own frustration and anger, confronting him with clenched fists. "How dare you think you control this relationship or my daughter?" she ripped out, keeping her voice low. "Deny it all you want—you couldn't have handled the truth back then. You left without speaking to me for three months, then showed up expecting me to drop everything because you decided you missed me? And when you heard about the baby, you never once wondered at the timing? How dare you judge me? You barely looked at us for two years, and I was supposed to tell you about her?"

"Yes! Because I'm her real father!" he shouted. "Becca is mine!"

"You're my dad?"

Sydney gasped and whipped around. Her daughter stood framed in the doorway, dressed in pink Hello Kitty pajamas, hair springing wildly around her head, those sleepy eyes huge as she stared at both of them, blinking furiously. Sydney clapped a hand over her mouth, swallowing her cry.

A shocked silence filled the kitchen. The room spun, tilted, then steadied. Dear God, how much had she overheard? What had they done?"

Sydney walked over, dropping to her knees and grasping Becca's hands in a tight grip. "Baby, I'm so sorry we were yelling. What did you hear?"

"Just what Tristan said. That he's my dad. Is it true?"

Her body shook as if feverish. Her lungs barely squeezed breath out, throwing her into a panic. She realized this was a moment she'd planned for Becca's whole life. Yet this wasn't the way she wanted her daughter to find out the truth. Fear choked her, but she pushed it aside and swore she'd do whatever possible to make it right. To make sure Becca wasn't scarred from finding out this way. "Becca, look at me."

Her daughter gazed into her eyes.

"I love you. I love you more than you'll ever imagine. Do you believe me?"

"Of course. Mommies always love their children more than anything else."

She blinked back the sting of tears. "That's right. You may get mad at me for not telling you the truth sooner about your dad. And the reason I didn't want to tell you was because you were too little to really understand. There was a lot of grown-up stuff going on."

She paused, glancing at Tristan to make sure he was ready. That he'd support what she was about to tell her daughter.

His face. Oh, God, his face was full of the divine as he stared at Becca, drinking in her presence as if she were water to his parched soul. Eyes lit with gentleness and pure love, as if he still couldn't believe she was part of him.

And then she knew it had to be done. Tristan deserved to be a father to Becca. She'd taken that from him, and it was time to reunite them, no matter how difficult it was going to be. She couldn't lie to her daughter to buy more time.

"Grown-up stuff about my dad?" Becca asked.

"Yes, baby. There's something you didn't know because I didn't tell you. You actually have two dads. Your first dad was here for a little while. He married Mama, but then he had to go far away for work."

"I know. That's why I never see him."

"That's right. But you have a second dad. Your real dad. And the only reason he didn't come back to see you is Mommy never told him he was your real dad."

Becca frowned. "What do you mean? Why wouldn't you tell him he was my dad?"

Sydney gathered up her courage and took the leap.

"Because we had a big fight before you were born, and I didn't think he wanted to be a dad. But I was wrong, Becca. He did want to be your dad, and I made a mistake."

She ached to snatch her daughter and wrap her arms around her body. But she remained still, knowing Becca needed to process this information in her own way.

"So my real dad never came to see me because he didn't know?"

Sydney spoke past the lump in her throat. "That's right."

"He knows about me now, and he wants me?" she whispered.

This time, tears filled her eyes, and she couldn't fight them off. "Yes, baby. He wants you so badly. He never wants to leave you again."

Those beautiful green eyes filled with such hope Sydney's heart shattered. She gazed at Tristan. "Is it you?" she whispered.

Tristan crossed the room and dropped to his knees in front of Becca. Slowly he reached out a trembling hand and cupped Becca's cheek. His voice was full of gravel and broken yearning as he spoke the words that changed everything.

"Yes, Becca, it's me. I'm your father. And I want you more than anything in the whole world."

The room was drenched in silence. No one moved, or breathed, as father and daughter gazed upon each other for the first time.

And then with a cry, Becca launched herself into his arms, clinging to him and crying, and Tristan held her like the most precious, treasured gift in the world.

Sydney watched them hold each other, the past and present merged in a moment of time that broke her completely and healed her in one perfect twist.

He sat with his daughter curled in his arms, the coconut scent of her shampoo drifting to his nostrils. They hadn't wanted to leave each other's presence, so he answered her endless questions as best he could, with Sydney running interference, perched on the edge of the sofa.

He studied her small, graceful hands, marveling at how little they were wrapped in his, her nails topped with pink glitter polish. He'd expected anger or resentment. He'd prepped for her reserve and distrust, struggling to understand why he'd suddenly shown up seven years later with an intention to become part of her life.

Instead, she'd humbled him with her open joy and affection, allowing him to steep himself in her presence and accepting him fully. He couldn't have timed it more perfectly when Becca asked if they were going to get married now that they weren't mad at each other anymore.

He'd immediately told her yes, cutting off any denials Sydney tried to scrape up.

Becca had squealed in excitement, sealing their fate. He spun a romantic tale to make things easier, painting an image of star-crossed lovers from a Disney movie, reuniting years later to get married and live happily ever after.

At least, Tristan could offer the marriage part.

Sydney took it all in with a forced smile on her face, but he saw the deep-seated panic beneath the surface. Things had gotten real. Becca had accepted him and was excited about them becoming a real family. Now it was time to move forward with the plan and make things legal.

Sydney seemed to sense his determination and cleared her throat. "Becca, I know this is going fast, and it could be really confusing. Tristan and I don't have to get married right away. We could wait and take things slow. You're never going to lose him again, sweetheart."

Tristan waited for Becca's answer. If his daughter communicated confusion, he'd back off. There was no way he'd do anything to upset her.

"No! I'm so excited! I want Dad to live with us right away," Becca stated. "Can I be the flower girl? Can we get a dog?"

He burst into laughter. He would've bought her a damn puppy right away if he'd known how easy pet bribery was with kids. "Your mom and I will talk about it and let you know about the dog. And I'd say you'll be the main star at the wedding, so yes, you can be the flower girl."

"So cool. Mama, can I tell Lyndsey and Callie? It's not a secret any longer, right? I can tell everyone that we found my real dad and you're getting married and it's like a true happily ever after?"

Sydney paled, but her lips curved in a smile. "Of course, honey. We want you to be as happy as we are."

"And can we live in the mansion? Please?"

"No, I don't think—"

"I think that's a great idea," he interrupted. "Uncle Cal and Uncle Dalton have already left, and we don't want to sell the place. Would you like to live here, Becca?"

Sydney cleared her throat. "No, we—"

"Yes! Oh, yes, yes, I love it here so much! This is the best day of my whole life!"

Tristan grinned and hugged her. It made perfect sense to move into his family home. It was her legacy and big enough for them to get as many dogs as she wanted.

"I'll be right back," Sydney said, practically stumbling out of the room in her haste to leave. He frowned, but Becca didn't catch on to her mother's distress. She was too busy spinning daydreams of decorating her bedroom and filling the place with puppies.

With one last hard hug, he lifted her up off his lap. "Let's get some breakfast. I think we promised you some bacon."

It didn't take him long to fry up some eggs and bacon. He poured her a cup of orange juice and refilled his coffee mug, noticing Sydney still hadn't returned. When Becca's plate was clean, he gave her a smile. "Wanna watch some TV while your mom gets cleaned up?"

"Yes. Are you coming home with us today? Or tomorrow?"

He caught the worried glint in her eyes and leaned over the counter so their gazes met. "Becca, I'm not going away ever again," he said quietly. "I intend to marry your mom, and we're going to be a family. We have a lot of time to make up for, so you're gonna end up getting really sick of me."

She smiled back and her small shoulders relaxed. "Okay. Can I watch *SpongeBob*?"

He made a note to study all relevant children's shows for the future, then nodded. "Absolutely. I'll set it up and we'll decide what we're going to do today."

When she was happily settled watching a strange yellow

sponge go on adventures, he headed to the bathroom and tapped on the door.

"Be right out." Her voice was happy, yet strained.

"Syd, open the door. It's me."

He waited a few moments before the door swung open. Her face was a bit swollen and her eyes were red. He caught the evidence and tried to push the need to hold her aside. If he broke now, he'd be setting up the rules of their relationship. He swore he'd treat her well, but he was done offering up his bruised heart for her to slice and dice. He'd never trust her with that part of his anatomy again, and he needed to build some decent brick walls before he put a damn ring on her finger. He refused to be a chump in the name of love again unless it was for Becca. He'd give all his affection to his daughter, who was safe.

"I fed Becca breakfast and she's watching TV. Want to talk?"

She nodded, and he stepped inside, shutting the door behind him. The bathroom was really a majestic powder room decorated in black raspberry and rich silver. It boasted a mini chandelier, a makeup counter with padded stools, and tapestried walls in textured velvet.

She leaned against the porcelain counter, her image reflected in the dual mirrors. He stood a few feet away from her, needing the distance. "I think it went well. Better than I could have imagined, especially since we didn't plan on telling her right away. What about you?"

Pushing her hair back from her face, she lifted her gaze. He stared into haunted, jade-green eyes. "Me? After my panic, I realized I've never seen my daughter look like that before. Like Christmas and birthdays all rolled up into one. Like she was finally . . . complete."

"You don't seem happy about it," he said quietly. "Did you want her to reject me?"

She gasped. "No! Oh, God, Tristan, no. The way you looked at each other? I'll never forget it. But this thing between you and me is too much. I can't just move in with you and plan a wedding in record time. Maybe we should let things settle before moving forward."

"No. All Becca needs to know is we want to be together as quickly as possible. And I want her to have my name. She's a Pierce, and our marriage will make that official. The wedding will be simple, just family. I think it's important she's involved and a part of it. We can get married next Saturday, and I'll set up everything to get you moved in."

She shook her head, fists digging into her temples. "Stop it! You're doing it again. Moving forward with plans without even consulting me. I am not getting married a week from now during one of the biggest jobs I've ever headed, and I happen to like my house. I don't want to move here. It doesn't belong to me."

He grasped for patience and kept his tone even. "I know it's moving fast, but we have no choice. Do you really want to stretch out a long engagement? It's a small town. There'll already be gossip—dragging this relationship out too long will hurt Becca. I also refuse to move in with you before we're married."

A small groan of distress escaped her lips. "I didn't think about the gossip," she said in a small voice. "Damn small towns for their nosiness."

"It's bound to happen. The quicker we get married, the faster talk will die down. As for the mansion, it just makes sense. I don't want to bully you, but it is Becca's heritage and has tons of space. I know it's a bit stuffy for you, so you can change anything you want. Hire a designer or do it yourself—it doesn't matter to me."

"It was your mother's house, and I loved her. I don't want to take away any of her memories."

He quickly hardened his heart against the surge of tenderness. Knowing how much Sydney respected his mother's space touched him, but he kept his face impassive. "She hated the formality of the house, but my father insisted it be a model for our work. I think she'd love you putting your own sense of design into these rooms. You both had similar taste."

She nodded, but she looked like the shock had begun to hit her. Tristan knew the best course of action was to forge ahead like in a battle, refusing to let her think about things too long. The quicker he made plans and shot down her objections, the quicker he'd be living with his daughter full-time.

"How can we hold a wedding before Morgan's? This is crazy. I refuse to take the spotlight off her. She's worked so hard to make her wedding perfect."

"Morgan will understand. Our wedding won't compete. We'll get married here at the house and have a small reception with just family. Simple and tasteful. No big party or church needed. There's no reason we can't have it on Saturday. I can contact everyone. If you want a planner, we can hire one."

She chewed at her lip. "No, there's no need. I can have it catered by the Italian deli here in town."

"I think Raven may want to do it."

"I don't want her to be working. She's family."

"Fine. I'll leave the details to you, but if there's any issues, let me know. I can cover you at the site for an afternoon if you want to take Becca dress shopping."

He tamped down on his annoyance at the green tint to her skin. Was marrying him so horrific to her? She'd married another man who was practically a stranger rather than tell him the truth. Had she really believed he wouldn't have wanted the baby?

He pushed aside the disturbing thought. "Let's make sure Becca knows we're excited about this new life we're about to embark on. There's no reason to let her sense any stress."

Her chin snapped up. "I know how to take care of my daughter," she practically growled.

He took a step toward her and ate up her space. Lowering his head, he studied her rapidly panting breath, parted lips, and big green eyes. Already he felt his dick harden and the overwhelming need to back her against that wall and punish her by using that sweet body until he'd wrung out all his frustration and anger. But that would open up the path that led to emotion and a deeper feeling he couldn't seem to fight around her.

He was done.

He'd marry her. He'd treat her like a wife. He'd eventually fuck her.

But he'd never let his heart open to her again.

"She's my daughter, too," he ground out. "You're not running the show any longer. Any decision regarding Becca will involve me, whether you like it or not."

Furious tears stung her eyes. "Why are you being so ruth-less? So cold? It doesn't have to be like this."

He drew back, retreating behind the familiar wall of ice. "You did this to both of us with your lies. This is the only way it can be."

She rose on tiptoes, jabbing her index finger at his chest. "Back off. I'll agree to marry you for Becca's sake, but don't you dare take a righteous attitude with me. I've been protect-ing her since day one, and you never gave me any reason to trust you with the truth. Not the way you treated me."

He growled, reaching for her, but she spun out of his grip. "You'd better rethink your interpretation of the past. Is that how you lived with yourself these past seven years?"

"If you keep acting like a coldhearted bastard, I'll take my chances on a legal battle rather than marrying you. Think about that."

He didn't have time to answer.

She marched off without a glance back, leaving him alone in an empty bathroom.

chapter seventeen

I now pronounce you man and wife. You may kiss the bride."

She watched the man who was now her husband lean over and press a hard kiss to her lips. It was formal, brief, and cold.

Just like he was toward her.

She forced a smile at her daughter's burst of clapping and delight, trying to focus on the good things. Becca had been living in a dream. The past week had been a blur of activity with little sleep. A group of movers showed up on Monday morning with instructions to pack and organize her entire house in a few days to move into the mansion. Charlie and Tristan rallied to give her two afternoons off to buy dresses and arrange catering, flowers, and the wedding cake. She barely saw Tristan. Instead of the sitter, he picked Becca up from school, made her dinner, and left promptly when Sydney returned home late from work.

They'd been able to play up the excitement and busyness of the wedding, but Sydney worried once the smoke cleared, her daughter would pick up on the crackling tension between them.

She walked back down the short aisle, smiling and accepting congratulations. The farce looked perfect: from the flower girl dress in a light shade of blush with a puffy skirt Becca adored to her own Carolina Herrera dress in a long slinky V-neck, with just enough lace and shimmer to make it feminine. The back dipped low in a row of pearl encrusted buttons, emphasizing her natural curves without apology. Her shoes could make a grown woman weep. Combining mesh with crystal, the four-inch open-toe pumps glimmered with each step, Gianvito Rossi at his best. The mansion was decorated with dozens of lit candelabras and pink teacup roses in small vases—tasteful and romantic. It was the exact type of wedding she had once dreamed of when she thought of marrying Tristan, yet today she felt trapped in a nightmare.

She'd been so stupid to think they could move forward after she told him the truth. She'd gotten wrapped up with dreams of forgiveness, especially since they'd been falling in love with each other all over again. But for the last week, everyone had treated her with a polite distance, refusing to spend more than a few minutes in her company. Even now, meeting Morgan's and Raven's gazes, she felt their quiet judgment, a simmering resentment that shredded her heart. Cal and Dalton no longer smiled at her, keeping their interactions brief. In the past week, she'd gained a husband but lost an entire family.

Determined to be happy for her daughter's sake, she headed to the formal dining room, where trays of food tempted guests and a champagne fountain cranked steadily. Tristan already held Becca's hand and was guiding her through the buffet line, putting food on her plate. The real problem centered around how little food she allowed on her plate.

"I thought you liked pasta," she heard him say with confusion.

"I do, but only when it's got the red sauce. That has white with green stuff in it."

"It's really good. Do you want to just try a bite?"

"No, thanks. Where are the chicken fingers?"

"I don't think we ordered any. How about sausage and peppers?"

Becca gagged. "I'd die."

"Meatballs?"

"No, thanks."

The man actually looked stressed. Sydney held back a sigh and marched over. "Young lady, there's bread, meatballs, and chicken."

"But the chicken has mushrooms and sauce on it!"

"You've had it before and you liked it. And I want you to have some of those green beans."

Becca gasped. "I hate green beans!"

"Not all the time. Have just two and I'll be happy."

"But, Mama!"

"If you want to try the wedding cake, I want to see you eat two green beans and the rest of the list I mentioned. Understood?"

She got the look, but Becca finally nodded. Tristan looked relieved and began spooning things onto her plate. Sydney headed to the champagne fountain for another refill. She'd decided there was only one thing to get her through this whole charade without collapsing.

Alcohol.

She grabbed two flutes and filled them both, deciding to

double fist. There was no way she'd be able to eat with her stomach churning. She leaned against the wall at her own wedding, watching family and close friends talk and eat, laugh and chatter, and had never felt so alone in her whole life.

God, she wished Diane were here.

"You okay?"

She turned. Cal held a plate, looking at her with a glint of concern. It was the first time he'd sought her out since he'd heard the truth. They'd stuck mainly to business because it was easier for both of them.

She forced a smile and refused to allow tears to burn her eyes. "I'm great."

"Liar."

"Well, that's what I am, right? A liar. Someone not to be trusted. Someone to be shunned. I get it, but since this is my big day before I embark on a fake marriage, I'd appreciate it if I can just drink quietly in my corner, and I promise to cause no further trouble."

"Syd." His voice broke, and he reached out to lay a hand on her arm. "I hate to see you hurt like this."

She took a gulp of champagne, embracing the burn in her throat. "Too bad. I'm a bit emotional today. The thought of you hating me, Cal, tears me up inside. I can take so much, but seeing you and Dalton despise me? Well, that may just be the icing on this crappy cake."

His face softened. "Sweetheart, we don't hate you. None of us do. But you dropped an atomic bomb on this family, and it's going to take us some time to deal with it. To understand. To forgive."

She nodded. "I didn't keep her a secret to hurt anyone,

Cal. It wasn't to get revenge or payback for Tristan leaving. I honestly did the thing I thought best for my daughter. I won't apologize for trying to protect her. You have no idea what I was going through or what stuff was going down between Tristan and me. Things were complicated, and I was so damn young. So scared. Diane wasn't around. I felt . . . lost."

His gunmetal eyes blazed with raw emotion. "It was a bad time for all of us," he murmured. "I love you like a sister, Syd. We all do. It just hurt us to know this whole time Becca was our blood niece and we never knew." He paused. "Tristan said he came back. Asked you to go with him to New York again. Did you want to tell him then?"

She'd never forget the image of him framed in the doorway while she committed herself to a life with a man who'd promised love and forever and happily ever after. "Yes," she said softly. "But then I saw the way he looked at me. Like he'd missed me because he was in a new place and was lonely. I always gave him what he needed without asking for anything back. I couldn't live like that any longer. And I knew, in my heart, he'd end up resenting us both if I tried to trap him in Harrington."

Understanding passed between them. "I get it." They stood together while she drank champagne and he drank his beer. "You didn't want to get married, did you?"

She gave a deep sigh. "I don't want this marriage to be a battleground. I understand he wants to give Becca the Pierce name and be part of her life. I just don't want to be the casualty in his quest for revenge."

"Syd, I know things are complicated with you both now. And you're right—Tristan didn't tell me the details of what went down, so I can't judge. But he came to see me the night he found out about Becca. I've never seen him so shattered." He shook his head, looking as if he was trying to find the words. "Something broke inside him. He's always been the most complicated out of all of us. His mind is so damn strong it mixes up his emotions. It's like he's responsible for the whole fucking world, and if he fails his mission, we all go down." A grim smile touched his lips. "Intense, but true. I also know no matter what he didn't say or do, he loved you. He just didn't know how to handle it. Hearing about Becca turned his world upside down, and he's trying to find his way back."

Her heart ached at the description of the man she'd always loved. "James Bond," she muttered under her breath. "Pain in the ass."

Cal laughed. "Yeah, that's about it. I'm asking you to give him a little time and patience, Syd. That's all."

Slowly she nodded. Cal understood better than anyone. And maybe he was right. Because that was why she'd married him. Even with the long shot, she wanted one last chance at his heart. At a future. At a happily ever after. She had to take it, or she'd regret not trying forever. "Okay. Thanks."

"Welcome."

"Do you think Morgan and Raven will come around soon?"

"Yes. It was hard for Morgan, since she can't have kids. The idea of keeping one from her biological father hurt her. She doesn't know about your past with Tristan, or the crap we all went through after Mom died. I explained to her, and with some time, she'll eventually come and speak with you."

"And Raven?"

He snorted. "Good luck. That woman is scary as hell. Confronting her alone may be better than avoidance."

"I love you, Cal."

He pressed a kiss to her forehead, then grabbed a flute of champagne from the passing tray. "Love you, too. Now, I'd advise you to get drunk and smash wedding cake all over your husband's face."

With a wink, he walked away. Some of her grief lessened. He understood. Which meant he and Dalton would forgive her eventually. So would Morgan and Raven.

It was her husband she was worried about.

She thought about what Cal had told her. Imagined Tristan breaking down in front of his brothers, the way he had that night with her after Diane had died. Her heart ached at the memory. God knows she never wanted to hurt him. Somehow she'd have to find a way to convince him of that.

On cue, he suddenly appeared before her. She stared at him with a stupid, glazed expression because he was so damn sexy her vision hurt.

Dressed in a black tuxedo, narrowly cut to emphasize his powerful, lean body, he gave off waves of masculine sensuality and elegance that Bond himself could barely keep up with. His redwood-colored hair was brushed away from his brow, falling in perfect waves. The scent of the ocean wafted from his clean-shaven skin. His face was carved in beautiful symmetry, from his high cheekbones and slashed nose to his full lips. His voice drifted to her ears, gritty with sand and coated with caramel.

"You don't look like a happy bride."

She choked out a half laugh and took another sip of champagne. "Forgive me. It's been a long week."

He studied her with a hard expression. There was no longer any softness or tenderness when he looked at her. She mourned the loss as much as his sudden distaste at touching her. If they happened to brush hands, or stand too close, he stiffened and immediately stepped away. "Well, it would be easier for all of us if you pretended you didn't loathe your new husband."

Her gaze snapped to his. The alcohol fueled her blood and gave her false courage. "Me? How about you? Everyone can tell you'd rather marry a—a—a zombie than me!"

He lifted a brow. "How much champagne have you had?"

"Not enough."

His gaze narrowed. He plucked the glass from her hands and gave it to a passing waiter. "Can you get my wife some water, please?"

A shiver crawled down her spine at the possessive inflection of the word. His *wife*. Thank goodness she was mad enough to fight off the sudden weakening of her knees at his arrogant expression, looking her over like she was his new possession. "You disappoint me," he said. "Usually your insults and innuendos are much more clever. I'm sure you can rise to the occasion once you sober up."

She gave him a smile full of white teeth and little humor. Then grabbed another glass from the fountain. "Trust me. The only way to get through this debacle is champagne. Lots of it."

He gritted his teeth and leaned in. A muscle ticked in his jaw. Good. She'd rather see him mad. Anything to battle the ice man. "Don't push me," he whispered silkily. "We just embarked on this marriage. I'd advise you to soothe the wild beast rather than inflame it."

She pursed her lips. His gaze dropped. She closed the distance between them until they were a hairbreadth away. Her blood heated from his closeness, the smell of his skin, the leashed violence hidden beneath the elegant tuxedo. "What beast?" she drawled. "I see the same type of man I always did. Cold. Distant." She uttered each word against his gorgeous, carved lips. "There must be ice in those veins, Tristan. How admirable to always be able to control your emotions. Us lesser folks struggle to own such restraint."

His smile was pure male, pure sin, and pure triumph. In seconds, he lifted her easily up into his arms, her lacy veil cloaking them from the world in their own private domain. "Maybe it's time I show you how lucky you are I own this restraint," he uttered against her mouth. "Wife."

His mouth crushed hers.

Startled, she gasped, giving him the opening for his tongue to dive deep and claim her. Her hands gripped his shoulders, clinging for dear life, as he lifted her up in the air, at the mercy of his hold, of his mouth, of the hunger he ignited deep in her gut, a crazed need that overtook all logic and swamped her. Her tongue met his in the stirring, dark kiss, and for a few moments, nothing else existed but this man, this moment, this kiss.

He tore his mouth from hers. For one moment, she caught the primitive glint in those amber eyes, and she thought there was hope. Hope this marriage could be more than about Becca or his sense of justice. But then it was gone, like a trick of the light, and he turned from her, smiling as a blinding flash went off in her face.

"Smile for the camera," he commanded. "I think we deserve a formal wedding picture. Don't you?"

Anger crashed over her in waves. She blinked at the photographer, who gave her a thumbs-up at the pose, and then he dropped her back to the ground and let go of her like she'd burned him. The kiss had been a simple setup—and another deft attempt at punishment. Humiliation burned at the easy way she'd responded the moment he touched her.

"Don't push me, Syd," he warned.

Her smile was full of fake cheer and her own warning. "Ditto, Tristan."

He narrowed his gaze in surprise, studying her for a few hard, shattering moments. Then he walked away and disappeared into the crowd. His family surrounded him, chattering and laughing, and Becca stood in the middle, soaking in all the attention, her face glowing with happiness.

Sydney choked back the searing pain and reached for another glass of champagne.

He shouldn't have kissed her.

Tristan stayed within the safe circle of his family and fought for composure. Her sweet taste still lingered on his lips. His pants were uncomfortably tight, and the chatter around him was like bees buzzing, a distant hum in the background.

He still burned for her.

The fact ate away at his gut. This attraction wasn't going

away. He'd thought the anger and betrayal would set his dick on the right path, but when it came to Sydney Greene—now Sydney Pierce—he'd always had a weak spot. Eventually he'd have to bed her. There was no way he could go years in this marriage without sex, but he needed some time to come to terms with being a father and a husband to a wife he intended to never love or trust.

He glanced over to find her staring at him. With a mocking smile, she lifted her glass and saluted him before drinking more champagne. Damned if he had to strangle back his laugh of amusement. She was such a ballbuster. Even after he'd deliberately humiliated her, she fought right back.

She was so fucking beautiful.

His heart had literally stopped when he saw her poised in the doorway in white. The dress was simple and elegant, flowing over her body and emphasizing the ripeness of her breasts, the curve of her buttocks, the hourglass of her hips. She sparkled so brilliantly he had to blink several times to make sure she wasn't just a vision. That glorious red hair was pinned up loosely, allowing waves to cascade down her back, fire peeking through the lacy white veil.

Her hand trembled in his as she recited her vows. He caught the gleam of panic in her emerald eyes as the words *I do* trembled on her lips. For a few seconds, he held his breath, tightening his hand on hers in slight warning. Once she said them, satisfaction flowed through him in riotous waves, along with something much more dangerous.

Possession.

He wanted to mark her as his, growl like an animal, and show the world she belonged to him. He'd never had such primitive emotions regarding a woman, but in his gut, Tristan knew he'd always known she was his for the taking, ever since she was eight years old and trailing him around in pure adoration.

He'd finally made it a reality.

He just had to keep from loving her.

Dalton clapped him on the shoulder, jarring him from his thoughts. "Raven said it's almost time for cake. You doing okay?"

"Yeah, thanks."

His younger brother gave a snort. "Listen, dude, if you're ready to wrap up, we'll follow your lead. Cake, coffee, home. This wedding is like a dream. No ridiculous dancing, throwing the bouquet, or garter shit. Think we can convince Morgan to follow your lead?"

"No." Cal took his place in the circle. "Though I doubt there will be any bouquet or garter shenanigans. Morgan thinks it's primeval."

"But there'll be dancing, right?" Dalton asked.

Cal sighed. "Yeah. A lot of it. Bad stuff, too. She was actually talking about a *Grease* reprise."

Dalton shuddered. "Not me, man. I don't care if I'm in the wedding party. I'm not parading like a trained pony."

"Yes, you are." Cal glared. "You'll do whatever she tells you or my life will be shit. She gets one day. I get the rest. I can't wait till I'm back in charge. This whole wedding thing has been exhausting."

A smooth Southern voice cut into their conversation. "Y'all are the sweetest. I mean, giving me a whole day to do what I want?" Cal froze as his fiancée ran a hand down his arm, batting her eyelashes in mockery. "Since my entire life is going to belong to you, Charming, I'd better make this count." Her blue eyes sparked with evil glee. "I'm thinking we can reprise our first meeting at the reception. I already picked you out a prince costume so we can surprise the guests. You'd look so sexy in tights."

It was the first time Tristan spotted pure panic in his older brother's eyes. "Umm, princess, we were only joking around."

"I'm not," she whispered. "Catch you boys later."

She sashayed away in her pink dress and kitten heels, leaving them in shocked silence.

"She's mean," Dalton finally said. "It must be the Southerner in her."

"You're such an asshole," Cal muttered. "You just had to push her."

"Me? I'm not the one who stated I'd be in charge for the rest of her natural life. That's like red to a bull, dude. She'd better not tell Raven, either, or I'll be pissed."

Tristan laughed out loud, a rush of sibling affection cutting through the mess. Damn, he loved them, even though they were batshit crazy, especially since they'd found the women they loved.

"Daddy! Is it time for cake?"

His daughter's voice warmed his ears, and he scooped her up for a brief hug, appreciating her giggles, before releasing her back to the ground. He noticed his brothers' surprise at her easy endearment. They'd had a long talk, and he'd been willing to wait as long as it took for Becca to call him Dad. Hell, as much as it hurt, he'd have taken Uncle Tristan or even his first name. He never wanted to push her into anything she wasn't comfortable with.

But damned if she hadn't asked him right away if it was okay. Even now, his insides felt all mushy when he heard it. His beautiful, perfect daughter wanted to claim him as hers, and he'd never been so proud in his whole life.

"Yes, let's get your mom. Think she'll let me smoosh the cake in her face?"

"No! That'd be mean." Her green eyes twinkled merrily. "But funny."

"I think her revenge may be too scary," he confided.

Becca nodded. "Once, my friend—who is not really my friend—was bullying me. She liked to tell me to do stuff and then push me down when no one was around. She made me cry, which made me so mad. I finally told Mama, and she called my not friend's mom, and said some really scary things to her. Then she went to the teacher at school and it all stopped and I was so happy. Emma—my not friend—still hates me, but she never pushed me again. And then I met Lyndsey and Tracey and they're my best friends."

Tristan frowned. The idea of anyone hurting Becca made him nuts. He didn't know what he'd do. There was so much negotiation in the world of parenting today, and things were so different. His father had used brutal force to gain discipline, but his mother had always been his soft spot in the world. Sydney was so like her. He saw all the qualities of good parenting and fierce love in Becca. He only hoped he could rise to the occasion and be the father she deserved. "So, your mom kicked some butt. Like Black Widow."

"Who?"

"Oh, umm, Wonder Woman."

Becca laughed. "Yeah! Or Batgirl!"

He made a note to coach her on the coolness of superheroes and expand her knowledge. "Then I'm definitely not doing the cake thing."

Becca grabbed his hand and pulled him toward Sydney. "I won't tell Mama you even thought about it," she whispered with a mischievous grin.

And just like that, they shared their first secret.

It was an epic moment.

chapter eighteen

Sydney stiffened as the door shut behind her.

The last of the wedding guests had finally departed. The caterers and servers had cleaned up. The kitchen sparkled, the leftovers were neatly packed up, the remains of the cake had been stored in the freezer for their first anniversary.

No trace remained of the wedding, which only made the day seem more like a dream than reality. She swayed on her bare feet and squinted as Tristan's image blurred into two.

Yep. Shouldn't have had that last glass of champagne.

Oh well, screw it. She was bone weary and sick at heart and craved some isolation and a soft bed. Maybe tomorrow she'd be stronger and more capable of dealing with the future. "I'm going to tuck Becca in," she announced.

He walked into the kitchen. He'd shed his jacket. Unbuttoned the first buttons on his snowy-white shirt. His tie was unknotted. Her stomach did a low, slow flip at the strong column of his throat and the sexy mussed-up look of him. "We both will."

She bit back her protest and forced a nod. "Fine. Let's go."

She turned a bit too fast, swayed again, and he clamped

a hand on her arm. The shock of his touch skittered through her. "Need help?"

Damn him. She stuck her chin up like she wasn't tipsy and aroused. "No, I'm fine."

He dropped his hand. She stalked out of the kitchen, up the stairs, and found Becca in her new room. The walls were a muted pink, and she'd gotten a new furniture set in white. Her butterfly comforter was bright and colorful, and already she'd arranged her stuffed animals and books in neat piles on the shelves, hinting at an OCD trait she'd seemed to inherit from her father. She was dressed in her favorite Belle nightgown, with a frilly collar and a hem that hit the floor. Sydney sat on the edge of the bed, and Tristan stood behind her.

"Hey, baby. Did you enjoy today?"

"I loved it. You looked beautiful, Mama."

"Thank you, but not as pretty as you."

"Definitely prettier than Belle," Tristan said seriously. She watched her daughter flush with pleasure. Emotion tightened her throat. Already the bond was tight between them, growing every hour they spent together. She was so happy the truth was revealed, and they were both free to love each other. Tristan was everything her daughter needed in a father now. She wondered whether everything would've been destroyed if she'd told the truth back then. They'd never know. Somehow, someway, Tristan needed to forgive her, or they'd end up tearing each other apart all over again.

Sydney sought her words carefully. "I know this was a big week for you, and lots of good things happened. We moved into the mansion and I got married, and you have a brand-new dad. Even though this is all great stuff, it's okay to feel a bit nervous or stressed. You can talk to us about it. We won't get mad or upset. We just want to be here for you."

Her daughter frowned, thinking hard. "I was worried I'd have to go to a new school if we moved, but I didn't, so I'm happy about that."

"Good. Anything else?" Tristan asked.

"Can we get a dog now?"

"No," Sydney said.

"Yes," Tristan said.

They looked at each other. Becca turned hopeful, pleading eyes toward her father to break the tie.

"We'll talk about it," Sydney finally forced out. It was time to learn about compromise. She didn't expect to keep making all the decisions regarding Becca, but she also didn't want her daughter to feel like she could get anything she wanted because Tristan ached to make her happy. "Teeth brushed?"

"Yes."

"Good girl." She leaned over and kissed her, snuggling into the warmth of her body. "Hmm, minty fresh," she teased, tickling her a bit. Becca giggled. "I'll leave the night-light on. Mama will be next door if you need anything or get scared."

"I have Mr. Ted Bear," she said, hugging her teddy bear.

"I grew up in this house, honey," Tristan said, switching places with Sydney. "Never saw a monster or bad thing in my life. Neither did Uncle Cal or Uncle Dalton. This is the safest place you'll ever be."

Becca smiled and held out her arms for a hug. The look on Tristan's face stole Sydney's breath. She backed up, shifting her gaze. It was just too . . . much.

"Love you, Daddy."

"Love you, too, Becca. Night."

They switched on the night-light, shut the door halfway, and headed right. Sydney's hand paused on the doorknob, exhaustion seeping into her muscles. The throbbing in her head warned of more to come. "Well, good night," she said, refusing to turn. "See you in the morning."

She tried to close the door behind her, but he followed her in.

"What are you doing?"

He lifted a brow and began unbuttoning his cuffs. "Going to bed. I'm tired."

Her eyes widened. She must be imagining things. "Oh, I'm sorry, I thought this was going to be my room."

"It is."

With deliberate movements, he began removing his shirt, heading over to the dresser and opening the top drawer. The lean muscles of his back flexed as he riffled through items. She shook her head to clear it, then tried not to wince. "Wait, then why are you in here?"

"This is our room. We're married now, and I refuse to use separate rooms. I won't have Becca wondering why her parents aren't sleeping in the same bed or questioning our commitment."

It took a moment for the true knowledge to sink in.

"Oh, hell no," she growled. "I am not sharing a bedroom with you! We never agreed on this, and you're not going to bully me like you always do. You can set yourself up in the next bedroom. Becca won't notice."

He didn't even turn around. Never missing a beat, he un-buckled his belt and dropped his pants, leaving his gorgeous, perfect ass on display, cupped in black briefs. Her mouth fell open. Some weird sound came out, but she had no idea what it was—a protest or sigh of pleasure. Why, oh why, did he have to own a legendary ass?

"She will notice. Trust me, I'm too tired to ravish you tonight. The bed is a California king so as long as you don't roll over, you won't know I'm there. Though you've always been known to be a cuddler."

"I'm not sleeping with you!"

He shrugged. Mostly naked, he turned to face her, his drool-worthy body on display for her greedy gaze. Reminding her of how good it was between them. How her thighs had ached deliciously in the morning. How her breasts were so sensitized just the brush of her cotton shirt made her tremble. How his fingers had coaxed her to orgasm so quickly and fully she'd begged him for more and more and more . . .

"Your choice. But you will be staying in this room. Take the floor or the chair, if you're scared you can't keep your hands off me. I'm taking a shower."

Her mouth dropped open. He pivoted on his bare foot and disappeared into the bathroom.

A low moan escaped her lips. No. This couldn't be happening. He dared threaten her? He couldn't force her to sleep in the same bed with him, could he? Her mind was fuzzy and her intentions unclear. Her body raged to sneak into the bathroom, join him in the shower, and to hell with the consequences. But she refused.

Was she really going to allow him to bully her like this?

Hell no.

Setting her jaw, she changed in record time, ripping off

her wedding dress and putting on stretchy yoga pants and a long-sleeved T-shirt in dull gray. The most unappealing wedding night outfit ever created, she thought with satisfaction. She craved a shower, but she'd have to sacrifice for freedom. Tomorrow, when her head was clearer, she'd go over the rules of this relationship and set the boundaries. The water was still running, so she darted out of the bedroom and headed down the hall to the opposite end, grabbing an extra toothbrush and paste from Becca's adjacent bathroom. She quickly brushed her teeth, washed her face, and ripped the pins out of her hair, tugging her fingers through the tangles. Each knot made a moan of pain rumble from her chest, but she was done in record time. Tiptoeing, she picked the second door on the left.

It was a more masculine-type bedroom decorated in rich burgundy and gold, outfitted with heavy teak furniture. She locked the door, stripped back the covers, and lay down in the crisp white cotton sheets.

Heaven. Safety.

Take that, Tristan Pierce.

She fell into sleep with a satisfied smile on her lips.

The dream unfolded like the mist shrouding a sunrise: slowly, completely, overtaking all the light and softening all the sharp edges to wrap her in comfort, urging her to let go and surrender to sensation.

The hot, hard length of his body pressed against hers. Her tight nipples dragged across his chest, causing her to arch upward for more. She sighed and softened. No need to fight in a dream. She was safe here. A sense of dizziness overtook her, and she clung harder to him, digging her fingernails into his muscled arms. Her name echoed in her ears, but she frowned, not wanting to wake up yet. She was so tired, and he felt so good. No one would know how badly she craved him.

She floated briefly in the air, then fell back into softness, cloaked in the delicious scent of ocean waves and clean soap. So good. She buried her face in his neck and breathed deep, scraping her teeth down the ridge of his throat, wrapping her legs around his so they were pressed hip to hip, thigh to thigh, and his erection pushed against the material of her pants. Her name echoed again, more urgently, trying to break the spell. No, she didn't want to wake up yet. Just a few more minutes and she'd get Becca to school. Just a few more minutes . . .

A masculine groan rumbled in her ear. She spread her thighs wider in invitation, running her tongue along the length of his jaw, relishing his slight shudder. "Kiss me," she demanded.

His lips crushed hers. His tongue dove deep and gathered her taste. She kissed him back, nipping his lower lip, soaking in the dirty curse words that emitted from his carved lips, wanting him to do everything bad to her, every delicious, sexy fantasy he'd ever had . . .

"Baby, if you don't want me to rip off those pants and slide inside you right now, you better wake up and tell me no."

Her hands slipped down and squeezed his pulsing length, so hard and thick, so ready. God, she loved dreams. He thrust into her palms, and then his mouth was taking hers again, pressing her hard into the mattress. Loose strands of her hair tickled her face, and she felt reality bite into the fantasy, a warning in her brain springing to life, telling her to wake up, wake up, wake up . . .

Her eyes flew open. Whiskey-colored eyes blazed into hers, fogged with lust and a fierce hunger that drove the breath from her lungs. Lips an inch away, face tight with tension, as if he was just holding himself back from the edge. Sexual arousal beat from him in waves. She stiffened, suddenly fearful. Blinking furiously, she tried to catch up, tried to remember why this was a bad idea, and then—

"No!" Panic hit. He'd carried her back to the master bedroom and laid her on the bed. She frantically tried to push him off her, and that hungry gaze narrowed in warning. "Don't touch me."

He raised himself up on his elbow, staring at her with a hard ruthlessness that stripped away her barriers. "That's not what you were just telling me a second ago," he reminded her. His gaze swept over her needy, aching body. Her nipples poked from the thin material of her shirt, begging for his mouth.

"I was sleeping and you took advantage of me." She pushed again, trying to scramble out from underneath his body. Oh, God, she ached everywhere. Her panties were soaked, and her heart beat so hard she swore he saw. His nostrils flared as if he caught the scent of her arousal, and a hard smile touched his lips.

"Liar."

"I mean it, Tristan. I'm not sleeping with you." Her body raged in protest at her words, wanting him so badly she had to grit her teeth and hang on.

"You have to. I will not have my daughter questioning why her newly married, happy parents don't sleep in the same room together. Do you really want to confuse her like that?"

She bristled with frustration. "No. But I'm not about to let you use me to slake a physical itch you have."

His lower lip twitched. "Physical itch, huh? And you're saying you don't have the same spot you'd like scratched?"

"That's right."

"Then answer me one question."

"What?"

His eyes burned a hot whiskey gold. His voice dropped to a husky whisper. "If I slipped my finger into your panties, how wet would I find you?"

She let out a cry of outrage and punched at his chest. He only grinned in amusement at her temper, easily holding her off. "Get off me now!"

"Sure, baby." He rolled over, his impressive erection straining his briefs. With a casual disregard, he walked to the other side of the bed and crawled under the covers. He let out a deep sigh and turned to his side. "Don't worry, I won't bother you. Unless you ask nicely, of course. But just know, I happen to have a master key to every room in the house." He plumped the pillow and let out a sigh of contentment. "Oh, and try not to snore tonight, okay?"

"I don't snore!"

"Yeah, you do. Hopefully I'm too exhausted to care. Been a hell of a wedding day."

She fumed in silence, her body stiff and unyielding as she lay beside him. If he even thought of trying to touch her, she'd kill him. Her heart pounded wildly as she listened to his breathing. Within minutes, Sydney realized he was fast asleep.

Oh, she hated him. Still pissed off, she climbed out of bed, gathering up all the extra pillows from the closet. She carefully stacked them down the middle of the bed, creating a wall between them. The temptation to sneak out again was great, but she was so damn tired.

She got back into bed, and her body slowly relaxed into the mattress. She was wet and achy between her thighs. Maybe she'd sleep for a bit, then leave. She'd have to find the damn skeleton key first. Still, when he woke up and found her gone, it would teach him a valuable lesson. He had a point about Becca, but she hated the way he ordered her around. He needed to be taken down a few pegs. She'd sleep with him when she was ready—on her terms. One day.

Yes, just a few minutes and then she'd prove her point.

In just a few minutes . . .

She drifted off to sleep.

chapter nineteen

"I think we should take Becca horseback riding."

Sydney regarded him over her coffee. It had been two weeks since the wedding, and they were still dancing around each other. Every night she snuck into a different room, and every time, she woke up back in his bed. Once she'd hid in the library with a blanket on the leather armchair.

He always found her and carried her back to bed, then rolled to his side without touching her and went back to sleep.

At least the wall of pillows was always there.

It had become a game between them and a way to show him she refused to buckle under his orders. She liked the way his usual wall of ice crumbled in the face of his aggravation, especially when he spent over an hour to find her. Pushing him seemed the best attack to get him to deal with her on a more emotional scale. He kept his promise, though, and left her alone.

Unfortunately her body seemed to seek his out like a missile to a target. Every morning she woke up with her legs and arms entangled around his, her face pressed to his naked chest, and the pillows scattered around them like rubble on a battlefield. When she regained consciousness, she pulled away in horror, disentangling herself and rolling back to her own side, but it'd be too late.

His knowing gaze raked over her body with amusement each morning, relishing her hot cheeks and refusal to look at him. It was pure torture, and she didn't know how to keep herself away from him. The ache in her gut was growing worse, along with the need for him to touch her. To say more than a few surface words to her. To give her a real smile.

They worked side by side during the day, staying out of each other's way and remaining polite. In the evening, they ate together, spent time with Becca, and then went to their separate computers to work. They couldn't keep on this path or one of them was going to break.

Sydney bet it'd be her.

She needed to force him to deal with her away from work and the bedroom. Horseback riding seemed the perfect opportunity.

"You mean for the lessons I bought for her birthday?" he asked.

"Yes, I think we can all use a day together."

He was sorting his briefcase for the day ahead. Dressed in a crisp black suit, red tie, shiny wing tip shoes, and engraved onyx cuff links, he emanated male grace, power, and hotness. Hair pushed back from his brow in brushed waves, jaw clean shaven, his ocean scent filling the air. Mornings were always hectic, but he kept completely calm through breakfast madness, her regular argument regarding Becca's wardrobe, the lost library book, and the toast he'd made too crunchy without melting the butter until it was invisible. Instead of getting annoyed, he remade it to perfection and discovered the missing library book tucked in the couch cushion.

Sydney finally got her off to the bus on time and scrambled back to gulp a last cup of coffee before heading out. "When did you want to go?" he asked.

"Saturday. I'd like for us all to go together. But you don't have to ride if it makes you uncomfortable." She threw out the challenge in a casual manner. He looked up from his briefcase with a frown.

"I can ride a horse."

She fought a smile. He'd always been so easy to bait. "Really? Somehow I can't picture you on a horse. It's messy. And I thought you were afraid of horses."

His frown deepened. "I'm not scared of horses. I can handle them just fine. It's a good idea. Let's go."

"Great. I scheduled the tile installation for Saturday, so maybe we can go early? I can set up a nine a.m. ride, and we can go for brunch. Then we can drop Becca off at Morgan's so we can stay late at the site."

"Fine."

She nodded. It was time to see if they could make this work together. Becca needed them to be comfortable with each other and make up a solid family unit. She deserved Sydney's best effort. "Are you coming to the site dressed like that?"

He cocked his head. "I have a real estate deal to close first. I'll meet you over there in a few hours."

"Do you need me to bring you some old clothes?"

He frowned. "No. This is my old suit."

She let out a sigh. "Of course. How did I not notice?"

He lifted an eyebrow. "Funny. What's that smell?"

She motioned over to the Crock-Pot. "Stew. It simmers all day so we'll be all set when we get home to eat without a lot of prep. I'll throw a salad together with it."

He lifted the lid and stared into the pot with something close to wonderment. "And it just cooks together in there?"

Her lip twitched. "Yep. Like magic."

"My mother loved making stew."

"It's her recipe. Of course, it's not as good. I wasn't too interested when she tried to show me how to cook, but I did keep all her recipes."

They stayed quiet for a bit, lost in their thoughts of Diane. "I appreciate you cooking. It's never been my strong suit."

"It's okay. I actually like cooking."

"It's Wednesday. Are you going to poker night? I know you haven't gone in a while."

She shifted her feet. Raven held poker night every week at My Place, and it had been a safe haven for Sydney. Laughing and talking with her friends allowed her to blow off some steam and soak in the power of female friendship. But since the truth about Becca came out, Morgan and Raven avoided her. She didn't know if she had the guts to go back, even though she was a bridesmaid in Morgan's upcoming wedding. "I don't think so. Things have been a bit strained between us."

He studied her for a while, as if trying to come to a decision. "I'll talk to them, Syd. I don't want them holding a grudge. It doesn't help anyone."

Irritation prickled her nerve endings. "I don't need you to

fight my battles any longer," she said. "I appreciate it, but this is something I need to take care of myself."

"Then go tonight. They're your friends, and you owe them a conversation."

He was right. It had been easier to avoid the confrontation, but it was time to say her piece. She owed her friends that much, and then they could make their own decision whether or not they wanted to continue the friendship. "I'll think about it."

He nodded, accepting her decision. "Fine. I'll check in with you later." His tone morphed back into the cool, clipped manner she was getting accustomed to. Her soul mourned the softening and intimacy between them before she'd told him about Becca. She wondered if she'd waited longer to tell him, would their bond have been more unshakable?

No. Any type of foundation they had laid crumbled to dust the moment he learned she'd lied to him. Sydney wondered if he'd ever be able to truly forgive her, let alone trust her again. She answered him with a quick good-bye, then left the mansion with a heavy heart.

Work was a balm to her soul. The hours flew by as she directed the renovation, got her hands dirty, and saw real progress being made. She was able to leave at a decent hour, help Becca with her homework, get dinner on the table, and change in time to get out to the restaurant. Tristan walked in minutes before she was due to leave.

"Daddy!" Becca flew into his arms, and he caught her, whirling her around in the air. She leaned against the wall and watched them. Heads bent together, smiles framing similar faces: Sydney soaked in the beauty of seeing them like this. It was so obvious how Becca's eyes were more gold than green, and her nose had that same sharp look. They were both lefties and allergic to strawberries. They were stubborn and sarcastic and beautiful, and each day they grew more bonded. Sydney had wondered if she'd feel any type of jealousy since Becca had been hers alone for so long. But she didn't. It was as if all the broken pieces had finally been mended together in a picture of sheer beauty.

"Mama put dinner aside for you. You're late again." Becca wrinkled her nose, but her father kissed her forehead, and her frown immediately smoothed out.

"Sorry, sweetheart. Mama and I are doing a big project, so things will be busy for a while. But I've scheduled your horse-back riding lessons for Saturday, and we'll all go together. How does that sound?"

Her daughter squealed and jumped with glee. "Yes! Oh, I can't wait, it's going to be so much fun. But are you sure you can ride a horse?"

He puffed out with pure male pride. "Of course I can. I'm like a regular horse wrangler."

Becca glanced over, and Sydney shook her head. "Lie," she confirmed. "Your father has never even seen a stable, let alone horse poo."

That made her break into giggles. "Mama, have you ridden before?"

Sydney shook her head. "Nope, this is going to be new to me, too. We'll learn together."

"Like a family!"

Tristan cleared his throat. "Yes, because we are a family." He shrugged off his jacket and moved toward the kitchen. "Thanks again for leaving me dinner. You heading out?"

Her palms sweated, but she was determined to face down her fears. It was time to see if her friends would stick by her side. "Yes. Don't wait up."

He lifted a brow. "I will, anyway," he said with a touch of warning. Was that a gleam of mischief in his eye, or was she hallucinating? No. Playing hide-and-go-seek every evening wasn't Tristan's way of having fun. He was too damn mad at her still.

"Suit yourself. Bye, sweetheart. See you in the morning."

"Bye, Mama."

She left them cozying up at the kitchen table and drove to My Place. Poker nights on Wednesday consisted of only females, and ranged from five to ten people on average. When she walked through the saloon-type doors, the sound of feminine laughter and scents of sweet potato fries, bacon, and good old-fashioned grease filled the air. As she neared the table, a chorus of greetings echoed in her ear.

"Sydney! It's been a while since we've seen you. Congrats on the wedding," Carla said, jumping up to hug her. She was a sweet-natured librarian with a tendency to get crazy during high stakes and reveal her fabulous potty mouth.

"Thank you," she said, hugging back.

Morgan gave her a tight smile. "Good to see you, Syd," she said quietly. Her gaze quickly dropped, as if she couldn't stand looking her in the face.

Sydney's heart ached, and she swallowed back fearful nerves. "You, too."

Raven came from around the bar and slid a Sweet Hot Chris cocktail across the table. Her famous champagne mixed drink was a favorite on poker nights and was dubbed for all the sexy celebrities named Chris she lusted after, such as Chris Hemsworth, Chris Pine, Chris Pratt, and Chris Evans. Dalton always laughed and said she'd named it before she met him, or it would've been the Sweet Hot Dalton.

Raven actually agreed.

"Thanks," Sydney said, searching her friend's dark eyes for any type of understanding or compassion. She found only distance. "Raven, I really wanted to talk to you tonight. With Morgan."

Raven nodded slowly. "I think that's a great idea."

She swallowed. "After poker?"

"Sure. Let's play a few rounds, and I'll cut the night a bit early."

"Thanks."

She slid into her seat, opened her purse, and bought her chips. They were just about to begin the first round when the door opened and a woman dressed in snug jeans, a cashmere cardigan, and Ugg boots waltzed in. Her soft brown hair was swept up in a fashionable ponytail. Her makeup was flawless, and she sported her signature bright red lips.

Sydney almost closed her eyes in horror.

Not her. Anyone but her. She just didn't have the energy tonight.

But when she peeked back, the woman hadn't left. She was talking with Raven, who nodded and motioned her to take a seat at the table.

Cynthia.

The one she'd battled with after the ballet and Tristan's new enemy. Right away, the woman's dark brown eyes focused on her. Was that a glint of evil glee in her eyes or was she being paranoid? Oh, God, why had she lost it and brought Christian Grey into their fight?

"Sydney Greene-Seymour," Cynthia purred, strolling over to take the seat next to her. Had she emphasized her last name on purpose? "Fancy meeting you here."

"Hi, Cynthia. I didn't know you played poker."

"Oh, it's been on my bucket list for years, so when I heard about this little weekly gathering, I thought it would be fun to try it out." She handed Raven a large bill and took her chips. Raven introduced her to the women, who engaged in casual chatter, and Morgan began to deal the cards. Sydney decided the entire evening was cursed. She'd concentrate on playing poker and try not to draw any extra attention. Small circles of conversation rose up around her. Cynthia sipped her wine, and they played the first few rounds. She began to relax. Maybe Cynthia really did just want to play cards and make some friends. Maybe Sydney had overreacted. How many times had she warned Becca not to look for trouble until it bit you on the ass?

Well, not in those same exact words.

"Jacks are wild," Morgan called out, dealing another round. Sydney glanced at her cards.

"Rumor has it you got married two weeks ago," Cynthia said casually, her glossy red fingernails sorting through her cards. "Tristan Pierce, huh? The man who took Becca to the ballet recital? The one you said was just a *friend*?"

Oh, yeah. She'd been right all along. Cynthia had just been biding her time.

"That's right."

"Congratulations."

"Thank you."

"Lucy told me Becca was saying in school he was her real father. Imagine my surprise when I heard. How did Becca take the news? I mean, I think we all assumed her father was your ex-husband."

A hot flush of anger flooded her. She swallowed and tried not to engage. "I'm glad the truth is finally out and that we can all finally be together," she said simply. "Becca is happy. We all are."

"How wonderful." Cynthia tapped a finger against her cards. "But I'm sure Becca was rather confused regarding your short marriage. Has she forgiven you for lying about her father?" She gave a mock shudder. "The whole thing must've been so stressful. Keeping such a big secret in a small town and all. Such awful gossip. What made you finally tell the truth? And get married?"

Sydney stiffened. Becca was excited to tell everyone her parents were now married. Excited about having Tristan in her life. Taking such innocent happiness and twisting it into hurt was wrong on too many levels. She knew then the only reason Cynthia had come to poker night was to get her nasty gossip and spread it around the school. She'd hoped to find Sydney here. It had been no coincidence. The woman wanted to play in the gutter?

Fine.

She'd play.

"Two, please," she told Morgan, flipping down her cards. She scooped up the next two and studied her hand. "Becca was very excited to be reunited with Tristan. We're happy now, and try to protect Becca. There're many people out there who are quite vicious and want to hurt a poor little girl just for some gossip. You know the type. Right?"

"One," Cynthia said. She perused her cards with an air of casual confidence. "How terrible. Who would be so mean? At least you figured out who her father is. Sleeping with two men at the same time can be quite tricky, but I'm just over the moon it all worked out. He even married you! Now, that's a man with honor right there. I always knew the Pierce brothers took responsibility seriously."

A red mist blinded her. Her hands clutched her cards. What would this woman think if she threw out the known fact her husband was cheating on her? Not that she'd ever go there. She could make her point a bit more subtly.

"You know a lot about that sort of responsibility, don't you, Cynthia?" she asked innocently. "Isn't this your fourth marriage?"

"Third," Cynthia gritted out.

"Ah, that's right. My bad. It's so nice you were able to take a risk that many times after failure. I admire you. I truly do. I want to be that brave one day."

The woman's gaze swiveled around and locked with hers.

"Call," Morgan said.

"Me too," Carla said.

The other two women folded, along with Raven. All gazes swung to Sydney. "Raise." She threw in three chips. Everyone whistled.

"Cynthia, you can fold or see Sydney's raise to stay in the game," Raven explained.

A bloodthirsty smile curved her lips. The woman flicked her wrist, and three bright red chips fell onto the green felt table. "I'll see your raise."

"Back to you, Syd," Morgan called out.

"Raise," she muttered, putting in more chips.

Cynthia shrugged and gave a fake laugh. "How fun. Things are getting interesting." More chips fell to the center of the table.

"I raise again," she said.

And it began. Each of them kept raising the other until a staggering pile of red chips lay in the center of the table, and they had nothing left to bet. The women stared in shocked silence.

"Umm, guys. That's a lot of money. Are you sure about this?" Raven asked, a frown creasing her brow.

Carla cackled with glee. "It's too late now! They're all in. Show your cards, ladies!"

Sydney showed her hand. "Straight. Ace high," she declared.

"Cynthia, what about you?" Raven asked.

Everyone held their breath. Sydney's heart pounded in a mad jungle rhythm. She had to win. In some weird way, it would be symbolic for her, and prove everything would work out with Tristan. She hated the way Cynthia made the whole thing seem ugly, even though she knew it could be the truth. He'd married her to give Becca a family, not because he loved her. But with this one hand, maybe her fate would change. Good would triumph. Maybe it would show they'd always been meant to be together. Maybe . . .

"Full house."

The table exploded with noise, and Cynthia gave her a triumphant smile. Sydney stared helplessly at all the lost chips and her cards. Stupid tears clogged her throat.

Ridiculous. It didn't matter. It was only a game and proved nothing.

"Are you okay?" Raven whispered in her ear. "You look weird."

She blinked and forced a smile. "I'm fine. Congrats, Cynthia. Great hand."

"Thanks." Cynthia bent over so she could utter the next words softly against her ear. "Don't push me. Already your daughter is the subject of gossip at the whole school. It could get worse, or better, depending on if I step in." Her smug smile made Sydney sick. "Next time you want to talk about my many marriages, remember I didn't have to play eenie meenie miney mo when it came to figuring out who the father is."

Sydney jerked back. With a mocking wink, Cynthia stood up and gathered her purse. For one moment, pain hit her in the gut. The idea of anyone talking about Becca because of Sydney's mistake made her want to howl like a wolf and tear Cynthia limb from limb. She'd kept her life simple for the past years, so no one had stirred up gossip. Now she was being picked apart and analyzed because of her past.

It was all her fault.

Suddenly Raven stepped in front of Cynthia. "Hey, what did you say to her?"

Cynthia waved her hand in the air. "Oh, nothing. We know each other from the school. Our daughters go to ballet together, right, Sydney?"

Sydney rose to her feet. Very quietly, she looked the woman in the eye. "Yes, that's right. Our daughters are also in the same class together at school. They're friends."

Cynthia never flinched. Didn't matter. Sydney wasn't going to make matters worse or put her daughter at risk of being teased or bullied. Morgan walked over and stood shoulder to shoulder with Raven. "Bullshit," Raven said calmly. "I heard what you said to Syd."

Morgan joined in, her Southern accent taking on a twang. "Are you trying to hurt a little girl because of your need to gossip and spread rumors?"

The woman gave a nervous laugh and took a few steps to the side. "No, of course not. You must've misunderstood."

"We don't allow mean girls to join our poker table." Raven's mild voice contradicted her badass attitude. In her jeans, black boots, and black tank top showing off her shoulder tat, she cut an intimidating figure. "Sydney is family. I think all of us have issues in our past we'd rather not discuss, especially with people we can't trust. Do you have a problem with this?"

Cynthia's mouth fell open. Sydney bet not many women challenged her with such stark honesty, ready to defend rather than tear apart. "No. As I said, it's just a misunderstanding. It was lovely to meet you ladies. Good night."

"Cynthia."

She looked back at Raven with wariness. "Yes?"

"Don't come back. And if you keep spreading gossip about Becca, I promise the Pierce family will make you regret it."

They watched Cynthia scurry out of the bar and slam the door behind her.

Morgan shook her head. "Goodness gracious, that woman is loathsome. Imagine using little girls to get attention. Plus, she took all our money!"

Sydney laughed, reaching out to take each of their hands and squeeze. God, she'd missed them. Forgotten how powerful a group of women can be when they unite. She'd had no idea how truly lonely she'd been without having girlfriends to talk to. "Thank you. I wasn't up to my usual fighting standards."

Raven squeezed her hand back. "I'll set you up with Xavier any time. For now, you have us."

"Always," Morgan said.

They took her side even when they were mad. Between fighting her feelings for Tristan and the whirlwind wedding and losing her friends, the emotions roared up and strained against the wall she'd erected for protection. Her lower lip trembled. Morgan and Raven shared a look. "Uh-oh. She's gonna break. Let's get the others out of here," Raven instructed.

"Done," Morgan said.

In a matter of minutes, the other ladies left, and she found a shot glass of whiskey in front of her at the table. "Drink," Raven ordered. "It'll settle you."

With trembling hands, she tipped the glass back and finished it in one swallow. Raven lifted a brow. "Nice. You've been practicing."

Sydney choked out a half laugh. "I hate crying. I feel all weepy and emotional lately. I feel so damn . . . weak."

Raven dropped into the seat next to her. "Nah, not weak. It's just all that ugly mess of truth coming up to be dealt with. There's been a hell of a lot going on in your life this past month."

"Yeah." She struggled to find the words. "I know you're

both mad. But thank you for sticking up for me tonight. It meant a lot."

Morgan blew out a breath and shook her head. Her smart bob swished across her shoulders. "You lied to us. You lied to Tristan. I needed some time to sort it out so I can talk to you without losing my temper. You know I can't have children. So when I heard you kept a child from her biological father, on purpose, it hit all my hot buttons."

Misery flooded her. Yes, she'd had her reasons, but her friends didn't know. She'd never told them the truth of her and Tristan's past relationship or the issues. To them, she'd done it with a cruel casualty and hurt the Pierce family. "I know. I kept the truth to myself for so many reasons, but I also know it may not be enough for you to understand. All I can do is explain my side of the story. I didn't keep Becca a secret to hurt anyone, especially Tristan. I was trying to protect them both."

"Tell us," Raven said simply.

So, Sydney did. She told them about their past and that disastrous night Tristan left. She told them about her first wedding, the end of her marriage, and the decision to raise Becca on her own. She poured out her heart and soul, refusing to hold back, until finally her voice trailed off into silence. Drained, she slumped in the chair, but her soul was light. These women had shared their own secrets over the past year, but she'd always held back. She saw now how clearly a friendship deserved true give-and-take. It took trust.

Raven gave a sigh. "I was running wild with my best friend, Izzy, at the age you got pregnant. There'd be no way in the world I could settle down and deal with a baby. I was too hurt from my father's death. Too broken. And I know for a fact Dalton, Cal, and Tristan were in no shape to build a solid future or be a parent then."

Morgan nodded. "Their family was ripped apart. Cal said all they did was fight. I can see how scared you'd be to tell him about the baby when he was desperate to leave."

"I did the best I could at the time," she said softly. "I honestly felt like I had no other choice when Tristan left. And when Becca was born, I knew I'd do anything to keep her safe and happy. I never had that feeling about anyone before."

"I don't know if I would've made the same decision, but I respect your choices," Morgan said. "And I'm here for you whenever you need me."

"Me too," Raven said.

"Thanks, guys." The tears broke free and ran down her cheeks. She wiped them away with a laugh. "Ugh, I'm acting like such a girl."

"We forgive you. Take another shot." Raven refilled her shot glass. "It's the good stuff I keep tucked away for female emergencies."

"I won't be able to pass the Breathalyzer test." Raven administered her own DWI test at the bar to make sure everyone could drive safely after poker night, or she called a cab.

Morgan pushed the glass toward her. "I'll drive you home, sweetie. Drink up."

The next glass warmed her stomach and settled her nerves. Finally she was able to take a breath without sniffling. "Thanks."

"I think the big question is where you and Tristan are with all this. Do you still love him?" Morgan asked.

"Yes. I never stopped. Even though he's acting like an asshole lately," she added. Her mind steeped in the memories. "I think I loved that man the moment I met him at eight years old. Diane used to tell me to be patient. Even after everything that happened, I felt we had a shot at something brand-new, but then I told him about Becca and everything is different. I don't think he ever loved me the way I did him. Maybe it's time I try to live with it. Stop torturing myself."

Raven burst into laughter. Sydney frowned. She thought it was funny? "Hey, I'm bleeding for you here and you're amused?"

"No, I'm sorry. Don't you know he loves you, Syd? It's so damn obvious. The way he looked at you on your wedding day. The times he'd stomp around all mad at you because you wouldn't listen to him. The goofy expression he gets when he spots you with Becca. The man is certifiably nuts about you."

"I agree," Morgan jumped in. "I knew there was something big that had happened between you, and now it all makes sense. Plus, your chemistry is off the charts. You two in the same room together makes me want to jump Cal immediately."

Sydney groaned. "No, that's just sex. We've always had mind-blowing, amazing sex. Tristan wants to base our marriage on sex and raising Becca and working together. In theory, it sounds solid. Reasonable. But in my heart—"

"It sucks," Raven finished. "Because you want his love, not his dick."

Morgan giggled. "Well said, sister."

"Well, I want both," Sydney admitted. They all shared a glance and burst into laughter. "Right now, I refuse to sleep with him. We've spent the last weeks either barely talking or fighting. I'll get all mixed up with the emotional versus physical thing. Men never get that."

Morgan sighed. "Emotional stuff is harder for them. Their brains get a bit foggy when things get complicated. They solve a lot of their issues through sex."

"A pleasurable but less effective way of communication," Raven added. "The problem is Tristan wants you just as bad as you want him. He's just not able to sort it out. I understand so much more now, Syd. Why you kept Becca from him. How he pulled away from you. But I've also never seen Tristan so hurt before. In his mind, I think he was ready to give you everything he had, and when he found out the truth, it dragged him back to the past and made him question himself. I think he's scared shitless."

Morgan nodded. "I agree."

Emotion clogged her throat. Her friends were right. It took him so much to allow himself to be vulnerable that he'd shut himself away from any possibility of loving her again. The knowledge of how deeply she'd hurt him broke her inside. And still, the main question haunted her. Could they find their way back to each other? Could he learn to let go and allow himself to love her the way she deserved?

"What should I do?" she asked. "There's still a chance for us."

"I know this advice may suck, but maybe he just needs more time. Time to build back the trust and make him see how important you are to him."

"Or you can seduce him until you have him wrapped up tight and then torture him till he admits he loves you?" Morgan suggested.

Raven whistled. "I love your ruthless side. It's just so badass."

Morgan smiled. "I'm learning from you."

"I think for now we need to focus on Becca and spending time together," Sydney said. "He's been so distant."

"Another good reason for sex. It breaks down the barriers," Raven said.

"I just don't know if I can handle that type of hurt again," she said softly. "Maybe he'll never really love me the way I need."

"Maybe he's just being stubborn," Morgan said. "The only way to find out is time. But I wouldn't hold back. You're fighting for something greater here. If you open up a bit, he may not be able to push you away anymore."

"You could be right." Tears stung her eyes. "Thank you for listening. All this time, I've had no one to talk to. With Diane gone, and having to keep my secret, I've been so lonely."

The women linked hands. "We're always here for you. There's never any need to be lonely again," Morgan said firmly.

"We're all family now," Raven said. "Sisters. How cool is that?"

Morgan caught her breath. "Is it almost official? You and Dalton?"

Raven grinned. "I found the ring hidden in one of my shoe boxes." She shook her head. "Don't men know never to hide anything with a woman's shoes?"

Morgan and Sydney clapped their hands with delight. "I can't wait!"

"Yeah, it's kinda fun to imagine when and mess with his head."

Sydney grinned. "You're so bad. Okay, love you guys. I

have to get home. Between the poker, Cynthia, and spilling my heart out, I'm exhausted."

"I hear ya," Raven said. "It's been a hell of a day. Started for me way too early. Guy at the bar was spiking his coffee with Baileys and went nuts. Had to throw him out."

"What did he do?" she asked.

"Mooned me in front of my customers."

Sydney pressed her lips together, trying not to laugh. "Well, that's not too terrible. I haven't seen a good mooning in forever."

Raven raised a brow. "From the front."

They paused for a moment. Then burst into laughter.

Lord, she'd missed her friends. Knowing they were back on her side made all the difference.

Morgan drove her home, and after quickly checking on Becca, she hesitated in front of the master bedroom. She didn't have the energy to try hiding in another room tonight. But she wasn't ready to have sex with him, either. She needed to sort through some of what Raven had told her regarding Tristan and figure out if she could break through the walls he'd built around his heart.

Squaring her shoulders, she marched in. He was sitting up in bed, the television droning low in the background. A book lay open in his lap. He had an obsession with Steve Berry books. He looked up from the page. "How'd it go?"

She lost her voice for a moment. All that gorgeous toasty skin displayed by his bare chest stole rational thought. Her nipples peaked, ready to come out and play, so she casually crossed her arms in front of her breasts to hide them. "Good. We talked. I'm glad I went. How's Becca?"

He broke into a genuine, happy smile. Those white teeth flashed and showed off the result of Diane's insistence he wear braces through the seventh grade. "She ate all the stew, even though there was stuff mixed together."

"How'd you get her to do that?"

Guilt flickered across his face. "Bribed her with a second dessert."

Her lips twitched. She'd tried that tactic before but it had stopped working. Guess it was different with Tristan. "Works for me. Sometimes I feel like I'm on a battleground and have to make certain decisions to offset blowing it all up."

"Got homework done and watched *America's Funniest Home Videos*."

"Ah, that's one of her favorites. Here's another hint: Anything on HGTV puts her in a trance. She loves it."

"You're kidding."

She laughed. "No, I'm serious. She's definitely going to take after you. Besides redesigning her room on a rotating basis, she adores *Fixer Upper* and says she'd love to have her own show one day."

His eyes glinted with a rush of emotion that threatened to burst her heart. "She kind of amazes me. I'm just afraid she may be smarter than me one day and then it's all over."

They shared a smile, and the surge of connection lit between them. The air sizzled with electricity and sexual awareness. Suddenly her muscles loosened, and liquid heat warmed between her legs. His gaze narrowed, raking over her figure, as if he already scented her arousal and was thinking of crossing the room to pull her into his arms, take her mouth, spread her thighs, and—

"Sydney?"

His rough growl stroked her ears. She shuddered. Blinked.

"I'm gonna—gonna—take a shower. Don't wait up."

She dashed past him and dove for the door, shutting and locking it behind her. She waited breathlessly as the minutes ticked by. Finally the light clicked off and she sagged in relief.

She'd be safe another night.

They were playing a dangerous game. And eventually, someone was going to lose.

She pushed the thought out of her mind and turned on the shower.

He listened to the running water and wondered whether she was looking for her vibrator.

Groaning, he rolled over to take the pressure off his aching dick. When he'd hired the moving people to pack up all her stuff, he'd made sure to retrieve her personal toy from behind the basket of nail polish. He kept it in his side bedroom drawer, tucked under his briefs for safekeeping. He figured it'd come in handy one day.

He was looking forward to it.

His hand craved to slide down his body and give relief, but he didn't know how fast she'd return. He hoped to God he didn't have to go searching for her again in a different bedroom. Since that first night she'd begged for his kiss, she hadn't woken up when he placed her in his bed and tucked her in. It had taken him over an hour to find her last spot— in the damn closet with the goose down comforter on the third floor. It would've been funny as hell if he hadn't been so pissed at the thought Becca could wake up and find her mother hiding from her father. He'd growled and threatened, but she just stuck her chin up in the air and told him she wanted a separate bedroom.

She was so damn stubborn.

The water finally stopped. He imagined those naked curves glistening as droplets clung to her white skin. Imagined sliding his fingers through her neatly trimmed fiery hair and stroking her to climax. He'd make her pay for forcing him to play this waiting game. He didn't think he could take much more. Eventually one of them had to break and dissipate the crackling tension. Once he got her back in his bed, maybe they'd be able to settle into a more normal routine. A marriage that made sense. They'd blow off all this lingering steam and move forward as partners, in both business and parenting.

He stiffened as she tiptoed inside, listening to him in the dark. He deliberately evened out his breath until she moved past him and dressed. Her hourglass shadow tempted his vision when she dropped the towel, and he held back a groan at the thrust of her hard nipples and luscious curve of her ass. He waited, and sure enough, the wall of pillows began taking form behind him. His fingers itched to tear them apart and grab her, but he was able to tamp down on the urge and continue breathing. Finally the closet door squeaked, and the sound of fabric whooshing down drifted in the air. Then she climbed on the bed, dragging a blanket over her body and settling on the farthest edge of the mattress.

She hadn't gotten under the covers.

Tristan was torn between wanting to strangle her and laughing. Did she really think she was safer that way? One tug and he'd smash the line of pillows, grab her, and swallow her protests with his kisses until she begged for him to take her. But now wasn't the time. He still wanted to take it slow for both of them, so when he finally claimed her body, he wouldn't have any lingering ideas about love. After learning about Becca, he felt way too vulnerable, which scared the crap out of him. Even this past week, she'd come dangerously close to thawing him out. He loved watching her face light up when she spoke with Becca, the soft glint in her eyes reminding him so much of his mother. He admired her adept and sometimes ruthless ability to deal with multiple suppliers and workers on the job site populated mostly by men. He ached to take her in his arms and comfort her when she rubbed her temples with exhaustion but still managed to make dinner without complaint. And when she smiled at him, forgetting they were temporary enemies, his gut clenched into a hard ball of need.

No, he couldn't risk his heart with her again. When he finally made his move, it would be about sex, plain and simple. No more getting his heart all messed up.

It was so much easier this way.

chapter twenty

Sydney looked up at the huge chestnut horse and took a step back. "Hey, why don't you two go and I'll wait here?"

Becca giggled. Perched on top of a white pony, her pink helmet strapped under her chin, she looked happy and at ease. Unlike her mother. "You can do it, Mama. Don't be afraid."

The horse wrangler patted the horse's rump. "Bam Bam is very gentle. He won't hurt you. Now, swing your leg up and over."

She looked to Tristan for help, but he only raised his brow in pure challenge. Damn. The man looked sexy as hell riding a sleek black horse, hands loosely fisting the reins like a pro. Dressed in jeans, brown boots, and a plaid button-down shirt, he should've seemed more approachable. Instead, he gazed at her from behind a pair of aviator glasses, reminding her of some macho Western cowboy refusing to bend to society's rules.

So hot.

She shook off her thoughts and followed orders. Her cushioned butt sat in the saddle, and she listened to the instructions on how to keep her heels down and direct Bam Bam by using the reins. Their teacher, Jim, seemed relaxed and in charge, keeping up a conversation with Becca as he guided her around the field a few times to get comfortable. Tristan was situated in the middle, and she was at the back. Seemed Bam Bam was the ultimate follower and preferred to go at a slower pace.

Fine with her.

They started out on the trail at a leisurely walk. Spring had kicked in and turned the trees back to vibrant green. Buds exploded into eye-popping colored flowers, and the sky was a deep powder blue with fat fluffy clouds. The breeze tugged at her hair, full of earthy, woodsy smells. The creak of the leather saddle and the steady tread of hooves soothed her ears. After a few minutes, she realized Bam Bam wasn't about to go charging anywhere and settled in.

Tristan slowed his pace and spoke over his shoulder. "Morgan called. Asked if Becca wanted to sleep over tonight at the new house. Is that okay with you?"

Bam Bam stopped to tear at some tasty leaves, munching with slow precision. She tugged, but he didn't move. "Sure. Morgan spoils her rotten, and that will give me an opportunity to work later."

The wrangler called out, "Kick with your right foot and pull your reins up! We don't want them eating on the trail."

"Great, I'm already in trouble," she muttered, tugging harder. "Bam Bam, let's go."

He shot her a bored look and tore another leaf off the branch.

Tristan grinned, easing his horse closer. "Kick him harder, Syd. At the same time, tug up sharply."

She did, and the horse practically rolled his eyes before

allowing himself to be guided back in line. "How come your horse is named Dancer, Becca's is Champion, and mine is from *The Flintstones*?"

"He senses your unease," he told her with a laugh. "Keep your legs tight to his belly and a shorter grip on the reins. He needs to know you're in charge."

"How the heck do you know about this stuff?"

"My father used to watch John Wayne movies."

She shook her head, fighting a grin. "Funny."

"Thanks."

Becca was up ahead, chattering away to her new friend Jim. Sydney cleared her throat. He deserved to hear what Cynthia had told her Wednesday night. "I wanted to tell you there may be some gossip going around at Becca's school. About you being her father. We just may need to keep an eye on her and make sure she's not getting harassed."

His voice turned hard. "How'd you find out?"

"At poker night, Cynthia joined us."

"Who's Cynthia?"

"Bad Mom from the recital."

"Crap. Are you serious? Tell me she wouldn't hurt Becca just to spread mean-spirited gossip."

"She might. I was going to have a talk with the principal, but I don't want to cause attention needlessly. I just wanted you to know about it in case Becca says anything."

He muttered a curse. "I'll put a stop to it if she tries to spread rumors."

"Raven and Morgan already threatened her. Scared Cynthia to death. Told her not to mess with the Pierce family. It was epic."

"I bet. Though I'm sure you didn't need it. Becca told me about your confrontation with Emma's mother."

"Ah, yes. I'm afraid Becca overheard some of my, er, colorful language."

"But it worked." He paused. "I'm glad you spoke with Morgan and Raven."

He sounded genuine. At least, he didn't want to see her punished by his family. It was something. "Me too."

The horses eased down a small hill into the woods. Thick trees blocked the sun. Sticks and twigs snapped under the horses' feet. A sense of peace flowed through her, a balance of nature and quiet, and being with the two people she loved most in life.

"Everyone doing okay back there?" Jim called out.

"We're good," Tristan said.

"Excellent. We're heading up this hill to the clearing. Just follow me."

The other horses pulled ahead, but Bam Bam paused in front of a large branch and shot her a look. "Come on," she urged him. "Just walk over. It's not big."

He snorted. Ducked his head and began eating more leaves. Frustration nipped at her nerves. "Bam Bam, go!" She kicked and pulled the reins, but he ignored her. Suddenly he lifted his head and stood stock-still. A terrible smell hit her nostrils. "Ugh, yuck." The sound of poop hitting the ground made her want to gag. So did the scent. "You're eating too many leaves, dude. Let's go."

His stomach emptied, he began to go forward, then took a sharp right.

"No, not that way—this way." She tugged, but he was

heading directly past a large pricker bush. Tons of deadly thorns stuck out at wicked angles. "Left! Go left, Bam Bam—ow!"

Her left side got dragged past the bush, the needles poking into her clothes with wicked darts of pain. The horse gave her a sideways look and opened his mouth to gnaw on his bit. Was he laughing at her?

Tristan suddenly appeared before her, looking like a god on the Black Stallion. "You okay?"

"No! He pooped because he keeps eating leaves, and he dragged me into a pricker bush. He's mean."

His lips twitched in amusement. "He's just looking for direction. Come on, Bam Bam. Follow me." He whistled, leading his horse a few paces forward, and Bam Bam began walking again, closing the gap between them. "See? Just keep urging him ahead with kicks."

Oh yeah, he was playing her for a fool. She wasn't stupid. This horse didn't like her. "Is Becca doing well?" she asked.

"She's doing great. Don't you think this would be fun to do on a regular basis? Fresh air, family time, and Becca learns about horses."

Ugh. No way. "Great," she forced herself to utter. "Fun things are supposed to be stressful."

"What do you mean? Don't you remember the time you came with us camping?"

The memory hit full force. "Oh, my God, I'd forgotten about that debacle! Your father had some crazy idea about going river rafting on the Esopus and decided camping out would be fun."

Tristan shook his head. The sun bathed him in a gorgeous light, giving him an almost ethereal halo. "He thought it would be easy but had no clue what to do. Dalton fell off the raft and almost floated away."

"Yes! And your mom freaked out and dove in after him, almost crashing on the rocks. I was so scared I just hung on to the raft and prayed to survive."

"Then the tent collapsed in the middle of the night during the thunderstorm."

"And we were covered in mud and freezing cold," she added.

"Cal and I had a big fight over who got the last hot dog."

"We had to walk almost a mile in the pitch-dark to get to the bathrooms, and your mom and I were freaking out about bears."

"And Dad lost one of his shoes and declared we were all going home the very next morning," Tristan finished, his golden eyes full of mirth.

She fought past the giggles. "No one talked to each other for the rest of the day, and we were hungry and tired and wet and miserable. And I swear, I think it was a raccoon that got Christian's shoe. Remember how he had to drive barefoot?"

Tristan laughed with her. "See, not every family outing is a good thing. Worst vacation ever."

Another memory flickered and teased her vision. "You kept me safe," she said quietly. "Do you remember?"

"What are you talking about?"

"In the raft. After Dalton went over the side and your mom dove in after him. I was scared and clinging to the raft, and you came right over. Wrapped your arms around me and told me you wouldn't let me fall off."

God, it was all coming back to her. The feeling of being safe with him, knowing he'd never let anything happen. His shoulders stiffened, and his voice sounded strangled when he finally spoke. "I don't remember."

"I do. Your dad and Cal were trying to help Diane, so I was left alone. You took care of me." The words stirred the air, wrapping around them like the breeze that sighed through the trees. Becca's chatter came from far up ahead. "Did you always feel like I was a responsibility to you, Tristan?"

He stopped the horse. Turned around. She sucked in her breath.

His eyes glittered with a fierce golden light, raw with emotion. "You were never a responsibility to me. You were a fucking gift. Never forget that."

And in that moment, she knew she'd do anything to win him back.

She loved Tristan Pierce with her heart and soul. Somehow she needed to believe he felt the same way. She had to fight to make sure they got their second chance, even if it meant pushing past uncomfortable boundaries and forcing him to take a risk.

"Mama? Daddy? Catch up!"

Turning back around, Tristan tapped his horse and closed the distance. "Come on, Bam Bam," she sighed. "Let's catch up." She gave him a kick.

Nothing.

He kept his bored, slow pace, and if she tried to kick, he got slower. The ride continued to get worse. Every time Tristan got ahead, Bam Bam would eat leaves, push her into trees, and jerk his head when she tried to tighten the reins.

"You're a big bully," she hissed against his ear. "I'm not giving you an apple unless you treat me nice."

He ducked his head low as if to jolt her off, and she let out a half shriek, clinging to his mane. Just as quickly, he rose back up and was standing with perfect innocence once Tristan turned around.

"Syd, you okay?"

"He's the devil," she accused. "He tried to knock me off!"

"I have an idea. Why don't you get ahead of me in line? Then I can help from the back."

"Fine. I can't believe you're taking the horse's side. He's lying."

Bam Bam docilely walked around Tristan, and the rest of the ride went without a hitch. She enjoyed her daughter's excited chatter and relaxed until the ranch came back into view.

Jim turned around. "We're going to try an easy trot up this hill. Nice and easy. Just follow me."

Jim's and Becca's horses fell into a graceful trot, and her daughter's giggles rose in the air. Bam Bam began to move at a bumpy clip, and Sydney's ass slammed up and down in the saddle, her body being thrown side to side as he seemed to deliberately make choppy movements and hit every rock and pothole along the way.

Tristan's horse lengthened his pace until he passed her, legs gracefully pumping into an almost canter with smooth, graceful motions that looked like poetry in vision.

And that's when it happened.

Bam Bam gave a mad snort and trotted faster, throwing her off balance until she clutched the saddle and prayed. She pulled up madly on the reins, but he ignored her, charging forward and then—

Stopped short.

Her ass collided back in the saddle with a sharp slap. Her teeth clattered together. Her body shook, off balance, and then he jerked his face around, saliva dripping from the bit he chomped madly on, brown eyes glinting with glee as he pulled back his lips and grinned at her.

"You did it on purpose!"

He snorted. Turned. Then began walking calmly the rest of the way, while the others gave her a thumbs-up sign.

They reached the top of the hill. "Did you see what he did?" she asked wildly. "He stopped short when no one was looking! He's manipulating you all!"

Jim, Tristan, and Becca gazed at her with a hint of sympathy and plenty of amusement. "Bam Bam has never caused any problems on the trail," Jim said with a frown. "He's one of the best horses we have."

"Yeah, Mama, look at him. He's sweet."

Bam Bam cocked his head with a mournful expression.

Tristan shook his head. "Umm, it's okay, Syd. It was your first time, and you didn't know what to expect. Just don't blame your inexperience on the horse." He patted Bam Bam on the head, and the horse gave him a gentle nudge for more. "See? Sweet as pie. Let's get you an apple, boy."

"No apple! I told him no apple!"

Becca gasped. "Mama! Don't be mean!"

Jim tightened his lips and helped her swing down from the saddle. "Not everyone is an animal person," he said with a touch of indignation.

"I love animals," she said. "I swear."

"Sure."

With one last look, he led Bam Bam back into the stable along with Becca and Tristan, leaving her behind. But not before his tail rose and an awful stench shot right at her.

She clapped a hand over her nose and gagged.

Ugh, gross.

She could hear his laughing whinny as he walked away.

Horseback riding sucked.

Tristan walked through the renovated kitchen of house number seven, looking for any imperfections. The cocoa-and-cream-splashed granite melded perfectly with Tuscan brown walls and Italian tile. Expensive looking but lower in cost than a consumer would expect. The wall removal gave it the much-needed open concept, and Sydney's suggestion of crown molding on the outer doors gave it a touch of elegance. They'd stripped and refinished the wood floors, going darker, and added a built-in shelf to help modernize the space.

Cushman would fucking love it.

He headed out the door toward the next job site. Sydney stood before the old, torn-up fireplace, already seemingly in deep negotiations with the bricklayer. He was amazing with brick design, and Sydney was focused on retaining his services. For the right price.

He stayed a few feet behind and listened to their discussion.

"I'm not laying out a whole wall of brick for wholesale," Paul said. He was a stocky guy with sandy-brown hair, a goatee, and light blue eyes. His business was thriving in Harrington, but Tristan bet dazzling Cushman could only grow his portfolio. He wondered whether Sydney would take that approach. If not, he'd be here to step in.

"Not the whole wall," she pointed out. "I'm going to do a detailed edge about two inches down."

"Still not enough. I hear this developer has deep pockets. Why screw your local contractors for a big-city guy?"

Sydney crossed her arms and studied him intently. Tristan knew what it was like to meet that emerald stare, full of determination and stubbornness. She ended up wearing down her opponents from sheer grit. It was sexy as hell.

"Let me tell you what I see, Paul. I see you hovering to expand, but there's not enough jobs in Harrington alone to break out yet. You do this job, and I'll make sure Cushman sees this as the focal point of the home. He's ready to buy up a hell of a lot more houses, as is Pierce Brothers."

Paul considered, stroking his goatee. Leaned forward a few inches. Why was he getting so close? "Land is scarce. Not gonna be much more property to buy."

"Yes, you're right, around the marina. It's time to build up the outskirts, and we're right in the center. Get on board with me now, and you'll get a piece."

Pride stirred. Nice work. She was smart, but she also knew exactly how to present her case without getting anyone defensive. It was critical when working with so many male egos.

Paul chuckled. "A solid argument. As usual." His gaze seemed to narrow with interest. Tristan shifted his feet, suddenly uneasy with the man's intensity. "I'll come down another twenty percent. No more, or it's not worth it."

Her smile dazzled, gripping at his heart. "Done. You won't regret it."

"Hope not. Maybe we need to go over more details over dinner. Tonight?"

A growl rose from his chest. He managed to strangle it back just in time. Had Paul just asked his wife out on a date?

Her laugh was a tad nervous. "Oh, I'm sorry, Paul, I guess you didn't know. I'm married."

"Oh, crap, sorry. I didn't see a ring."

She stuck her bare finger up in the air, smiling wryly. "Yeah, I forget to put it on sometimes."

Paul frowned, as if trying to decide if there was still an opportunity to take her on a date. Anger pumped through Tristan's system, blinding his vision. She'd forgotten her ring? Was she fucking serious?

Refusing to wait another second, he strode over until he stood beside her. Then got straight to the point. "Did you just ask my wife out on a date?"

Paul took a step back. "Sorry, Tris. Didn't know she was married. Didn't mean to step on any toes."

Sydney shot him a warning look. She waved her ringless finger in the air to calm him, but he was like a bull seeing red. "No need to apologize, Paul."

Tristan nodded, forcing a grin at the man. "Yeah, no worries. I'll have to get her a ring on a string so she can wear it on the job site," he said casually.

They laughed together. Sydney frowned and tried to ease away. He tucked his hand firmly under her elbow. She stiffened and shot him a look. Then deliberately lifted her arm in the air in one neat motion and sidestepped.

Oh, he was going to punish the little minx for this one.

"Well, congrats. You're a real power team now. This work has been solid. Looking forward to working with you."

"Thanks, appreciate it."

The moment Paul disappeared, she whirled on him, her eyes shooting green flames.

"What was that about?" she hissed. "A bit territorial, don't you think? I had it handled."

He took a step toward her and leaned in. His breath rushed over her lips. "Oh, I see how you're handling this, all right. Why aren't you wearing your ring?"

She blinked. "I leave it off on the job. I forget to put it on."

A flash of pure male temper hit him hard. "From now on, you will wear your ring every damn day. Understood?"

She jerked away from him, chin tilted, and spoke in a furious whisper. "Don't threaten me. I'll wear the ring when I want. And I don't appreciate you bringing our marriage onto the job site. I've worked hard to get here on my own, and I don't need you playing the game of whose dick is bigger on my time. It affects my relationship with my suppliers. Understood?"

"Maybe it's time you treat our marriage with some respect instead of hiding me like a dirty little secret," he growled back.

She jabbed his chest with her index finger. "Back off, buddy. Let's keep the focus on work, shall we? Remember, this isn't personal. Take a moment to cool off and then we'll head home. We're both exhausted and need some rest."

She marched off without a glance back, leaving him in shock.

Had she just called him buddy? And told him to cool off?

His skin stretched tight over his muscles. He tried to breathe to force his blood to stop boiling and resume pumping normally. He'd made a big mistake. By giving them both space and refusing to force intimacy, he'd let her believe she was in charge. She didn't wear her ring. She didn't sleep with him in the same bed voluntarily. She didn't have sex with him. And she practically waved off the fact she was married when asked out on a date.

This morning, their horseback riding expedition had reminded him of everything good they had together. There wasn't another woman who made him laugh like Sydney. Her insistence on her horse being evil not only amused him but helped him appreciate her many layers. Remembering that camping trip reminded him of how important she'd always been to him. Trying to keep her at a distance had only emphasized his physical ache for her. A few conversations over dinner and at the site was not what was needed—for any of them. They needed to bond on a deeper level to make this the family Becca truly deserved.

The realization of what he needed to do washed over him, bringing back a sense of calm and purpose. It was time to make this a real marriage and show her who she truly belonged to.

It was time to finally claim his wife.

chapter twenty-one

He was starting to freak her out.

Sydney tried not to study him under her lashes as he competently broke down the empty pizza box and stacked the salad plates in the dishwasher. Since Becca wasn't home, they'd decided to get takeout. They'd eaten at the counter and talked solely about work. He seemed calm again, as if that strange blowup on the site had never occurred.

Except Sydney knew something had changed.

Each word he spoke was accompanied by a glint of determination in those whiskey eyes. He seemed to be studying her, like a predator would assess his prey before striking. The air hung heavily with tension, but she couldn't figure out what seethed beneath the surface.

Was it the ring?

The moment he'd slipped the three-karat diamond on her finger, she'd felt weighted down. Knowing the marriage was fake, it hurt to wear it, so she became used to leaving the ring behind in the velvet box. Working the site was a perfect excuse. He'd never noticed before. Was it because Paul had tried to ask her out?

The idea of Tristan being jealous thrilled her, but she doubted that was it. Probably more like a claiming territory sort of thing. Her mind spun with possibilities. She couldn't keep dealing with the push/pull of this relationship much longer.

"Refill?" he asked, pointing to the bottle of expensive French wine he loved.

"Yes. Nothing like a great vintage with pizza," she said. He poured her another glass. The rich aromas of blackberry and smoke rose to her nostrils. "It's been a long day."

"Becca loved the horseback riding. I'm glad you suggested we all go together."

"Me too. But next time I want a horse that's not named Bam Bam and doesn't secretly want to try to kill me."

"Why aren't you wearing your ring, Sydney?"

She stiffened. Uh-oh. She should've known he'd get stuck on this issue. She kept her voice cool. "Does it really matter? I'm sorry if you took it personally, but it doesn't make sense when I'm working at the site."

He nodded and sipped his wine. Contemplated her words. "You didn't wear it yesterday, either, when you were strictly at the office. Or at poker night. Where is it?"

She practically gnashed her teeth together in frustration. Damn him for pushing. "In the box. Where it's safe."

"I wear mine every day." He lifted his hand. The ring flashed in the light—a dazzling gold with intricate carved ridges. Her heart dropped at the symbol of love and devotion for a couple who committed without doubt. Not like them. Not like a shotgun marriage performed seven years later because of a child. She buried the pain and concentrated on anger. It was so much simpler.

"Well, goody for you. Maybe you're more careful than I am."

"Have you changed your name legally yet?"

She glowered. She was excited Becca would have the family name, but it terrified her. How many times had she lost herself in the pursuit of Tristan Pierce? Having his name was a hollow victory without his heart. She tried not to squirm under his relentless gaze. "I'm waiting for Becca's new birth certificate. It should come in the mail in a few more weeks."

"And yours?"

"I haven't had the time to go to the town office yet. It's a lot of paperwork, and I've been busy."

He propped his elbows on the counter and regarded her. "Hmm." Slowly his finger tapped against the edge of the glass. The air lit with electricity, and she struggled for breath. He was so damn virile. From those lean muscles and tapered fingers to those carved lips, the man oozed sex appeal.

She snapped her mind into battle mode. "What does that noise mean?" she challenged. "You don't believe me?"

"Oh, I believe you've been busy. But I also believe you don't want to change your name. I think you're pretending we have a convenient arrangement and refuse to admit this will be a real marriage."

"It's not a real marriage! You made me do this."

He lifted a brow. A flush hit her cheeks. Deep inside, she'd dreamed of marrying him her entire life. Of being his wife. Unfortunately, she'd gotten her wish in the completely wrong way. She'd tried to protect herself by keeping her distance, but nothing seemed to work.

Maybe it was time to change her plan.

Maybe it was time to go after what they'd both wanted.

"I think we tried it your way for a while and now we're going to try it mine."

His soft tone caused goose bumps to shiver along her skin. Her heart began pounding so loud, she knew he heard it. "What do you mean?"

A smile touched his lips. "I think you know."

She got up from her seat. Poised for flight, she trembled, staring at him in half unease, half fascination. He seemed completely calm and in control of the whole situation. The air hung heavy with sexual tension. She regarded him with heavy-lidded eyes, knowing this was a turning point for both of them. Tristan intended to get her into his bed.

And she intended to be there.

But it couldn't be on his terms.

She tilted her head, as if considering his words. She was not going to just meekly acquiesce to his primeval threats. The thrill of the game sent shivers of anticipation down her spine. "Maybe I do know." She tossed him a challenging smile. "But I don't think it's going to happen tonight. Better to tell you that right now before things go any further."

He placed his glass down on the table. Slowly rose from the chair and stretched with an animallike grace. "Maybe it's best if I lay out the actual plan of the evening." He shrugged off his jacket and hung it neatly on the back of the chair. "First, I'm going to remove all of your clothes. I'm going to lay you out on the bed and spend endless hours tasting you. Touching you. Biting you. Licking you." He unclipped his cuff links and laid them on the counter. "When you've come at least twice, I'm going to fuck you. First hard and fast.

Then real slow. Until you weep and scream my name over and over." He rolled his cuffs up his forearms. "Then I'm going to do it all over again until you remember to wear your ring every damn day."

Her mouth was as dry as a barren desert. His dirty words caused a tsunami of sensation curling in her belly, fogging her mind with a gripping need that blasted away her defenses. Dear God, he was good. Already she craved to give in and to hell with a chase.

She fought to rally. Took a step back, her hands in front of her. "No. I mean it, Tristan. Stay away from me or you'll regret it."

"Too late. You're my wife and it's about time I claimed you as such. In my bed."

She gulped for air. Whiskey-colored eyes narrowed in on her. He loosened his tie, unknotted it, and slid it off his neck. The red ribbon dropped to the floor in sheer seductive glory. Her thighs squeezed, and her panties dampened. Holy shit. She was soaking wet, and he'd only taken off his jacket and damn tie.

She glanced to the staircase, counting the number of steps necessary to get her to safety. If she moved fast, she'd be able to lock herself in the bedroom. That would show him. She prepared for flight, only to be distracted when he began unbuttoning that snowy-white shirt, unveiling a line of hard muscles and intriguing hair that traveled down his chest, over eight-pack abs, and disappeared under his slacks.

His lips twitched at her hungry stare. "You want this just as bad as I do."

His arrogance took her breath away. She gathered her

temper and flung it at him like a witch casting a spell. "I'm sure you'll tell yourself that to justify forcing me."

His laugh made her curl her hands into fists. "Oh, baby, this won't have anything to do with force. In fact, I won't be satisfied until you beg me." He unbuckled his belt, slid it from the loops, and dropped it. The metal hit the wood floor, causing her to jump. "Do you remember how well you used to beg, Sydney?"

She raised her chin. Her nipples were tight and achy, pressing against the thin material of her shirt in a demand to be freed. Her core heated and softened, ready for him. "Maybe this time you'll be the one to beg," she threw out. "'Cause I'm done."

"You've been driving me crazy for way too long." He drew the tab on the zipper down slow. The hiss hit the air like bacon sizzling in a pan. "It's time I take what belongs to me and teach you a valuable lesson."

She seethed with frustration and arousal. "I'm not your possession."

His eyes flared with a hungry, raw lust that kept her chained in place. He stalked her like a predator, and she moaned low in her throat. "Yes, you are," he declared. "You're my wife. You're mine, whether you like it or not. The moment you said those vows, I owned that sweet body, and it's time I show you who the real boss is around here."

Did he really think she'd surrender that easily? She'd make him work for it. "You'll have to catch me first."

The dare hung in the air between them. His pants drifted over his hips and hit the floor. His erection strained against his briefs, and her mouth watered at the gorgeousness of his body, the hard strength standing before her. Toasty-golden skin covered with dark hair and bulging biceps and muscled thighs braced apart. He was *David* incarnate: proud and strong and graceful, and she'd never wanted him more in her entire life. And they were still in the kitchen? Why hadn't she moved yet?

"Sydney?"

She blinked away the haze of primal lust. "Yes?"

"I'll give you one chance." He paused. His grin was slow and feral. "Run."

Adrenaline hit. Heart racing, she dove for the stairs and scrambled up with speed but little grace. Fingers closed around her ankle, but she gave a frantic yelp and ran faster, bare feet skidding on the hardwood floor.

No time to look for a room. Her hand brushed the knob of their bedroom, and she flung it open, pivoting in one swift motion in an effort to shut the door and lock it behind her.

Too late.

He grabbed her around the waist and lifted her high in the air. She fought like a wild thing, desperate for escape, but he only laughed and held her easily, keeping her tight against his chest, then tossing her onto the bed.

She rolled to the left and feigned escape, kicking out with her right leg to connect with his shin. He pulled back for a few precious seconds. Putting all her energy into one last-ditch effort, Sydney bolted off the bed and launched herself into the air, ready to crawl into the bathroom to safety.

Midair, she suddenly changed course and found herself pinned to the mattress by a very hard, very pissed-off, very dangerous male.

"You've always been a pain in the ass," he muttered. His forehead was damp with sweat. His bare skin pressed against every one of her curves, his cock wedged intimately between her thighs. Her breasts lifted and strained against her. "I'm so going to enjoy making you pay, baby."

"Fuck you!" The stinging words were contradicted by her ragged breaths and hard nipples.

He made a tsking sound, golden eyes lit with hunger and the thrill of the catch. "I plan to."

His mouth crashed over hers.

The moment their lips met, the fight drained from her body, to be replaced by a raw, savage need that heated her blood. She moaned, biting his lip hard, and he gripped her hair, holding her head still, as his lips ravaged hers in the soul-stirring kiss. All her promises and insults and defenses shattered with the thrust of his silky tongue and the intoxicating taste of him.

He wasted no time in tugging off her clothes, until she lay naked beneath him. His hair-roughened legs entangled with hers, holding every inch of her still as he kept kissing her, devouring her whole.

When he ripped his mouth away, she was panting. Her skin burned like fire. Eyes dazed, she looked into his beloved face and slowly reached up to cup his cheeks. "What are you going to do?" she whispered.

He pressed his thumb against her swollen lip. A shiver of fear bumped down her spine at the intensity in his eyes. "Everything."

His fingers suddenly plunged between her thighs.

She cried out and arched under the delicious sensations of his fingers deep in her pussy. There was no finesse or seduction, just the primitive thrusts driving her upward in brutal determination to make her explode. She clung to his shoulders, barely able to hold on, his palm dragging across her clit as he pressed straight into her G-spot over and over until—

She came hard, her body seizing around him, sinking her teeth into his shoulder. He grunted in satisfaction, refusing to slow down, forcing her to milk out every last shimmer of her orgasm before removing his fingers.

Boneless, she blinked up at him.

"That's one."

"Tristan—"

He lowered his head and took the hard tip of her nipple in his mouth. Helpless to fight, she offered herself up to him, drowning in the intense pleasure of his wicked tongue licking, sucking, the sharp edges of his teeth raking across her nipple until she was swollen and so sensitive, it bordered on pain. He murmured in satisfaction and moved to her other breast, giving the same treatment, until she was hot and aching again, desperate for him to slide inside her channel.

"I love your breasts," he growled. He blew air over her tight, wet skin and watched her nipples harden even more. "Do you know how many times I fantasized about unbuttoning those proper white blouses and cupping my hands over you? I dreamed you'd sit on my desk in your tight little skirt, bare breasted, just for my pleasure."

"I used to have my own fantasies," she whispered in his ear, biting his lobe, blowing gently.

"Oh, yeah? What about?"

"This."

Taking him by surprise, she wrapped her legs around him and rolled, pinning him to the mattress. Sliding over his body, she pulled down his briefs, releasing his heavy erection. Her hair spilled over his muscled chest and she cupped him with both hands, stroking and squeezing, loving the feel of his hot, silky skin stretched tight over his hard cock. "Taking you deep in my mouth while you begged me to stop." She lowered her head, her breath rushing over him in warning. "While you begged me to continue."

Her name was uttered like a curse and a prayer.

She opened her mouth and took him deep.

His hips shot up as she pleasured him, sucking and licking, scraping her teeth delicately over the wet tip, then taking him back full between her lips. His fingers clenched in her hair and she sucked furiously, wanting him to slide over the edge. She hummed, letting the vibrations intensify his sensations, nails digging into his hips as she worked him closer and closer—

He flipped her back over in one neat motion, until she lay helpless underneath, blinking in confusion. "Hey, I wasn't done!"

He chuckled, moving down her belly. Kept her pinned down with two hard hands. "Witch." His tongue dipped in her belly button, his teeth scraping across the sensitive skin of her hip, inner thigh, and around the landing strip of hair she'd left for him. "Get ready for number two."

He spread her thighs wide, holding her open with his broad shoulders, and dipped his head. His tongue licked with a teasing insistency that made her crazed. Her clit throbbed for attention, but he refused, spending long minutes nibbling, sucking her labia, scraping his teeth over her swollen flesh until she writhed helplessly under him, desperate for contact.

"Tristan!"

"Ask me nicely." Around and around his tongue circled, refusing to give her the pressure she craved. Her vision blurred, and she clenched her fists in the tangled sheets.

"No."

He laughed low, pleased. "I was hoping you'd say that."

Oh, she burned. His tongue teased her with a ruthless determination, until the edge of pain and pleasure blurred. Her whole body clenched, kept on the precipice of falling apart, and she moaned deep in her throat, going halfway mad with need. "Tristan."

"One word."

"Bastard."

His teeth scraped. His thumbs danced. "That's not it."

"Please."

"Very nice." He opened his mouth and sucked hard on her clit.

She exploded, jerking against his lips, caught in waves of sensation. His name came out on a sob. She was dying and he hadn't even entered her yet.

She heard the tear of a wrapper. He knelt on the bed, sheathing himself with the condom, staring down at her with a fierce satisfaction that gave him the look of a conqueror. She waited for the shame to hit, her easy acquiescence the moment he touched her, but it was buried underneath the throbbing ache for him; to have him inside her one more time, to truly belong to him.

"You're so damn beautiful," he said in a husky voice.

He grasped her ankles, pushing her feet up. She reached out her arms to him, but those lips curved in a half smile, full of male triumph. "No, baby. I said the first time would be hard and fast. Remember?"

"But—"

With one swift motion, he flipped her onto her belly. Head spinning, she had no time to think or protest, because he dragged her to her knees, pushed her legs far apart, and entered her in one full thrust.

For a moment, she fought him. The burning stretch of her muscles as he filled her completely, buried to the hilt, shook her to the core. His hands gripped her hips, palms on her ass. Head bent over the pillow, propped on her elbows, she was suddenly, achingly vulnerable, open to anything he wanted to do, and she shook in a combination of thrilling abandon and crippling fear.

Then his head ducked, pressing kisses over her shoulder, his voice hot and steady in her ear. "Hold on, baby. I got you."

Her body relaxed, accepting him fully, and he muttered a vicious curse. Then began to move.

He took her just as promised—hard and fast. Deep strokes that left her no place to hide, a show of domination that was primitive, sexual, and so arousing, she was shoved immediately to the edge of her next climax. Sydney pushed back with her hips, demanding more, and he gave it to her, reaching between her legs to pluck at her clit. She panted, arching, and he sank his teeth into her shoulder, throwing her over the edge.

This time, when she came down from her climax, she was on her back, staring up into his whiskey-gold eyes.

"I can't get enough of you." He paused. "I've never been able to get enough of you."

The words ripped at her heart. With no barriers to protect herself, tears threatened, and she looped her arms around his neck and buried her face against his damp, hot skin. He pressed gentle kisses everywhere, stroking her body with slow, calming touches, bringing her back up step-by-step. His lips took hers, tasting, giving, cupping her cheeks with a tenderness that made her ache.

The final time, he made love to her with slow, drugging precision, refusing to rush. He kissed and licked every inch of skin, worshipping her. She explored on her own, reveling in the hard muscles of his biceps, nipping at his tight stomach, her fingers squeezing his cock, like silk covering hard steel. Time stopped, blurred, faded to nothing under the aching intensity of flesh melding with flesh. When he finally entered her, their gazes locked, their breath a mingling whisper. She hovered on the edge of the cliff, mesmerized by the carved features of his face, then fell into the heat of his gaze and said good-bye again to her heart, which had never been hers to begin with.

It had always been his.

She shattered into tiny pieces, and he held her the entire time. Her name was a groan from his lips, and then he pulled her tight against him, both of them seeming to be unable to break away from the searing contact of skin and bone and flesh. Without a word, she closed her eyes and fell into sleep, already knowing sex had changed everything.

chapter twenty-two

Tristan sat in the chair, sipping his coffee, and watched his wife.

She slept hard, just like she did everything else. Mouth open. Hair springing merrily around her face. Tiny snores emitted from her swollen lips. The sheet was twisted around her naked body, and one full breast peeked out. Her strawberry nipple was hard and practically begging for his mouth.

He shifted as his arousal came back full force. It was never enough. He'd taken her multiple times during their marathon, and his body still ached for her. She was like a drug he couldn't get enough of. At least they didn't have to fight the attraction any longer. Last night, they'd charted a brand-new path for this marriage, and a bond had been re-formed.

Memories of the night hit him. Oh, the sex had been off the charts, but it was the tenderness that he kept remembering. The look on her face as she gazed into his eyes. The way she stroked his body with a reverence that humbled him. The way she gave herself, over and over, without thought as to taking for herself.

Uneasiness stirred. He'd been concentrating on moving their relationship back to a physical level. Her keeping his daughter a secret had broken them, and though he'd learn to forgive, he wouldn't forget. He needed to keep his heart safely tucked away, and everything would work out fine. He'd be able to give her enough of himself to keep her happy.

It was a win-win.

Then why did he feel like last night had changed everything?

He bit back a groan, trying to sort through his tangled emotions. He'd begun believing he was in charge and could seduce her. Instead, she'd seduced him, ripping away his carefully erected barriers and challenging him on every level. Buried deep inside her body, his gaze locked on hers, fingers entwined, his entire being had shuddered with a sense of rightness. Belonging.

Homecoming.

He'd made a big mistake believing sex would finally sate his hunger. It had only made him ferocious for more of her, and he didn't know what he was going to do.

Her eyes flew open. She blinked, frowning, and he remembered she was always a bit grumpy in the morning before coffee. She slowly sat up, pressing the sheet against her, and stared at him with confusion.

He stiffened, waiting to meet her challenge. Would she deny last night? Still try to keep separate rooms? Pretend to ignore the whole encounter?

"Where's my coffee?"

He relaxed, a smile curving his lips. He wanted to kiss that pout off her mouth, but he knew the conversation had to happen with caffeine. "I didn't want it to get cold, since I didn't know how long you'd sleep. Be right back."

He poured her a mug and walked back into the bedroom. She snatched it, allowing the sheet to fall, and he happily feasted on the vision of her perfect bare breasts, nipples pebbling in the cool morning air. "Thanks," she muttered into her mug.

"How are you doing?"

She grunted. "Between horseback riding and you, I'll be hobbling around today."

Satisfaction curled in his gut. Good. A man had done his job if his woman couldn't walk the next day. "Now you're just flattering me."

She snorted a half laugh, still sipping. "I need to call Morgan and check on Becca."

"As soon as you get dressed, we can go together." He studied her, looking for any sign of tension or defense. "Do you want to talk?"

Amusement flickered in her emerald eyes. "Do you?"

Damn, she was hot. His heart squeezed. He adored her smart-ass ways and her constant surprises. "Yes. I feel like I need reassurance."

This time she gave a full laugh. "We're married already, so it's not like I can call you a one-night stand."

"Will you stop sneaking out of our room at night?"

"I guess," she muttered. "Though it was starting to get fun."

"I'll find a new game we can both enjoy."

Her brow lifted. "Like last night?" she teased.

"Yes. Like last night. Though I'd rather not have to chase you through the house next time."

Her smile slowly disappeared. She dropped her gaze, and a strange fear clutched at him. Was she having second thoughts? He didn't want to force her into his bed every night. He needed her to want him just as bad. "Syd? Look at me."

She raised her chin. A strange mixture of emotions swirled in her emerald eyes. Was that a glint of sadness or just a trick of the light? "I can't fight this anymore," she said quietly. "I want you. There's no use denying it. But I also can't have you doing this to—to get back at me. For hurting you. I can't play those types of games."

He put his mug down and went to the bed. Grasping her arms, he leaned over her and met her miserable gaze. "Baby, that was no game last night."

"I can't take the coldness anymore. There's no way I can be in your bed and deal with such distance in the morning."

He let out his breath and took her in his arms, hugging her tight. Yes, he was still struggling with the truth about Becca, but she was right. They couldn't go on with him holding her away because of lingering resentment. He tried to put it in words. "I'm sorry, baby. When you told me about Becca, I was so angry I didn't know how to act. It was easier to push you away and keep you there until I wrapped my head around it. I'm still struggling with knowing you kept her from me, but I want you just as badly as you want me. I've never been able to fight our connection. It's not about revenge, Syd. I want to try to move forward in this marriage for all of us. Especially Becca."

She nodded against his chest. "Okay. We can take it slow, day by day."

"Deal." He tipped up her chin and pressed a hard kiss on her mouth. "Finish your coffee, and I'll call Morgan."

As he left the bedroom, his spirits lifted. Everything had slid into place. He'd have Sydney in his life, and in his bed.

He began to whistle as he picked up the phone to call his daughter.

Sydney sipped her coffee and stared at the empty doorway.

Last night he'd finally given her hope. The stirring tenderness and blinding intensity as he made love to her told her what words never could.

He still had feelings for her.

He was her husband. He was in her bed. He was involved in her day-to-day life and was a wonderful father to Becca.

Last night she'd realized he'd broken through every one of her defenses, and they'd never be rebuilt. She couldn't fight him any longer. Maybe if she accepted him fully into her life, he'd eventually open his heart again.

She was going to try to make this a real marriage and win back his trust. One day he'd have to understand that she'd kept the truth from him about Becca to protect her daughter. She'd never wanted to hurt him. Time would build trust. Forgiveness.

Time would bring hope.

Sydney dragged in a breath and set her shoulders for the biggest battle she had ever waged.

The battle for his heart. She couldn't accept any less from him.

It was all or nothing at all.

chapter twenty-three

"Goodness, gracious, I'm getting married, y'all."

Sydney laughed at Morgan's incredulous expression, like it had finally hit her right before she was about to walk down the aisle. Raven flanked her on the other side, looking gorgeous in the sleek buttercream dress with her dark hair pinned up high. Thank God Morgan had chosen a sophisticated color palette that emphasized her Southern roots and elegant simplicity.

Plus, Sydney could actually wear the dress again.

"You look beautiful," she whispered, fussing with Morgan's train.

"You do, kitten." Morgan's father gripped her elbow, his full mane of white hair, blue eyes, and crisp tuxedo giving him a dignified air. Sydney had fallen in love with Morgan's parents and wished her mother would stick around. Diane would've loved her, with her classic breeding, sly humor, and obvious love for her daughter and Cal. Sydney imagined the two women chattering late into the evening while they watched their children walk off hand in hand.

"Showtime," Raven announced, turning toward the heavy

wooden doors. The music poured into the foyer of the church, and Raven headed down the aisle.

Sydney bent down to whisper in Becca's ear. "Ready sweetheart? It's your cue."

"Ready, Mama."

Excitement lit her gold-green eyes, and seeming perfectly poised, she began slowly walking down the aisle, scattering blush-pink rose petals. Her dress was the same color as the roses, and with the baby's breath braided through her hair, she looked stunning. There was a tittering in the crowd as everyone watched her, and Sydney puffed up with pride. Two weddings in under a year. Becca was practically an expert.

She studied Tristan's expression as he watched Becca walk down the aisle. Her whole being pulsed with joy as the two people she loved most joined at the altar. He motioned for Becca to stand all the way to the right. She nodded and gave him a thumbs-up, which threw the guests into laughter, then moved to her place.

Her turn.

She walked with slow, steady strides to join her daughter. Dalton and Tristan stood beside Cal, dual best men, devastating in their sleek black tuxedos. Smiling at her husband, she turned toward the main event, and the crowd stood as "The Wedding March" began to play.

Morgan floated down the aisle, her gaze trained on the man she loved, her face wreathed in a joyous smile. Wide blue eyes shone behind the weblike lace of her veil. The Vera Wang gown was a classic, with a full skirt and a high neck encrusted with an array of pearls, emphasizing the graceful length of her neck and her delicate bone structure. Her shoes shimmered in a peekaboo toe in pure glass.

Damn. She wore actual glass slippers, just like the princess Cal called her.

She reached Cal, and her father gave the bride away, blinking back tears. Cal hugged the man, then took his bride, joining their hands together.

Her lower lip trembled. Oh no. Not this early. She would not cry. No, no, no . . .

Tristan met her gaze across the room. Whiskey-gold eyes pierced into hers, a gleam of understanding and desire closing the distance and squeezing her heart.

Then he winked.

She pressed her lips tight to keep from laughing. The gesture was so unlike him; she knew he'd done it for her. She certainly didn't want to be blubbering the first five minutes and ruin all her makeup for photos.

God, she loved him.

The ceremony unfolded, wrapping the guests in memories of love and hope for the future. When they were announced man and wife, Cal picked Morgan up high in the air and spun her around, laughing with such open joy the guests burst into wild applause.

They lined up outside in the receiving line, greeting guests and posing for pictures in the gorgeous June sunshine. Tristan entangled his fingers with hers and Becca's, standing as a unit through the wedding formalities of pictures, toasts, and getting to the reception. Becca was still freaking out at being able to ride in a limo, and Morgan treated her like her own, making sure Becca had a glass of apple cider when they drank on the way to the country club.

They pulled up to the Harrington Club, a five-star resort on a stunning golf course with rolling green acres. After a few more pictures, Sydney made a beeline for the waiters and began pulling madly from the trays.

"You bringing those to Morgan?" Tristan asked, his hand resting on her waist.

She paused in the act of taking her first bite and groaned. "I'm evil. Hell no, I wasn't thinking about Morgan. I'm starving."

He grinned. "Eat first, then feed her. You'll be no good to her if you pass out from starvation."

"I'm a terrible mother. I forgot about Becca."

He took the bite-size bacon-wrapped scallop and popped it into her mouth. She half closed her eyes in delight. "She's fine. I got her situated in the bridal party room with a tray of chicken fingers and mozzarella sticks. She may never leave."

"You rock." She took the next few minutes enjoying bruschetta, shrimp and grits, various cheeses and vegetables, and mini spring rolls. "Okay. Now I can take care of Morgan."

"I think Cal has her covered."

She turned. Cal stood in the corner with his bride, feeding her slowly and pressing kisses to her mouth in between bites. It was an image from a movie poster, so tender and real everyone around them stilled to watch. The photographer jumped into action, snapping pictures with a mad glee, but they didn't notice. They gazed at each other, lost in the world they'd created for themselves.

Raw yearning gripped her. Her breath whooshed out, and for a few precious moments, she ached with bone-jarring jealousy. Their obvious love for each other beat in their auras, and Sydney almost fell to her knees in a mixture of grief and want.

It had been three months since her own wedding day, and she was no closer to Tristan falling in love with her than when they'd begun. Oh, the coldness had finally drifted away. He looked after her and Becca with a sweet concern that brought tears to her eyes. But he still held back.

Every night, he took her in his arms and wrung excruciating pleasure from her body. He reminded her of his possession, of his claim, yet after the orgasm settled and he fell asleep in her arms, she was left with an aching emptiness that was slowly devouring her.

"Baby? You okay?"

She shook off her thoughts and forced a smile. "Sure."

Becca raced across the carpet, her mini train trailing behind. "I'm back. Did I miss anything?"

Tristan swung her up in his arms, and they stood together in a tight circle. "Nope. Is your belly full now?"

"So full." A tiny frown creased her brow. "We've done the ceremony and pictures and ate and did a toast. What's next? Cake?"

Sydney laughed, and Tristan pressed a kiss on top of his daughter's head. "Something much more important and a heck of a lot more fun."

"What, Daddy?"

He leaned close to whisper in her ear. "We party, sweetheart."

Tristan glanced around. Coast was clear. He darted to the side door and escaped outside. He sucked in deep breaths of fresh air. His shirt was stuck uncomfortably to his skin, his tie was too tight, and his shiny stiff shoes hurt like a bitch. Pressing himself against the far wall, away from the smokers, he relaxed for a few seconds and hoped no one would find him. He refused to become a spectacle in this *Grease* thing Morgan had lined up. No one could make him do it, either. How could such a classy Southern woman stoop to such a level as to force a musical rendition on her guests?

The door banged open. Dalton came out, spotted him, and darted over. "Thank God. I'm not doing that shit, man. The DJ is looking for a Kenickie, and Morgan's already pissed 'cause they can't find Cal to be Danny."

"Well, don't lead them out here to me," Tristan hissed. "You always sucked at hiding. Did anyone see you?"

"Nah, I checked for tails."

"Did you bring beer?"

"Yeah, here." He shoved an extra bottle into Tristan's hands. The cold brew felt like heaven in his palm, and he pressed it against his forehead. "I'm so fucking tired. I hate dancing. And why are there so many relatives I don't recognize? They keep telling me how big I got."

"Yeah, Dad never kept up with his side of the family. They haven't seen us since we were ten."

The door squeaked, then flew open, and Cal trudged out, looking like his usual grumpy self. "I'm not doing it. Fuck Danny. Fuck *Grease*. There are certain levels of humiliation you can't go past, even on your wedding day."

"Did anyone see you come out here?" Tristan asked. "I found this spot first, and I'm not anyone's sacrifice."

"No, I had someone plant a clue I was in the bathroom, then I raced out here."

"Good job," Dalton said.

Cal glared at them, then took a swig of beer. "Some best men you are."

"We had to save ourselves. Morgan is scary," Dalton said. "Who's playing Danny now?"

"Her father. Uncle Bob is Kenickie, and some twelve-year-old is Sonny."

Tristan lifted a brow. "Umm, if Morgan gets mad about your nonparticipation, will you get a wedding night?"

Cal rubbed his head. His hair fell in disarray across his brow. "Don't know. I think I have enough moves to get her to forget."

Tristan snorted. "You hope."

"I'm not putting on a fake leather jacket and lip-synching 'Summer Nights.' There are people I know out there. Men I work with. I won't be welcome on a construction site for the rest of my life."

Tristan met Dalton's gaze and burst into laughter. "Sorry, man, that sucks. We'll tell them you got sick and needed some air."

Cal gave a brusque nod. "Now you're talking."

They stood against the wall, drinking beer, looking at the night sky. A sense of peace settled over him. "You happy?" he asked Cal.

His brother turned and grinned. "Hell yeah. Are you?"

Tristan nodded. "Yeah. I am."

"Things seem to be working out with Sydney. Have you been able to forgive her? Move on?"

He shifted his feet. Thought about the question. Had he? Since the night he'd chased her into bed, their relationship had shifted. They were closer, the physical union sparking a deeper emotional bond he hadn't been prepared for. When he felt as if he was slipping too far, caught deep in her jade-green eyes, he managed to yank himself back from the precipice. So far, he'd been able to control it. They were being real with each other. No words of love or false promises. Things were just about perfect.

Except for the sadness in his wife's eyes.

He caught her now and then, staring out the window, a melancholy aura hanging heavily around her figure. Sometimes she'd look into his face, and he'd spot a glimmer of pain that tore at his heart, but when he looked harder, it disappeared.

He shook off his thoughts and tried to answer the question.

Tristan was surprised at his honest response. "Yeah, we've been able to move forward. We're finally giving Becca something real."

Cal nodded. "Good for you, Tris. It's always been obvious how in love you two are. I'm glad you both finally admitted it."

Tristan held up his hand. "No, we're not in love. That's a place I'm never going again."

His brothers stared at him. "What are you talking about? You married her. Have a daughter. You're sleeping together, right?" Cal asked.

"Yeah."

Dalton gave a laugh. "Dude, you're kidding yourself. You love her. She loves you. What's the big deal? You're already married. It's usually the opposite way—men terrified of committing forever."

His gut clenched. Loving Sydney put their relationship

on a whole other level—one he never intended to reach. The word only brought confusion and too much damn vulnerability. "Love is how things get fucked-up," he said brusquely. "Much better to keep things the way they are."

Cal snorted. "Yeah, good luck with that. Sydney loves you. No rationalization is going to make that fact disappear."

"The longer you deny your own feelings, the worse things will get," Dalton warned. "Believe me, I figured that out from experience. Just man up and admit you love your wife."

"And if I don't?" he challenged.

"Then either you're scared shitless you'll get hurt or you haven't really forgiven her," Cal said.

Dalton nodded. "And either one needs to be dealt with, or things can begin falling apart. Don't let that happen, man. You and Sydney deserve to be happy."

He opened his mouth to deny both charges, but it was too late.

The door banged open.

Three pissed-off females stood framed in the doorway. They all wore pink satin jackets over their dresses and bright pink sneakers. Fake cigarettes dangled from their fingers. Gazes narrowed in feminine temper, they stepped outside like a gang about to kick some ass.

Ah, shit.

Morgan stuck out her lower lip and blew her lace veil off her face. Blue eyes glinted in warning. "Charming, if you're not inside to finish up this dance in two minutes, tonight will not be what you expected."

Cal's mouth dropped open. "I told you I didn't want to do this! Isn't it my wedding, too?"

Raven practically snarled, looking mean in her pink satin. "Morgan has been dreaming about a *Grease* song for years. You're telling me you can't take a few minutes from your life to make her happy on your wedding day?"

Tristan blinked. Damn, she was good. Dalton was in big trouble.

Sydney joined in, her index finger jabbing through the air. "Have you been trying to hide the groom from us?" she asked suspiciously.

Tristan threw his hands up. "No! I came out for a quick break, and they followed me!"

"Traitor," Cal and Dalton growled.

"Well, I don't care. All of you get inside, put on the leather jackets, and let's do this. Becca is jumping up and down with excitement, and Uncle Bob needs to take his medication, so he can't dance any longer," Sydney snapped out.

Suddenly Morgan's face fell. Her lower lip trembled. "You don't want to do this with me?" she asked pitifully.

And just like that, Cal crumbled.

"Aww, princess, don't get upset. I'll put on the jacket. Okay? But I'm not dancing. I'll stand there, and you can dance around me."

She smiled brilliantly. "Perfect. Thanks, Charming. Love you."

He sighed. "Love you, too." Cutting his brothers a furious glance, he trudged inside.

Sydney tapped her pink-clad toe and jerked her thumb. "Let's go, T-birds."

Tristan paused, lowering his head to whisper in her ear. "Get ready for payback later, Pink Lady."

She grinned. "I'll look forward to it."

He followed his brothers toward the dance of hell, pushing their conversation from his mind. Cal and Dalton were wrong. His marriage was perfect exactly the way it was.

No need to bring love into the equation and mess it all up.

chapter twenty-four

Sydney turned on the water and stepped into the shower, leaning against the Italian-tile wall. The mansion sometimes made her feel like she was Cinderella swept to the castle not to clean, but to live. The walk-in steam shower was equipped with so many jets she didn't know how to work half of them. She groaned as the heat began to work her tired muscles. The wedding had been perfect, but she wasn't used to staying out till two a.m.

Becca had barely roused when they transferred her from the car into her bed. Tristan volunteered for tucking-in duty, so Sydney had run straight to get changed and cleaned up.

She'd just squeezed bodywash into the loofah sponge when the door suddenly opened.

"Tristan?"

She squinted through the thick steam. Heart pounding, she waited, frozen, as he tugged off his clothes and stepped into the shower. His large naked body dwarfed the massive space, and her mouth went dry at the sight of his impressive erection and hard mass of muscle in full masculine glory.

What was he holding behind his back?

"Hey, baby. Thought I'd join you."

Those golden eyes held a wicked glint that made her suspicious. She squirmed, hating the bright light that showed off her stretch marks and full thighs. Yes, she was comfortable in her body, and Tristan made her feel adored, but she'd never showered with him. It seemed extremely . . . intimate.

She crossed her arms over her breasts and tried to act casual. "Umm, maybe this isn't a good idea? Becca could come looking for one of us."

He ignored her, stepping closer so the spray hit his chest and they were an inch apart. "She's fast asleep and won't be waking up any time soon. I locked the door. Why are you covering yourself?"

She bit her lip. "I'm not. Umm, I'm done, so I'll wait for you outside."

He blocked her path, gazing down at her with raw intensity. "Are you shy?"

"No! No, I just have to—"

"You're fucking adorable. But you're not going anywhere. I owe you a punishment." He turned quickly, giving her a view of his gorgeous, tight ass, and placed something on the low tiled bench. Then forced her arms down to pull her against him. Her hard nipples dragged across his hair-roughened chest, and she gasped.

"What punishment? I didn't set up the *Grease* medley!"

"You were part of the plan and enjoyed it too much. If I find myself on YouTube, I promise you'll regret it."

She gave a *hmmph*. "What did you put on the bench?" she asked, trying to crane her neck.

"Something you'll like. Something you've missed."

She frowned. A warning rang out in her head, but she was foggy from hormones. Her hands opened and stroked his wet skin, kneading his shoulders and biceps, then moving to caress those eight-pack abs that made a woman drool. There was simply nothing as sexy as a man who dressed in a suit to reveal such glory underneath the civilized veneer. "I've missed you," she admitted, squeezing his cock, fisting him slow underneath the spray of water.

"Missed you, too," he murmured. He jerked in her hands and uttered a curse. "Too much. God, I love your scent. Sometimes, when I'm away from you, I swear I can smell orange blossoms, and I get hard as a rock, wishing you were there."

It was more than he'd ever said before. His head lowered and he kissed her deep and hard and long. When her legs sagged with the effort to stay upright, he grabbed the sponge and soaped her up with thorough motions, then cleaned himself. Her body became sensitized from the sting of the spray, the heat of the steam, and his magical hands as he stroked and explored her naked flesh. Slowly he turned her around.

"Put your hands flat against the wall," he commanded.

Her belly dipped to her toes. Swallowing, shyness long forgotten under burning need, she obeyed. He eased her legs apart and adjusted the sprays so each one hit her nipple, and a softer mist drenched her stomach, rivulets trickling down the crease of her legs and over her clit with a light teasing touch.

He tugged her wet hair to the side and bit her earlobe. "I have a surprise for you."

"I bet you do."

He chuckled, kneading her ass. She felt him move away, then he was wrapping his arm around her waist, holding her tight. Suddenly a low buzzing cut through the air. She froze, trying to turn, but he kept her still.

Oh, my God.

He had her vibrator.

The steam had nothing on the flush that hit her cheeks and body in sheer embarrassment. She'd panicked after the movers had left, realizing she'd left it hidden in her bathroom cabinet where anyone could find it. After unpacking, she'd been horrified to realize it was gone. She'd tried not to think of the missing article, telling herself it had probably just been thrown out by mistake.

Her husband had it the whole time.

"Where did you get that?" she squeaked, still trying to fight his grip.

His low laugh caused wicked shivers to race down her spine. Her clit pounded for attention. "Let's just say I had it for safekeeping. It did bring up some interesting questions, though. For instance, do you like using a vibrator in the shower rather than the bedroom? Or was it strictly for noise-level reasons?"

She was going to die.

Sydney shook her head, face hot, and refused to answer. He ran his tongue down her neck and moved the hot pink vibrator down her belly to trace the line of her pubic hair, running ever so lightly over her throbbing center.

She stiffened, her hips arching of their own accord. "Why are you doing this to me?" she moaned. "I can't answer that."

"Sure you can. And I'm doing this because I've been fantasizing about playing with your toy for too damn long." He ran the buzzing head up and down, then in small circles until her fingers curled and she rose on tiptoes, desperately trying to get closer. "Now, tell me."

"I—I like it in the shower. Plus, Becca's bedroom was right next to mine, and I didn't want her to hear."

"Understood. You won't have to worry about any noise tonight—this room is practically soundproof." He played with her breasts, still moving the vibrator in a steady pattern. "Besides, I intend to make you scream very, very loud tonight, baby."

"Oh, God."

"Oh, yes." With one quick thrust, he took her from behind, his cock buried deep into her wet, swollen channel. She gasped, pushing back against him for more, caught between the need to get closer to the vibrator and the ache in her body for him to fill. He chuckled with satisfaction, slowly pushing in and out of her with steady strokes, then laid the toy right against her clit.

She jerked with sharp waves of pleasure.

He removed the vibrator.

"Tristan."

He started the torture over again. Deep thrusts in and out. Vibrator rotating in small circles. She cried and begged, and he finally pressed the pink toy against her hard nub.

She grasped for the climax, hovering with shattering, brutal tension.

He removed his hand again.

Panting for breath, going mad from the sexual torture,

she let out a keening wail, bending over to force himself to bury deeper inside her. "Damn you," she whispered. "Take me now."

"I want you to scream."

He plunged inside her and held the vibrator at the highest setting directly against her clit.

She climaxed. She screamed. She bucked as the shattering release poured through her. He forced her to ride out the very last convulsions, then picked up her shaking body. Quickly drying her off, he carried her to the bed and laid her down gently. His knees straddled her as he climbed onto the mattress and pressed a kiss to her lips. Her lids closed, the satisfying weight of her orgasm making her limbs weak. She felt her legs drift apart, and the hard tip of his cock poised at her dripping entrance, ready to fill her.

"Look at me, baby."

She did.

Whiskey-colored eyes blazed with fierce possession and male satisfaction. Jaw tight, lips set in a thin line, he shook with primal lust, barely contained by his usual control. "Tell me what you want," he demanded.

And suddenly she didn't care anymore about holding back or being safe. Her entire being pulsed with the need to give him the truth. "You," she whispered. "I can't fight this any longer." She reached up and gripped his hair, looking deep into his eyes. "I love you, Tristan. I just want you."

The words ripped through the air. Tristan held himself over her in perfect stillness, breath coming out in ragged pants, sweat gleaming from his brow, his gaze piercing into those gorgeous emerald eyes, naked with raw emotion, stripped of all barriers.

Everything inside shifted, cracked open, and poured out of his soul.

She loved him.

In one swift movement, he pushed her legs up and claimed her in one hard thrust.

He pressed his forehead to hers, his entire body shuddering as he fought for control. Buried to the hilt, he felt her squeeze his cock mercilessly with her wet heat, and her nails dug deep into his shoulders, drawing blood. He clutched her hips, holding her in place as he pinned her to the mattress, his hungry gaze devouring her face, devouring her submission.

Her name sighed from his lips.

Then he moved.

He fucked her with total abandon, giving her as much as she gave him, claiming her completely with each hard, deep stroke. Lowering his head, he took her mouth, plunging his tongue inside the silky wet cave, drunk on the taste of her. Her body tightened underneath him, and she cried out in a throaty gasp he swallowed whole. When she shattered completely, he threw his head back and roared with abandon, emptying his seed, jerking helplessly from the brutal release.

Afterward, he held her tight, his hand stroking her hair. They lay in the darkness, not speaking, limbs entangled, breath mingling together.

She loved him.

He couldn't deny how the words affected him. His soul

practically shuddered with satisfaction and the knowledge they belonged together. There'd never been another woman in his life who completed him. Each one before was a shadow of Sydney, a reminder of what he'd never be able to have again.

But now he could.

It was as if she'd held the secret part of his heart for all these years and had given it back tonight.

She waited for him to return the words and end the complicated game they'd been playing for too long. He needed to tell her he loved her.

The declaration hovered on his lips, just like it had that night eight years ago, when she asked him for something bigger. Something to make her go with him. Something to make him stay.

And once again, he said nothing.

They were married now. They were happy. They'd become a true family in every way it counted. Wasn't that what was most important?

Tristan pulled her closer with shaking hands and tried to pretend it didn't matter.

Eventually they fell asleep without saying another word.

chapter twenty-five

"Can you drive Becca to gymnastics tonight?" she asked, sliding blueberry waffles into the toaster. "I have a few meetings and a conference call with Adam."

He paused to study her, a slight frown creasing his elegant brow. "Sure, but this is the third night in a row. Do you need some extra help?"

She forced a smile, pouring some orange juice for Becca. "Just nearing crunch time. Want to make sure everything's perfect, and I need to help Charlie a bit at the office."

"You're doing an amazing job, Syd," he said seriously. "We've already got three houses complete and right on schedule. Cushman is happy. The suppliers are getting what they want. I'm just worried you're pushing yourself too hard."

"I can handle it." She rechecked Becca's backpack, slid in an extra bottle of water, and called her down to breakfast. "Appreciate it."

Her daughter skipped down the massive staircase, hair in a perfect ponytail. "Look, Mama, guess who did my hair this morning?"

Sydney stopped to study Becca, tapping her finger against her lip. "Hmm, Mr. Ted Bear? Or Barbie?"

"Daddy! Didn't he do good this time?"

Sydney laughed, taking in her husband's beaming face. "Yes, he did great," she said, her heart wrenching a bit. "You've come a long way since the recital."

"I just stay away from pink sparkles."

Becca giggled, sliding into her chair and keeping up her chattery morning conversation. Sydney concentrated on the familiar chaos, loving the banter among them all around the breakfast table. They had finally settled into their own routine. Days slipped by and melted into one another in a blur of happiness, laughter, and productivity. Tristan embraced his role as father and husband with a grace that humbled her. As time passed, Sydney admitted that from the outside, they had a perfect marriage and family.

Yet she still longed for more.

Every night, he wrung orgasms from her body and she spilled words of love from her lips. Every night, he gave her his body with a fierce devotion and passion she couldn't fight.

And every morning, he slipped a little further away from her.

Her marriage was a facade. It was as if the years had dissipated and left her the same young woman who allowed him to protect his heart for too long before walking away. Back then, it had been enough. She would've settled for any crumb of his affection.

Now Sydney knew she deserved more.

Soon she'd have to make a decision.

"I'll meet you over there this afternoon?" he asked, straightening his tie. "I have a closing today."

"Fine. Good luck."

He paused beside her chair. Then tipped her head up. "I'll see you later. Have a good day." He kissed her, slow and thorough, with a tenderness that made her whole being sigh with pleasure.

"Ew!" Becca said. "Kissing is gross!"

Tristan grinned. "I'm glad you think so, sweetheart. Keep on that track for me, okay?" With a wink, he left, leaving her staring at the closed door.

She finished breakfast, got Becca on the bus, and headed to the job site to get an early start. The day and evening passed quickly, and she took her time driving back home, lost in thought.

She had committed herself to this marriage because she loved him. Believed with enough time, he'd begin to trust her again. Open his heart. Love her the way she loved him. But months later, he still shut himself off. She was losing herself a little bit more every day, and it might be time to confront him. It was time Tristan Pierce took a risk with her and laid his heart on the line.

When she walked into the mansion, the downstairs was quiet. Kicking off her shoes, she headed up the staircase to check on Becca. As she approached her room, she heard them talking and paused in the doorway. A smile rested on her lips as she listened.

"Why does the princess always marry the prince at the end of the fairy tales?" Becca asked. "Do you always have to marry someone you kiss?"

Tristan's low chuckle warmed her heart. She heard the rustle of bedcovers. "Definitely not. Fairy tales were written a long time ago, when women had no other opportunities other than getting married."

"They couldn't be CPO like Mama?"

"CFO. And no, not back then. They'd marry, have children, cook, clean, and stay home."

"That sounds boring. I thought I wanted to be a princess, but I think I'd rather be an animal doctor. Or work on houses like you and Uncle Cal and Uncle Dalton and Mama. I like HGTV."

"You are so much smarter than those princesses," he said.

"Yeah, 'cause if the prince gets me mad, I have my own money to go somewhere else."

Tristan's laugh pumped up the room with joy. Becca laughed with him. Sydney shook with mirth, ready to step in and give her daughter a high five, but Becca's next question halted her mid-stride. "If you don't get married because you kiss, then why do you?"

"Because you love someone."

"We can't get married! But you love me, right?"

She squealed out loud. He must have been tickling her. "Silly girl, of course I love you. Parents always love their children, though. Adults are the ones who fall in love and decide to get married."

"Like Mama, right? You love Mama?"

She froze. Heart beating madly, she stood poised at the door, straining to hear his answer. A short moment of silence fell heavily in the air. Her breath caught as she waited.

"I love our family, Becca. And I love you more than anything in the whole world. Get it?"

"Got it."

Their voices mingled. More laughter. Sydney backed slowly away from the door. Very quietly, she entered her bedroom and sat on the edge of the bed. Everything around her remained the same. Inside, everything felt different.

"Hey, I didn't hear you get in. How was your day?" He stepped inside, shutting the door. He'd changed out of his suit into a pair of faded jeans and a simple black T-shirt. The scent of the ocean filled her nostrils. He was barefoot.

This man finally belonged to her. Her husband. The one who claimed her heart and made her body weep.

But it wasn't enough.

She made sure her voice didn't wobble. "I overheard you talking to Becca."

He smiled and shook his head. "Now, that was an interesting conversation. Decided she didn't want to be a princess. She'd rather have a job and make money. Who do you think she learned that from?" He walked to the dresser, removing his silver watch.

"You told her you loved your family."

"That's right. I do."

"But not me."

He stiffened. She watched him while he seemed to gather his composure before turning back around. "What are you talking about? I told her I loved our family and her."

"Yes, but when she asked you directly if you loved me, you didn't answer."

His brows snapped in a frown. "Semantics. What are you getting upset about?"

"I think you know."

He stilled. Studied her figure. Already the familiar distance shrouded his form, wrapping him up in protection. This time, she wouldn't allow it. His voice held a touch of defensiveness. "Sweetheart, let's not do this tonight. Things have been good between us. Have I done something to show I wasn't committed to this marriage? To you?"

A sigh broke through her lips. "No. Commitment isn't what I was questioning. Neither is responsibility. What I'm questioning is your feelings for me, Tristan."

He braced his legs apart, placing his hands on his hips. His pose reminded her of a warrior ready to do battle. "We've moved forward. We're happy. I don't know how you could possibly doubt my commitment to you."

Temper coursed through her veins. She stood from the bed and faced him. "There's that word again. *Commitment.* Oh, you've done your duty well, marrying me to be with Becca. You've said you moved on. But have we really, Tristan? Or do we just keep replaying the past, over and over?"

"I don't know what you're talking about. I forgave you for keeping Becca from me!"

"I don't need your forgiveness for doing something I was pushed to do! God, don't you remember how cold you were when you left? How you treated me like we'd never grown up together or been a part of each other's lives? Like a responsibility you didn't want anymore? You came back because you were lonely, not because you truly wanted to be with me. I had no choice, and I'll back up my decision to the very end because I did it all for Becca."

"How do I know you ever planned to tell me?" he asked. "How am I ever supposed to trust you again?"

She blinked back angry tears, shaking her head. "I don't

know. All I can tell you is when Becca was older, I always intended to give you both the truth. When we began to grow close after I made CFO, I saw a different man. One who was ready to really open up his heart. I knew it was time, so I took a leap of faith. But then it happened again. You shut down and closed up, and I'm fighting for something bigger, Tristan. I'm fighting for us."

"You want me to say the words? Will that help everything go back to the way it was so we can move on?"

Pain shredded through her, but she kept her gaze steady on his. Even now, his golden eyes swirled with a hint of fear, as if losing control was beyond him. Diane had always told her he was the one she worried about the most, and Sydney knew why. It was so hard for him to admit vulnerability and give trust. To be open enough to say *I love you* without holding back. Losing his mother had just made everything worse, made it easier to shut himself off.

Was it even possible for him to take such a risk?

"You still don't understand," she said softly. "Or you don't want to. If you can't give me your heart completely, we don't have a chance. I thought I could do this, but I can't. I can't be mad at you for not feeling the same way. For not loving me like I've always loved you. But I can't pretend not getting it isn't destroying me a little bit each day. Is this what you want? Don't we deserve to show Becca how two people should truly love each other?"

"Becca is shown every day how two people should treat each other. Why do you always have to push for more? For things I can't give you!"

Shock carved out his expression as he threw out the

words. The truth seeped into her skin and bones and soul. He didn't love her the way she needed. She'd believed this marriage would give her the time and space to win his heart. But the waiting game couldn't go on forever, especially when each day she'd resent him more for not loving her enough.

"I understand."

"No, you don't understand, Sydney. I didn't mean it like that."

A sad smile curved her lips. "Yes, you did. I'd rather have the truth than a lie. We can't keep doing this, Tristan. Eventually we'll hurt Becca, and she deserves more. You're an integral part of her life now, and I don't think you ever have to be afraid of not being involved with her on a daily basis. But being married to you? I can't do it anymore."

Was that panic she spotted in his expression? He took a step forward, his hand reaching out. "No. We can work this out. Dammit, do you really want to lose what we've had? What we've built?"

"Yes, I do." She squared her shoulders and told her own truth. "Because I deserve more than you can give, Tristan Pierce. It's about time I realized that."

She walked away with her head held high.

This time, when she went into another bedroom for the night, he didn't come after her.

chapter twenty-six

The house was quiet.

He paused in the kitchen, looking around. Syd had taken Becca to ballet this morning. The cleaners hadn't come yet, and the space still held the joyous clutter of two females. Glossy catalogs and colorful magazines lay scattered on the counter. There were remnants of chocolate chip cookies by the stove. Two high-heeled shoes and one pair of pink flip-flops had been kicked underneath the table. A pink unicorn with long hair and a gown-less Snow White took up two chairs. The scents of orange blossoms and coconut drifted in the air. A *Frozen* ChapStick and a bottle of pink nail polish sat lined up neatly next to his expensive bottle of French wine.

His throat burned as he poured himself a glass of water. They'd gotten used to horseback riding on Saturdays, but Sydney had canceled this one. It had only been a few days since their confrontation. He'd been hoping things would go back to normal after she settled down and realized what she meant to him. Instead, she'd spent last night at Morgan's, informing Becca she was having a grown-up sleepover party and they'd have a father-daughter night.

As much as he adored being with Becca, he'd missed his wife. He didn't try to push her, thinking with some time and space, they'd be able to work things out. He recognized the panic and fear clawing at his gut at the thought of her walking away from him but was still unsure how to handle it.

He should just tell her he loved her. It would solve the problem. But then he remembered the hurt in her eyes, the shattered expression on her face when she confronted him. Nausea hit his gut. Still, she never backed down. God, when had she gotten so brave? She'd stood in front of him, admitted her deepest feelings, and declared she could do better.

She'd walked away.

What was he going to do?

Smothering a groan, he set the glass in the sink and picked up the pile of mail. Sifting through, he studied an official brown envelope and slit it open. Two documents fell out with a letter.

Becca's new birth certificate had come in. The name change was official. His daughter was now known as Rebecca Pierce.

Fierce satisfaction uncurled. He glanced at the document, then noticed they'd also included a copy of the original birth certificate. His gaze stopped on the line that asked for the father's name.

Tristan Pierce.

His heart stopped. Slowly he read it again, the truth skittering on his consciousness to finally blast him full force.

Sydney had listed him as the father on Becca's birth certificate.

She'd never tried to hide him. Anyone could have pulled

the document and found out. She'd never lied and put down her ex-husband, though everyone had naturally believed him to be the father.

Dear God, she'd told him the truth. She had been planning to tell him one day. It was right there in black and white.

The papers dropped from his fist. The memory rose up like a tidal wave, gripped him, and threw him over into chaos . . . into the past . . .

He felt her gaze on his back but refused to turn around. Quickly he dressed, ignoring the sick ache in his gut. Lately the urge to run after he made love to her swamped all thoughts of decency. What was happening to him? It was as if he was twisted inside with the need to be with her versus the need for space.

"I thought you were going to stay."

Her husky words drifted across the room. He stiffened, but pulled on his T-shirt before meeting her gaze. Emerald eyes sparked with confusion and a need that drove the breath from his lungs. That type of need was dangerous. Could he ever truly give her what she wanted from him? Why didn't she crave more, like he did? Why didn't she want to run away from Harrington and never look back? And why did she have to tell him she loved him?

The questions caused a flash of resentment to cut through him. "I can't," he said shortly. "I have an early day tomorrow. Better to get our sleep."

Her face reflected a deep hurt that only inflamed him further. "Okay. My grandparents want you to come over for dinner Thursday. I thought that would be nice."

"I already said I'd meet some friends at the marina Thursday night."

She blinked. Dragged the covers closer to her naked body, like she realized she needed to hide from him. "Oh. That will be fun. Want me to drop by?"

He saw how much those words cost her to ask, but he shook his head. "You're not drinking age yet. Remember?"

He'd gotten her into the bar before but didn't want to go through the hassle this time. He just wanted a quiet night out so he could stop thinking about his mother and the shit storm that made up his family. He needed to get away from the responsibilities strangling him, which now seemed to include Sydney.

Why are you treating her like this?

The voice had hints of his mother, faintly scolding, but he pushed it away. He was so tired of thinking all the time. Was it so wrong to want things to be simple again? To start with a clean slate, alone, with no one to judge or want more from him?

"I'll tell them we can reschedule," she said. He noticed her voice wobbled just a bit.

He gave a curt nod. "Thanks. I'll see you tomorrow."

"Tristan?"

"Yeah?"

"I love you."

His gut lurched. His skin burned. The words got stuck in his throat, rising up but dying before they left his mouth. He couldn't do this right now. He couldn't handle her need for him when he barely had enough sanity to deal with himself. He couldn't commit his heart to her when tomorrow was completely out of his control. He'd already lost his mother. His family. Why set himself up to lose her, too? At least this would be on his terms.

"Good night."

He left her in the bed, skin still warm from his touch, lips still bruised from his kisses, and hated himself.

But not enough to go back.

The memory dissipated like smoke.

He let out an animallike groan. His body trembled at the sudden burst of realization that tore through him.

Had it been easier to see the past from his own viewpoint rather than accept his actions? Over the years, his memories had spun to cast her in the role of betrayer. The role of a liar bent on keeping the truth from him for revenge or selfishness. But maybe it had been so much bigger than that.

Maybe he was also in the wrong.

All those times he'd walked away, knowing he was deliberately hurting her but unable to stop it. The more she opened up her heart to him, the faster he ran. The easier it was to push her away, not wanting any more messy emotions to tear him apart. The night she was going to tell him about Becca, he'd announced his intention to leave for New York. Yes, he'd asked her to come, but had he ever given her any indication he *wanted* her to come?

No.

Because deep inside, he'd wanted to do it alone. Yes, he'd come back for her months later. But was it because he'd been lonely and aching for someone to love him? Had he been the one who set her up to be the ultimate giver, with him as the taker? What had he ever given to Sydney?

Not his love. Not his trust.

He'd given her great sex. Then expected it to be enough because he was so used to taking what he wanted from her.

His breath choked his lungs, and he stumbled outside,

needing air. Opening the door, he walked onto the porch, staring into the sunny summer morning. He'd never loved her the way she truly needed him to. And if she'd told him about the baby, he could've destroyed them both.

She was right. He would have burned with resentment and stayed in Harrington. He would've taken out his rage and emotional emptiness on his child instead of finding himself and taking the time to heal his wounds. He hadn't been ready for anything eight years ago but refused to admit it.

He dropped his forehead into his open palms. What was he going to do? He'd pushed her to the breaking point, and there was no other place to go. She wanted to leave him. He needed to take the ultimate risk—for Becca. For Sydney.

For himself.

Raw emotion swirled inside, overtaking him, and he let it all flow through, finally accepting his fate.

He loved Sydney. She was his soul mate. His wife.

His entire life had been a series of steps to bring him to this moment. To her. His stupid fear and need to control almost ripped his future from his grasp. Somehow, he needed to try to make things right. Make her see how badly he needed her. Trusted her. Loved her.

It was time to give her everything he had and see if it was enough.

In a daze, he pulled out his phone and called his brothers.

"Mama, there's Morgan!"

Sydney paused from settling her daughter into her booster seat and cocked her head. Her friend walked over to the car, dressed in her usual polished white suit with kitten heels. "What are you doing here? Looking for ballet lessons?"

Morgan gave her a hug, then popped her head in the back to talk to Becca. "Hey, darlin'. I've come to ask if Uncle Cal and I can take you to the aquarium today."

"Yes! Oh, yes, Mama, please? Can I go? Please? The last time I got to pet a real stingray, but he didn't bite, and I want to do it again!"

"Raven and I thought we'd have an old-fashioned sleepover with Becca," Morgan continued. "Some girly DVDs. Popcorn. Painting our nails. Would it be okay if she slept over?"

Sydney frowned, trying to keep up. "That's really sweet of you. Do you want me to come, too?"

"No. You'll have other plans."

"Mama, please! I got new pajamas and pink slippers to match!"

"I cannot wait to see them," Morgan said with a smile. "In fact, why don't I swing by the house and pick up her overnight bag, and I'll check in with you tomorrow?"

Sydney shook her head, then looked around. "Oh no. Are you setting me up for some type of reality television thing? I hope it's not that one where you find out you've been dressing horribly and they buy you a whole new wardrobe."

Morgan's blue eyes flashed with excitement. "Nope. I'm under strict orders to send you to these places the rest of the afternoon. The appointments are already made, so don't be late."

Sydney glanced at the list her friend thrust in her hand. *WTH?* Her mouth fell open as she read it. "I don't know what's going on, but I can't do this stuff today. I have to stop at the dry cleaners and make cupcakes for the PTA. Then I have to stop back at the site. Who set this up?"

The answer slammed into her as soon as she asked the question.

Tristan.

Disappointment cut deep. This must be his last-ditch effort to try to mend things. Send her to a few beauty salons and everything gets better. Unbelievable. She shook her head. "No. You can tell Tristan I'm not interested."

Morgan leaned in, keeping her voice low. "Syd, I don't ask you for much, do I?"

A frown creased her brow. "No."

"Well, I'm asking now. Just do what the list says. That's all. Do it for me."

Her mouth fell open. "You're on his side?"

"No. I'm on the right side. You're going to have to trust me. Please."

"Mama! Can I go, please?"

She stared at her friend for a while, then slowly nodded. "Okay. For you."

Morgan gave a ladylike squeal and grabbed Becca out of the car. "Come on, sweetie, we're going to have some fun today. I got your booster. Say bye to your mama, you'll see her in the morning."

Sydney kissed and hugged her daughter, then watched her disappear with Morgan across the parking lot.

Well, a promise was a promise. As ridiculous as this whole thing was, maybe Tristan needed to truly understand their relationship would never work. Not when he couldn't give her what she needed.

Tamping down a sigh, she got in the car and drove to her first stop.

Three hours later, she realized this was on the level of *Pretty Woman*.

Tristan was serious.

She'd been treated to the full works at the beauty salon, including a trim, color, mani, and pedi. From there, she'd gone to the spa for a facial and mud bath thing that detoxed her skin and made her glow. The bikini wax wasn't her favorite thing in the whole world, but she had to admit it was worth it when she saw the sleek results. Her final stop was at the department store, where she was instructed to head to the women's department. A matronly woman named Emma fussed over her as she tried several dresses in the fitting room. Since she had no idea where she was going, she left it up to the experienced saleswoman and finally settled on an emerald-green gown with a square-cut neckline. The material shimmered, hugged her curves, and swept out in an elaborate train. The jewelry section was already prepared for her, an associate immediately clasping an elaborate diamond necklace around her neck. Of course they added the matching earrings and bracelet. Sydney was afraid she'd end up beeping past the monitors and spend the night in jail for shoplifting.

But she got through just fine.

The shoe department presented her with gold platform sandals with emeralds twisted around the ankle strap. Finally, three women pampered her by doing her makeup, giving her long lashes, a pouty lush lip, and a gorgeous green shadow dusting over her lids. When she looked in the mirror, she had been transformed into a ravishing, polished, pampered woman who looked about ready to go on a romantic date.

Wow. She gave him props for going all out, but a sadness clung to her the entire time she was getting prepped. She had to tell him tonight. They had to part ways before things became worse. It was the best thing for all of them, including Becca. Her daughter was strong and had two parents who adored her. She'd be fine with both of them working together.

When she exited the department store, a sleek black limousine was waiting for her at the curb. A driver dressed in a tux bowed and opened the door, handing her a glass of champagne.

"We're not going to the set of *The Bachelor*, are we?" she called out.

"No, ma'am. Just sit back and enjoy the ride. We should arrive shortly."

She shrugged, drank her champagne, and wondered where they were going. The opera? The ballet? When they finally pulled up to the familiar restaurant, her heart jumped.

Il Cenácolo.

It had been Diane's favorite place: a mix of old-world food, intimate atmosphere, and elaborate gardens in the back. Patrons felt as if they'd entered Tuscany. The waitstaff was legendary, along with the restaurant's five courses, and it took months to get a reservation. After Diane died, the family had stopped coming here for dinner. Tristan always said it was too painful and wreathed in memories.

She glanced around as she exited the limousine, noticing the parking lot was empty. The limo driver bowed, then motioned for her to climb to the top of the stone stairway. Moving carefully in her golden heels, she pushed open the double doors and stepped inside.

Then caught her breath.

Tristan stood before her dressed in a sleek black tux. He screamed of polished elegance and masculine grace. His hard, lean body was barely contained by the expensive fabric, and already her hands itched to touch him, push back his thick, wavy hair, caress his smooth, square jaw. His whiskey-gold eyes blazed across the room, stealing her breath. He'd brought his A game tonight—a game of seduction and charm. He wanted her to stay, but he still had no idea how to give her what she truly wanted.

"You look beautiful," he said huskily.

"Thank you." She cleared her throat, trying to make herself speak. Already her heart wept and her body ached to be close. The connection would always be there, but she'd have to learn how to deal with it. "What are you doing, Tristan?"

His smile dazzled; those straight white teeth flashed in the shadows. "What I should have done years ago." He reached out his hand. "Will you come with me, Sydney? Just one last time?"

Cursing her weak heart, she nodded and reached out her hand.

One last time.

He led her into the main banquet room, which had been transformed. Dozens of candelabras and flowers spilled through the space, creating an intimate atmosphere that wrapped tight around them. A table with blinding-white linens and sparkling crystal was set in the center. The sensual sounds of Frank

Sinatra played softly on the speakers, reminding them of love gone wrong and second chances. He pulled out her chair and invited her to sit, handing her a glass of red wine.

Her hand trembled as she sipped. She stared at him in the flickering light.

And realized she couldn't do it.

She loved him too much to spend an evening with him in such intimacy. Blinking furiously, she shook her head and took a step away from him. "I can't do this. I can't pretend to have this perfect evening with you when it's all a lie."

"I know."

"You have to let me go, Tristan." She promised it would be the last time she ever begged him for anything. "Let me go."

His eyes filled with raw pain and grief. He closed the distance between them and cupped her cheeks, tilting her head upward to meet his blistering gaze. "I can't."

"Why?" she choked out.

"Because I love you."

She stiffened. "Don't do this. Not now. Not like this."

In shock, she watched those beautiful golden eyes fill up with unshed tears. "I'm asking you to listen to me one more time, Sydney. I need to say this, and you deserve to hear the truth. Please."

He dropped his hands and took a step back, waiting. Allowing her to reject him or leave. Giving her the choice.

Frozen in place, she managed another nod.

"I found Becca's original birth certificate today," he said. "You had me listed as the father all along. I realized then you had always planned to tell me I was Becca's father, even back when you got married."

Sadness overtook her. She was glad he'd finally realized her true intentions and might have some measure of peace. She also knew his knowledge didn't change anything between them.

"I've been thinking a lot about our past. Over and over, I sifted through our interactions, defending myself for my choices. Thinking about how you hurt me. I'm pretty good at taking care of me, Syd. Always have been. You've been with me for so long, I never questioned your feelings for me. Whether it was friendship or love or passion or support, you gave it all freely, without taking. And I gave you sex."

His face crumpled in self-disgust. Sydney wrapped her arms around her trembling body.

"Sex. I thought it was enough. And when I came back because I was lonely and missing you, I felt betrayed when you'd decided to go on with your life. Even then, I felt as if you belonged to me. But it wasn't in the right way. It wasn't about protecting you or wanting to see you happy. It was about you making *me* happy. And I'm going to have to live with that. Knowing how I failed both you and my mother."

She pressed her lips together to keep from interrupting. Before her, she watched the protective walls crash down, finally showing her the man inside, the man she'd always longed for, the man she loved.

"I took you for granted my entire life. I made excuses to force you into this marriage that had nothing to do with Becca and everything to do with me. Because I always knew, deep inside, that you are the woman who can save me. It was only with you I felt complete and whole and happy. And I destroyed that by constantly taking and never giving."

Slowly he knelt in front of her. Stunned, she watched the man she loved humble himself before her. A tear trekked down his cheek, but he looked her straight in the eye and never faltered.

"I don't deserve you. I never did. But I'm asking if you will give me one more chance to show you every day how much I love you. To give you every part of me—good and bad—and be your husband, your partner, your everything. I swear to you, my love, I will give you my all for the rest of my life. You will never doubt my love for you again." He reached into his pocket with trembling hands and took out a ring box. It was a new ring—three sparkling diamonds lay against the black velvet. "I'm asking you to marry me, Sydney. For the right reasons. Because I love you. Because every road in my life has always led to you."

Sydney stared at him on bended knee, golden eyes filled with a raw vulnerability and naked love she'd never seen before. Choking back a sob, she stepped forward and reached out her hand. Entangling his fingers with hers, he rose, and she reached out to trace the tear on his cheek, pressing her forehead against his.

"Yes," she breathed against his lips. "Yes to everything."

His mouth closed over hers, and he kissed her deeply, with a reverence that shook her to the core, and she wrapped her arms around his neck and kissed him back.

"I love you," she whispered.

"I love you, too."

And she smiled as her husband slipped the ring on her finger and finally claimed their happily ever after.

epilogue

Tristan sat on the front porch and sipped his red wine. Cal and Dalton flanked him, with Dalton drinking a Raging Bitch and Cal nursing a snifter of expensive whiskey. Darkness blanketed the lawn, and the thick woods were alive with singing crickets. Stars exploded from the sky. The sounds of feminine chatter drifted in the air from the open door.

"Things are good," Dalton announced.

Tristan grinned, still a bit surprised at the depth of happiness that had settled inside him. Since Sydney had accepted his new marriage proposal, his life had shifted. A lightness he'd never truly experienced before poured through him. It was as if by finally letting himself open up, he'd discovered a new strength and joy he'd been keeping himself from.

A soft voice echoed in the wind, caressing his ears.

"I'm proud of you, my son."

He sent back his own message, knowing she heard. *"Thanks, Mom. I love you."*

Cal stretched out his legs on the battered wicker table that should've been replaced years ago. "About time things worked out for all of us. It's been a long journey."

"And it's not done yet," Tristan added. "We're getting a new member of our family."

"Sydney's pregnant?" Dalton asked, leaning forward in excitement.

"Not yet. We're hitting the rescue shelter tomorrow to get Becca a dog. I finally convinced Syd."

His brothers laughed. "Nice work," Cal said. His eyes burned suspiciously bright as he reached in his back pocket and pulled something out. "But I may have you beat on this one."

Tristan frowned, taking the paper and unfolding it. "What's this?"

"Initial adoption papers. Morgan and I are adopting a baby girl from China."

Tristan clapped him on the back, loving how his older brother was fighting back emotion. "Dude, congratulations. We're so happy for you."

"Thanks. It's still a long road, but we're going to be patient and have trust. In the meantime, we'll spoil our new canine nephew or niece. And Becca, of course. Morgan loves being an aunt."

"So does Raven," Dalton added. "Guess it's time for my news?"

Cal and Tristan waited.

"Gonna ask Raven to marry me tomorrow. I have the ring. Got the whole setup. Al's going to help me do it at My Place, since that's where it all started for us."

Tristan gave his brother a half hug. "Congrats, it's about time. We've all been waiting for this."

"You sure she's gonna say yes?" Cal teased.

Dalton groaned. "Dude, don't make me more nervous than I am."

"Let's just make sure she doesn't do a *Grease* revival at your wedding," Tristan added.

As if they'd heard the conversation, Becca's giggle echoed in the night air, followed by Morgan's, Raven's, and Sydney's.

"I think Mom would've been happy," Dalton said quietly. "I know it may sound silly, but sometimes I hear her talking to me. Especially when I look at the stars."

Tristan nodded. "I hear her, too. And I think she would've told us the same thing. That she's proud of us."

"Me too," Cal said. "We found our way back to each other and found the women we love. Doesn't get much better than that."

"Agreed."

"Agreed."

They shared a glance and clinked their glasses together.

Then they all settled back on the porch for a long time in comfortable silence.

acknowledgments

This part may get a bit emotional.

First off, a big thank-you to my crew, the "moonies": Catherine Bybee, Marina Adair, Shelly Alexander, Julie York, Sofia St. Angeles, and Diana Orgain. Experiencing that type of feminine bond over a conference weekend is special and I'll never forget it. Simply put, you guys rock.

I won't be able to thank my editor, Lauren McKenna, enough for getting me through this book. You carried me to the finish line barely functional, but what we created together is pure art. I LOVE this book so hard, and you helped me get there. Your talent is breathtaking.

A big thanks to the team at Simon & Schuster; my agent, Kevan Lyon; my publicist, Jessica Estep; and my assistant, Lisa Hamel-Soldano. It always takes a village, folks. And it's good I have some of the best in mine.

Finally, ending this series is bittersweet. I've loved spending my time with the Pierce brothers and the incredible, strong women who matched them. I loved diving into the HGTV world and conquering it my way.

Saying good-bye is hard, in all things in life. But like anything, there's a brand-new chapter ready to be started lurking around the next corner—for all of us.